MICHAEL HEAD

Table of Contents

PROLOGUE

Magical flames crackled in the fireplace, casting harsh, unnatural blue light across the room. They lacked any heat, but that made no difference to the inhabitants of the chamber. Arched windows overlooked beautiful snowcapped mountains, where no human had stepped foot in living memory. The altitude made it impossible to survive for long, the air too thin to support life. Unnatural creatures that called the barren mountaintops home would have cut short any expeditions foolish enough to try.

Four figures huddled over a table covered in maps. They were unnaturally still, despite the chill. A living person would shiver uncontrollably if they were subjected to such extremes, but the four had long since left such trappings behind.

"Sir, the battle at the second entrance resulted in a cave-in. We don't have a way to get through in time." The speaker was the shortest of the group, but he was as broad as any two of the others combined. A thick, pale finger shifted a wooden flag on the map several inches. "If our team repositions to the third entrance, there's still a chance. It's a longer route, but we know the way is clear."

The lone woman of the group picked up the pair of wooden flags in the center of the map the group was focused on. Her long silver hair reflected the blue firelight, giving her an ephemeral appearance that carried more weight than her slight stature would suggest. "It seems to me there's no point in throwing more troops at a lost cause. We overplayed our hand, and the demons took advantage." Setting them aside, she pointed at a map that had been shoved off to the side. It showed a large city surrounded by smaller villages, with population numbers scrawled in the margins. "We can replace our losses in a few weeks and try again."

It isn't that easy. The third speaker was almost skeletal, barely more than skin and bones, wearing a worn, moth-eaten robe. Instead of an actual voice, its words entered the minds of those around it like an insidious whisper straight from a nightmare. Their eyes glowed with a green eldritch fire that scorched the sunken sockets of its skull. *Handing them pitchforks and wood axes won't be enough.* He motioned to the short figure. *Even the duergar can't produce weapons and armor at the type of speeds you're asking for, and opening a portal to their world already costs more than you're willing to pay. You're talking about throwing away our best-equipped units like it's nothing, and I for one won't—*

Off to the side of the room, a rune-encrusted marble orb carved to mimic a globe on a wooden stand started to grow warm, giving off wisps of steam in the chilly air. The fourth figure, who had yet to speak, snapped his head around the moment he noticed the change. All conversation cut off, and the man slowly walked over to observe the device.

"What's happening? Are the demons making another incursion?" The woman took a tentative step backward, putting the skeletal figure between herself and the magical artifact.

"No. This is something different." The man concentrated, holding out a hand and nearly touching the surface of the globe. "It feels like a portal is being opened somewhere on our continent, but not like anything I've encountered before. Perhaps a new faction making themselves known." His voice was deep and resonant, which matched his classic noble features and proper attire. While he watched, a portion of land started to glow. The heat caused the runes on the globe to deform, and the man hissed in annoyance, displaying elongated canines. "Someone is interfering with the location spell. The runes can't lock on to where it's opening." His frustration caused his composure to slip, and the force he contained within himself made the other three in the room shift in discomfort. He held up a hand, quickly forming a series of symbols that left lines of vibrant red light in the cold air. "We'll see if they know what they stand against."

As the vampire's spell finished, it drifted toward the globe. The moment it touched, a catastrophic reaction resulted in an explosion that obliterated the orb. All the windows in the room blew out, which allowed the arctic air to blast through the chamber, throwing the entire area into disarray and extinguishing the magical fire.

"Milord!" The shortest of the four ambled forward, afraid that the man had been destroyed in the spell backlash. As the smoke cleared, and the winds scoured clean the room, the noble was still standing. A faint red shield surrounded him, shooting out sparks that scorched the stone floor, as if they were a direct reflection of his anger. "You-you're okay?"

"I guess they knew what they were doing, wouldn't you say? Using a fixed runespell in place of a willpowered conjuration was foolish." The woman's smirk was laced with equal parts humor and scorn. Her elegant features were revealed to be cruel by her twisted smile. She displayed a set of elongated canines almost as fierce as the noble's. "What are you going to do for an encore? Perhaps destroy our stronghold below? Collapse the cavern holding my ship?" She tapped her lips with a perfect finger. "I know. You could challenge the dragon to single combat again, since that worked so well last time. I'm sure the demon hordes would love to cheer the two of you on."

The noble snapped his fingers, dismissing the shield. His displeasure at the woman's sharp words were ignored as he focused on the more pressing issue. "This is direct interference from the other side. We have to answer this incursion immediately. A new set of interests can't be allowed to intrude at such a…*delicate* time." He pointed at the skeletal figure. "The spatial distortion is located nearest to your territory, and you will enforce my will."

What would you have me do? The skeletal figure took a few steps to separate himself from the other two. He had been singled out, and didn't want to squander the opportunity this represented.

The noble looked at the table where his maps had been before the wind had blown them away and waved his hand. An exact carving of the lands far to the south quickly took shape in the expensive wood, and the two stepped close to look over it. "I wasn't able to pinpoint the exact location, but the portal must've opened somewhere near here. Flood the region in undead. Twist the living to our purpose, if you see fit. Force whoever this is into the open. And when you do, end their interference however you prefer."

The skeletal figure turned to leave, but was stopped by the heavy hand of the vampire on its bony shoulder.

"As I said, however you see fit. But they *will* meet their end. Or you will."

It will be as you say, Destitute. The green fires left the eyes of the skeletal figure and flew out of the open window, as the now inanimate body collapsed into dust.

The noble figure, known as the Destitute, turned back to the other two still in the room with him. There were more immediate issues that needed to be resolved.

CHAPTER 1

Not another one. I sighed in defeat as I trudged into town. This was only the third village I had come across since coming here, and all of them seemed to follow a similar pattern. In front of me, a scene that could have been in a spaghetti Western played out before my eyes. I told myself to ignore what was happening. That I would be better off if I just kept on walking. All that went straight out the window the moment my gaze met with the insolent, angry eyes of the child.

"My lord, please forgive him!" The screaming mother dropped to her knees into the muddy road, tears blending into the rain running down her face. "He is only a boy, and doesn't know how to act around his betters!"

"Then the fault lies on your head, woman." The rotund noble was barely old enough to be called a man, but the years of opulence and non-restricted rations had already given him jowls. They were painted pink at the self-inflicted outrage from a four-year-old boy who was foolish enough to bump into him on the streets. "Your lack of proper education has cost this child his hand."

The mother whimpered in fear, knowing what the future prospects of a maimed boy would be.

"Just be happy I haven't decided to take his head instead!"

"Th-thank you, my lord. For allowing my boy to keep his life." The woman kowtowed in the mud, slamming her forehead into the filthy muck that was ankle-deep everywhere in this gods-forsaken dump of a town. "Your generosity will carry on the winds to the ears of the ancestors!"

"Of course it will, foolish woman. Now, guard, give me your sword." The noble held out his hand, and the hilt of a heavy curve-bladed dao was gently placed in his soft palm. He almost dropped it when the guard let go, but the noble managed to keep its gleaming length out of the mud.

The guard was already going to have to spend hours cleaning it once they got back to the jumped-up hut the nobleman called his manor, so keeping the mud off it was a small mercy.

He looked at the mother. "You, hold out his arm."

She looked up from the mud with a face twisted by horror, silently shaking her head.

The noble stomped in the muck, splattering himself.

The second of the three guardsmen who were playing bodyguard for the man in silk robes grimaced and stepped forward, kicking the woman out of the way. "I'll do it, Counselor. She's too weak to hold him properly anyway."

The noble thought for a moment before nodding in agreement. "Fine."

The guard looked away as he held out the stick-thin arm of the boy.

"Good. Now, don't move. I don't want to miss, and accidentally dent your armor."

Looking at the face of the boy, I made the same kind of decision that I always made. The worst kind. The kind that always ended with me in trouble. I tightened my weapons belt more firmly about myself as I swaggered more fully in view of the ridiculous noble. The scene I created only needed a set of spurs, some six-shooters, and the sun to be at high noon to really flesh it out. "The real violation of justice here is your wardrobe, mister." I gestured at him from head to toe, taking in all of the slovenly noble as I worked my face into a dramatic grimace. "Who wears silk robes in the mud and rain? I mean, seriously. That's a *special* kind of stupid."

While the noble sputtered in indignation at my interruption, I paid attention to the eyes of the little boy. The white-hot rage burning in their depths was what made me decide to interject myself into the situation in the first place. Like I said, it was the worst kind of choice to make, but even after all these years, I was never as heartless as I needed to be. I saw a little of myself in the boy, which was why I opened my damn fool mouth. "And cutting off the hands of children? Does that make you feel important, somehow? Come on, guy. That's the worst type of person you can be."

"How *dare* you speak to me that way!" The soft-skinned noble sputtered, his formerly puffy pink cheeks turning almost as red as his silks. "Guards, bring me that man's head on a pike!"

"Sure, why not immediately jump to killing the armed stranger who just strolled into town all by himself?" I sighed, pulling the end of my staff out of the mud to shake the end clean. I didn't bother unclipping the mace dangling from the right side of my belt, opposite the straight-bladed ninjatō sword on my left. "I mean, he clearly was capable enough to travel alone through monster-infested lands, managed to make it past all the bandits, and *still* pulled off looking this good, but yeah, attacking him is the definite go-to for your classic pompous villain." I tilted back the straw hat protecting me from the worst of the steady downpour, giving them my best smile. It was important to me that they understood I wasn't lying about looking good. I even tossed a wink at the lady peeking out of the door to the general store this drama was taking place in front of for good measure.

"Counselor, maybe we should try talking first." The third guard was the oldest of the bunch, and clearly the only one with a brain. His battle instincts must be ringing alarm bells if his sudden shifting posture were any indication. "We don't even know what clan or guild he comes from!"

"Yeah, you don't even know what clan or guild I come from, Mr. Stick-Up-My-Butt. You wouldn't want to make somebody mad by accident, would you?" This time, I winked at the nobleman.

He didn't appreciate it nearly as much as the lady did.

"I don't care! Kill him, so I can feed his body to the pigs!" He was shaking now, and I half expected him to keel over from a brain aneurysm. "Now!"

The boy scampered back to his mother the second the guard let him go, and the two took off.

Man, the thanks you get nowadays.

I turned my attention back to the three guards slowly approaching me, all with naked steel in their hands. The oldest guard—probably close to my age, which made me wince internally—held out an official badge and started to speak.

"By order of Counselor Bri—"

I cut him off with a backward spin of my staff. The tip hit a clump of mud near my feet, and I flung it at his face. I didn't feel like listening anymore.

"Get him!" The guard to my right was outraged by the dirty trick, and charged with his dao raised above his head for a mighty downward chop.

I twisted my staff up high, slapping the side of his blade and knocking the sword sideways. The momentum of the heavy lump of metal meant it ended up buried at least a foot deep in the thick muck. A quick diagonal quarter-swing brought the tip of my staff upside his head, and the guard face-planted in the muck.

He was gonna take a little sleepy-time break.

"Now, I know what you're thinking." I did my best not to sound too sarcastic, but it was hard, given the situation.

The older guard was still doing his best to wipe the mud out of his eye. I almost felt bad about it, because he was certainly getting pink eye after this. After all, we're talking genuine fantasy-world poo water here. The guard to my left had paused when he saw what happened to his friend, and was carefully watching his partner to see what he would do.

"What you *should* be thinking is, 'Do I feel like drowning in the mud and manure of the street like my friend is right now?' But what you are really thinking is, 'I can probably take this guy. I'm a better fighter than my friend, and I have a chance!' Well, guess what, bub." I thumped his unconscious friend on the back with the end of my staff. "You really aren't better than your friend, and you will most definitely drown if you try me." I took five quick steps backward, almost losing one of my boots to the mud. "If you want to save him, roll him onto his back, you and your friend pick him up, and you go on home. Maybe have a cup of hot coffee or something."

A spark of intelligence burst forth, and the man did the unthinkable. He listened. I didn't say anything while he rushed forward to save his compatriot, and he dragged his friend to the nearest wall and propped him up against it. The older guard finally got to the point where he could see, and quickly joined the other two, out of my way.

"What are you doing?! You have to listen to me! I told you to kill that man, so kill him! I am a *Counselor*, and I will not be ignored!" The noble shook in impotent rage, and he pulled a short dagger from his belt as I got closer to him. "No, yo-you stay away from me! Don't come any closer!"

"In all the worlds I have traveled. In all the lands I have walked. I don't know if I've met someone as stupid as you." I was most definitely lying. I had met some *incredibly* stupid people before. "Now, are you right-handed, or left?"

"Worlds you have traveled? Are you insane? And what does me being right or left-handed have to do with anything?" The noble was taken aback by the rapid shift in subject and tone. "And why should I answer to the likes of *you*?"

"I'll answer those in order. No, I'm not insane. At least, I don't think I am." With a twist of my wrists, a foot of almost paper-thin pointed metal shot out of the top of my staff and snapped into place, turning the wooden rod into a very dangerous spear modeled after a Japanese yari. I sliced it downward, then horizontally, removing the noble's hands at the wrists in a blur of movement. The blade was so thin, the noble didn't even understand what had happened until his appendages flopped in the mud.

The counselor's jowls quivered as his mouth opened in a silent scream and blood fountained from his severed limbs. From past experience, I knew the pain hadn't hit yet. He was just in shock. His voice came out in a trembling whisper, choked with the agony he knew was about to hit. "It was…my…right…"

"I guess it doesn't really matter which hand is dominant, since you don't have them anymore."

The blood loss caused him to fall over onto his side, but he still watched me.

"Honestly? I just wanted to get your hopes up and show you the same injustice you visit on others. As to why you should answer? Well, first off, if you had, I would have only taken the dominant hand. But the real reason is because I am stronger than you, and there is nothing else that truly matters in this world, as you have so aptly demonstrated before my arrival." I could have thrown some titles I had earned at him to lend some legitimacy to my words, but I didn't see any point in it. He wasn't really listening to me anyway, considering his eyes had rolled back into his head.

I turned away and walked toward the door to the general store. I needed some supplies if I was going to make it to the next village, and I was pretty sure the cute lady had smiled at my wink. Definitely something to check out. I ignored the guards as they rushed forward and tried to stem the blood still erupting from the man's wrists.

By reflex, I checked to see if the quest I had been given long ago had finally completed. I wasn't shocked to see it still staring me in the face. It hadn't changed in a long, long time. Twenty years, twenty worlds, and no end in sight. Still, I had to know. "Status."

> **Name**: James Holden (Earth v7)
>
> **Title**: Chief Justice/Arbiter/Justicar/Executioner/etc.
>
> **Level**: 100/MAX
>
> **Age**: 27 (Physical) 47 (Actual)
>
> **Class**: Warrior/Soldier/Knight/Paladin/Mage (5/5)
>
> **Profession**:
> Healer/Alchemist/Blacksmith/Runesmith/Judge (5/5)
>
> **Status**:
>
> **Strength** – 50
>
> **Flexibility** – 50
>
> **Vigor** – 50
>
> **Mind** – 50
>
> **Mission:**
>
> **Mythical Quest**: Deliver Justice – World Count 20/???
>
> **Legendary Quest:** Return Home – Requirements not met
>
> **Epic Quest**: Find out why – Requirements not met
>
> **Rare Quest**: Track down Silver Star – Ongoing

Well, that confirms it. I'm still screwed.

CHAPTER 2

After confirming that I was, in fact, still very screwed, I took a deep breath and let it out slowly. Getting grabbed by a shadow while walking down a dark alley wasn't supposed to be a literal problem from where I was from originally, but I had come to learn that it was definitely a serious issue on most planets. Sure, most places, the shadow would just eat you. I suppose I was just the unlucky idiot who found the only hoodoo, magical, sci-fi-fantasy wormhole portal shadow on all of Earth to exist, and I woke up with a blue screen over my eyes and the worst version of a front-row-seat-at-a-rock-concert-while-simultaneously-suffering-from-a-hangover headache in history. It had sucked.

That was twenty years ago, and my life from before felt more like a dream than anything real by this point. It had been hard to make the adjustment to my new reality, but I had only been given two options. Either figure it out and live, or don't. Full stop. Considering I hadn't wanted to die, I chose to figure it out. Well, I should be honest with myself. I had worked out enough to keep breathing, but the last two decades hadn't given me many clues to what had actually happened to me. Ultimately, it didn't matter. I had a quest that said it was possible to make it home, and that's exactly what I was going to do.

Not that I was sure what I would find back home. I mean, if there's wormholes, or portals, what about time dilation? What if my world was destroyed, and I was only here because it no longer existed? After twenty years, I had thought up a lot of random crap.

Certainly, my cat had died of old age, same as my dog. The girl I had been seeing probably moved on a few weeks after I vanished. At least, I hoped she had. We had only been on a few dates before I was yanked into a different world, and if she was still waiting for me after all this time, that screamed stalker vibes. Which, in my experience, might lead to great sex, but wasn't a good recipe for a lasting commitment. Really, the only people who would probably even remember me would be my parents, and they would be getting close to seventy years old at this point. Still, they deserved to know what had happened to me, even if they locked me in a loony bin after I told them where I had disappeared off to.

"Welcome, sir. What can I do for you?"

I was snapped out of my inner monologue by the woman standing behind the counter.

"Are you looking for something in particular?"

"That depends entirely on what's available." I pulled off my hat and set it on the wide countertop before looking her up and down. Mid-twenties, black hair, dark eyes, and pretty enough to help boost sales numbers. I turned up the wattage of my grin. "Specifically, are you? Available, I mean. Any boyfriends or sheepherders in the picture?"

"Oh, she's single, but not to a traveling ruffian like you."

I turned to face the newcomer, who had stepped out from behind a curtain that sectioned off what I guessed was the storeroom.

"Why don't you go to the back and finish up the inventory, Vikie. I'll handle this customer."

"But Dad, I can handle—"

"No buts, young lady. Get back there, before I call down your mother."

The store owner—who didn't like me for some unknown reason—gave me the stink-eye. He was *definitely* the lady's dad. They shared enough features that he didn't need to worry about a paternity test. The biggest difference between the two was their size. The daughter had been willowy and graceful. The father was burly and weathered, with a dusting of white at his temples. I instantly knew he would put up more of a fight than the guards had managed. He exuded a certain type of competent confidence that made me instantly like him.

"Now, what can I get you, so you can leave?" He pulled out a scrap of paper and a stick of charcoal to take notes.

I shook my head in defeat. This was one battle I knew I wouldn't win. "Enough trail rations for two people to make it five days. Two balls of twine. Three vials of lamp oil. Two shaving razors. One bag of sugar. Two bags of salt. One bag of flour. A rack of healing potions, mid-grade or higher. I don't want a case of the runs from some knockoff crap."

He nodded without looking up, and underlined a section of his notes.

"A short hunting bow, if you have one."

He continued to nod without looking up as he wrote down my list.

I let out a short sigh of relief. My last bow had been broken in the battle with the cave dwellers three days ago, and it had made getting fresh meat almost impossible. "Three dozen arrows, wrapped and sealed in wax paper. Goose feather fletchings, with metal tips. One dozen broadheads, the rest pointed. Do you have any silver?"

He looked up at that request.

"Silver?" The shopkeeper squinted at my belt buckle, where the people of this world normally kept their clan or guild affiliation.

Mine was from the court of King Sloban, a ruler two worlds ago who had adopted me into his court. I hadn't changed it out yet, considering the sentimental value it held. Well, sentiment, and the secret compartment inside it was nice, too.

"That doesn't look like a hunter sign to me."

"I'm not from around here." If only he knew how much of an understatement that was. "Do you have any? I won't be stealing any contracts from anyone, but I have a long road to travel, and running away from things isn't an option."

He wrote down a few things, and looked back up at me. "Fine. I'll show you what I have in stock. Just don't go causing problems around here. I don't know you, and I'll tell anyone who asks that you bought them from me if there are Questioners or White Wardens involved."

"That's fine." I nodded and tossed a heavy purse onto the counter next to my hat. "Last thing." I swallowed hard, holding out hope that there might be some on this planet. "Do you have any gunpowder?"

He looked at me with obvious confusion.

"Maybe you call it fire powder, or boom dust. Anything like that?"

The shopkeeper paused before answering, glancing at the purse. "If I did have any fire powder, I would only be able to sell it to those who carried a writ. Do you have a writ?"

I pulled my pack off my back and thumped it on the ground, secretly trying to hold in my internal sense of glee. I reached into a small pocket sewn into the side and pulled out a single green gemstone the size of my thumbnail.

After I placed it on the counter, the shopkeeper's eyes widened, and he swallowed hard. "Looks like a writ to me. Give me a minute to get everything ready. Have a look around while I'm in the back. You might find something else you need."

"Don't take all day. I want to eat a hot meal and get settled at that inn on the other side of town before the sun goes down." I looked out the open window, gauging how much daylight was left. It was hard to tell with the cloudy skies, but I guessed it was a little more than an hour before everyone would need to be inside. I was happy to see the counselor and his guards were nowhere in sight, and less happy about the crowd that had gathered to inspect the pair of hands left in the mud. I turned back to the shopkeeper, my eyes glancing to the door where his daughter had fled earlier, arching an eyebrow suggestively. "Unless you want me to spend the night here?"

"That won't be necessary." The burly man scooped up his notes and hurried to the back.

While he was gone, I looked over his wares. They were geared toward farmers and ranchers, for the most part.

I did pick up a small collapsible spade that would fit in my pack, and grabbed a length of rope. Three cakes of soap went in the pile, and I kicked myself for the hundredth time about not getting some before leaving the last town. There was a small cleaning kit meant for farm implements that would work well for any kind of metal that I added to the pile, and I stopped to rearrange my pack with my homemade wristband on top. If the powder was high enough quality, I would be able to wear it again.

"Well, it took a bit, but I think this should do the trick!" The shopkeeper rolled out a cart loaded down with enough items that my back was already hurting just looking at it. "Will this work for the silver?"

He laid out a lacquered box on the counter and flipped open the lid. Inside were five rows of five silver crossbow bolts. They were undersized, meant for a one-handed pistol crossbow favored by lycanthrope and undead hunters who worked in more urban environments. I would need to melt them down, but the sheer amount of material was perfect.

"They'll work, even though I don't have the proper weapon to use them with." I scooped them out and added the bolts to the burlap bag holding the three paper sacks of salt, flour, and sugar. I pulled out the flour and inspected it. "There are weevils in this." I tossed it back on the counter with a puff of white dust. "What kind of business are you running here?"

"I'll have Vikie sift it again, but that's the best you can get in these parts. The next crop won't be ready for another month, and the damp has molded most of the stock. All that's left is what was stored in the barrels meant for sea rations." He scooped up the bag and headed for the back once more. "The counselor won't ask for assistance from the city lord, because it means he didn't have the storehouses properly sealed. Those funds went to his new wardrobe." Before he disappeared behind the curtain, he turned back around. "You didn't make any friends with what you did to him, but you didn't make any enemies, either." He left to make the flour at least a little more edible.

I inspected the rest of the gear, finding it to be acceptable. The pointed arrows weren't the best, but I would only be using them to hunt small game. The broadhead arrows were similarly mediocre but serviceable for hunting larger game. The rations were sealed, so I cracked one open to check the contents. Dry biscuit, dried mystery meat, and a small packet of dried vegetables and spices. All the ingredients needed for trail stew, the staple diet of all travelers across the universe. I had told him enough for two people to travel five days to throw him off a bit. I really wanted ten days for just myself. The hope was, he would think I wasn't traveling alone, and that my destination was only five days away. Which, of course, wasn't anything close to the truth. I had no idea where I was going yet.

I put the package back on the counter to get resealed, and set the small powder keg and rack of potions in front of me while double-checking that I was alone for the moment. I had found out at the last town that casting spells was seen as a bad thing on this world, so I didn't want to do it with witnesses present. It made sense, considering the presence of gunpowder. It seemed almost universal that if they were advanced enough for gunpowder, they hated magic. No gunpowder, and magic was fine. The correlation was one of those things I had always wondered about, but never really had the time or inclination to truly study.

What *wasn't* universal was how magic worked. No magic was exactly the same from planet to planet, but a few spells stayed consistent no matter where I ended up. I made a fist, then stuck out my pinky and ring finger before concentrating on the activation word. *"Identify."* A blue screen popped up in my vision, and indicated the two items I couldn't otherwise test without making a mess.

Item: Potion

Type: Healing

Grade: 4/10

Description: An alchemical mixture of herbs that speeds healing over a short period of time. Purity level is low. More than one potion used in a thirty-minute period will result in adverse side effects.

Item: Fire Powder (Gunpowder)

Type: Black Powder

Grade: 7/10

Description: A dry powder that combusts when introduced to open flame. Primarily used in the current world as a mining tool. Military and offensive purposes are limited to specialized units found only in the largest cities.

The extra bit of information on the gunpowder was nice to have. The system was spotty with little nuggets of information like that, and I was genuinely happy to see it. I had only been on this world for a few weeks, and learning all the subtle ins and outs of their culture was still something I was working on. The fact they even had gunpowder made me almost giddy with joy. I had just left a world that didn't have anything similar, and had run out after only a few months of dispensing 'justice' to the people of that planet. Making my own just wasn't worth the trouble when I could throw a fireball. Plus, playing around in bat guano was disgusting. At least they hadn't had lycanthropes there. Just a bunch of undead that were controlled by a lich I had finally killed a few days before getting pulled here.

"Well, we've sifted the flour again, but it isn't much better. It's all I have though, so you'll either have to take it, or leave it." The shopkeeper came through the curtain, and I dismissed the screen with a wave of my hand to clear my vision. He held out the bag of flour for me to inspect. "Is this good enough?"

"Considering the abundance of options, I guess it will have to work." I plucked the bag from his fingers and wrapped it up tightly, doing my best not to sigh. Extra protein in the worst possible way. My life was filled with endless joy. "Can you seal this back up, and reseal the trail ration I opened?" I indicated the packet off to the side.

"Sure. Let me get the candle and wax kit." He wandered off, this time with a smile on his face.

I guess pawning off his bug-infested flour on me made him happy. While he was gone, I walked back to the shelving and found a small copper canteen that had a narrow mouth. It was probably meant for measuring out some type of ingredient in a kitchen, but it would work well as a powder horn for me.

The shopkeeper came back and got to work sealing everything up, taking his time to make sure everything was waterproofed. I appreciated the extra time he took on the packets of arrows, and mentally added a small tip to my purchase total. He was much faster at tallying up the cost of everything, and silently slid the bill over to me.

"Seriously?" I looked over everything I was buying, mentally adding up what the cost should be. "That's about double what I was expecting."

"Well, it might be a bit higher than average, but that's my only keg of fire powder, and I shouldn't be selling you that silver at all. Any of the guilds hear of it, and I could get stuck paying the contracts for anything you kill with those." He crossed his arms defiantly, and I subtracted the tip I was going to give him.

"Fine." Tip revoked. I yanked over the coin purse I had tossed on the counter and started pulling out thick copper disks. After counting out nine of them, I topped it off with a thin gold coin that physically hurt me to touch. Not because gold affected me in any way. I just hated being broke. "That should do it."

"What kind of coins are these?" He looked them over closely, inspecting the symbols stamped on each side. "I've never seen the like."

"The kind that spends. I told you, I'm not from around here." I pointed to a dusty set of scales on a shelf behind the counter. "Feel free to weigh them if you want. It should end up being about the same. Your scales *are* accurate, right?" I placed my hand on the hilt of my sword and arched an eyebrow.

"I'm sure it's fine." He scooped the coins off the counter, making sure to include the gemstone I had put there earlier. "Now, you better get moving if you want to make it to the inn before the sun goes down."

I looked out the window. It was definitely getting dark. "I'll be off, then. Tell your daughter I said goodbye." As I walked out the door, I had the distinct impression from the frown on his face that he wouldn't be passing along my message.

CHAPTER 3

The walk through the muddy streets was far worse than when I had first stepped inside the general store. My almost empty pack was now overstuffed, and I sank deep into the muck with every step. I used my staff to keep me upright, eventually stumbling through the thick wooden doors of the inn just as full dark was setting in.

"And who might you be?"

The common room was almost empty, not counting the innkeeper and his two serving girls who were cleaning up. I only saw a group of three figures hunched over their drinks in the far corner, their features hidden in shadow. The sense of danger I got from them distracted me from answering the innkeeper right away, and his hand dropped behind the bar before he repeated himself.

"Stranger, I don't appreciate being ignored, especially by someone who comes in right before we lock the doors for the night. It makes a man wonder about your status, if you catch my meaning. Now, let me ask you one more time. You looking for a room, or are you looking for trouble?"

"My apologies, innkeep. I was distracted for a moment." My eyes drifted over to the far corner again, my instincts screaming danger at me. "I'm just a traveler, looking for a meal and a place to rest through the night. And a bath, if you have one."

"Mattie, get the man a plate of whatever's left in the kitchen, and grab the room key for number six."

One of the women nodded quickly and dashed off to do as ordered. The second serving girl continued to clean, doing her best to stay away from the three in the corner.

The innkeep looked back at me, his bald head shining in the lamplight. It was warm in the room, and the thin man was sweating profusely. "It will be six brass for the night, two for the meal, and two more if you want a bath prepared."

"A whole copper for just one night?" I shook my head. This whole village was run by crooks. After briefly remembering who had been in charge, I suppose I wasn't all that surprised. "I'll leave off the bath, and if there are bugs in my bed, I'll only pay half."

"We don't have bugs here, but you pay up front. Otherwise, you can leave." The innkeeper shrugged and turned back to wiping down his bar. "Don't matter to me either way."

"Fine then." It was hard not to grit my teeth, but I walked over and put down another thick copper coin on the bar top. "I'll have the bath, and there better be an ale included in the price of that meal."

The innkeeper swapped the coin for a mug of foaming ale, once again shrugging. "That's fair enough, I guess." He snapped his fingers at the other serving girl, and pointed at a doorway on the opposite wall. "Jess, get the boiler going, and prepare a bath. Worry about the tables later."

She left, making sure to walk next to the wall opposite the people in the corner. At least I knew it wasn't just me who didn't like them. The first serving girl came back from the kitchen and set a large platter in front of me. It was mostly steamed vegetables, with a few chunks of what smelled like mutton mixed in. A loaf of crusty bread—obviously speckled with weevils—was set on top. Not exactly the best value for my money, but good enough that I couldn't complain.

A wrought-iron key with a symbol carved in the side was next to my fork. I guessed it was their written form of the number six. I had long ago given up trying to figure out how to read and write all the various kinds of languages I had come across. Whatever magic moved me from world to world only included the ability to speak whatever was most common for the region I ended up in. Learning a new one every year was pointless. If I really needed to know, the Identify spell would usually tell me what something said. It was amazing how far context clues could get you in life.

"Bath's ready."

The soft voice at my elbow made me jump. I turned to look at the serving girl, truly noticing her for the first time. She was mostly unassuming, except for her eyes. They were slitted like a cat, and I had to stop myself from lashing out at the sign of a lycanthrope. If she was working here and openly unafraid of showing her eyes, it meant she was safe to be around. Either an evolved form that could hold off her shift, or the child of a woman bitten while pregnant, and couldn't shift at all.

"It's this way."

"Thank you." I hurriedly finished my plate of food, and downed what was left in my mug before following her.

She had similar features to most people in the region, slender with dark hair, but her eyes made the more subtle differences stand out. She moved almost silently, and her motions were almost unnaturally fluid. The tips of her ears had a tiny point to them and were slightly oversized for her frame. It wasn't quite as pronounced as the elves had been on the eighth world I was sent to, but still noticeable. My guess was some kind of cat shifter.

"My mother was bitten while she carried me." She turned to look at me as she held the door open. "I could feel you staring at me." I opened my mouth to apologize, but she shook her head and looked down at her feet. "It's okay. Everyone does it. I'm used to it by now."

"Can you shift?"

My question seemed to surprise her. Apparently, most people didn't continue talking after finding out she carried the taint.

"I-I can't." She shook her head and looked back down at her feet. "Even on the full moon, the most that happens is my fingernails growing really long."

"That's probably a good thing. I imagine some of the hunters out there wouldn't stop to ask questions if you could manage more than that." I moved past her into the room, placing my hand on the doorknob. "Thanks for preparing a bath for me."

"It's my job." She shrugged and pointed at the knobs hanging over the wooden tub in the center of the room. "The white handle is for hot water, and the black one is for cold. To drain it, just pull on the middle one. Soap is on the rim of the tub, and towels are in the cabinet." Before I could say anything else, she turned and left.

"Not one for conversation, I suppose." I dropped my pack, and jumped into the steaming water with all my clothes on. It had been a month since I had used a bar of soap, and what I was wearing needed a good scrubbing too.

After draining and refilling the tub three times, I finally felt clean enough to get out. Then I had to scrub and wash the three pairs of even dirtier clothes in my pack, which then caused me to need another bath. While it was draining for one last rinse, I was doing my best to wring out my sopping clothes, the whole time debating in my mind what I would be willing to give up for a functioning washer and dryer. Before settling on what was an acceptable loss, my thoughts were interrupted by a scream. I froze, trying to gauge whether it was an 'I'm about to die' scream, or an 'oh, I saw a spider' scream. There is a difference, and while it is neither subtle nor nuanced, you still need to be listening carefully to tell them apart. A second scream confirmed it was the 'I'm about to die' version, and I took off running for the door.

On the way out, I only had time to grab my mace leaning against the door. It was the weapon I had the most experience with, and I had brought it with me for the past eleven worlds. It was a custom piece I had made myself, modeled after a flanged mace I had seen in a museum once. The whole thing was one solid piece of blessed star metal, with six thick ridges of metal for the head and a spike poking out the top. When I had first made it, the blades had been sharp enough to cut silk with only a touch. That changed immediately after I walked with it for the first time, and the heavy end banged against my calf as it hung from my belt. Really, who needs sharp blades on a mace? It didn't make much of a difference, especially when I was using all fifty of my Strength stat to pulp whatever I was hitting.

As I rushed into the room, naked as a jaybird, I entered just in time to see a vampire rip the throat out of the serving girl named Mattie, who had brought me my food. The innkeeper was backed up against the closed door to the kitchen, holding back two vampires with what looked like a silver letter opener. The other girl, Jess, peeked over the edge of the bar, her eyes flashing in the lamplight.

"Get back!" The innkeeper swiped at the outstretched hand reaching for him, leaving a burning gash on the palm of the vampire. "Damn you, Tren! How dare you turn, and then come into my place after. Get back!"

"No need to get upset, Frons. It isn't like I want to drain you. I just want to bite you! We're supposed to recruit some folks, and I thought of you first!" The undead creature snapped his fanged jaws at the innkeeper before leaping clear of the silver swung in his direction. "Trust me, you'll love the change. You won't believe the rush!"

"Liar! Back, you unclean thing!" He tried to swipe at the vampire a second time, but the other one darted forward and smacked the letter opener out of his hand. "No! Trinity, save me!"

"Look, I didn't like the movie *Twilight* very much, but I was a big fan of the Blade franchise. So, if I were you, I would turn around and walk out like a bunch of good undead, and wait for me to come and kill you in your lair." Giving away the element of surprise was a dumb move, but even I couldn't make it across a room filled with tables and chairs in time to save the surly innkeeper from two apex predators. Well, three apex predators, but the other one was busy drinking someone. Everyone in the room turned to look at me when I spoke, and I couldn't help but smile at the widened eyes peeking up from the bar area. Naked victory poses really put me in the best possible light. Hopefully.

The vampire formerly known as Tren looked back at the innkeeper and pointed a thumb at me. "Who's the crazy naked guy?"

The innkeeper shook his head. "No idea. Just stopped by for a night. Charged him double, though. Didn't like the look of him."

Tren nodded at the innkeeper's reply. "That's plain ol' good sense. You gotta make crazy people like him pay to be around normal folks."

The vampire drinking from the serving girl formerly known as Mattie poked his head up from behind the table he was crouched behind. "I can see why. He looks shifty."

I shook my head in disbelief. "You're kidding me, right? You're vampires. You murder people and drink their blood." I pointed my mace at the innkeeper. "And the two of us are going to have a discussion about fair business practices."

"Enough stupidity. Let's just kill the crazy guy and turn your friend. It's a long way back to the Mausoleum, and the Destitute will be angry if we're late." The vampire who had knocked the letter opener out of Frons's hand finally spoke up, his dry and raspy voice marking him as an elder vampire.

That made him the biggest threat. The older the vamp, the more powerful they became. I had no idea who or what a 'Destitute' was, but I definitely recognized it as a title.

"I have some questions you are going to answer before I kill you." I thought about the threat for a moment. "Kill you again, I guess."

The vampire drinking Mattie dropped her and threw a table at me, so I took a step back in the doorway and let the wall catch the heavy hunk of wood. The plaster walls barely held up to the impact, catching the table and momentarily blocking the rush of undead as all three charged me. It was ripped out of the way by Tren, who I introduced to the head of my mace in as violent a manner as I could manage. He spun away from the doorway, missing most of his face and throwing black blood over the sawdust-covered floor. The vampire flopped bonelessly to the ground and didn't get back up. Which, apparently, was a big surprise to the other two.

"Back! His weapon can hurt us!" The elder vampire hissed at me after shouting to his friend, and backed away as I walked through the door. "Who in the demonflame are you?"

"You mean besides being incredibly awesome?" I flipped the imaginary switch in my head that changed me from James, into the man given an endless quest by faceless and uncaring gods. I swung the head of my mace into the back of Tren's neck, pulping the spine and finishing off the undead creature. I made a fist, lifting my middle finger and thumb in a snapping motion that activated another spell that seemed to work no matter where I was. The blessed star metal of my mace glowed a vibrant blue before I even said the activation word. "I'm what this world has been missing. My titles are many, but most know me as the Chief Justice, appointed by the gods of many worlds to judge those who commit any gross wrongdoing, and mete out the proper punishments they have earned." I lifted my glowing mace and pointed it at the two undead cowering before me. "Your judgment, for the crime of murder, is *Purification.*"

One of only four active spells given to the Paladin class I had earned on my sixth world activated, and light blazed from my weapon like the noonday sun. With nothing more than a flick of my wrist, the light left it like a lightning bolt, destroying the vampire who still had blood from Mattie dripping down its chin. Only a scorched mark on the floor of the inn marked its death. The purification spell also scalded the elder vampire, crisping its exposed skin as it forced out a rasping scream of pain. Not the 'I just saw a spider' kind of scream, either.

I knelt down next to the monster, gently placing the spike on the head of my mace on its temple. "Now, like I mentioned earlier, you and I are going to have a little talk."

CHAPTER 4

After a brief conversation, I made my way back to the bathing room to wash off all the new gunk that always managed to get on me when I fought. At least I didn't have to wash any clothes. While scrubbing off the black blood from the vampire, I weighed the pros and cons of just fighting naked all the time. I mean, what were the real downsides? It was really just an extension of the washing machine debate I had with myself earlier, and I grumbled quietly as I put a set of still-damp clothing on. There was a spell I knew to warm things up, but plenty of experiments had ended with a bunch of burned clothing.

"What are you?"

The voice that came from behind me was barely audible, but it still scared the crap out of me.

"Stop that!" I tried to get my heart rate back to something close to acceptable and stuck my finger in Jess's face. "Do you enjoy scaring the bejesus out of everyone, or is it just me?"

"I don't know what a 'bejesus' is, or what a 'movie twilight' could be, and a 'blade franchise' is no weapon I am familiar with, but whatever you are, I want to come with you."

She had stumbled over the unfamiliar words, but I heard the conviction in her voice. Which was a problem.

"Look, Jess, I'm sure you're a great girl and all, but this just isn't working out. It's not you, it's me." I started stuffing things back in my pack, trying to hurry back to my room. Or, if necessary, out of this town.

"What does that even mean?" Jess gave me an exasperated look, which I completely ignored. "You don't understand what it's like to grow up lycan-touched in a village this small. No one wants to talk to me. No one even wants me around them. Parents threaten their children with bribing me to bite them when they act against their wishes!" Her catlike eyes brimmed with tears, and she choked down a sob before continuing. "And the counselor, he…he is a bad man, who hurts people."

"Whelp, gonna go cut off some more bits from that guy in the morning." I tightened down the straps to my pack and grunted as I lifted it onto my back. "Look, you aren't the first person to try to follow me around. You aren't even the tenth person. And you know what happens to every waif who tries to learn from the random traveling master who swings by and stirs up trouble?" I opened the door and stepped out to head to my room. "They always end up horribly scarred, maimed, or dead. Not necessarily in that order. You have good survival instincts, a roof over your head, and food to eat. That's more than you would have following me around. Just do yourself a favor, and stay here."

I left her fighting back tears, secure in the knowledge that keeping her from joining me was the better choice. It wasn't an exaggeration to say that everyone who joined me on my quest ended up physically worse off than they were before they met me. Not *all* of them had died, but only a few had survived long enough to benefit from becoming someone like me. Only five of the nineteen worlds I had been on before this one had a Judge left behind to successfully continue on the work, and none of them were fit for fighting in the field.

After making it through the thoroughly messed-up common room, I matched the symbol on my key to the one on the door to my room. I made sure to check it for bugs, and I was happily surprised not to see any. There was a plain bed, a small table, and a chair. Simple, but clean.

"Well, better get started." I dropped my pack on the ground and pulled out the silver crossbow bolts, along with the mold I had perfected back when I was trying to get my Runesmith profession. It was a large funnel attached to what looked like a miniature ice cube tray. Only, instead of ice cubes, it made silver bullets. It clicked together with easy familiarity, and I set it in the center of the small table on top of a ceramic plate so I didn't damage the wood. I held out my hand, palm facing downward, and brought my ring finger down to my thumb, making sure to keep the other fingers perfectly straight, and said the activation word. "*Heat.*"

After waiting for the metal funnel to turn cherry red, I dropped in three of the silver crossbow bolts. They gradually softened and melted into a puddle in the bottom of the funnel. I used a piece of wire to scrape off a thin layer of impurities, then slid aside the lever that opened the funnel's bottom. The liquid silver poured into the bullet mold, and I made sure all nine spaces were evenly topped off.

It only took a few minutes for the bullets to cool once I cut off the spell. They popped out of the mold, and I inspected them for any imperfections. After seeing the first batch was good to go, I repeated the process until I had melted down all the crossbow bolts into an even fifty bullets. With the amount of powder in the small keg, I would be set for a long time.

Reaching back into my pack, I pulled out my wristband. It was a contraption that had taken a lot of trial and error to get right, but it had been worth all the pain and powder burns. To the unknowing observer, it looked like a thick leather bracelet with three black metal tubes that ran across the back of my hand. Each tube was about three and a half inches long, with a diameter of about a fourth of an inch. They rested between the knuckles of my hand, only sticking out about an eighth of an inch past my fingers when I made a fist. A thin copper band stabilized the three tubes and wrapped around the edges of my hand.

The contraption looked odd, and felt awkward at first, but it was more than worth it. When I pulled on a pair of custom fingerless leather gloves, no one would even notice it beyond the very tips sticking out when I curled my fingers.

Loading it took some time, and was the biggest issue I had with it. There was no way to reload in the midst of a heated battle, and the accuracy was only good for about twenty feet. It was also the best secret weapon a Judge could ask for. A flicker of fire magic, and you could kill three enemies in as much time as it took to move your arm between targets. It had saved my life a countless number of times.

I had tried to make an actual firearm several times, but each attempt had failed miserably. The only metal I had that could handle the forces involved was the same blessed star metal that I used to make my mace. There was barely enough of it to make the tubes, so after months of experiments, I had settled on what I could get.

After filling my new powder horn, I measured out a load into each tube, dropped in a thin piece of parchment paper, and packed it all in place with the bullet. I used a plug of wax to keep it dry, and then put everything away.

By now, the sky was already starting to lighten, and I needed at least a few hours of sleep before I left for the next town. My goal was to reach a major city and learn what the serious injustices the people of this world were dealing with. I had seen several examples of rural leaders abusing their power, but that was the same story the world over. Well, *worlds* over, really. If things got too out of hand, the people would rise up and solve that problem on their own. What I was looking for was the kind of thing that only someone with my capabilities could change.

Right off the bat, I had figured out one thing that needed fixing. The stranglehold the various hunting guilds held over the people needed to change. But before I went and started burning down buildings and such, I wanted to have at least a basic understanding of what the political landscape looked like. And if the guilds were this bad, what else was going on? I needed to find out, preferably without anyone important knowing I was a new player in their games of intrigue. At least, not until I wanted them to know.

I was self-aware enough to realize that I was a hammer, so to me every problem was a nail. That wasn't likely to change anytime soon. What I *had* learned through several experiences in the past was that there was always more than one hammer out there, and I didn't want to get crushed by hitting the wrong nail at the wrong time. Knowing *when* to strike was just as important as knowing *how* to strike.

After settling down and propping the chair under the doorknob to stop potential intruders, I climbed into bed and closed my eyes. Tomorrow was going to be another day out in the wilds, and I had no doubt I would need my rest.

CHAPTER 5

I woke up to the sound of someone hammering on my door. Sitting up, I shouted for them to hold on. They ignored me, and only pounded harder. I fought free of the sheets and stumbled over to the door, ripping it open to see what was going on.

"See! I told you, he runs around naked like a crazy person!"

The innkeeper stood behind two men wearing a higher quality of armor than I had seen so far on this planet. It was a mix of leather and lacquered steel plate, with chainmail protecting their joints. The complete set was a pleasant shade of blue with gold highlights, with a golden hawk engraved on their chest plates over their hearts. Both soldiers were cut from the same cloth, with chiseled, rugged jawlines designed to make any woman swoon.

"You better arrest him, before he grabs his weapon. I saw him use it last night, and it has to be enchanted! And he doesn't even have a guild crest! That means I get the guild bounty for turning in an imposter, right?"

One of the soldiers held up his hand to silence the innkeeper and looked back at me, making sure to maintain eye contact. Probably a good choice, considering my state of undress. "Are you the traveler who assaulted the village counselor yesterday, and illegally hunted three of the advanced undead, which resulted in the death of an innocent bystander and destruction of personal property?" He was standing with his weight slightly forward, balanced on the balls of his feet, with his other hand resting on the hilt of the short sword hanging from his belt. Two stripes below his chest emblem probably made him the higher ranked of the two. The other soldier had a halberd that was too long for the low ceiling of the hallway they were in, so he held it horizontally, pointed in the general direction of my chest. These guys were no pushovers, and definitely came from a different group than the village guards.

I straightened up a bit and gave a quick glare at the innkeeper, who took a flinching step backward. I was definitely getting a refund. I turned back to the soldiers. "Do you mean, am I the traveler from distant lands who stopped the Counselor from cutting off the hand of a little boy, and then killed three vampires before they could murder everyone inside this establishment? Yes, that would be me."

The soldier with the halberd lowered his guard a little and glanced over at his leader. "None of that was in the report, Corporal. Or what the innkeeper told us."

"I'm aware, Private." The corporal looked back at me. "We'll get to the bottom of this. Why don't you put some clothes on, and meet us in the common room."

It definitely wasn't phrased as a question.

He turned to the private and nodded at the innkeeper. "Why don't you pull him aside and ask some more *pointed* questions about what happened last night, while I speak to the suspect."

"As you say." The private turned around and wrapped a muscular arm around a suddenly white-faced innkeeper. "Come with me, sir. We have some things to discuss. Is there a more…*discrete* place where we can talk?" The two walked out of sight, the innkeeper stuttering to answer as he dragged his feet.

"I'll be waiting." The corporal walked away, the whole time keeping his hand on the hilt of his sword. Before he left the hallway, he turned back and looked at me. "If I were you, I wouldn't try running."

"Wouldn't dream of it." I gave him a flippant salute and slammed my door. Getting dressed took longer than normal, mostly because I was being an asshole and taking my time. Intellectually, I knew it was a bad idea to insult the soldiers. Viscerally, I didn't care. They had been rude, if professional. I paused a beat… Professionally rude, I decided.

Packing everything neatly took two tries before I had it just the way I wanted it. The balance had to be just right if I wanted to avoid being sore at the end of the day. Once I was ready, I put on my wrist gun, gloves, and strapped on my weapons. I walked into the common room, using my staff like a walking stick.

"I was just about to come and check on you." The corporal was behind the bar, pouring some tea for himself.

I noticed a lack of a second cup for myself. So, I joined him around the counter and poured a mug of ale from the tap. I didn't like tea very much anyway. At least the soldier waited until I had walked back around, dropped my pack, and sat down before he started in on the questions.

"I need you to tell me exactly what happened yesterday, from the moment you walked into town, until the time you laid down for bed." He leaned forward over the bar, intruding into my personal space. "And don't leave anything out."

"First, I want to know who you are, and why I should even be listening to you. Like I said earlier, I'm not from anywhere around here, and I don't recognize your uniform." I took a drink and grimaced. "Please tell me this is just another poor example of the region's beer, and not the norm?" The other towns I had been to so far had ale that was equally as bad as this one.

"I don't drink, so I couldn't tell you."

I almost choked on the crappy beer, shocked to hear of a soldier on *any* planet who didn't drink.

The corporal waited for me to stop coughing before continuing. "I'm Corporal Leedy, squad section leader of Blue Branch in the Western Wardens, brother organization to the Eastern Marshals." He seemed shocked when my expression showed I clearly didn't recognize either of the names. "You have never heard of us? *The* Western Wardens. Tales of our deeds stretch from shore to shore in these lands!"

"Not from around here, remember?" I shook my head, finishing off my ale and pouring the foamy dregs on the sawdust-covered floor. "I'm sure you're important and everything, but that still doesn't tell me why I have to listen to you."

"We are the single most powerful branch of the Hunters' Guild, funded jointly by three kingdoms, and tasked to keep order across all regions of the Untamed Lands from the Sea of Solitude to the banks of the Mighty Reka, the river that divides the continent." He looked at me skeptically. "And you have never heard of us?"

"Nope." I shook my head and stood up to go poke around in the kitchen to find something to eat. Leedy followed me, leaving his tea on the bar. I didn't find anything immediately ready to eat, but a chunk of pork belly hanging from the pantry ceiling was calling my name. "You want some bacon?" I pulled it down, along with a pan that I put on top of the rack in the fireplace. "It's just as easy to fry up some for two as it is for one."

"But…you aren't lying." Leedy shook his head in disbelief, absolutely flabbergasted by my complete lack of knowledge. "How is this even possible? Did you grow up under a rock?"

"Yep, that's exactly what happened. Born and raised under a rock, until I grew tired of the scenery, and now I'm ready to explore. Or—and I know this might be hard to believe—maybe you aren't as big of a deal as you thought you were. Now, do you want some bacon or not?"

I mean, come on, man. Prioritize your life already!

He still didn't answer, so I used my folding pocket knife to slice the pork belly into ten thick strips, and placed them evenly throughout the pan. They sizzled almost immediately, and my stomach rumbled in anticipation. The ale might suck, but their bacon was on point. I guess this world wasn't a total loss. "Now, I take it that you are tasked with enforcing local laws, protecting the people, and generally keeping the peace. Would you say that neatly sums up your organization's role?"

"I think that's an accurate way to describe what the Western Wardens do, yes." Leedy seemed to snap out of it, finally getting back into his job as this world's version of the police.

Well, considering they operated across borders, maybe they were more like the FBI. Mentally raising his standing in my estimations, I decided to take him a little more seriously.

"Okay then, I agree to answering your questions, even though I'm still on the fence about ceding to your authority." I could tell that didn't make him happy, so I kept talking before he could raise an argument. "So, yesterday afternoon, I came into town in time to see a man about to cut off the hand of a child. He declared himself as the counselor of the region, and demanded that I be killed when I interrupted him."

The corporal nodded along, clearly having heard this part of the story before. Now, I hit him with the ol' okey-doke.

"Obviously, I determined him to be a liar, since no true leader of the people would stoop so low as to needlessly hurt a child, or order the murder of an innocent traveler. Since he was clearly some kind of criminal, I defeated his dastardly sidekicks and cut his hands off, to stop him from hurting children and innocents in the future."

The corporal's mouth dropped open slightly, completely blindsided by the way I described events.

"Tell me, Corporal Leedy, did you find and apprehend the man already? Or did he die from the wounds I inflicted?"

"Apprehend him?" Leedy winced, and all of a sudden, he couldn't look me in the eye. "Actually, he survived, and is at the Healing House now. I was ordered to arrest you for maiming the *real* counselor, and I am to take you to stand trial at the nearest branch of the Hunters' Guild as soon as possible." He was obviously ashamed after hearing how I saw events, and I almost felt bad for the man.

Almost.

His bacon privileges, however, were firmly revoked.

"So, you're telling me that the man who tried to hurt a child is actually in charge around here?" I shook my head as I flipped the bacon over, making sure it didn't burn. "Maybe I should have stayed under my rock, because where I'm from, you're arresting the wrong person. I guess your job doesn't include protecting children, then? It's okay to kill kids, but you have to leave the adults alone or you go to jail? Maybe that's why I haven't heard of your group before. Where I'm from, under that 'rock,' you would be seen as cowards. No, not cowards. Accomplices, who encourage people to hurt the innocent when the fancy strikes them."

"What? No!" Leedy looked a lot less sure of himself now and took a few retreating steps backward. "It isn't like that at all! The Western Wardens protect everyone. Especially children!"

"Oh really? Well, there's a saying where I come from. Actions speak louder than words. And your actions? They say that it's okay to hurt children, and the people who protect them are the criminals." I pulled the pan off the fire, dropping it onto the bar top. "Are we done here? Because if you aren't going to do your job and arrest the counselor for hurting children, I am going to eat this, track him down, and cut off some more parts of him for assaulting young women." I leaned over the bar, looking for a fork so I could eat my meal. "You are free to join me, unless you don't protect young women, either. I understand if you have to follow the laws that only protect the people in power, of course. Since that's what your 'guild' seems to really do anyway."

"You can't—I mean, we don't—!" He sputtered, clearly overwhelmed by the truth bombs I was dropping on him. "We do more than just protecting the people in power. We help everyone!"

"Whatever you say, Leedy. Pretty words, no substance, from what I can tell. Now, how about you run off and see what your man found out from the innkeep, while I finish my breakfast." I had given up on finding a fork, and just used my fingers to pluck a strip of bacon from the pan. It was hot, but I was willing to suffer minor grease burns for the crispy piece of delicious fat and meat. I was exaggerating, of course. Fifty points in Vigor meant that minor splashes of grease would be healed before I felt the pain, but I still remembered the pain of cooking a rasher of bacon in nothing but my underwear. I shuddered. Mistakes were made. "I won't run off yet, I promise."

The corporal, so sure of himself before, walked off without saying anything.

I was being overly harsh, but this was part of what I had to do when I arrived at each new world. Pointing out the hypocrisy and injustice in irrefutable terms to the people who actually enforced the laws was the first step in tearing down the system that perpetuated the problem. It had taken some trial and error to figure it out, but that was the fastest way I had found, and resulted in much fewer pitchforks and torches at the end of the day. People were people, no matter where you were. Most wanted to do the right thing. You just had to lift the veil that was blinding them to the truth.

"That wasn't very nice."

I almost jumped off my barstool when Jess spoke, and I spun to face her.

"Would you stop that!" I pointed at the pan in front of me. "I could have whacked you with that by reflex, and we would all be upset. You would have a nasty headache, and I would waste perfectly good bacon!"

She looked over my shoulder and reached over to snatch a piece. I had made enough for two people, so I didn't mind. "That Warden is only trying to do his job, and you are giving him a hard time." Instead of taking just one piece of meat, she took three.

That was less okay.

"Am I giving him a hard time, or forcing him to see how twisted the values are that he fights for every day?" I grabbed two slices of bacon this time, making sure I got a fair amount. "I think I'm being very nice, when you look at it that way."

"Sure, whatever you tell yourself." Jess fell silent, turning to look over the common room.

I let the silence settle. It gave me time to finish eating.

"Were you serious about what you said?"

I cocked an eyebrow, not sure what she was referring to.

"About cutting off more parts of the counselor. Are you really going to do that?"

"Deadly serious." I nodded, gripping the hilt of my sword with the hand not covered in grease. "That's what I do, Jess. I balance the scales. When someone does something bad, I do something worse back to them, so they know not to do it again. If they don't learn that lesson the first time, I don't give the bad people a second chance."

"Is that why I can't come with you?" She turned back around to face me, her feet scuffling on the floor. "Because you go after bad people?"

"One reason, yes." I stood up and walked back to the kitchen, so I could wash up at the stone sink I had seen. Jess followed me, scooping up the rest of the bacon. "There are a bunch more besides that one."

"What if I want to protect innocents from bad people, too?" Her cat eyes flashed, catching the morning sunlight that streamed in from a narrow window above the sink. "I saw what you did to those vampires last night." She lowered her voice, and leaned in to whisper conspiratorially. "You used *magic*." Jess swallowed hard, clearly intimidated by the thought of someone using a kind of power she didn't understand. "Would you teach me?"

"I'm not a wizard, Jess." Technically, I wasn't lying. I was classified as a mage, after all. "And even if I was, teaching a random serving girl I just met any form of magic would be crazy."

Jess nodded, probably in a mixture of regret and relief. "I understand. I guess that does make sense. You barely know me. If you were going to teach anyone, you would need to make sure they were worthy of such a gift."

"Exactly. See, I knew you would understand." I finished washing my hands and went to pick up my gear. Leedy was taking too long, so I decided to just pop out for a minute to visit with the counselor and come right back. The Wardens wouldn't even notice I was gone. Until they talked to the counselor again, of course. When he was speaking with a higher pitch, they were sure to notice something.

CHAPTER 6

My trip to see the counselor went about as well as you might expect. Lots of screaming, followed by death threats, and finished up with a lot of tears. At least he wouldn't bleed to death, considering I cauterized the wound. That's what caused most of the crying. On the plus side, I was pretty sure he was learning his lesson.

Don't do bad things, or they happen to you.

I was still waiting for some kind of title that said 'Bringer of Karma,' but it hadn't happened yet. Maybe on one of these worlds, I would meet the hidden requirements and get the title. If it even existed, of course. That's how I had gotten all of the ones I had already. Either as a reward for completing a quest, or just randomly after doing something. They had no rhyme or reason, so far as I could tell.

At least they gave bonuses to my skills and abilities, when I managed to get one. Right now, I was using the title 'Bloodletter' to remove the stains from my clothing as I walked. I had gotten it after cutting the throat of a wereleech on my seventh planet. That had been a really rough year, even if it had been great for leveling my stats. Everybody hates leeches, and the human-sized versions were even worse than they sounded. The title I gained gave me the ability to wash 'bad blood' off just about anything, as long as it was still fresh. It only worked on blood, but with my job, it was still a lifesaver.

By the time I made it back from visiting the counselor, everyone was waiting for me in the common room. As I opened the front door, the shouting coming from inside cut off abruptly. From the sounds of things, several people were very upset. All eyes turned to me as I shut the door quietly, pulling it closed and latching it gently. Being quiet didn't seem to defuse the situation very much.

"What happened to 'I'll be right here when you get back,' *sir*?" Corporal Leedy appeared to be angry with me. It might have been the sarcastic way he said sir that tipped me off. Or the way he was swinging around a set of shackles in one hand, and a bared sword in the other. "You have been gone for an hour!"

"No, what I said was, 'I won't run off yet, I promise.' And I didn't run off. I'm still in town, aren't I?" I pulled off my pack and dropped it near the door. If things were about to get a little spicy with the Wardens, I didn't want it weighing me down. "Besides, I did tell you exactly what was going to happen. I finished my breakfast, and then went and saw a man about changing his ways."

"Oh? Who did you talk to?" The private spoke up, covering for the suddenly pale corporal. "Was it a nice chat?"

"It doesn't matter!" The innkeeper nearly exploded in frustration, his features twisted and angry. "Why are you even talking to this criminal? Just arrest him, and give me the bounty!" His eyes flickered to my heavy pack and weapons. "I'll hold on to his belongings for payment of the damages, and the unpaid bill he ran up while staying here."

"Don't listen to him! The warrior paid double the going rate for staying the night." Jess spoke up for me from behind the bar, earning herself an angry look from her boss. "What? He saved your life, Frons. You should be thanking him, not trying to get him arrested!"

"Charging me double didn't cover the cost of breakfast this morning?" I shook my head and rested my hand on the hilt of my ninjatō. "Do we need to have a sit-down about the right way to treat paying customers? We still haven't had our discussion about fair business practices, and now you are compounding the issue."

"*Enough!*" Corporal Leedy pointed his sword at me, and despite his frustration, its tip didn't waver. "Private Murphy, please go and check on the counselor. See if he's still alive." He turned, pointing his sword at the innkeeper. "And you, stop lying! It's clear that this man was not actively trying to unlawfully steal bounties from the Guild, so stop pushing him to be arrested for Guild violations."

"But what about carrying enchanted weapons?" Frons pointed at the mace dangling from my belt. "Magic held by anyone without a guild sign means immediate arrest!"

"I haven't confirmed if he has magic or not." The corporal turned to look back at me. "But there are plenty of other reasons for me to arrest him, so for now, please go about your day as normal, and let us do our job!"

"Fine." The innkeeper stomped his foot like a petulant child and stormed off to the back. He grabbed Jess on his way out, pulling her along behind him. Before they disappeared behind the curtain, he turned and looked back at the Warden. "Don't come crying to me if he magics you into a toad!"

"A toad?" I shook my head, heavily debating on just turning around and leaving. "I'm not a sorcerer, or a druid. I won't be turning anyone into animals."

"You. Sit." Leedy pointed to a chair in the center of the room. "We have more things to discuss before I decide what to do."

I propped my staff against the wall next to my pack before walking over and sitting down. There was a bracelet that I thought about grabbing from one of the pockets lining the outside of my pack, but I decided against it. If the corporal was going to check for magic somehow, it would immediately set off whatever tool or spell he used. At least inside the lining of the pocket, nothing would be able to detect it. As far as I knew, anyway. This world might still surprise me.

"Now, what would you like to talk about, Corporal?" I leaned the chair back on two legs, ignoring the creaking protest of the cheap wood. "I'm an open book. Ask me anything."

He waited until the private walked out the front door before saying anything. "First, before he gets back, is there anything you want to tell me about what you were doing while you were gone?" Leedy sat down in a chair opposite mine, just barely out of easy reach. Instead of leaning backward like me, he sat on the edge of the seat, his sword point digging into the floor between his feet. "Did you really do something to the counselor?"

"I haven't lied to you once." I had to pause to hold back a yawn. It was shaping up to be a long day, and it was barely after breakfast. "When I said I was going to cut off more of his body parts for assaulting women, I meant it. You won't do anything to him, so I did my job, and Judged him for his crimes."

"And just what is your job? I thought you were just a traveler from far away, not doing a job." Leedy paused, squinting at me. Maybe it was more of a grimace. I chose to go with squinting. It felt nicer. "Wait. I don't even know your name yet."

"That's because you haven't asked until now." I leaned forward again, dropping my chair onto all four legs. "My name is James, and I'm the Chief Justice of the Order of Judgment, tasked by the gods to balance the scales on whatever world they decide to send me." I frowned, thinking about the newest quest I received, when I stepped onto this world. "And I am on a quest to find the 'Silver Star,' whatever that might be."

Corporal Leedy laughed, then stopped when he saw I wasn't smiling. "Wait. You're serious?" He squinted at me. "There wasn't a lie in anything you just said, but my ability only tells me if you *know* you are lying. It doesn't mean it's true."

"Well, I might be crazy, but that has no bearing on reality. I was sent here to right the wrongs of this place, and that's exactly what I'm going to do." I leaned back again, almost hoping that the chair would break and cost the innkeeper a little more money. "The 'Silver Star' thing is new for me, but I'll figure that out too."

"Everyone knows about the legends of the Silver Star. You aren't the first treasure hunter to try to track down the Lost Airship of Princess Starnight." Leedy waved his hand in a generally northern direction. "It was supposed to have been lost in the mountains north of here, but no one can make it through them without freezing to death. Otherwise, the single most important mixture of magic and technology ever created would have been found ages ago. It's probably nothing but a pile of splinters by now, anyway." He stood, stretching his lower back. "The storm that caused it to disappear was old news when my father was just a youngling, still trying for the Guild Academy. Besides, you won't be heading north anytime soon."

"Oh?" I rocked back a little farther, subtly balancing without my feet touching the ground. It was a display of very advanced balance and physical ability that could have been considered showing off. "And why is that?"

"Because I'm going to arrest you, to stand trial for assaulting the counselor." Leedy stood, pointing his sword once again at me. "At first I thought you were making some valid statements, but now I know you're just some crazy treasure hunter. Stand up and remove your weapons, then place your hands behind your back."

"No, I don't think I'm going to let you arrest me right now, Leedy." I didn't move, maintaining my balance. "Don't you want to hear what the Private has to say first?"

"That isn't necessary. It's obvious what you are now, and my job includes making sure people like you don't go around disrupting the peace. Treasure hunters are all the same. Desecrating temples, destroying tombs, running off and leaving their families for their next big score. I won't allow this to continue." Corporal Leedy took a step forward, closing the gap between us. "Now, on your feet. I will force you to comply if you don't listen."

"Oh, I'm listening, all right." I rolled backward out of my chair and sprang to my feet. I pulled my ninjatō free of its sheath, the runes along its length glowing a subdued red. That told me there were a whole lot of enchantments on Leedy's gear. At least it wasn't glowing blue or green. Those would have signified something much worse. "I think you've misunderstood who is in control here. The one with all the leverage in this situation isn't you. It's *me*."

"You want it the hard way then? Fine. That works too." Leedy's armor seemed to brighten, and his sword suddenly darted for my legs as he lunged forward. To a normal person, it would have been so fast that reacting in time to stop him would be nearly impossible.

I was not a normal person.

I shifted my hips, taking the blow on the metal haft of the mace hanging from my hip. I could have slashed Leedy across the face with my sword, but I held back. Instead, I slapped him with the flat of the blade. On the ear. Which I knew had to hurt like the dickens.

"Now Leedy, you should stop before someone gets seriously injured."

He touched his ear, wincing in pain. A thin trickle of blood from his earlobe was proof enough that I had already won this fight. He knew it, I knew it, but his pride hadn't given up yet. Another lunge, this time aimed for my face, forced me to spin out of the way. I used my ninjatō to guide his sword to the side, forcing an opening to his midsection. Once again, I didn't take advantage of it, instead poking him in the chest hard enough to stop him in place. Three inches higher, and it would have been buried in his throat.

"I mean it, Leedy. Knock it off."

"*Warden's Wall!*" The corporal didn't listen to reason, instead activating some unknown device or spell that forced me back into the tables and chairs behind me.

I wasn't expecting him to have such a strong defensive ability, so I was unable to counter it before I was tripping over broken furniture. At least some of the innkeeper's stuff got broken.

While I was unbalanced, Leedy threw the shackles at me. They were heavily enchanted, and somehow snapped into place around my wrists when I raised my sword to block them from hitting me in the face. The shock must have shown on my face, because Leedy let out a low chuckle.

"That's right. There's a reason why the Western Wardens are feared across the wilds. We can bring down any foe, kill any monster, and capture any criminal—" He was cut off by the scream of shearing metal, as my runed ninjatō sliced through the enchanted chain connecting the two bracelets of metal. It was an awkward angle for me to cut, but my magic-eating sword had no problems dealing with the thick links. The more magic used when making something, the easier it was to cut through. Although swords weren't my first choice in a weapon, when I had found this one, there was no way I was going to pass it up.

Slicing off the bracelets around my wrists only took another second, and when I was done, the clinking sound of them falling to the ground seemed to break the hold on Leedy. He rushed forward, swinging his sword at me as if I were some kind of tree that he desperately needed to chop down. Considering I wasn't a tree, it didn't go like he wanted.

Each swing of his sword I blocked with my ninjatō, though I refused to move my feet. I was once again showing him how outclassed he was, using my maxed stats to overpower him. I didn't know yet whether this world had stats and classes like some of the others I had been to, but I would guess they were in the high teens or low twenties. Double what a normal person on my Earth could manage. It was still less than half of where I was now.

Finally, I got tired of fighting. I didn't want to kill him, so putting him down to cool off seemed like the best option. I waited for him to wind up for a mighty downward slash, and drew forward enough to crack him across the jaw with my elbow. He dropped to the floor like a puppet with his strings cut.

"Well, that was quite a show." Private Murphy poked his head inside the inn, and stepped fully inside when he saw I wasn't going to finish off his leader. "Did you have to hit him so hard?"

"He wasn't listening." I shrugged and moved to the bar to get an ale. The burst of physical activity had caused me to work up a little sweat. "I take it you talked to the counselor?"

"Yes, sir. He told me to not get in your way, and under no circumstances were we supposed to try to arrest you." Private Murphy walked over to check on Corporal Leedy. "Is he going to be okay?"

"He'll be fine. Just let me drink this terrible excuse for an ale, and I'll check him over." I took a long drink and got a refill from behind the bar. "Did the counselor say anything else?"

"Well, he wasn't much for talking, sir, but he did say he was sorry. Kept repeating it over and over, mumbling it under his breath." Murphy shivered, a faraway look in his eyes. "I don't know what you did to him, but I hope I'm never on your bad side."

"Me too, Murphy. Me too." I finished my ale and knelt down next to the corporal. "Before I help him, can you tell me of any towns farther north?"

"Oh, sure. If you go down the eastern road to the next town, there's an old trail that heads north." Murphy used the butt of his halberd to draw a rough map in the sawdust on the dirty floor. "There's three or four little hunting outposts in that direction, but you gotta look out for the werebeasts and undead. Not to mention the ogres, goblins, and such. I even heard a rumor of some witches living in the foothills of the mountains stirring things up recently, though most people don't go that far north. It's too dangerous." He drew another line, going farther east from the intersection with the northern path. "If you go another three days this way, you could visit Greendown. It's a proper city, and finding a guide would be easy. You might even be able to hire some folks from the Hunters' Guild to help you handle the really bad stuff." He looked me over, pointedly observing my lack of armor. "It's a good place to find some proper gear, too."

"Thank you, Murphy. I appreciate it." I touched Leedy on the forehead with my index finger, tracing an invisible letter '*J*' before drawing a circle around it. My very first profession, Healer, kicked in, and a trickle of energy left me, causing Leedy's head to glow a faint yellow. "Now, I best be off, before he wakes up."

"You're a healer?" Murphy took two steps away from me. "Why didn't you say you were in the Healers' Guild? That would have shut that innkeeper up right quick. And the corporal wouldn't have tried to arrest you, that's for sure."

"I'm not *in* the Healers' Guild, Murph. Not yet, anyway." It was definitely something I needed to check into once I got to this Greendown, especially if it would help me cut through the political red tape of the region. "Thanks again. I'll be sure to check out the city before I venture any farther north." I got up after making sure Leedy was going to be okay. "See you around, Murph."

Murphy winced at my shortening of his name before looking down at the unconscious corporal. "I'm sure I will, sir. I'm sure I will."

CHAPTER 7

"Commander Gleason, I think he's fallen unconscious again."

The man wearing the uniform of the White Wardens, the investigative division dedicated to rooting out criminals violating the laws set forth by the guilds no matter where they might hide, dropped the mundane leather whip he was holding and glared at the man who had spoken to him.

"Do I need to explain everything to you? Have the healers look him over. I want answers, and he's not allowed to die before I have them." Gleason waved his hand in irritation at the sergeant assisting him for the day. "No, don't untie him, idiot! Bring the healer *here*. I want him *alive*, not given *relief*."

Chastised, the Warden rushed off, leaving the bleeding man tied to the post where he had been for the past several hours.

Gleason was relentless when he suspected a man of wrongdoing, and wouldn't stop until he found the truth he was looking for. The prisoner should feel lucky, despite his reluctance to confess. At least he wasn't using his enchanted weapons. The training yard he was using at the moment near the front gate made it more difficult to interrogate prisoners, but his usual location was under renovations after the last…*incident* that occurred. His temper had gotten the best of him, leading to a few walls needing repairs.

"Making more friends, I see."

Gleason looked up to see the only Warden in the city who might have the slightest chance at matching him in power besides the Commandant. The man was on horseback, wearing the uniform of a Blue Warden, with the armor and rank of a captain.

"Don't you tire of beating on innocent civilians and ordering around underlings, Gleason? You should join me outside the city on a hunt sometime. It might do you good to fight a real monster or two for once."

"Innocent?" Gleason snorted in derision. "This man is a member of a conspiracy dedicated to undercutting the Potters' Guild. Do the starving families of hundreds of potters seem so trivial to you, Captain Cross?"

"I'm not trying to do your job, Commander. All I'm saying is that getting out of the city would broaden your horizons about the threats we face." The Blue Warden shrugged and turned to leave. "It's your choice, of course. Anyway, I'll leave you to your work. The Commandant has me on a special mission, so I best be off."

Gleason's brow furrowed. "A special mission? Why would the Commandant select you over me for something like that?" After all, Gleason knew he was the better choice. He could perform more powerful magic and had won far more duels in both the Hunters' Guild and Warden tournaments.

"I'm not supposed to talk about it." Captain Cross put a gentle heel to his horse, sending it walking slowly toward the nearby gate. "This isn't exactly a secure area to speak of such things."

Not one to give up so easily, Gleason kept pace with the Blue Warden's horse. "Look around. No one is foolish enough to listen in on one of *my* private conversations. They wouldn't dare." Of course, a quick glance proved him right. Not a single person was close enough to eavesdrop. "You might as well tell me. I'll find out anyway."

Captain Cross winced, aware of the things the commander might do to uncover a secret he wanted to learn. "Fine. I was requested specifically by *The Oracle*. There's a new threat that has cropped up, and I was chosen to put it down, no matter the cost. I've had word from some of my men who have pointed me in the right direction, and now I'm going to take care of it."

Gleason stumbled, almost tripping over his own feet. "*The Oracle* requested you, over me?" The Blue Warden nodded his head in acknowledgment, and Gleason could feel his heartbeat in his ears. "I suppose I should wish you well. Trinity's blessings make your path easy."

"Thanks." Captain Cross raised a hand in farewell, spurring his horse onward. "I'll tell you how it goes when I return."

"You do that!" Gleason waved, the smile on his face not reaching his eyes. Once the Blue Warden was out of sight, he turned back to the yard where his prisoner was still tied up. The healer had finished applying some salves and stood off to the side, where his sergeant waited.

As Gleason approached, the sergeant stepped forward to speak with him. "Commander, the healer said—"

Brushing past the Warden, Gleason picked up the blood-encrusted whip off the ground. As he unfurled it, the words of Captain Cross ran through his head. Rage bubbled up in his chest. Why would *The Oracle* not choose him, the strongest of the White Wardens? Why wouldn't the Commandant want his best on a mission to put down a threat that warranted the attention of the Trinity? Had he not proven himself, time and time again? Was there more he needed to do? What more did the gods demand? Did he need to—

"Commander!"

Gleason looked over to see his sergeant had grabbed his arm, stopping him from swinging. When had he started whipping the prisoner again?

"Commander, I-I think he's dead. You can stop now."

The courtyard was covered in blood and gore. Streaks of it ran across his white robes, staining their pristine appearance. Both the sergeant and healer looked at Gleason with fear in their eyes. His prisoner was barely recognizable as human. He looked as if he had been shredded in an animal attack. Taking a deep breath, Gleason let go of the whip and freed himself from the sergeant's grasp.

"Clean this up. I need to change." As Gleason left the courtyard, he stopped and glanced back at the sergeant. "On second thought, toss the body to the side, but leave it in plain sight. Then, bring in the next one. His brother, I think. I still need to know who else is in their group."

Gleason wouldn't let such a minor setback stop him from completing his mission, especially now that he knew he still had to prove his fidelity to the Trinity. And prove himself he would. One evil criminal's pound of flesh at a time.

CHAPTER 8

As I left town, I noticed a dark and heavy cloudbank moving in from the west. It looked like I was about to get soaked. Now was the time to pull out the bracelet. I waited until I was out of sight of the town before digging it out of my bag.

It was a simple black band with a line of runes carved down the center, and it had taken me almost a full year to get right. Gaining Runesmith as a 'Profession' within the system forced upon me—instead of the regular version of a profession—meant I had to make something worthy of a proper Runesmith, not just a Blacksmith who knew some engravings. The bracelet had been the item that helped me make the jump from dabbler into professional.

When I put it on my right wrist, opposite my hand cannon, it grew on its own enough to close around my wrist. It was a constant drain to wear it, but I had just gotten clean, and having a personal shield to keep me dry was worth it.

The bracelet glowed a dull green, letting me know I was alone. It would glow yellow if someone who could use magic was close, and red if it was actively defending against an attack. I had added that feature after dealing with a group of psionics who didn't use visible magic. Just thinking about those assholes gave me a headache. Ain't no head pain like a brain-sucker attack.

As soon as it had drained enough mana from me, the bracelet activated. A soap-bubble-thin film wrapped around my body like a second skin, protecting me from the rain that started to fall. It had taken an embarrassing amount of time to get the shield enchantment to contour to my body instead of turning me into the mystical equivalent of Bubble Boy. Which was not someone you wanted to be.

I'd learned that lesson the hard way, after being smacked down the side of a steep mountain by a war troll on my twelfth world. I was sent rolling downhill, plastered to the inner wall of my shield for an eternity before finally slamming into a tree thick enough to stop me. Never again.

The shield was strong enough to block one or two major attacks, five or six minor attacks, or keep the rain from soaking me for about half a day. It had kept more than one arrow from killing me, especially after I had made a name for myself on a new planet. Those who were afraid of the changes I represented always thought of using an assassin at some point. Usually right after trying to assault me in a dark alley somewhere. Which wasn't a very nice thing to do, really.

Hearing the rain drum against the barrier had a soothing effect, and soon I found my mind drifting back to a few days ago, when I had been transported to this new world.

"Are you sure you have to go?" Sinthia stood in front of a group of children, cradling a broken arm. Her golden waves of hair glinting in the moonlight only enhanced the beauty she projected, despite the dirt and injuries from the final battle we had barely won. "We still need you here."

"This isn't my choice. The gods determine when I go, and I'm no better than a leaf caught in a hurricane." I fought back the urge to kiss her, knowing that I would leave a piece of myself behind if I did. "As long as you don't allow things to regress to the way they were, life will be better for everyone, like it should have been in the first place."

"I would change everything back to the way it was if it meant you could stay." A single tear traced down her cheek, creating a streak of clean skin through the grime and blood. It was the only clean spot on the battlefield covered in the bodies of our friends and the forces we had barely defeated. "None of it matters if you aren't here."

"Don't say that." I reached forward, healing her injured arm with a push of my recovering mana. She grimaced in pain as the bone set, but she suffered in silence, the grit and determination that was one of a thousand reasons for me to love her, making my heart ache. "This is about more than just you and me. We have changed the world with today's victory. Freeing children who can do magic will make all the difference."

Before she could answer, a hole in reality ripped open behind me. The pull wasn't strong enough to drag me through yet, but I knew from experience that it would grow stronger the longer I avoided going through the portal.

"It isn't fair!"

Sinthia reached out for me, and I took a step back, afraid of what would happen to my already fragile heart if we touched. The look of anguish on her face almost broke me.

"There's so much I want to tell you. So many things I should have said. We deserve to be together!"

"What we deserve and what we get are seldom the same thing." I nodded to the dozens of freed children cowering behind her. "Get them somewhere safe, and teach them what you have learned. They are the future this place needs."

"I will!" The wind forcing me backward almost drowned her out, its pull growing faster than ever before. "I love you, James!"

My eyes never left hers as I was dragged through the portal, leaving yet another piece of my soul behind.

I wiped at the moisture dampening my cheeks. Stupid shielding must have sprung a leak. While I scrubbed at my face with my sleeves, my system dinged with an alert.

> **New Title Earned**: Hide-and-Seek Loser
>
> -Your lack of ability to sense those spying on you has gained the attention of the gods. Lucky you!
>
> **Skill Imparted**: You become 10% more likely to discover someone spying on you. An additional 10% will be applied if the entity spying on you has no negative intentions.

Another notification from the 'gods' who landed me here. For the thousandth time, I cursed the invisible entities who used me like a punching bag in some kind of perverse game I was forced to play.

The sound of someone rustling through the leaves off the road to my right reached my ears, and I sighed. It looked like someone from the town had followed me as I left. Considering the properties of the new title meant they were most likely friendly, I made a not-so-great intellectual leap and guessed who it was.

"Jess, you might as well just come out." I was surprised to see my bracelet flicker from green to yellow as she approached, but it settled back to green as she stepped out of the underbrush. "I told you not to follow me, remember?"

She got to the edge of the muddy road and stopped, unwilling to come any closer. "I know."

Her bedraggled appearance matched her tone, and I almost felt bad for her. Almost.

"You don't understand, though. When I stood up for you in front of the Wardens, Frons tossed me out. I don't have anywhere else to go." Jess had a small pack on her back, and she carried a staff that resembled my own, with a long dagger hanging from her belt. Without the super-cool additions I had made to mine, of course. Her clothes were thick canvas, dyed a dark brown and green to blend in with the surrounding landscape, and clunky boots with soles thick enough I had no idea how she managed to follow me for so long without making more noise.

I didn't see a waterskin, and the pack was too small to hold much food. She was soaked through, thin, barely old enough to be considered an adult, and short enough that she hardly reached my shoulders—basically, she looked as pitiful as a kitten forced to take a bath, in order to pluck as many heartstrings as possible. Whether it was on purpose or not, I had no idea. The universe could be downright mean sometimes.

"I take it you left in a hurry?" I leaned on my staff, feeling its tip dig into the mud a few inches before hitting something. "Because you aren't well-prepared for a journey through the wilderness."

"I grabbed what I could, but most of my belongings were loaned to me by Frons. This is all I have." Jess shrugged, her soaked clothing dragging down her shoulders. "My savings bought these clothes, and this dagger. It's supposed to be blessed, so it can hurt the undead." She indicated the simple bone handle, and I held out my hand to test it.

"Let me see." I took it from her, and admired the simple craftsmanship. Thick blade, sharp edge, and a faint blood-groove to keep it from sticking in an opponent. Also, definitely not blessed or magical in any way. "Yeah, you got ripped off. A vampire would shrug that off with no problem. You could still kill a zombie or skeleton, but you would need to crush the skull or remove the head, like any plain weapon." It also meant my bracelet activated because of *her*, not because of her weapon, which made me doubt what she said about not being able to shift.

"What?" Jess took it back, staring at the weapon as if it would bite her if she took her eyes off it. "All my savings, everything I had…"

"So, you want to join me, but you don't have any food, water, shelter, or effective weaponry." I turned to keep walking down the road. "I don't think this life is for you, kid."

Jess hurriedly sheathed her dagger and jogged to keep up with me. "I can cook, and clean, and wash your clothes, and I don't mind taking a watch during the night to look for predators." She stumbled, and I reached out to catch her before she did a facer into the mud. "And I… I don't have anywhere else to go." She shrugged out of my hand and looked down at her feet as they squished into the road. "Please, don't make me go back."

"I'm sure you are very good at all of those things, but so am I." I picked up the pace, forcing her to hurry to keep up. "I won't force you to go back. That isn't my place, and I do owe you a little for sticking up for me." I squinted through the rain, thinking hard about how to best balance the scales between us. "I'll get you to Greendown, and you can start a new life there. Sound good enough?"

Jess looked up, grinning large enough that I could see that her canine teeth had a sharper point than a regular human would ever manage. With her slightly pointed ears, slitted eyes, and sharp cheekbones, she looked more catlike than ever. "Deal!" She perked up, happy that she got her wish. "What's the plan to get there? Are we going to stop by each town and straighten them out too? Protect the weak, like you did in my village?"

"What? No." I thought about how things had been going since I stepped into this world. "Maybe. It depends on how they act."

"Yes!" She pumped her fist, excited about the prospect of getting into a fight. Just like every other young person who had never been in a proper fight before. "I *knew* it! We are going to fix the countryside first, and then, after they see the error of their ways, we can move into the big cities, and after that—"

"Stop." I shook my head, putting a kibosh on her imagined future of conquest. "You are going to find a nice job in Greendown, and I am going to go where my quest leads me. There won't be any 'fixing' of anything."

Jess looked at me sideways, clearly not believing me. "Sure, of course. You won't be bringing your *Justice* to everyone we meet. Right."

"It's not *my* Justice, Jess. It just *is* Justice. Justice is an impetus—a *power* with its own unstoppable momentum—an implacable force that both needs no arbiter, and demands it at the same time. There is a saying where I come from that states, 'all it takes for evil to triumph is for good men to do nothing.' I'm not a good man, Jess. I'm just working on that 'not doing nothing' part."

I sighed again, suddenly realizing I had been doing it a lot lately. Already, I started to make plans for how I could ditch her in the city without her knowing where I went. Her enhanced senses would make it hard, so planning now only made good sense. Her actions so far already proved she would follow me otherwise, no matter what promises she made here and now.

"Let's hurry. We need to pick up the pace if we are going to make it to the next village before our food runs out. I wasn't planning on feeding anyone besides myself."

Jess skipped happily as she gave me a thumbs-up.

It was hard to hold back the groan that wanted to escape over having to deal with someone who had 'pep.' I was too old and tired to deal with 'pep.' Young people were exhausting.

We walked for three whole minutes before she started talking again. "Where are you from?" When I didn't answer, Jess fell silent again. For about two seconds. "How did you get to be so good at fighting? You don't look very old, but you fight like you've seen a lot of battles."

My only answer was to speed up even more, my longer stride making her struggle to keep up.

"If we go too fast, you're going to walk right past the trail to the waypoint without seeing it."

She was breathing heavier, which genuinely surprised me. I would have guessed that her lycan ancestry would help improve her strength and stamina.

"What waypoint?" I looked around carefully, not changing my pace. "I haven't seen or heard of any waypoints along any of these roads, and I've been walking them for more than a few days now."

Jess sped up to get in front of me and held out an arm to slow me down. "I'll show you, if you would just slow down enough for me to check the trees." She pointed to a birch tree a few paces back from the trail. "See? That tells you it's close."

I had to move closer to make anything out. The water draining down my shield was like a car windshield without any wipers, making it harder to see. Once I got close enough, the worn and faded carving of a campfire was barely visible in the bark of the tree. I had never noticed any markings on the trees, because I didn't know it was already there. This was just one of hundreds of examples of the things that made traveling between worlds so dangerous. You just never knew about the kinds of stuff everybody else took for granted.

The two of us kept walking for almost a mile before she abruptly stopped. Not expecting it, I almost bumped into her, barely managing to avoid the two of us ending up in the mud.

Jess tilted her head and sniffed hard, nostrils flaring. "Do you smell that?"

My Mind stat was maxed out at fifty, meaning my perception was very good. That didn't mean I used it all the time. It had taken weeks to figure out how to ignore the incredibly loud sounds, sharp features, and even sharper smells my enhanced stats caused. The headaches were not fun. Once I got past thirty points, worlds without proper bathing facilities, plumbing, and deodorant were definitely my least favorite. Which was most of them. The process of dialing it down had been a kind of meditation at first, but now it was a natural reflex, deadening my senses to more normal levels unless I concentrated to bring them back to superhuman levels. I focused on my sense of smell, and immediately noticed the subtle scent of smoke. "I think so, yes."

"That means someone is already using the waypoint." Jess bit her lower lip in concern. "Do you think we should skip it? If we keep going until midnight, we could reach the next one."

"Just what is at these waypoints? Why can't we set up our own place to camp?" I looked around the wet forest, trying to assess what dangers might be hiding in the shadows. When I looked back at Jess, I finally realized she was shivering pretty hard. That wasn't good. If physical exertion wasn't working to keep her warm, she was brushing up against the risk of hypothermia when the sun went down. Which, according to my mental clock, should be in about two hours. It was another thing I needed to keep in mind. Having a maxed-out Vigor stat meant things that I could ignore might kill her if I didn't pay attention.

"There is a small shelter, along with a well for fresh water, and a few metal stakes in the ground to tie a mount to overnight." She was fighting not to expose how cold she was, determined not to let it show in her voice. "But the biggest benefit is having a few small wards, four sturdy walls, and a roof when full night comes. You never know what creatures prowl the roads at night."

"Is that so?" I turned to head toward the source of the smoke. It was muted due to the rain, but I could still follow it. "Let's go then and get out of the rain." She sighed in relief, and I frowned at her. "And next time, speak up if you have a problem. I don't want to spend the next several days nursing you back to health when it could be avoided by just telling me. I'm used to this kind of environment, and you aren't. Don't try to tough it out when a few minutes of self-care now could save us days in the long run."

"I-I'm sorry. It won't happen again." Jess was having difficulty stopping her teeth from chattering. "I'll be fine after I get warmed up a little bit." She pointed farther up the trail. "Why don't we just look for the path that leads straight to the waypoint?"

"Because that's the way everyone expects someone to come from." I turned and pushed deeper into the damp underbrush, still following my nose. Jess stayed close behind, making almost no noise as we went. I felt a little better about not noticing her following me now. I shouldn't have been surprised, especially with her annoying habit of popping up like a shadow all throughout the inn. It wasn't much longer before I stepped into a clearing, and I could hear laughter coming from inside a small rectangular log cabin.

It reminded me of a bunkhouse from a summer camp I had gone to as a child, back when my parents still cared about what happened to me. The acrid scent of body odor assaulted my nose, and I immediately turned down my sensitivity. When I say 'assaulted my nose,' I meant it. At least one person inside the building smelled like they were rubbing a bag of onions all over their body as a hobby.

"I d-don't know, m-maybe we should j-just keep going." Jess must have smelled the inhabitants as well, and didn't relish the thought of being in an enclosed area with them any more than I did.

"No, you won't make it to the next rest area. We could make our own camp if this place doesn't work out." I approached the heavy front door and knocked loudly with the butt of my staff. "Who knows, maybe they'll be friendly!"

The door slammed into me, bouncing off my shield and knocking me back two steps. A man large enough to have an ogre in his family tree, wielding an oversized meat cleaver, stepped into the open doorway. The intense smell of onions and garlic hit me harder than the door ever could have managed, making my eyes water. While I fought down the urge to gag, the stranger gave me a gap-toothed smile. I didn't appreciate how the nature of his smile changed when he glanced at Jess, but I was in the business of punishing people for their actions, not their thoughts.

"Ah, visitors! Come in, come in. It's wet out there, and you'll catch your death." He turned a thumb toward another man sitting by a stone fireplace inside the bunkhouse who was picking his toes with the handle end of a ladle. The source of the pungent odor was coming from the cast-iron pot sitting over the flames. Well, some of the odor came from the pot. There was still plenty coming from the man in front of me. "We're almost done making the Vampire Bane potion, and we can have the leftovers as soup!"

With a grimace, I motioned for Jess to head inside. It was obvious she didn't want to go, but the firelight called to her like a moth to the flame. I was not a moth, and would very much prefer to not have to wash every article of clothing I owned to get the smell of garlic and onions out, but I was responsible for Jess until we reached Greendown. That meant I had to go inside too.

Sometimes, doing the right thing really was a punishment.

CHAPTER 9

"So, what brings you two out here in weather like this?" The man who answered the door had waited for me to step inside before putting down his giant cleaver, and loomed over Jess and me as we sat down together on the bunk farthest from the fire.

Inside the bunkhouse, the layout was surprisingly comfortable. Eight beds were lined up against the walls, with a walkway running down the center. Opposite the doorway was the fireplace, with enough space for two benches that allowed people to sit close to the fire. It had two tiny windows on each wall, barely big enough to reach an arm through. The thick timber walls made it feel cozy, and I could see why Jess thought it was a good idea to stay in a place like this. If there weren't weirdos already inside, of course.

"You aren't cursed, undead, witches, magic casters, or otherwise a threat to the Trinity, are ya?"

"We're traveling to Greendown, where my friend will be looking for a new job." I glanced over at the other man sitting by the fire, still picking away at his feet. "And who might you two be?"

"You don't recognize who we are by our clothing?" He motioned at what he was wearing, which was some kind of blend of leather, chain mail, and odd copper disks so old they had turned green. "Haven't you met a member of the Tinkers' Guild before?"

"Nope. You're the first." I nodded toward his partner, who had finally stopped picking at his feet, and now ladled the smelly mixture into glass jars laid out in a row in front of him. "If you are tinkerers, why are you making potions? Isn't that the job of some other guild?"

The man laughed uproariously, apparently finding my question to be hilarious. "Why would another guild make Vampire Bane? Have ya seen a member of the Alchemists' Guild ever lift a weapon? They'd crap their pants at the first sight of an undead, especially one that's smart enough to talk!" He walked over and picked up a potion, taking a small sip and smacking his lips. "Ah, that's the stuff! See, only the Tinkers' Guild has enough hair on our chest to go out in the wild, face the evils of the world, and then…" He looked over at me, expecting me to finish his sentence. When I didn't, he let out a defeated sigh. "And then, we fix broken pots."

Having the Alchemist profession myself, I could attest to the fact that they did occasionally lift a weapon or two when needed. I personally thought it was more likely the Alchemists' Guild didn't make the 'potion' because it smelled like a strip club garbage can, and no, I didn't want to think about what I had been doing near one of those. Shame could be more than skin-deep.

"Not just pots." The other man spoke for the first time. If I had to guess, I would say he was at least distantly related to the first guy. Big, hairy, and terrible personal hygiene. "We fix anything with metal. I like to sharpen things." He pointed at the ninjatō on my belt. "Can sharpen that for you, if you want."

"I just sharpened it, but thanks anyway." I pointed at one of the jars cooling on the floor. "I wouldn't mind buying one of those off you, though. I've never seen a Vampire Bane potion before."

"We're in the Tinkers' Guild…we don't sell potions." The guy who liked to sharpen stuff shook his head, clearly disappointed about not getting to play with my sword. "I'll just give one to you, if you have somethin' else I can sharpen."

"How about this?" I pulled out my folding pocket knife and held it up. "It could use a good sharpening." He seemed confused, until I opened it, showing him the blade.

"Oooh, you must be rich. I've never met someone who could afford somethin' like that out in the wilds before." He walked over—giving me the new and fun smell of bare feet that smelled like rotten corn chips—and traded me my knife for a potion. "I'll have it ready before you know it."

"Thanks." I set the potion down on the bedpost, not willing to put it in my bag without knowing it wouldn't leak out all over my stuff. "How much for sharpening the knife?"

The first man sat on the bed across from us, making the wooden slats groan in protest. "Two coppers, and a promise to not waste that potion." He tried to give me a disarming grin, but his eyes couldn't help but drift over to Jess once more.

"Here's the money." I handed over the coins, not bothering to barter. "And I assure you, we won't waste the potion."

"Yeah, James killed three vampires all by himself just last night!" Jess seemed to be recovering quickly, the color in her cheeks already starting to come back. "He didn't need a potion to do it, either. Took care of all three with only his mace, and didn't get a single scratch!"

The tinkerer sharpening my knife didn't react, but the one sitting across from us didn't like hearing what she said. He looked me up and down with a frown, and the temperature in the room seemed to chill just a little bit. "Ya say he killed three? I don't see a guild badge." His eyes flickered to his cleaver leaning near the door. "It's illegal to take bounties without a guild badge."

"Oh, the Wardens already talked to him. It was self-defense, not hunting." Jess squirmed, obviously realizing her mistake. "The vampires tried to turn the innkeeper, but he stopped them before they could."

"Well, I would still watch myself if I were in ya shoes." He stood, making his way over to his weapon and walking over to join his partner. "If word got out that someone was killing the undead outside the guilds, it could end bad. Even if it wasn't *really* hunting."

"Thanks for the warning." I spoke up before Jess could, trying to keep her from making things worse. The dynamic of the guilds being in charge was most definitely the first thing I needed to figure out when we got to town. "We're planning on getting back on the road at first light, so we better get some sleep." I moved to lay down on the bunk the tinkerer had just vacated, setting my ruck down next to it.

The tinkerer turned back to get a bowl of their 'soup,' his offer to share it with us apparently no longer on the table.

I was perfectly okay with that.

While both of them were busy, I decided to see just how effective their homebrewed potion really was. "*Identify.*"

> **Item**: Potion
>
> **Type**: Defensive
>
> **Grade**: 1/10
>
> **Description**: Barely more than a poorly made soup, this tincture will repel vampires, lycanthropes with advanced olfactory senses, and most other creatures with a nose that come close enough to smell it. Purity level is very low. Adverse side effects when consumed may include intestinal distress, halitosis, and a temporary reduction in the Vigor statistic.

Seeing the side effects wasn't any kind of a surprise, but I was genuinely impressed to see that it was an actual potion. It wouldn't do much beyond slowing down an enemy temporarily, and I decided to give it to Jess instead of risking it breaking inside my own pack. She didn't appreciate it very much.

"Why do I have to carry it?" Jess wrinkled up her nose when I passed it over to her. "It stinks."

"That's why you have to take it." I pointed to my ruck. "Do you want that stuff to get on our food?"

"How about I carry all the food, and you take this?" She tried to pass it back, but I was already lying down and doing my best to ignore her. "Fine, but don't expect me to hold onto it forever. If I'm supposed to get a job in Greendown, I can't smell like *this*."

I was already halfway asleep, trusting in my shield to protect me if the tinkerers tried anything. Neither of them carried anything magical, which would give me at least some warning if they tried to hit me with something.

Soon, the only sounds in the bunkhouse were the crackling of the fire, and the stropping of the knife as the tinkerer sharpened it. I hadn't gotten a good night's sleep in ages, and it was hard to keep my eyes open, despite the smell.

A loud thump coming from the door jerked me awake, and I held perfectly still. It took a heartbeat for me to remember where I was, and I could feel every bone I had ever broken throb in response to the realization that I wasn't sleeping on a pillow-top mattress with actual sheets. And a pillow. Oh, how I missed pillows. It had been two decades, and I still had moments like this.

"What was that?" Jess hissed the question, doing an admirable job of keeping her voice down.

The fire had died down while I had slept, and it was pure darkness inside the bunkhouse. Another loud thump shook the door in its frame, snapping the two tinkerers awake.

"Wuzzat?"

The shout from the more talkative tinker let whatever was outside know someone was inside. Apparently, it *really* wanted to say hello, because the door started to rock as the unknown assailant pounded on the thick timbers. Whatever it was, it had to be strong.

"Wake up!" The tinker who had sharpened my knife hopped out of bed and started stumbling into everything, making even more noise that only excited our late-night visitor even more. "Anton, something is trying to get inside! Wake *up!*" He found his partner and thumped him hard on the chest to get him out of bed.

"Okay, okay! Keep ya shorts on!" Anton sat up, his burly outline barely visible in the dim light. "What's all that racket about, Ausin?"

In a moment of fantastic cosmic timing, a giant fist punched through the small square window near Anton, throwing broken glass all over the shirtless man. The pounding at the door only increased, meaning we had at least two whatever-creatures-of-fun-new-terror trying to get inside. I finally got out of bed, grabbing my staff so I could maximize my reach in the tight confines of the building. I was about to twist the locking mechanism to unleash the spearpoint when I had to jerk back from getting hit by Anton as he fumbled with his cleaver.

"Lycans!" Ausin threw something that glinted in the dark at the thick arm grasping around inside the bunkhouse. It made a meaty thwap as it hit the fleshy part of the forearm, and the arm whipped back outside, taking the weapon with it. He let out a grunt, and his silhouette turned to look at me. "Oh…uh, sorry. That was your knife."

"Seriously? I liked that one." I didn't really care too much about the blade at the moment. Especially considering the thing outside didn't react at all when it got stabbed. Most lycans would have let out at least a small roar of surprise or pain. Instead, there was only silence. Not counting the one at the door. It still banged on that hunk of timber like it owed it money. "Why didn't it make a sound when you hit it?"

Jess appeared near my elbow, her cat eyes flashing in the darkness. "Because it isn't shifters outside. From the smell, it's a pair of *wendigo*."

The two tinkers gasped, and I had to think furiously about what in all the hells a wendigo might be.

"It can't be a wendigo. They are almost walking skeletons!" Ausin pointed to where the window used to be. "That thing's arm was big!"

"Only starving wendigos look like skeletons. That one has been eating well." Jess pointed to her nose. "Trust me, I've smelled them before, and this is definitely a pair of wendigos."

This was another problem I had come across more than once. Sometimes monsters in one world were called something else in another. Or—and this was by far the worse option—they had entirely unique monsters that I had no idea how to fight, or what weaknesses they might have. And although I enjoyed fun new nightmares that could wake me up in a cold sweat as much as the next guy, learning to fight something new with zero preparation and innocents to protect was the opposite of how I wanted to spend my night.

"What are we going to do?" Anton seemed jumpy, and that was never a good thing. Especially when the jumpy person was holding a giant meat cleaver. "We don't have any wormwood, or lilac water!"

I squeezed between the two, making my way over to the fireplace. "First, we get this fire going big and bright. Fighting in the dark with unknown friends can be even more dangerous than fighting in the dark with enemies." A thin scar running along my ribs that no amount of focused healing had managed to get rid of was proof of that. Man, world number eleven really had sucked. "Once we can see, things should start looking better."

Jess came over and knelt to help me get the fire going again, because I could only use one hand while I had my wrist cannon on. Didn't want that cooking off accidentally. As we waited for the fire to build, she leaned in close to speak quietly with me. The incessant pounding at the door ensured the tinkerers couldn't listen in.

"James, what are we going to do? Wendigo are almost impossible to kill, especially without the weapons meant to fight them." Jess glanced quickly back at the tinkerers. "But, there are only two of them, and when they kill something, they stop and eat the whole thing before moving on to the next victim. We could hide, and as soon as they started eating those two, we could run far enough away that they would forget about us." She shivered, but it wasn't from the cold. "I don't want to get eaten."

"I know you are scared, but running away while someone else gets devoured isn't the right thing to do." I stood up from my crouch in front of the fireplace and offered her a hand back to her feet. "And that's the opposite of what I do, Jess. I'm here to do the *right* thing."

Jess took my hand, and I pulled her up. She leaned into me, and I fought down the automatic reaction to hold her as we pressed together. The gap in my chest where Sinthia belonged ached in response, and the pain must have shown on my face.

"I-I'm sorry." Jess pulled away and stood up straight. "I didn't mean—"

"It's fine." I cut her off, and turned to face the door. This wasn't the time or place to deal with events from the past, no matter how much they hurt. "Tell me everything you know about wendigo, especially what their weaknesses are."

"How do you not know about *wendigo*?" Anton cut in, doing his best to strap his armor on over his bare chest. "They are people possessed by hunger demons, and they eat other people. Nothing but a wormwood stake to the heart, or weapons coated in lilac water will hurt them!" He finally got his armor on and moved to brace the door with his shoulder. "Our only chance is to keep them out!"

Wormwood was a poisonous plant on my home world that was used to make a fantastic drink called absinthe, which meant it was something else on this planet if they were making stakes out of it. That one was out. Thinking hard, I tried to remember anything I could about lilacs. Something about them being antifungal or killing intestinal parasites was all I managed to pull from my memories. Maybe it helped with headaches somehow? I didn't have any idea whether I was right or wrong here, but if I needed some kind of antifungal or anticoagulant, my healing spells might work on one. Also, if it was a fungus or parasite that was actually turning people into insane cannibalistic monsters, this world *sucked*. I might prefer an actual hunger demon.

"Look out!" Jess shouted a warning as the window close to Ausin shattered.

He had been trying to put his own armor on, but fear had made his hands shake, slowing down the process. He was just within range of the wendigo's outstretched arm, and it backhanded him hard enough in the chest that I heard several ribs crackle from being crushed as he flew straight into the stone fireplace, where another loud crack meant more broken bones.

From the impact, I guessed his spine snapped right between his shoulder blades. Big ouch.

"Nooo!" Anton shouted, but didn't stop holding the door. It was starting to splinter around the frame, so that was definitely a good thing. "I'll kill ya, unclean demon! I'll kill ya!"

I looked at Jess and pointed at the door. "Go help him hold it. I'll try to fix all this."

She ducked below the flailing arm and ran to help brace the only thing keeping us from ending up in a wendigo's stomach.

I moved to crouch over Ausin, and ran a hand over his body as I chanted a spell that worked like a weak form of x-ray vision. It always gave me a headache to use it, but I needed to know if it was possible to even save him. Healing could only fix so much. *"See-The-Unseen-Let-Me-See-The-Unseen-Let-Me-See-The-Unseen-Let-Me-See…"*
As the spell kicked in and my head started to pound, I could see the faint outline of the internal injuries quickly killing Ausin. The internal bleeding was extensive, and the spinal injury might be too much for me to heal without knocking myself out for a day or two. I could at least stabilize him, though, and work on fixing him the rest of the way after the wendigo problem was taken care of.

Considering this needed more than Leedy's healing had, I needed to increase my connection to my patient. I spit on his bare chest and used it to draw both a '*J*' and '*H*' before making a large circle around the letters, concentrating specifically on what I wanted my healing energy to do the whole time. The moment the circle closed, a rush of energy left me. My recent lack of sleep made the hit to my system harder than normal, and I broke the connection with a swipe of my thumb through the spit.

I stood up, feeling light-headed and a little off-balance. Ausin was already looking better, though, and his wounds were closing up cleanly. I was surprised to see the spinal injury fix itself along with the ribs and punctured lungs, meaning I was either getting better at healing, or he was a very hearty individual. Most likely it was a mix of both. He was still going to hurt, though. I didn't do much to diminish the bruising. If anything, it would be a reminder to be aware of his surroundings, maybe duck next time. I don't know, I wasn't a fortune teller.

"Is he alive?" Anton shouted to me over the banging on the door, the strain of holding it turning his face red. "Or did that monster kill him?"

"He's going to make it."

Anton didn't look like he believed me, but a groan from Ausin seemed to change his mind. He must have missed me casting a healing spell, which I was okay with. I went to my pack and pulled out a piece of jerky to help with the dizziness while the arm through the window continued to flail about mindlessly. It was time to see how tough these things really were.

I twisted my staff and the thin blade snapped out, gleaming in the firelight. As I approached the window, the arm reminded me of a dangerous whipping electrical cable, flailing around and ready to destroy. I waited for the right angle, and swiped downward hard with the spear tip, slicing through the elbow joint. The forearm and hand dropped on Ausin's bed with a spray of black blood. The feeling of victory quickly faded when the severed arm didn't stop moving.

"Stop that!" Jess was crouched at the base of the door, putting her weight against it. "You are only going to make it angry!"

"Removing limbs only makes it angry?" I watched as the stump disappeared from the shattered window and was quickly replaced by the opposite arm of the monster. This time, it started tearing chunks out of the wooden wall with a determination that didn't bode well for the structural integrity of the building. "Ah, I see. They don't feel pain. Lucky them."

The still-moving limb was thankfully caught up in the thin blanket on the bed, so it wasn't able to get away when I moved closer to inspect it. The first thing I noticed was the smell. It was a musty, earthy scent that set alarm bells ringing in my head. Fungus. And fungus gave off spores. Which we were certainly breathing. This world was quickly trying to surpass number eleven for suck factor.

I immediately cast a healing spell on the tangled limb, keeping my body's fluids to myself this time. The weak version was still enough to cause a rapid reaction. As the limb started twitching, the spell tried to heal the infected flesh and I saw the blood leaking from the end gradually going from black to red. It still moved, which was freaky, but it wasn't moving as…vigorously. I couldn't be sure, but it sure was acting like a fungal infection. The wendigo wasn't happy about it either, and the process of the creature turning the wall into wood chips picked up speed.

Wait. Fungus. What kills fungus? A faint memory of my grandmother using a garlic clove on the toenails of my brother to cure the fungal infection he caught from wrestling bubbled up from my distant past, and I immediately turned to look at Anton. "Where are the potions you made?"

"What?" Anton looked at me with obvious confusion as he was bounced around by the wendigo on the other side of the door. "Those are for vampires. These aren't vampires."

"Just trust me! Where are they?" I hurried over to where he pointed at a burlap sack at the foot of his bed, and pulled out two jars of the stinking mixture as I dropped my spear-staff. "I think this will work."

"I already told you, these aren't vampires!" Anton looked down where Jess was crouched. "Is he hard of hearing?"

The opening in the wall was big enough for the wendigo to stick its head and shoulder inside the room, and the musty smell was nearly as overwhelming as the onion and garlic smell had been when we first got here. I saw the creature in the light for the first time, and I was surprised at how bestial it looked. Whatever this thing used to be, I was almost positive it hadn't started out as a vanilla human. Either a shifter, or maybe some kind of hobgoblin or orc had succumbed to the fungus, turning it into the monster it was now. Its lantern eyes blinked slowly as we sized each other up, and it let out a rasping hiss.

Yeah, I don't like you either, guy.

I popped the lid off the first jar and threw it in the wendigo's face, and gagged at the smell that hit me like a physical attack. The wendigo didn't even react, just tried squeezing itself farther into the window. Thankfully, it hadn't made a large enough opening to get its monstrous body through, and it appeared to be stuck. Not giving up, I bent down and picked up my spear-staff and slashed it across the face with a sweep of the thin point, cutting a narrow gash just above its eyes. It didn't even seem to notice until I tossed the second jar in the wound. Then, I finally got a reaction.

The wendigo flipped its shit. Big time. It flailed around like a rabid wolf caught in a bear trap, cracking the thick timbers holding it in place as its face started to melt. The monster managed to pull itself free, falling back outside of the bunkhouse, where it started a kind of raspy wailing that made my headache worse. I wasn't stupid enough to stick my head outside the window to check on it, especially once the constant pounding on the door stopped.

"What just happened?" Jess stood up and took a step back from the door that was mostly splinters at this point. "What did you do?"

"Did ya use the right potion? Or were ya hiding some lilac water up ya sleeve?" Anton didn't back away from the door. He clearly wasn't willing to risk letting the door go. "Why didn't ya just say—"

A fist punched through the ragged wood of the door and latched onto his shoulder before yanking him out into the dark in a spray of splinters.

Jess backed up until she bumped into me, and I let out a long sigh. "Well…fuck."

CHAPTER 10

I sprinted out the door, my right hand already hooked into a three-fingered claw. It was similar to the form for my heat spell, except the three extended fingers were curled halfway to my palm. It was too dark for me to target anything, so I made a throwing motion at the edge of the clearing at the tallest tree I could see. As my arm whipped forward, I growled out the activation word to help focus my mind. *"Fireball."*

The ball of flames that was launched at the tree was much smaller than I was used to seeing. Call it performance issues, but I was tired. Or fire magic was weak in this world. Either way, it was underwhelming considering the cost in energy it took from me. Instead of a basketball-sized orb of fire, I created something closer to a baseball. It was still enough to ignite the tree into a giant torch that lit up the clearing. The napalm-like flames ate into the still-damp tree like it was dry kindling. I had been hoping for a little more shock-and-awe, and I regretted doing it as soon as another wave of dizziness hit me. Learning new worlds was always a hassle, and I was quickly figuring out that my magic didn't recharge nearly as fast as it had in the last world. There was a flash of movement near the illuminated trailhead where Jess and I should have approached the waypoint, and I crouched to sprint for the tree line, thinking the monster must be using the narrow trail to escape with its human prize.

"Help!"

Anton's shout came from around the corner of the bunkhouse, on the side where the injured wendigo was still wailing in pain. I reoriented and ran around the corner, fighting off the nausea that threatened to slow me down. As I rounded the corner, my own shadow blocked most of the light from the burning tree. I was still able to see that the uninjured wendigo was dangling Anton upside down over its partner like it was offering him as a snack. The injured wendigo paused its wailing, somehow sensing there was a nearby meal being offered to it even though half of its face had already melted away. It tilted its head and opened its mouth, unhinging its lower jaw in a frightening display of teeth and dripping bloody saliva.

This world was definitely as bad as number eleven.

"Hey, ugly!" My shout made both wendigo turn to look at me so quickly that their movements looked blurred. Well, one of them looked at me. The other one's eyes had melted, so I guess it just moved its head in my direction. "You two freaks want to tango with someone your own size? 'Cause I got something special for creepshows like you."

The wendigo holding Anton threw him at me. The poor tinkerer smacked into my shield hard enough to overload it in one hit, and I stumbled backward as his limp form bounced off me. Before I could blink, the uninjured wendigo was in my face, and I desperately swung my spear-staff to block it. The thin edge of my spearpoint intercepted its fist, and it split the hand and arm up to the middle of the forearm like a peeled banana. I got a face full of black blood, and I clamped my lips shut so I didn't get any in my mouth.

I twisted the spear to free it from the monster's arm, and it kicked me in response. My shin lit up in agony, and I spun the butt end of my weapon into the bend of the wendigo's knee as hard as I could. My shin bone didn't break, even if it felt like it should have. The wendigo's knee folded like a wet paper bag. Yay, me. Winning fights through durability wasn't fun, but it was still a win.

The monster tried to use its split arm to brace itself to stand back up, and it fell flat on its face. I took the generous opening it gave me and cut its head off with a downward chop, causing another fountain of blood to erupt all over the side of the building. Poor Anton got coated in the stuff as well. Nothing I could do about it now, though.

I started to limp around the body to go finish off the wounded wendigo—wondering why people were so afraid of these things—when the headless body kicked me in the stomach hard enough to take me off my feet.

Oh. That's why.

A hard blow to the stomach from such a powerful monster would have probably ruptured organs on a regular person, but it still managed to knock the breath out of me and made me instinctively look for the license plate number on the bus that just hit me. I gasped for air as I rolled to my feet, spear-staff ready to block any follow-up attacks. The kick had knocked me between the headless monster and the injured wendigo, and both of them started to move for me.

The eyeless one was hunched over to protect its vitals, swinging its single arm side-to-side like it was a heavy club. I dodged out of the way and watched as it hit the headless monster that was doing some kind of shuffle-crawl with its two functioning limbs. They immediately started to duke it out, and I walked around their struggling forms to go check on Anton. My aching torso and shin were almost worth the show of the two creatures tearing into each other, and I watched in fascination as chunks of gray flesh and black blood went flying. Which was when a third wendigo came blurring in from out of nowhere and shoulder-checked me into the bunkhouse.

Now, being maxed out at level one hundred makes you incredibly strong, fast, and durable. But it definitely didn't make you invincible. I knew that at least one collarbone was broken, and it felt like my left shoulder, which was the side that took the hit, had been ripped out of its socket. I could only see out of my right eye, and I tasted blood from almost biting my own tongue off during the train wreck of an impact. There might have been some other broken things, but the wendigo choking me made them less of a priority. I guess I hadn't been seeing only flickering shadows earlier.

I used my right hand to hold its face away from mine, its fanged maw snapping only a few inches away from taking off my nose as its grip tightened around my throat. My neck bones creaked in protest, and I was already starting to black out from lack of oxygen to my brain.

Concentrating was hard, but I had plenty of practice casting the spark spell. It didn't need any motions or words to activate, and two of the three tubes on my left hand went off with a roaring boom.

My shoulder had popped out of place, so I couldn't really lift my arm to aim, but luck was on my side. The two silver bullets hit the wendigo in the hip and upper pelvis, blowing off its right leg and causing it to topple over, with me somehow landing on top. Whether it was that this one could actually feel pain, or maybe the shock of the noise and instantaneous limb removal, the monster let go of my neck to try to catch itself as we hit the ground.

I sucked in a lungful of air, grabbed my left wrist with my still-functioning right hand, and jammed the unfired barrel against the bottom of the wendigo's jaw. It went off with another spark spell, blowing the creature's head off in a fine mist of black blood and chunks of white bone. It spasmed, still mostly functional, but I managed to roll away before it could grab me.

Thankfully, it didn't get back to its feet. It flopped around on the ground, spinning in place and flailing its limbs in an uncoordinated mess.

I struggled back to my feet, looking around for my spear-staff in the flickering firelight.

Unfortunately, the two wendigos that had been fighting each other had figured out that they weren't enemies. The one with a melted face still had ears, and it was using them to try to figure out where I was. Setting off my hand cannon must have given it a good reference point, because it was already closing in.

Seeing the snapping severed head of the wendigo that had grabbed Anton, I limped over and punted it off to the side. The sound of it bouncing through the grass sounded enough like footsteps that the eyeless creature turned and tried to chase it down.

I finally found my weapon and picked it up. As I made my way over to check on Anton, I heard a rustling from behind me and spun around, dreading another attacker. Instead, I was greeted by flashing cat eyes.

"You're alive!" Jess rushed forward and slammed into me, giving me a hug that caused a hiss of pain to escape my lips. "Oh, I'm so sorry, James. I didn't mean to hurt you!" She fussed over me, wincing in sympathy as soon as she saw my arm hanging limply. "Are you okay?"

"I will be." I coughed and spit up some blood. "Well, that's not good." Another wave of dizziness hit me, and I used my spear-staff to help me keep my balance. "Go get the rest of those potions the tinkerers made, and throw them over everything. And I do mean everything. Anton, me, the wendigos, and anything their blood touched."

She gave me a sharp nod. "Got it. What about you? Do you need anything?"

"My waterskin, and one of the trail rations. I'm going to need it soon." I was having trouble catching my breath, and I started worrying about my left lung trying to collapse. "Hurry."

Jess ran off, and I traced a small circle over and over again on my forehead with my right index finger. It wasn't necessary for self-healing, but it helped me concentrate. Especially once the bones started to slide back into place. The lack of mana in the area meant it would take some time to get back to one hundred percent, and I wasn't looking forward to the migraine I was sure would hit once I bottomed out. I wanted to save the healing potions I had bought for emergencies, so a nasty headache didn't warrant their use.

I limped over to Anton as soon as I could breathe normally, and I let out a sigh of relief when I saw the rise and fall of his chest. From the awkward way he was laid out, it was obvious he had at least one broken leg. There wasn't anything I could do for him at the moment beyond making him more comfortable, so I did my best to straighten his limbs and ensure he couldn't choke to death on his own tongue.

A cold splash of stinking liquid hit me, and I jerked upright, wincing in pain as my shoulder popped into place with the sudden movement.

Jess stood behind me with a guilty look on her face. "I scared you again, didn't I?"

"I swear, I'm going to put a bell around your neck until you learn to stop sneaking up on me." The smell of onion and garlic was foul, but I ignored it as best as I could as it dripped down my back. "Start with the two wendigos, and I'll bring down the other one when it comes back from chasing the severed head of its friend."

Jess tilted her head, obviously confused at the odd statement.

"It's a long story. Just know that you are going to have to track down wherever that head went, and pour some potion on it too."

CHAPTER 11

The sun was well over the horizon by the time we were done finishing off the monsters and coating everything in the Vampire Bane potion that might have spores from whatever fungus caused the wendigo to form. I was pretty sure no one with a nose would ever want to use the bunkhouse again, even if someone repaired the damage.

Anton and Ausin were laid out on the floor in front of the fireplace, both snoring in blessed unconsciousness. Jess was out at the well, doing her best to clean off the smell before we left. I had given up and burned the clothes I had been wearing, and had already changed into a pair of brown linen pants and a pale-green long-sleeve shirt. All my clothing was starting to look a little worn, so I would need to buy a few new sets when I got to Greendown. At least this set would blend in a little better with the forest.

I was cleaning and oiling my gear after reloading my wrist cannon. While my hands were busy, my mind was keeping track of how quickly my energy levels were recovering. My guess had been correct about it taking longer in this world. Getting some kind of mental gauge on what to expect would take a few more tries, but a basic understanding put the recharge rate at somewhere near the fourth world I had visited. Basically, I wouldn't be able to use my Mage class whenever I liked. No waving my hand and winning battles automatically, like usual.

"Everything is ruined, and I hate my life." Jess stomped into the bunkhouse, holding the set of clothing she had been wearing away from her body while pinching her nose with the other hand. "These were my favorite pair of pants!"

"So, I take it cleaning things didn't go very well?" I dodged the sopping wet mess that she threw at me, trying not to laugh as it made a splat on the wall behind me.

"Didn't go very well? No! It *definitely* didn't go well!" Jess had changed into a set of my old clothes that were entirely too big on her. "Now what am I supposed to do when we get to the city? No one will hire me if I smell bad, or if they see me wearing these."

"We'll get things sorted, don't worry. There are a few small villages we have to pass through before we reach the city, and we can find you something different to wear there. Or maybe somebody knows a way to get the smell out." I stood up and stretched before moving over to check on the two unconscious tinkerers. "Once these two are back on their feet, we'll head out."

A quick healing spell on each of them wasn't enough to make me feel dizzy this time around, now that I knew my limits. And it was enough to make sure both were free of the wendigo fungus. I looked over to Jess, who was packing her things and getting ready to leave. "I do have something important to ask you."

"What is it?" Jess turned to give me her full attention.

I paused to think about how I wanted to ask my question. Finding out whether this world had a system similar to mine was always a touchy subject. Thirteen worlds I had visited had some kind of internal stat screen or device that produced a hard number system the people could use to measure their strength, growth, and abilities. None had matched mine perfectly, but their versions had all been comparable. In the six that hadn't shared a similar trait, keeping my own system secret had seemed prudent. The one time I had let it slip, everyone thought I was crazy. It had ended in a nasty mess I still regretted ever happening. Exorcisms are certainly real things, but pretty silly when you aren't actually possessed by anything.

"James, is everything okay?"

"Yes. I just wondered, if you had to measure, how strong do you think you are?" I had a second reason for asking. There was no basis for why I believed this beyond my own hopes and dreams, but if I ever made it to the world where my upgrade and stat screen system originated, I might be able to figure out who—or what—was responsible for yanking me away from my own world and tossing me all over the place.

"Oh, I don't know. Maybe as strong as a full-grown man who wasn't part shifter?" Jess flexed her bicep while clenching her fist. "I'm definitely stronger than I look, that's for sure."

A sigh of disappointment escaped my lips. She didn't quote from a stat sheet, or mention any numbers. This wasn't the world I was hoping for. "That's good to hear. Thank you."

She looked at me with a curious tilt to her head. "What's wrong? Did I fail some kind of test or something?" Jess picked up her pack and pulled it onto her back. "I promise you, I'll be strong enough to hold my own in a fight." She looked at the hole in the wall where the door had been and swallowed hard. "Against normal enemies, anyway."

"No test. I was just wondering." I picked up my own ruck and got it settled onto my back, ensuring all my weapons were in their proper place. I had even managed to get my folding pocket knife back. This world wasn't the one that would bring me the answers I was looking for, but that didn't mean I should slack off. "I need to check your health, and then we can wake those two before we leave."

She warily approached my outstretched hand, and I swirled a quick circle on her palm. There was a moment of resistance, and then a trickle of my magic pushed through her body. It detected some old injuries, along with a few minor points of resonance along her lower back. Old scar tissue from being whipped. Not enough of a concern for me to use my x-ray spell to see specifics. More importantly, there were no signs of a fungal infection. Jess would be fine. Any mental scars from a rough childhood were outside my abilities. I let the energy stay in her body, where it would repair the few spots that might still bother her.

"Am I okay?" Jess gasped as the knots of skin relaxed and smoothed over under her shirt. "Wha-what was that? What did you do to me?" Her stomach growled, and I turned around so she could reach inside my ruck.

"It was a light healing spell, to make sure you weren't infected with the stuff that turns you into a wendigo." I pointed a thumb at my pack. "There wasn't anything for it to fight off, so it healed some old injuries instead. The energy to do so mostly came from you, so grab a ration and get some food in you."

She rummaged around for a bit, and then she tugged hard on the straps to close it back up.

Instead of her being grateful, I was getting the sense that she was upset. I turned around to see her tearing angrily into the dry food. "What's wrong? Did I do something wrong?"

Jess paused and wiped her eyes, then took a deep breath before meeting my gaze. "You had no right to take away my scars." She turned sharply away before I could see fresh tears fall. "They were a reminder. A way for me to never forget…"

I let her trail off. Whatever she had been through, it must have been pretty bad if her job in the inn was an improvement. I reached out and stole a corner from the hard biscuit in her ration. "I apologize for healing you without your permission." The dry biscuit tasted like burnt crackers, and I took a swig from my canteen to wash it down. "But if there is anything I have learned through my travels, it's that holding on to the bad parts of your past will sour your future." She looked up at me as if she were going to argue, so I held up a finger to stop her. "I didn't say that you should forget the past. It's what shapes you in the now, but don't let it define who you will be. Wallowing in your misery helps no one. Learn from it, and be better than the old version of yourself could ever believe possible."

She turned away, eyes still brimming with tears. "What would you know? You don't know my past. What it was like growing up in the village—the only person with eyes like mine. You're barely older than I am." Jess hurried away, leaving me with the tinkerers.

Oh, how little she knew. Just because my body was stuck at twenty-seven didn't mean I couldn't feel every one of my nearly fifty years of life.

That didn't make her wrong, though. It had been wrong to take her scars away without permission. I couldn't give them back to her, but I could do my best to improve the rest of her life. She deserved better than what she had gotten so far. I would have to think over the best ways to make sure she didn't regret meeting me.

Instead of chasing after Jess, I shook awake Anton and Ausin. Both men were disoriented at first, but quickly got to their feet and prepared to leave once they saw what time it was. Neither man wanted to be in an unsecured building when the sun went down. They were both sore and stiff from the ordeal last night. Neither complained, though, and were more than happy to still be alive. They tried to pay me for their healing, but I waved them off. My lack of guild symbols probably helped keep them from prying. We exchanged goodbyes, and I took a letter of recommendation from Anton that he claimed would help me get through the city gates without paying a toll. I would have Jess look it over to make sure, since I couldn't read what it said.

Waving farewell to the duo, I headed in the direction of the path that would eventually take me to Greendown. The habitual damp from the daily rains made the forest smell like mold and rot when the sun managed to peek through the clouds and warm the wet ground. I made it back to the trail, expecting to see Jess waiting for me. She was, but she wasn't by herself.

"Well, it's about time you showed up." Corporal Leedy stood with his sword in his hand, a round buckler shield held in his off hand. Jess was bound and gagged, sitting on the edge of the trail nearby. "I was beginning to wonder if you had gone off and left the shifter to fend for herself."

"What do you want, Leedy?" I subtly activated the bracelet that formed a shield around me, but I held back on actually projecting the bubble shield. Instead, I waited to see what kind of light it would show. I was genuinely disappointed to see it flash a dim yellow four times. It meant there was more than just Leedy and Jess nearby. "Why don't you tell your friends to come out, and we can have a talk? Who else is out there? Murphy? I know there is at least one more besides him."

"This isn't about them. It's about *you* and *me*." Leedy hefted his sword and dropped into a crouch. "Once I beat you, I'm bringing you in for a trial."

"You disappoint me, Leedy." I made no motion to defend myself, instead deciding to lean up against the tree next to me. "Tying up innocent barmaids, springing ambushes on people, it really doesn't speak well to the kind of person you are. You'd impressed me with your professionalism and open-mindedness at the inn, right up until your incorrect conclusion that I'm some kind of treasure hunter, that is. What did 'they' ever do to you, anyway? Never mind. It doesn't matter. But this?" I shook my finger. "I'm not angry, Leedy. I'm just disappointed."

I squinted at a thick patch of foliage behind Jess that was the most likely hiding place for one of the Wardens. "What about my question, Warden? Does it make you feel strong, picking on an innocent woman who has done nothing wrong?" I snapped my fingers as though I'd solved a great mystery. "Oh, I get it now! She's a hostage, and you're going to kill her if I don't give myself up. You have to get the sword a little closer to her throat to really sell it though, Leedy." His face was only getting redder the more I talked. "Is this more of that vaunted Warden honor you told me all about? Makes me glad there aren't any of you where I come from. It would be terrible to have such evil around unsuspecting women and children."

The bushes shook, and Murphy popped his head up. "It ain't like that, sir. We really do help people. Honest."

"Shut up, Private!" Leedy was almost shaking with rage, and his eyes flickered to my left.

Ah, so that's where another was hiding.

Leedy took another step closer, his sword unwavering. "Don't listen to him. He twists everything we do and say, gets in your head, and then—"

"And then you start to see that what I'm saying isn't twisting anything. Just pointing out the hypocrisy of your Order, and what its true function is. Not protecting the people, but keeping them in line, while those in power abuse the same citizens they are supposed to look after." I shifted my weight onto my heels, making myself appear as even less of a threat. "Prove me wrong, and I'll go with you to the city to stand trial, no fighting necessary. But deep down, you know I'm not wrong. You are just going through the five stages of grief. Denial, anger—that's where you are right now— bargaining, depression, and acceptance. I don't blame you for it. In a way, you are dealing with the death of something you upheld as righteous and good. Seeing it crumble to dust before your eyes is certainly traumatic. No less traumatic than the death of a loved one."

Leedy's eyes widened, as something I said struck home. His sword started to dip before the person to my left finally made himself known.

"That's quite enough, traveler. You will submit yourself to us, and come without a fight." A man in armor that had far more gold highlights than Leedy's stepped out from behind a thick tree a few paces away.

The tension in the air ratcheted up to a new level, and I felt the weight of his gaze settle on my chest. This man was a heavy hitter. A genuinely powerful mage.

"Otherwise, I will be more than happy to use force."

CHAPTER 12

"And who might you be?" I finished activating my bracelet, and the shield shimmered in place around me. It wasn't fully recovered from being broken last night, but it was better than nothing. I noticed the newcomer's eyebrows raise as he saw it snap into position. "I take it you are the man in charge?"

"My name is Captain Cross. I'm in charge of the Blue Branch of the Western Wardens, with a full company of two hundred men."

The pressure in my chest doubled as he clenched his fist, and Jess whimpered behind me. My poor shield quivered as it tried to help.

"Now, lay down your weapons, and submit yourself for judgment."

"Judgment?" I had to shake my head at the irony of it all. "The judgment of a group that thinks it's okay to hurt innocent people?"

I saw Leedy out of the corner of my eye wince as he shifted behind me, his sword still pointed at my back.

Although I was pretty sure I could handle Cross and Leedy, I didn't know if I could do so without Jess getting hurt. Whatever the officer was doing, it affected the entire area, making my magic-eating sword useless to stop it. It was also a pretty good indicator that he would have more spells that did the same. Area-of-effect spell-users loved their big and flashy spells. It really only left me with one viable option.

"Look, I'll tell you the truth, *Captain* Cross. You're going to need a higher authority if you plan to pass judgment on *me*. Because as it stands, I outrank you. See you soon."

"Stop him!"

Captain Cross tried to catch me as I darted off to the right, sprinting between him and Murphy into the thick underbrush. Corporal Leedy seemed shocked, rooted in place as I left him far behind. The sounds of pursuit slowly faded as I weaved between the trees, using all my stat points to their full advantage. Unless they had some form of transport spell, there was no way any of them were going to catch me.

After a few more minutes of not hearing anything, I slowed to a standstill. The sun was still high overhead, and I was starting to feel warm as the humid forest increased in temperature. I took off my ruck and pulled out a ration, picking through it for the items that were heavy in protein. I would need it for what came next.

Circling back took much longer than my initial sprint, this time making sure I stayed quiet. When I got back to the point where they had confronted me, I found a series of tracks that led in the direction of Greendown. One set of hoof prints must have belonged to the captain, while the others trudged along on foot. Another pair of prints had joined them for a time, and broken off to go toward the village I had left behind. It must have been the tinkerers. Whatever they had said to one another hadn't changed the fact that Jess was still being held prisoner.

I followed them, leaving my shield bracelet turned off so it could charge. While I walked, I practiced going through several of the more basic spells I knew, to test how effective they were in this place. Almost universally, they were weaker than they should be. Ice Bolt, Stone Spike, and my version of Magic Missile were all about half as powerful as they were in world nineteen. Another pang of sadness hit me as thoughts of world nineteen flashed through my mind, but I pushed the memories down.

Not now.

After running through a few more of my go-to spells, I stopped testing them to allow my mana to recharge. I wanted to be ready for when I caught up to them. Although it was doubtful this Captain Cross was a genuine threat, I had been through too much to ignore an unknown danger. He could have an item or ability I had never seen before.

Eventually, the trail split into two directions. One continued onward to the east, with the second less-traveled path curving north. The Wardens had taken the northern trail.

"What could be in that direction?" From what Murphy had told me, there wasn't much up there, and all the hunting communities were farther west. I couldn't see the mountains in the distance due to the closeness of the trees, but I knew they were waiting in the distance. The markings that pointed toward a waypoint were nowhere to be seen, so it wasn't that they were looking for a place to stay for the night. Something didn't sit right with me, and the instinct that had kept me alive all these years was screaming at me that it was bad they weren't continuing toward Greendown.

I moved off the trail, deciding to keep out of sight in case they had stopped and made camp, or anticipated me trailing after them. Never assume you're facing a stupid enemy.

The sun was now creeping toward the horizon, and it wouldn't be long before night fell, in all its horrors. While walking, I came across several faint game trails, some with signs of things other than deer and rabbit. A goblin footprint looked the same, no matter what world I was on.

Finally, I caught up to the group. The reason for why my instincts had triggered was immediately obvious. They had taken Jess here to question her, and they weren't being very nice about it.

"I'm telling you, that's all I know!" Jess was tied to a thick post in the middle of a large clearing, at the base of a low hill. A hill with a cave opening. "Let me go! I didn't do anything!"

"That's enough." Captain Cross, who stood in front of her near the cave entrance, closed his fist as she gasped in pain. "Either you tell me what I want to know, or we leave you here for the goblins."

"Sir, I don't know about this. She was only with the traveler for a few hours, and she hasn't even had a trial." Corporal Leedy was standing off to the side, the normally robust Warden seemingly shrunken by the sudden turn of events. "This is supposed to be the punishment for murderers, not—"

"Did I ask for your opinion, Corporal?" Captain Cross stomped over to his subordinate, shaking his finger in his face. He also moved far enough away from Jess that he didn't notice the moment she started to struggle against the ropes holding her. "That *traveler* is stirring up notions and thoughts that we can't let spread. What he is spouting is a poison, one that infects everything it touches." Cross leaned forward, squinting in Leedy's face. "Did he poison you too, Corporal? Do you need to be cleansed as well?"

"Captain, I'm a loyal member of the Wardens." Leedy swallowed hard, clearly afraid of the man in front of him. "You don't have to worry about me. I swear."

"We'll see." Cross turned and looked at Private Murphy, who stood as far away as possible while still being in the clearing. "And you, Murphy? Do you need to be cleansed of the filth that man was spouting?"

"I'm a Warden, sir. Not a murderer. This ain't right, and you know it, same as we do." Murphy looked at his captain with pity, his muscular hands unwavering on the haft of his halberd. "Why don't we all head for the Guild Hall, where we can talk this over with the others."

Captain Cross, instead of exploding into a rage like I expected, seemed to deflate. "If only it was that easy, Murphy." Cross raised his hand, pointing his palm at the private. "This is out of my hands. The moment Leedy's report crossed the Commandant's desk, it was too late. I'm sorry."

A pressure built up in my chest again, and my ears popped. Murphy dropped to one knee, whatever Cross was doing too much for the stalwart young man.

"Enough." I wasn't willing to watch Cross hurt or kill Murphy, and the sun was already almost gone anyway. It was time for me to step in. "Even for an organization as twisted and diseased as the Wardens, this is too far."

Cross spun to look at me, but the pressure on Murphy didn't let up. "I knew you would be back. There is no way you would just run away, not after everything I've heard about you." He took a step toward me and raised his other hand, and I got to feel the same pressure Murphy must be experiencing. "At least I can wrap everything up now, without more collateral damage. I do hate this part of my job."

"You know, I always end up getting some pushback when I get to a new place, but it usually doesn't come around this fast." I straightened my back against the weight of his spell. It must have been some kind of gravity manipulation power. I would have to try to figure out how he did it later. "The thing is, people like you never learn. When the winds of change decide to blow, you either go with the flow, or get out of the way." I took three quick steps to close the distance between us, and his eyes widened in surprise. "But if you try to stop it, you only end up getting destroyed."

"How are you doing this?" Cross clenched his outstretched palm into a fist, redoubling his effort to stop me and flattening the grass in a wide cone extending from his hand.

I activated my bracelet in response, and it flashed red as the shield fought against his attack. I still felt some pressure, but it was manageable.

"You should be on your knees!"

"Nah, I don't want to get my pants dirty." I stuck my staff in the ground before I unhooked my mace from my belt and raised it to my shoulder. "Now, I'm a little on the fence about how to deal with you. Crushing your skull would be the easy way out, but I feel like leaving you alive to tell everyone what happened here will do *far* more damage to the people in charge."

"I don't think so." Cross released Murphy and shifted his other hand toward me, clenching it into a fist and increasing the pressure once more. "Your winds die with you, like nothing but hot air."

"Ha! I gotta admit, that was a good one." I really felt the pressure now, but it still wasn't enough to stop me. Especially considering I was using my shield to handle most of the weight of his magic with my will, instead of my body. I closed the distance between us, and I saw his eyes drift over to the post where Jess was tied up, most likely intending to use her to stop me. Where she *used* to be tied up, anyway. She had squirmed free about the same time Cross started crushing Murphy. "Sorry, bub. No hostages for you this time."

I lifted my mace and smashed it down on his foot, pulping it with the help of his increased gravity. He screamed, falling onto his butt and passing out at the backlash of his spell being cut off improperly. I looked over to see Murphy climbing to his feet, while Leedy looked at me with shame in his eyes. "Glad I caught up to you in time. I would hate to see the two of you killed just for meeting me."

"Captain Cross was just talking. He would never…" Leedy's words died in his throat, and he hung his head in defeat. "None of this went the way it was supposed to go. And then it was like he lost his mind, and when we had to tie up the girl—"

"What he means to say is, 'thank you.'" Murphy walked over and kicked Cross in the ribs. "Some leader he turned out to be. Do you want us to find out where the girl ran off to?"

"She'll be back, don't worry. Just give her a few minutes to circle back around." I bent down and started stripping the equipment off of the unconscious Warden. "As for this guy, don't take it too personally. He was under orders to do this." I pulled off the bracers around his forearms, noticing an interesting set of engravings running along the edges of the inside. I set them to the side for later inspection. "Who is the person in charge of him?"

"That would be Commandant Beck." Seeing what I was doing, Murphy started to help me take off the rest of the captain's armor. "He's in charge of the Blue, Black, and White Branches of the

Western Wardens." When I didn't respond, Murphy pointed to Leedy and himself. "We're in the Blue, so we travel across the lands to keep the peace. The Black do the same thing, but in cities where their abilities help with more than just fighting. They put out fires, keep rioters under control, and keep vermin out of the food stores."

I nodded along, making mental notes. The Blue were like their analogs for police, while the Black were firemen, guards, and government inspectors. "And what are the White?" I looked through the coin purse the captain had been wearing. There was a lot of gold in here, with a silvery piece that had to be platinum. Nice. It would certainly help supplement my funds.

"The White are…" Murphy paused as he yanked off the breastplate, flopping the captain onto his face. "There aren't many of them. The White track down murderers, uncover corruption in the guilds, and capture the people corrupted by power." He thought about what he wanted to say next for a few seconds. "They're the executioners. The people who punish the criminals beyond redemption."

"And what color does the Commandant originate from?" To me, it sounded like the White were this place's version of a detective, bounty hunter, and special forces all rolled into one. I would be shocked to hear if the higher leadership echelons were from any branch but the White.

"They always appoint someone from the White to Commandant. Black and Blue hold all the Captain positions." Leedy had finally come over, his eyes still downcast. "The Generals are all members of the Green." Before I could ask, he finished filling me in. "The Green are the strongest of us. There are never more than ten, and each of them are a force by themselves. Magic, fighting, knowledge—they are the best of the best."

"Any other colors I need to know about?" I shook my head, amused at the classifications these people came up with. At least it wasn't a bunch of 'A-Rank' this, and 'S-Ranked' that, like I had seen in several other worlds.

"The Eastern Marshals use different colors. Red, yellow, orange, and purple, but I haven't met one, so I don't know what they all mean." Leedy looked up sharply, where a rustle was coming from the nearby trail. "Someone is coming."

Before anyone got too worked up, Jess walked into the clearing, leading a horse. It must have been the one that belonged to Captain Cross. I stood and brushed my hands off before walking up to her. "I'm glad to see you're okay."

"I knew you'd be back." Jess looked worn out, but she was still whole. No fingers snipped off in some misbegotten form of torture. "I was waiting for you to show up before I made my move."

"You did a good job. Now, let's get the captain tied up to this horse so we can get out of here before the residents of that cave decide they want a fresh meal." I made it back as the two Wardens finished stripping their leader. Cross still wasn't awake yet, but it was only a matter of time until he recovered. His foot was dripping blood into the dirt, so I took a moment to bind it tightly. I could heal him if it looked like he was going to bleed out, but my experienced eye told me that I'd done just the right amount of damage. I tossed him over the horse and tied his hands to his uninjured foot to hold him in place. "Okay, are we forgetting anything?"

"Nope, got it all." Murphy had placed all the gear and armor in a sack that he hung from the back of the horse's saddle. "What are we going to do with him?"

"Make a spectacle at Greendown. If we announce what he tried to do in public—kill an innocent girl alongside his own men—the Wardens won't be able to touch you." I looked back at the post Jess had been tied to and pulled my staff out of the ground, making sure it was still working after the gravity fluctuations it had been through. "At least, not openly. You will have to watch yourselves if this was truly sanctioned by your Commandant." I made the hand motions for a fireball and cast an orb of flame the size of a golf ball at the post. It lit on fire with a whooshing sound, and I turned to leave. "No more using that for punishment. Okay. Let's get out of here."

The glint of eyes from the cave opening watched us as we left, and I returned their gaze with a wink. Nothing followed us back to the trail.

CHAPTER 13

We didn't make it much farther after reaching the path before needing to find a place to camp for the night. The sun dropped below the horizon, and the forest came alive with the sounds of predators hunting their prey. In some cases, it might have been predators hunting smaller predators. Either way, walking strung out on the trail felt like a bad idea.

"I know of a copse of trees nearby that will work as a makeshift campsite." Corporal Leedy was in front, with Private Murphy bringing up the rear. Jess and I walked on either side of the horse that had Cross on its back. "It'll provide more protection than setting up camp in the middle of the road."

I nodded in agreement as both Wardens pulled out torches and lit them using a flint and steel. "Works for me, then." The sound of two creatures meeting each other in an unhappy manner came from somewhere close behind us. And by unhappy manner, I mean screams, roars, tearing flesh—all the fun and exciting things you like to hear in a dark and suddenly scary forest. All of us looked at one another with wide eyes, and both Jess and I took some torches from the pack on the back of the horse to push the heavy darkness farther away from our little group. "And you might want to hurry."

There were more sounds all around us as we continued on, almost as if the sheer number of things hunting us was protection from all of them. They were so busy figuring out who was the deadliest predator, they didn't have time to actually attack us.

"Do you think we'll be okay?" Jess had to nearly shout to be heard over the background noises. "I've never heard of the trails being this dangerous before."

"When I was by myself between villages, it wasn't nearly this bad either. I think we stumbled on some kind of turf war." I looked back to Murphy, who was close enough to the back of the horse that

I was mildly concerned he was going to get kicked. "What about you, Murph? Is this normal?"

"No." Murphy kept turning around to look behind us, making sure nothing was sneaking up to pounce. "I think you're right, though. It sounds like a raptor pack ran across a bunch of pumas."

Jess nodded in silent agreement, tapping her nose to show her sense of smell agreed with his assessment.

"Well, that sounds awful." I looked up, making sure a big cat wasn't ready to drop on my head. Just because I would most likely win that fight didn't mean I wanted to get torn up by a giant cat. Pain still hurt, and I wasn't a masochist. Then, I had a brain stutter when I realized what he had said. "When you say 'raptor,' what exactly do you mean?"

"You know, giant lizard, big teeth, moves fast—you haven't seen one before?" Jess raised an eyebrow, answering before Murphy could. "Everyone knows what a raptor is."

"Oh, I know what they are, but that doesn't mean I'm happy to find out they are *here*." Movies involving resurrected dinosaurs from my home world flashed through my head. I had seen several large lizard creatures over the years—even lizard people, and a few memorable experiences with dragons—but an outright dinosaur? This would be a first. "How hard is it to kill a raptor?"

"Not hard. They like ambushes, so just stay aware of your surroundings." Murphy pointed to his throat and belly. "The scales on their undersides are weak, so just aim there."

I shook my head in disbelief. Definitely worse than world number eleven. "Thanks for the tip. I'll keep it in mind."

"They're also pretty rare this far west, and they are pretty easy to knock around. They aren't nearly as heavy as they should be, given their size." Jess smiled, trying to make me feel better. "People say it's because they have hollow bones."

"Hollow bones, huh? That certainly makes things easier." I shook my head again. I would just deal with them when the time came. "How much farther, Leedy?"

Leedy looked back at me and shrugged. "I'm not sure. There is no moonlight tonight, so I won't see the turn-off until we get there."

We continued for a bit longer, a cluster of tiny lights in a forest of shadows. The sounds around us started to die down, and I passed my torch off to Jess so I could use both hands to fight. If the victors decided they were still hungry, I would stay and fight them while the others got away.

Somehow, Lady Luck decided to smile on us, and we weren't attacked by pumas or dinosaurs. Even thinking that gave me a mild headache. Seriously, this was shaping up to be the worst world I had visited, and there were some doozies in my past. At least I hadn't needed to fight off a dragon in world eight until I was there for several months first. And I had a lot of help.

Finally, Leedy led us off the trail through a gap in the trees.

The trees here were older, and their thick branches had cut off enough sunlight on the forest floor that there was almost no undergrowth. It was obvious when we came to the place Leedy had mentioned, but not for the reason I had expected. The moment I stepped into the circle of trees, a rush of power hit me like I had slammed a Red Cow, two lines of coke, and licked a nine-volt battery plugged into a wall socket, all at the same time.

"Wow." I stopped in my tracks, trying to deal with the influx of energy that slapped me like I owed it money. "What just happened?" Mana poured into me, causing my body to shake. I heard a faint ding, and I pulled up my stat screen to see whether there were any changes. There were two, so I focused on those, and my screen updated to show only what was new.

Name: James Holden (Earth v7.1)

Status:

Mind – 51

Mission:

Unique Upgrade Quest: Find five places of power – 1/10

Reading it was hard because my eyeballs were vibrating in my head, but I was absolutely shocked at what I saw. Flabbergasted. That's the word for what I was feeling.

Not only had I gotten a new quest, but I had gained another point in one of my stats. Even more confusing, my initial 'Earth version seven' had gotten an update. That shouldn't have been possible. At least, I didn't *think* it was possible. In fact, up until now, I had always assumed that 'Earth version seven' was an identification number for my original planet. It had always been a conundrum to think that there were multiple versions of Earth, and mine was simply the seventh.

My entire worldview had just forcibly been shifted. Was it describing the software version of whatever created my status sheet? What was it about this particular world that allowed the update to happen? Do these places of power somehow serve as some kind of docking locations to a demented cosmic internet out there? They were clearly related to whatever it was that had been happening to me over the past twenty years. Perhaps the most important question of all, however, was could they somehow get me home? Or, even give me some control over when and where I transfer worlds?

Questions continued to rattle through my brain as I tried to contemplate the ramifications of this new discovery. I had only maxed out my level and stats recently. Did that somehow play a role in all of this? Could there have been more places of power on other worlds that I simply lacked the qualifications to access? I forced myself to stop the churn of questions and focus, zeroing in on what I knew.

My version hadn't changed since the first screen had popped up in my vision, and I had maxed out my levels and stats in world nineteen three months after arriving. No matter what I had done since, I hadn't managed to find a single way to increase my numbers.

Nine months of no change. Nine months of thinking I had hit the ceiling of how strong I could become. Now, after giving up any hope of further advancement, I gain a stat point for just walking into a circle of trees?

"James, are you okay?"

Jess had stopped to check on me. I hadn't even realized that I was sitting on the ground, leaning against a tree with water leaking out of my eyes. I was definitely not crying. Nope. Not a thing.

"What's wrong?"

"Nothing." I got to my feet, and almost face-planted from the surge of power increasing as I got closer to the center of the circle. "I'll be fine. Just give me a moment." It was clear that I was the only one who noticed anything different about the circle of trees. My body felt like an overflowing cup of water, except there was nowhere for the excess to go.

"Seriously, what's wrong?" Jess stood up on her toes to get a better look at me. "Your eyes are glowing, and you smell like burnt hair."

"I just got a huge spike of magic the moment I set foot in the circle of trees. I should be able to deal with it, as soon as my body adjusts to the power levels." I concentrated, trying to get the stagnant energy to stop filling me, and start flowing through me. It felt like trying to push a boulder up a hill using only my tongue, but after I managed a slight nudge, the mana started to move on its own.

Instead of flowing up my feet and slamming into the top of my head, the energy began to swirl through my body, running up and down each limb until it settled into my center, behind my belly button. There, it was like a tiny whirlpool, and it sank into a calm ball that slowly grew until it gradually came to a stop.

The edges of the ball seemed to stretch, and I felt a sharp warning stab of pain. By instinct, I tried compressing the ball, squeezing it together to avoid it rupturing. It relieved the pain, but the whirlpool only spun faster. I squeezed harder, hoping it was enough to hold everything together.

After what felt like an hour, but was probably only a few minutes, the flow of mana trickled to a stop. I opened my eyes to see Leedy and Murphy setting up a pair of tents, while Jess was trying unsuccessfully to build a fire using wet branches from the clearing. Cross was still unconscious, lying in a heap near the horse. I checked my status again, and I saw a new line, and even more changes to my stats. I looked at the whole sheet this time, to ensure I didn't miss anything.

Name: James Holden (Earth v7.1)

Title: Chief Justice/Arbiter/Justicar/Executioner/etc.

Level: 100/MAX

Rank: 1/10

Age: 27 (Physical) 47 (Actual)

Class: Warrior/Soldier/Knight/Paladin/Mage (5/5)

Profession:
Healer/Alchemist/Blacksmith/Runesmith/Judge (5/5)

Status:

Strength – 55

Flexibility – 55

Vigor – 55

Mind – 55

Mission:

Mythical Quest: Deliver Justice – World Count 20/???

Legendary Quest: Return Home – Requirements not met

Epic Quest: Find out why – Requirements not met

Rare Quest: Track down Silver Star – Ongoing

Unique Upgrade Quest: Find ten places of power – 1/10

Now all my stats had increased five points, and I was ranked one of ten. I had no idea what was going on. One conclusion I could make was the obvious connection between my Unique Upgrade Quest and my Rank. Were these places of power upgrading the system? If I get all ten, will it update to a version eight, increasing a tenth of a point each time?

A potentially more terrifying thought occurred to me, as I glanced once again at my improved stats. Was the quest upgrading *me*? Into what, exactly? Was I still going to be human? Everything about this world seemed geared to throw me for a loop.

First dinosaurs, and now this? I felt unbalanced, like my life as a Judge was changing into something different.

I'd taken pride in having seen and done it all after so many worlds, and I absolutely did not appreciate the feelings of ignorance this world kept giving me. I was going to fix that problem and figure out what exactly was going on, and I was going to start right here, right now.

CHAPTER 14

After helping Jess get the fire started, I volunteered for the first watch. I was still juiced up on energy, and there was no way I could sleep with all these recent developments hitting me rapid-fire. I needed to figure out what was happening to me.

I checked the ropes holding Cross, then sat with my back to the fire and concentrated on my stat screen some more, focusing on the new information. It had been a long time since I had actually looked at the pop-up screens that gave details on each bit of data. Nothing had changed in years, so there had been no point. The first one I looked at was 'Rank.'

> **Rank** – Designated status of personal mana source. Affects ability to cast spells and enhance physical potential. Accessible only to those with high aptitude and necessary resilience capable of containing the forces subjected upon the body and mind.

So, it looked like I could continue to level up through the growth of a personal mana generator? That went against almost everything I had learned from the Order of Elven Mages on the eighth world I had visited. They told me that mana came from the power of life around you, and certain people were able to harness that energy for their own use. Storing that power inside you was only temporary, like a battery that needed to be recharged. If my body was an electric engine, mana was the charge that the environment around me slowly replaced. This new 'Rank' system was like stuffing a diesel generator in the trunk and never needing to stop and pull over.

If it was only available to those with high aptitude and resilience, it made sense that I hadn't been able to unlock it until after I had maxed out my stats. The current version of myself was far different from the person who had first appeared on a foreign planet, with dreams of helping people through kindness and caring.

That James Holden would have exploded like a meat-covered bottle rocket if he stepped into the clearing and had the same power shoved into his body with a proverbial fire hose. That James Holden had also been an abject failure on his first world, and learned hard and fast how the universe really worked. My eyes had been forcefully opened, and I discovered very quickly that violence might not have been the best answer, but it was certainly *a* solution. One that I hated to admit was often an all too effective one, as well. Power respects power, so I gained as much of it as I could, as fast as possible. It made things simple. If all your problems were nails, all you'd need was a hammer and you'd never need to have any other tool in your toolkit.

I knew the pitfall I was seeing the Wardens fall into. I'd experienced it personally, and it had made me a better Judge—for all that it still haunted me. I relaxed my fists, realizing that I was clenching them hard enough to make my knuckles pop. Thinking about the first world I visited always made me angry, so I took a deep breath and shoved those thoughts to the side.

Next, I focused on my new quest. Which revealed nothing, like always. Okay then, thanks for nothing. Stupid mystery gods and their even stupider ridiculous quests!

Instead of getting worked up all over again, I concentrated on 'Strength,' to see if it was different now that it had gone past fifty.

> **Strength** – 55: The measure of your ability to employ your physical skills and abilities, carry heavy objects, and participate in melee combat. You have surpassed the maximum limits of all human analogs, and are broaching the barrier of the metaphysical.

The rest of my stats basically said the same thing. Breaking past fifty was some kind of threshold that made me more than a human was ever meant to be. If it meant *all* human hybrids by using the word 'analogs,' I was looking at becoming even better than the half-elves who had constantly shown me up when I was on world eight. Those had been some seriously brutal training sessions, and I had marveled at what they had been capable of doing.

"Are you ready to talk about it now?"

I was startled out of my stat screens by Jess, who had once again snuck up on me. I guess that stupid Hide-and-Seek Loser title wasn't good for much after all. She stood over me with her hands behind her back, rocking back and forth on her heels.

"There isn't much to talk about, Jess." I looked up at her with a frown, upset at myself for letting my guard down. "I'm just dealing with some changes to how I can cast spells."

Jess sat down next to me. "Would you show me? Maybe someone from the outside looking in can give you a new way to look at things."

I thought about it for a second and nodded in agreement. "Okay, I can see how that makes sense. Watch this." I held my hand in front of me with the palm facing upward, fingers straight except for my ring finger pointed up. A flicker of concentration, and a barely visible curved blade of wind the size of my hand shot into the sky. I didn't even feel the slightest tug on my energy levels, and it held its shape well beyond what I would normally expect. "See that? I didn't even need to say anything. To get a blade that big, I would normally need to at least mumble the activation phrase."

"Whoa…" Jess was looking up, trying to see where the blade had gone. "Will you show me how to do that?" I raised an eyebrow in answer, and she blushed. "Right, I'm an outsider looking in. And you need to trust me first." She looked around the clearing in silence for a bit before meeting my eyes. "Do the gods really speak to you?"

"They don't exactly speak to me, no. More like give orders and expect them to be carried out." I grimaced at how many hours of my life I had wasted shouting at the sky in an attempt to get any kind of reaction from whatever had stolen me from Earth.

"Well, if they want you to do things for them, maybe they are making it easier for you because they know you will need help." Jess looked out past the edge of the trees, where the darkness of the forest seemed to be waiting for our little fire to go out so it could rush in and engulf us. "Maybe the gods know better than you what's coming, and for you to do what they want, it means you need to be even more powerful than you've ever been."

I held back the shudder that tried to run down my spine. "I hope you're wrong, Jess." I got to my feet, dusting off my pants as I stood. I turned to make a circle around the edge of the area. "But I'm afraid you might just be right."

A twig snapping on the other side of the clearing brought both of us to high alert.

Jess sniffed hard, gritted her teeth, and hissed out a curse before looking at me. "*Vampire.* At least three, probably more."

"Wake up Leedy and Murphy. Don't untie Cross." I snapped the blade out of the end of my staff, then stuck the dull end upright in the ground next to me. After unhooking my mace from my belt, I took another step to the edge of the firelight in the direction where the sound had come from. "You might as well come out. We already know you're there."

"Ah, no matter. The hunt is always more fun when the prey sees you coming." A pale-faced man dressed like a farmhand stepped to the periphery of the trees, where the light of the fire stopped. He was big. Heavy muscles, with the height to match. "Why don't you come over here and we can discuss the events of two nights past? I have some questions I think you can answer."

I looked down, noticing that the vampire didn't step on the cleared ground. His bare feet were right on the edge of the circle the trees formed. "What's wrong? You can't come closer?" I smiled, spinning my mace before setting it on my shoulder. "I've never seen a vampire afraid of a location outside of a church or temple before. Is this blessed ground to you? Does getting any closer cook the stolen blood in your rotting veins?"

Another vampire joined the first, this one a woman dressed in the clothing of a minor noble, or maybe a wealthy merchant. Her clothing enhanced her figure, no doubt making it easier to entice victims to step into a dark alley with her. She whispered to the man, but my increased perception was able to hear what she said. "*It's weak, but it surrounds them completely. We can't get to them.*" After giving her report, she looked up at me. "Were you the hunter who killed three vampires at an inn?" When I didn't reply, she snarled at me, and I felt a mental shove against my mind. "*Answer me!*"

"Oooh, you trying to control me, little leech?" I gave her a genuine smile. I had almost forgotten the last time something had tried that. "If you weren't such a walking cliché, I might feel sorry for you." I twisted my free hand, flicking the power back at her. To the vampire's credit, she barely reacted to the attack. "Sorry, but those little tricks won't work on me."

"*Sorcerer…*" She hissed at me, lifting her own hand and casting a defensive spell that flickered in place around the pair with a dim red glow. "What dark god do you serve, that they would allow you to kill one of us? The Grimweaver?" She looked at her fellow vampire. "If he is owned by the Grimweaver, we cannot touch him without permission."

"Sure, let's go with that." I hated being called a sorcerer, but they were dropping all kinds of little nuggets of information. No sense in cutting that off if I didn't have to. After questioning the vampire at the inn, I was happy to increase my knowledge of the greater undead operating in the area. "Why don't you tell me why you care so much about the three vampires at the inn?"

The male vampire frowned, clearly picking up on my sarcasm about my soul being owned by a dark god. "You killed three members of our…organization, and our leader demanded an example be made."

"Oh, so you're some of the Destitute's people? I was hoping to run across more of you. I *really* want to know where your base is. Care to tell me the location of the Mausoleum?"

Both vampires took a step back, either from shock or surprise.

"I know it's to the north and east somewhere, but I'm still vague on the details."

"How do you—" The woman was cut off by a sharp glare from the man. "We don't know what you're talking about."

"Don't be like that! I had a *wonderful* conversation with your friend before he succumbed to his wounds." I tapped the handle of my mace for emphasis. "It's always hard to gauge how much damage your kind can take before they die. I've never been able to figure out that fine line between undead and dead, you know? Probably just need more practice. Now, you can either tell me what I want to know, or volunteer to be my test subject. Your choice."

Before they could answer, a shout from behind made me spin around. Leedy ran for the edge of the clearing toward another pair of vampires, his sword leading the way.

I sprinted to catch up to him, barely catching him by the belt before he could get himself killed. "Leedy, stop, dammit! Take a second and look around. They can't enter the clearing."

A hiss from the pair of disappointed vampires was echoed by another pair who stepped into sight. Leedy had almost ran straight into an ambush. But, instead of thanking me, he tried to jerk free of my grip and run to them anyway. "Let me go! I can take them. They're weak, and I'm invincible! Let me go!"

"What's wrong with you?" At first, I thought he might just have an ego that big. It didn't really fit with his general level of competence and experience, though, and I finally caught sight of his eyes. They were glazed over and unfocused, like he wasn't seeing what was actually in front of him. "Ah, they got you with a mind whammy, didn't they?" I had to put him in a choke hold for him to stay still, but I managed to draw a circle on his forehead and imbue enough mana to break the hold on him. He slumped in my arms, suddenly weak from the attack on his mind.

"I… I'm okay. You can let me go." Leedy stood on his own, holding his free hand to his head. "Thank you. That was much closer than it should have been."

"Are you going to be all right?" I stayed close, ready to stop him if they managed to give him another whammy. "These bloodsuckers aren't newborns. They're old enough to have developed at least some of their powers."

"I'll be fine. If I had just taken a moment to put on my helm, the inscriptions would have protected me from such a simple attack." Leedy stared balefully with bloodshot eyes at the undead crowding the circle. There were six of them on this side now, all of them crouched and ready in case he decided to get within range of their claws. "If we're safe in this circle, it might be best to wait for daybreak."

"You just make sure they don't get to the others." I looked over and saw Murphy already wearing his helmet, and Jess was wearing the one that had belonged to Cross. "Although it looks like they'll be okay."

Leedy stumbled off, still holding his head.

I made sure he got his helmet on before I turned back to the pair I had been speaking to. "Now, where were we? Ah, that's right, I was giving you the chance to tell me what I want to know, before I kill you all."

"I don't think so." The woman gave me a wicked smile, showing off her fangs. "Unless you want your friend to die, I suggest you answer *our* questions."

"My friends are all fine." I motioned to the trio standing near the fire, all safely protected by Warden helmets. "You can't get to them now."

"Are you sure about that?" Her red eyes flickered to the side, where a shadowy figure stumbled through the dark. "What about this one?"

I grimaced as the limping figure of Cross finally stepped into the light.

CHAPTER 15

Okay, well, moral values check time. Cross was a cog in the machine of this crappy world, nothing more than a product of his situation. But, he was also a massive dick about it. Unfortunately for me, the Judge aspect inside me was silent about what to do. I could let him die, or try to make a deal for his life. Decisions like these were why they paid me the big bucks.

"What do you want, blood-bag?" I hooked my mace back on my belt and took another step away from where my spear-staff stuck out of the ground. "I can spare a few minutes to listen. Can't promise I'll accept your terms."

The female vampire gave me another fang-accented smile. Probably imagining draining me. "First, you can answer some questions." She ran a hand down her captive's face, and Cross leaned into her touch. He was completely within her thrall. "Tell me what denizen of the hells you have made your compact with for power, sorcerer."

I had to grit my teeth at the question. Being called a sorcerer was like nails on a chalkboard. Not only that, but I really couldn't give her a good answer. If I told her the truth, I'd be giving her too much information, but I also couldn't lie about something as important as a sorcerer's compact. Saying something owned my soul with my own voice was never a good idea. She had been the one to talk about the Grimweaver earlier, not me. Time to improvise. I lifted my hands and formed an orb of fire in my right hand, and an orb of water in my left. They were both no bigger than a marble, but the power leaking from them was like a physical force that pushed against the senses. "There is no name for who controls my power. Even I can't speak its name." I was technically telling the truth, since no outside force controlled my magic, and therefore there was no name to actually give.

Gotta love semantics.

Thankfully, the theatrics seemed to have at least some impact. Both the vampires stepped back to confer, and finally the woman came back to speak with me, while the man held on to Cross. "We have marked your compatriot, and can find him anywhere he goes. Our team will return to the Destitute and tell him what we have seen."

The man shoved Cross across the invisible line of blessed earth that protected us, and I let him fall flat on his face in the dirt.

She frowned at my lack of compassion for my 'compatriot,' before regaining her haughty composure. "Once we know how to proceed, we *will* return."

"And when we do, I would recommend not running." The man smirked at me, flexing his fingers like they were claws. "You won't get very far."

Tired of their bullshit, I returned his smirk. "You won't be there at all." I flicked both hands forward, the two orbs of energy flying at the vampire so fast he barely had time to try to run. Fire and water combined, creating a flash of superheated steam that exploded with a crackling hiss. The attack was incredibly destructive, considering steam could get much hotter than fire alone. The smell of cooked rotten meat permeated the air, and the corpse of the undead monster fell to the ground in a heap of rubbery flesh and exposed bone. I looked at the surprised woman vampire and shrugged. "I don't like it when people threaten me."

"Release them!"

Her shout was the only warning we had before a group of freaking velociraptors rushed into the clearing. The vampires must have herded them toward us in a display of critical thinking skills I hadn't expected, making me realize I had been underestimating them. Just because the undead were blocked from entering the clearing didn't mean dinosaurs were in the same category.

I couldn't do anything to stop the vampires from retreating, considering the dazed Captain Cross was about to be eaten if I didn't help him. I grabbed him by the ankle and jumped backward, dragging him face-first through the dirt back to the fire.

"Get back-to-back!" Leedy had managed to get the rest of his armor on at some point, and he was positioning the others around the small fire. I got in position, completing the circle as I tossed Cross into the center next to the fire pit. Jess had snatched up my spear-staff for herself and was swiping at the raptors that had come rushing in from the other side of the clearing, the extra reach going a long way toward making up for her lack of familiarity with the weapon.

Private Murphy had already killed one dinosaur and was hacking the broad side of his halberd into the side of another. I unclipped my mace just as the leading velociraptor chasing behind my retreat caught up to me, so I was in position to give it an uppercut straight to the lower jaw. It was my first chance to get a better look at the dinosaur up close and personal, and it was everything the twelve-year-old still living inside me hoped it would be.

Thick scales, scary teeth with bits of flesh clinging to them, dangerous talons, it was the real deal. Seeing them gave me a thrill, but they were trying to eat me, so I didn't get time to enjoy it…much. I mean, it's still freaking dinosaurs. That distant child in my brain jumped up and down in glee, despite our situation.

After the first raptor caught my mace with its face, the next one in line jumped for my exposed left side. I was forced to use the middle barrel of my wrist gun to keep it from taking off my arm, and the sound of the explosive report was like pushing the pause button on the battle.

Leedy and Murphy had been swiping their weapons back and forth to keep the dinosaurs back, and the loud noise made both of them duck. It would have been a fatal mistake if the velociraptors didn't also flinch away. They must have been very sensitive to sound, because only the few still engaged in direct fighting stuck around. The others took off running, their croaking screams disappearing into the distance.

Jess had heard the wrist gun fire when I had killed the wendigos, so she was the first of the trio to recover. She slashed out with the bladed tip of her borrowed spear, opening up a deep gash in the side of the neck of her opponent. It fell back with a strangled cry, dropping to its side as dark-red blood poured out onto the ground.

The gunshot also seemed to break Cross out of his stupor, and he sat up, spitting dirt out of his mouth. He seemed upset, given the change of setting and general state of near nakedness he found himself in, not to mention his mouth being turned into a makeshift field plow earlier.

I shook my head. Some people were just so emotionally fragile. I ignored him, because the two raptors I had wounded were still in the fight. The one I had shot was in bad shape, the silver bullet lodged in its chest making it wheeze as it lunged for me.

I swung my mace sideways as I drew forward, smashing it across the side of its head. The mace got stuck in its skull, and I let it go to defend myself as the other raptor jumped. The one I had given a nasty uppercut to pulled a ninja on me and kicked forward, slicing its thick and ridiculously sharp talon across my side. The raptor I had hit in the head went all rubbery and stumbled away from me, and I formed a double wind blade with both hands that blasted into the dinosaur that had cut me.

My new power boost made me misjudge the amount of energy I put into the spell, and the creature fell to the ground in three pieces. I winced at the waste of mana, and promised myself to practice more as soon as possible to get a handle on it. The others were done finishing off their dinosaurs, making the clearing seem abnormally quiet as the only sounds suddenly became the crackling of the fire and the heavy breathing of exhausted warriors. My side was leaking blood, so I put pressure on it and went to retrieve my mace from the raptor that was now bleeding out near the edge of the clearing.

"What in all that is good and holy is going on?" Captain Cross was very obviously upset.

I ignored him and pried the bladed head of the heavy mace free, finishing off the raptor in the process.

"Somebody answer me!"

"Sir, there was a vampire attack, and then there were the velociraptors, and you were taken by them—"

Leedy stopped talking as Cross waved his left hand in a swatting motion, and I heard a loud slap.

Cross had a spell made just for slapping? That was definitely a first for me. Either that, or he had fantastic control of a kinetic spell. Probably the latter, but I would make sure. I could definitely use a slapping spell. It opened up all kinds of possibilities.

The raptor dying at my feet caused a message to flash across my vision, distracting me from the drama unfolding by the fire.

> **New Title Earned**: Dinosaur Hunter
>
> -Killing majestic and beautiful creatures has earned you a reward. Congratulations on helping dinosaurs go extinct on one of the last worlds they still exist!
>
> **Skill Imparted**: Dinosaur and dinosaur-adjacent creatures do 5% less damage. An additional 5% will be applied if there are multiple opponents.

Not the worst reward, although the extinction comment wasn't exactly fair. They had started it. Kinda.

I hooked my bloody mace onto my belt and cast another healing spell on myself as I walked back to the soap opera still playing out near the fire. I sighed at the veritable explosion of healing magic that surged through my body, almost immediately sealing any injuries and leaving the jittery energy of unused magic humming through my body. I really needed to get a handle on my new capabilities, otherwise I could give myself a tumor or something.

"You will return my belongings immediately, Corporal, or I will see you in the stocks!" Cross was still giving Leedy grief, and I must have missed another magical slap because both of his cheeks were swollen and red. "And you can start with my bracers!"

"Nope." I spoke quietly, but Cross snapped his head around as though I had shouted. He tried to get to his feet as I approached, his injured foot giving him problems. "Don't bother getting up. You lost, and your actions back at the clearing invalidated any authority you might claim to hold."

"It's clear you don't understand your situation, wanderer. You don't get to decide what authority anyone has. You aren't even a part of a guild!" Cross finally got back to his feet, and I saw him cup his hand as if he were going to cast another spell.

I held up a clawed hand and allowed a fireball the size of a basketball to form. It was almost too easy, the energy inside me practically jumping at the chance to escape. And I hadn't even used an activation word. Definitely needed more practice. "If you cast anything, I'll burn your face off, then heal it back without eyes."

The combination of suddenly putting out a large amount of power and wild threat put Cross on his back foot. He just gaped at me, so I added a little more mana, and the color of the flames turned from orange to blue. I wasn't actually a devout believer in the 'might makes right' camp, but Cross clearly was, so I would speak a language he could understand. "Are you going to calm down, or am I going to have to use this?" I tossed the now blue-white flame up and down once in my hand as Cross tracked the mini-inferno with his eyes. "As for your question about guilds. What are guilds, at their heart? They are a crutch for power. An effective crutch, but a crutch nonetheless. It is the accumulation of the strength of many to impose their values on the world, and whose ultimate authority is derived from the implicit threat of violence. I am stronger than you, and thus you must do as I say. But what if one person possessed both the strength and implicit authority of the many? To be more clear, what if I could kick both you and your guilds' asses? What permission could they offer me that I could not take for myself, Cross?"

"How are you so strong?" Cross looked at my wrists and shook his head. "You didn't steal the bracers, so how are you able to draw that much power?" I pulled my hand back like I was about to toss the fireball at him, and he held his hands up in surrender. "Okay, I will not cast spells. But don't tie me up again."

"Jess, go and grab those bracers. I think I just learned what those runes carved on them are for." She ran to grab them as I turned back to Cross. "First, I would have your word that you submit, and won't attempt to harm anyone here, or attempt to escape." I started to absorb the mana from the fireball back into myself, and whispered the activation to one of my Judge abilities. "*Detect Lies.*"

"I give my word as an officer that I will not purposefully harm anyone in this group for the duration of this journey, or try to escape while we travel."

My ability gave me a slight flicker of untruth when he spoke, making his lips look purple to my eyes. It wasn't a complete lie, though, so he at least wasn't thinking about hurting anyone. Probably planned to subvert his Wardens back to his side, and then capture me. It was what I would do in his shoes.

"Is that acceptable, wanderer?"

"You aren't being completely honest, but I don't think you are going to break your word right now." He flared up like an angry peacock when I called him a liar. I didn't care. I felt my Judge skill fall away, its short time limit running out. I wouldn't be able to use it again for a few hours. Another of the odd rules I wish I knew more about. "Now, why don't you sit down and tell me who ordered you to execute Jess and me before we could reach Greendown?"

Cross spluttered, his face going pale. "No one ordered me to kill you!"

I didn't need my Judge title or skills to tell me he was lying.

"Why would you think someone would order that?"

"Look, I'm tired. I've had a really weird couple of days." I motioned at a dead velociraptor near the edge of the firelight. "Vampires, Wardens, wendigos, more Wardens, then more vampires, and now fucking *dinosaurs*. How about you just cut the bullshit, and we level with each other."

He looked down at his hands, refusing to meet my eyes.

"Cross, I know you didn't act on your own. It's possible you didn't even *want* to kill us and were only doing what you were told. Although that's a very thin excuse, no matter who you are."

The Warden grunted, agreeing without coming out and saying so.

"I also want you to know that I could *make* you answer me, but I don't want to do that if I don't have to. So just tell me."

Cross hobbled over and sat next to the fire, a defeated look on his face. Jess came over and handed me the bracers, and I hooked them on my belt to check out when I was done with Cross.

"I'm going to skin the velociraptors while you talk to him. We can sell the hides at Greendown."

I gave her a nod and she left, grabbing Murphy to help her drag bodies into the firelight.

Leedy just stood there, looking tired and forlorn.

"You aren't going to believe me."

I sat next to Cross, who was now looking into the fire and absolutely ruining his night vision.

"This goes higher than anyone would ever suspect."

"Trust me, Cross. I've probably heard it all before. Was it your guild leader? A noble? A royal? The king himself?" I sighed, thinking of all the crap I had dealt with on my first world. Political intrigue was more dangerous than dinosaurs, that was for sure. "Just tell me."

"My orders…" Cross swallowed hard, closing his eyes. "The order to kill you came from the gods themselves."

My eyebrows tried to crawl into my scalp at his words. Well, way to prove me wrong. I guess I *hadn't* heard it all.

CHAPTER 16

"So, the 'gods' demanded you execute us?" I shook my head, trying to reconcile the idea with what I knew about celestial and infernal beings. Believing that an actual god was giving orders to mortals was a little unbelievable to me, but the things we called angels and demons were a different story. One of them could easily pull off calling themselves a god, because there wasn't anyone around who would call them out on it. At least, no one who would survive the experience if they were there in person on a world as magic-starved as this.

Getting my Mage class had unlocked celestial and infernal magic, but I hadn't used any of it beyond a few blessings and curses. The elves on my eighth planet had libraries filled with books that told stories of how horrible it could—and did—turn out when you messed with incredibly powerful beings from other planes of existence. Lawfully Good was frequently just as dangerous as Lawfully Evil, and I wasn't in a rush to mess with the insanity of either. "Why don't you tell me which 'god' wants me dead?"

Cross cleared his throat roughly, and Leedy passed him a canteen without him having to ask. After taking a long drink, Cross finally got on with it. "Many people don't know this, but our guild wasn't always the most powerful in the west. We had help to get where we are today. The ancient home and headquarters for our guild is many leagues to the south and east, in a small port town called Swordsworn on the banks of the Mighty Reka."

Leedy silently nodded along with Cross, telling me the man was being honest.

"I'm not surprised to hear it. Every organization has to start somewhere." I thought of the few worlds I had managed to create an order based on my Judge profession, and the struggle it had taken to get there. "So, what helped you become the leading guild? And what does that have to do with your orders?"

"That's what I'm trying to tell you." Cross leaned forward, his face deadly serious. "What allowed us to rise to power, and where most of our orders originate from, is *The Oracle*." He waited, trying to see if I understood the gravity of the information. When I didn't react, he frowned and kept talking. "*The Oracle* is a book. An ancient tome that is connected to the Trinity. Whatever they say always comes true. It allows our leadership to write questions, and the gods will answer, if they deem the request worthy."

I snorted, unable to contain my scorn. "So, your entire guild listens to whatever a book says? A book that *anyone* with a strong enough transference spell could write in? With advanced thought processes like that, it's a miracle this place isn't a burning wasteland already."

"You scoff, but the power of *The Oracle* has been proven true over generations. You can only dismiss it so easily because you don't understand its real power." Cross picked up a stick and poked at the fire. "There have been plenty of wizards over the years who have tried to control the messages *The Oracle* gives us, but it always ends in their death."

"And is it common for your book to order the murder of innocent civilians?" I tossed more wood on the fire, as it was getting colder. "Or are Jess and I lucky enough to be the first?"

Cross winced, looking down at his hands. "I don't know every order *The Oracle* has given over the years, so it's possible there are more." He looked up to see me frowning at him. "But yes, you are the first I know about."

"No argument about the innocent part? Maybe there's hope for you yet. How many people received these orders? Am I going to have to worry about fighting every Warden I come across from now on?" I didn't say it out loud, but this also changed the plan about exposing him to the local populace at Greendown. It wouldn't be nearly as easy to show up with him tied up and denounce him as an attempted murderer if he was following orders.

"Not many know of the orders passed down by *The Oracle*. It isn't a secret that we have the book—especially in certain circles— but we keep the actual messages it gives us as quiet as possible." Cross paused to think, looking for answers in the fire. "The one who passed the message to me was the Commandant. I don't think anyone else knows about it. Once news gets out that I failed, the Wardens will either send more of our own people to hunt you down, or hire members of the Button Guild to handle it. Since there aren't many Wardens more capable than I am in the region, I would guess they do the latter."

"Button Guild? What kind of guild is that?" Images of button collectors and seamstresses armed with scissors following me through the woods flashed through my head. "It doesn't sound very threatening."

Leedy had walked over to the saddlebags near the hastily erected tents and returned with a set of clothes for the nearly naked captain. He answered before Cross had a chance. "The Button Guild has the best assassins of all the guilds. They don't do cloak-and-dagger style like the Thieves' Guild, or poison like the darker side of the Alchemists' Guild. All their kills are made to look like accidents."

"Oh, now that is scary." I deadpanned my reply, but I actually meant what I said. An assassin competent enough to kill someone without making the death obvious that it was a murder meant they were truly dangerous. Some real Final Destination kind of stuff. "So, you are saying that we need to look out for runaway wagons and loose roof tiles?"

"Something like that." Cross took the clothes from Leedy and put them on gingerly, still in pain from his injured foot and various scrapes and bruises from being dragged roughly across the clearing. I didn't offer to heal them. He could suffer a bit longer. "What are your plans now that you know?"

"I'll have to gauge that based on what I see when we get to Greendown." I looked over to where Jess was skinning another raptor. "Finding a safe place for Jess to go will probably be my first priority. After that, I don't know. Not that I would tell you, even if I did have some idea."

Cross looked away from me, refusing to meet my eye. "It…it's not a good idea for you to separate from the lycan-touched. She isn't going to last long without your help."

"What do you mean by that?" I sat forward. A flash of anger ran through me. "Was she named in the orders from your stupid book? I thought it only wanted you to kill me."

"It didn't name you. Just described you, and what your message to the people you met would be." Cross still wouldn't look at me. "But I did name both of you when I sent in my report after we spoke with the innkeeper."

"You stupid piece of shit." I took a deep breath and tried to calm down. "You signed her death warrant, knowing what it meant."

Cross finally looked up at me, and it was all I could do not to shoot him in his dumb face. "I should just kill you for that. For everything you've done."

"I was only following orders." Cross barely whispered his words, knowing how hollow they sounded. "The Wardens are a force for good, and *The Oracle* says you threatened that. I did what I had to do to protect us."

My inner Judge finally came to a ruling on his actions. I *wanted* to kill him outright, but I knew it wasn't the right choice. I could feel my voice deepen as the aspect of my Judge profession came to the forefront. "Captain Cross, you claim to have only been following orders, but you know you violated your conscience. Your actions were that of a murderer and reflect the evil inherent in your organization. Instead of choosing to do the right thing, you chose the easy wrong. By the authority vested in me through the Office of Chief Justice, Arbiter, Justiciar, and Judge, I condemn you. As punishment, I claim your ability to perform magic, so that you may no longer use your power for evil. Since you've raised your hand against your brothers in attempted fratricide and against the innocent in attempted murder, let this punishment be a reminder of the responsibility you bear, and may it prompt you to lift your hand only in the pursuit of good."

Before he could react, I had already stood, unsheathed my ninjatō, and removed his left hand with a hard chop. The same hand he used when slapping Leedy earlier. I held back from removing his right hand, even though it left him with the ability to learn spells with it. Magic was a finicky thing, and I knew that he would carry the mental scars of losing the primary hand he used for casting. It would be nearly impossible for him to ever become as powerful as he was before.

Cross stared down at his hand in shock, not even reacting to what I had done. I grabbed his wrist, cutting off the spurt of blood before he could die. I stuck my sword in the ground next to me so I could use the free hand to draw a circle with both a '*J*' and '*H*' inside it, channeling a healing spell into Cross. I made sure not to allow the hand to regrow, instead healing it into a stump. Now, no one would be able to fix it. The loss of the hand was permanent.

Leedy had lurched back, but rushed forward with his sword drawn. He stumbled to a stop when he saw me healing Cross. "Wha-what have you done?!"

"I've removed his ability to cast spells. From now on, anytime he thinks about hurting someone who doesn't deserve it, he will remember the consequences of his evil choices." I looked down at Cross, who had gone deathly pale. "Your Judgment has been passed. Don't make the same mistakes a second time."

"You just ended his career!" Leedy was still holding his sword, but it was pointed at the ground.

I could sense Private Murphy standing off to the side, ready to step in. I had no idea which of us he would fight for, but the unusually wise young man held himself back. Leedy didn't show the same restraint.

"He can't serve as a captain without a hand! You have no idea how much you have weakened this region. The number of monsters that can now roam free without him there to stop them will result in the death of—"

I snapped my full attention from Cross to Leedy, my eyes boring into the Warden. "He ended his *own* career the moment he thought it was acceptable to kill Jess just for being associated with me." I pulled my ninjatō from the ground and wiped it off before slamming the straight blade in its sheath. "And he only compounded his sins when he sent out a message that he *knew* would end in her death, even if he personally didn't do the deed. As for the monsters, the Commandant will have to do his job and protect the people. *Without* his captain's help."

Leedy backed away, sheathing his own sword. "I don't like this, James Holden. You did this without him being brought before a tribunal, and decided on your own to—"

"When will you learn?" My voice was quiet, but the intensity was enough to silence the corporal. "I *am* the tribunal. I am a *Judge*. This is what I do. It is my responsibility to decide the punishment for the crimes others commit. Do you think the burdens and responsibilities I shoulder are light and easy? Let me tell you the truth about our line of work, Leedy. Because your job isn't supposed to be all that different from mine. When you swore the oath to become a Warden, you became a servant of Justice. That Justice requires discernment and firm resolve, and you had better make *damn* certain that you understand the moral compass that you are using to execute righteousness." I pointed to Cross, still on the ground in shock. "The same measurement you use to judge others will be used to judge you. Can you handle that? Because I know that

I can. I—*we* are both the judge and the judged, and have to acknowledge that reality every morning that we get out of bed. If you don't like that, then you are free to return to the corrupt organization that allows the injustices of this world to fester."

The corporal turned away, moving to go help the others with the dead raptors. He didn't look at me the whole time.

"What…what am I supposed to do now? You didn't just end my career." Cross finally looked up at me, still clearly in shock. "You've killed me. When those vampires come back, I'm finished."

"No, I removed one of the weapons at your disposal. Do you have other weapons, besides your magic?" I stood over him, purposefully being as imposing as possible. "You misused your magic. Perhaps you can change, and use your sword for good, now that you can't use spells for evil."

I turned and walked away, finding my own dead raptor to clean. There was no guilt for what I had done. Cross had made his bed, and now it was time for him to lay in it. I was more concerned about what I was going to do with Jess. There was no way I could send her off on her own now, not if an entire guild of assassins was going to come after her. I looked down at the bracers I had gotten from Cross and started to plan.

Out of the corner of my eye, I picked out Cross examining the stump of his arm. My keen ears picked out his contemplative whisper. "The judge *and* the judged…"

CHAPTER 17

"What's wrong?" Jess walked next to me, the two of us trailing the three Wardens. We were leading the disgraced captain's horse, which was loaded down with raptor hides and other various bits. "You haven't said much since we left the clearing."

"There are two things that are really bothering me." I had come up with several ways to keep Jess from getting killed, but only one of them gave her a genuine chance at survival. It was the plan I disliked the most. "And I don't see a way to fix the biggest issue without a lot of pain, sweat, and tears."

"Well, tell me what's bothering you. Maybe I can help." Jess slowed a bit, opening the gap between the Wardens and us. She leaned in to whisper. "Is it because of those three?"

"No. The biggest problem I have is what we are going to do to keep you alive." I explained what I had learned from Cross, and told her my concerns about leaving her in Greendown. "So, you see why I'm unhappy."

Jess didn't answer right away, instead taking a few minutes to think about her reply. "The best thing would be for me to go east, outside the region that the Wardens control." The corners of her lips turned down into a frown. "But the Eastern Marshals are close enough to the Wardens that they might as well be the same thing." She fell silent again, her nose scrunched up in thought.

I considered Jess for a long moment. She was strangely calm for someone who had just learned she was being hunted by a kingdom-wide organization of law enforcement. I waited for her to work through the problem. While we were walking, the forest thinned out enough that sunlight was able to reach the forest floor, making the ground warm up and creating a low fog that hugged the earth. Both Leedy and Murphy were quickly red-faced and overheated in their armor, but the hearty Wardens refused to slow down. Cross seemed to still be in a daze, occasionally glancing back at me with a blank look on his face. I'd healed his foot back at the place of power, so it was easy for him to keep up with the rest of us.

"Of course!" Jess winced as soon as she realized she had shouted, breaking me out of my observation of our surroundings. "I could just change my name when we get to Greendown. No one will know who I am, especially since I'm from a small village." She seemed proud of her idea, walking with a bit of a strut.

Until I burst her little bubble.

"So, there are a lot of pretty shifter girls around your age, height, and weight in the area?" I raised my eyebrow, already seeing her wilt. "I suppose if you can blend in with a group of people who look just like you, it should be easy to hide."

"You don't have to be so sarcastic." She looked down at her feet. "What am I supposed to do then? Hiding in the wilderness until they forget about me sounds terrible."

"No, I have something much worse in mind." It was hard not to smile as Jess seemed to pull in on herself in fear. Served her right for sneaking up on me all the time. "I'm going to teach you magic. At least, enough to protect yourself from mundane assassins."

Her eyes went as wide as saucers, and her mouth dropped open, exposing her elongated canines. "Y-you are going to teach me magic? Real magic. The kind that you do." I nodded, and she whooped with joy. "Yes! I'm going to be a real wizard!"

"It's wizardess, and that's not what I'm going to train you to be." I shook my head as she tried her best to calm down. She almost managed, but she couldn't keep her hands still. I ignored it and got on with the first lesson. "I'm going to teach you how to be a mage. Not a wizard, wizardess, sorceress, druid, warlock, or witch. A *mage*."

"What's the difference? I mean, I know a druid talks to animals, and a witch makes potions and love spells. But it's wizards who cast real magic." Jess was finally settling down, the conversation leveling her out some. "Aren't warlocks and sorcerers the same as a wizard?"

I almost growled in frustration. It drove me crazy when people got it all wrong. "No, they are not the same as a wizard, and a wizard isn't the same as a mage." I paused, expecting another interruption, but she surprisingly stayed quiet. "A wizard performs magic through rituals and memorized spells. They usually need some kind of focusing object, like a wand or staff, that they have enchanted somehow."

"Yeah, that's what I want to do." Jess did the fluttery thing with her hands again. "This is going to be so amazing!"

"No. We don't have the time for you to spend the next decade memorizing the necessary incantations and rituals required to be a wizard. And although a mage uses enchanted items, they use them to *enhance* what they already do. They don't require them like a wizard does." I held out a hand and snapped my fingers, shooting a bolt of electricity into a nearby tree. It was much stronger than I expected, but I played it off like I completely meant to blast the bark off an innocent walnut tree. "See that? Only some concentration and an activation movement, and I can do magic. A wizard can't even manage that much without some kind of tool to help them. Mages directly control the power of the universe through willpower and mental focus."

"Wow. Okay, I get the point. I want to be a mage." Jess walked over to inspect the damage while I waved off Leedy and Murphy.

The spell had made them stop short, expecting an attack. I gave them a shrug in apology and the two of them turned around. Cross hadn't stopped walking.

Jess returned from looking over the tree, and we fell in step behind the Wardens. "What about the other kinds of magic users you were talking about?"

"I don't want to get bogged down explaining everything right now, so I'll just go over the bare minimum. Sorcerers make a deal with a powerful entity of some kind and borrow their power in return for something. Usually regular sacrifices, their own soul, or promises of future favors. You can see why I don't like being compared to one of them."

Jess nodded to show she understood.

"Good. Now, druids are similar to sorcerers, but they make deals with nature or earth spirits for power. Sometimes the primal gods of old, if they have any power left to share. Those are the ones that can turn into animals like a shifter, without all the downsides of being a lycan. Usually, a druid is a force for good—as long as you don't trash what they are protecting. The bad part of being a druid is the limit on how far they can go. They promise to protect nature, or some sacred region. If they stray too far from their place of power, they get weaker and weaker until they are forced to return."

"What happens if they don't go back?" Jess looked around the forest as if she expected a druid to pop out from behind a bush or something. "Do they die?"

I shook my head. "The compulsion to return would get stronger and stronger, until they couldn't ignore it anymore. And them leaving their place of power is pretty rare, especially if they have a big region to cover. Like this forest, or a mountain range. That isn't the important part for you to remember, though."

"Okay, what's the important part?" Jess was still watching for a druid instead of looking at me. "Don't shoot trees with lightning?"

"Well, you're not wrong, but what I was going to say was to try to avoid fighting a druid on their own turf. They are always tough." I remembered the crazy old druid I had fought on world ten. I had been trying to gather rare ores so I could gain my Blacksmith profession, and he had taken exception at my digging. It had all worked out since that's what led to my blessed star metal mace and hand cannon. At the time, it had been less than fun.

I realized Jess was staring at me and cleared my throat. "Anyway, the last two you need to know about are warlocks and witches. They don't just make love potions and cackle over a black cauldron."

"Oh, I was just kidding about that. I know how evil witches can be. There is a coven to the north that rules over the orcs and goblins. Some people even say they control the weaker undead." Jess shuddered. "I definitely don't want to be one of those."

"Well, I don't know how true all that is, but I do know not all witches and warlocks are evil." Jess opened her mouth to argue, so I held up a finger to stop her. "There are white witches and black witches. White witches aren't very common, which is why most witches get a bad name. The difference comes from how they get their power. Black witches get their power from sacrifices, like a sorcerer, but they manipulate the spent life energy directly instead of trading it with a demon or something similar." I shuddered, remembering the great sacrifice of the Seven Shade Coven on world eleven.

"If that's how black witches get power, how do white witches use magic?" Jess was guiding the horse around a divot in the road, doing her best not to step in the mud packed on the edge of the trail. "Do they sacrifice bad things?"

"Nope. White witches get magic through prayer and dedication to benevolent entities, and they use spells through runed objects and potions. They can and *do* use blood sacrifices, but the blood and energy is their own, and magic seems to recognize the significance of that." I thought about world seven, and the woman the people had known as simply the White Witch. I had called her Lizbeth. She sacrificed her own life and power in a burst of raw magical might that was still unmatched in my experience to date, short of a nuclear explosion. There were no black witches on the *continent* after that day. I still debated with myself about whether it was worth it or not. Lizbeth had been one hell of a woman, and the universe was a worse place without her.

"That sounds a lot like a druid, except without the promise to stay in one place." Jess finally got the horse back on the trail after managing to get mud up past her ankles. "Do they have limits like druids?"

I thought for a minute about how to best explain it, considering how close they were to a druid. "You know how most healers are a priest of some kind? They heal through prayer to a god they worship. Well, not all gods work that way. Some are in between the gods of nature and the gods of light and dark. Those are the ones a white witch deals with. That means they are usually weaker in a direct confrontation. Their actual power lies in the wide array of abilities and potions they have."

"Like what?" Jess hopped along next to me, trying to knock the mud off her feet. "Love spells?"

"What is it with you and love spells?"

She just shrugged at me.

Ugh. "Yes, things like love spells, seeing the future, tracking spells, potions for strength, speed, invisibility, breathing underwater, charms of all types, the ability to speak to spirits, all kinds of things."

"Okay, I get it. They are powerful, but not in the same way a black witch or warlock is. It sounds to me like becoming a mage really is the best choice." She squinted at me, her face turning serious. "When do you start teaching me?"

"Now, if you want." I waited for her to stop dancing with joy before I finished talking. "First, I need you to hold out your hand and let me test you."

"What are you testing me for?" Jess practically shoved her hand in my face. "Are you going to teach me how to throw a fireball? Oh, how about turning invisible! I've always wanted to do that."

"Let me test you first, and we can go from there." I took her hand and gently pushed a tiny puff of mana into her body to check how resistant she was to it. At least, I tried to make it a tiny amount. The burst that shot into her was enough to jolt her as though she had been shocked, and her hand yanked out of mine as she gave me an uppercut to the nose.

"Wha-what was that!" Jess trembled, and I was pinching off a bloody nose.

The girl had hard knuckles.

"Are you trying to kill me?"

"I could ask you the same thing." I drew a few small circles on my forehead to stop the bleeding, then pulled out a rag to wipe away the blood running down my face. I was genuinely impressed she could hurt me. "I gotta say, you have a solid punch."

"Remember where I worked? I had to be able to defend myself." Jess shook her hand, trying to get feeling back into it. "What did you do to me? My hand is asleep."

"That's because you have my mana in your hand instead of your own. Where does the numbness stop?" I moved closer as Jess indicated a spot just below her elbow. "Hmmm, that's interesting."

"Interesting good, or interesting bad?" She was still flexing her fingers. "Is there something wrong?"

I shook my head and took her by the hand again. "It's just interesting. Not necessarily good or bad." I tried to pull my mana back out of her hand again so she could get feeling back in her arm, but it wouldn't come free. "Well, it looks like your first lesson is going to be how to purge your body from foreign mana instead of a fireball. I think it might be because of your heritage making you different, but I can't reclaim my mana from you."

"Different? How does being lycan-touched make me different?" Jess seemed to curl up on herself.

Another person telling her there was something wrong with her because of a situation she couldn't control. I was going to have to break her of that mental trap at some point. Might as well start now.

"Stop acting like being different is bad." I shook my finger in her face.

She looked up at me, clear trepidation in her eyes.

"Being different is what separates you from the chaff. Like I was saying, your body seems to hold onto mana much better than anyone

I've ever trained. It will make it much easier for you to gather energy for powerful spells. Controlling them is going to be your issue."

"Y-you mean I can still cast magic? I'm not going to go full shift or something and lose control of myself?" Jess perked up, her ears almost vibrating with excitement. "I can be a mage?"

"Actually, I didn't even think about you shifting. That's something we'll have to keep an eye out for, but I'm not worried about it." I put a hand on her shoulder to calm her down. "Even if that does happen, I won't let you hurt yourself, or anyone else. Have faith in your new teacher."

She took a few deep breaths and gave me a sharp nod of agreement. "Okay. I trust you." Jess held her hand up, flapping it around like an injured potato. "Can we fix this now?"

I laughed and let go of her. "Sure. First, I need you to imagine that your body is an empty vessel. Like a Jess-shaped vase that doesn't have anything inside it."

She squinted, concentrating on what I was telling her. We were getting farther away from the three in front, but I was okay with that. Just in case something didn't go as planned, some extra space was probably a good thing.

"Now that you have that image in your mind, do your best to sense the mana I pushed into you. You should see it as a kind of mist or fog that fills up the numb part of your arm."

Jess grunted, and beads of sweat popped out on her forehead. "I see it. It's like a blue-green fog, with yellow lightning running through it."

Well, the lightning part was new. I would have to check on that later, when I was alone. "Good. Now imagine opening up a hole in your palm, almost like popping the cork on a bottle. Then push the fog out of it and seal the hole back up when it's all gone."

Jess lifted her hand and pointed it off into the forest, away from the rest of us. Her arm started to shake, and she bit down hard, gritting her teeth. After a few seconds, a burst of cyan light shot out of her palm, gouging out a deep rut in the ground and sending dirt flying with a booming shockwave I felt in my chest. Jess dropped to her knees before passing out.

I managed to catch her before she could face-plant into the hard-packed trail.

"What are you doing back there?!" Leedy had stopped, his sword out and ready. "Would you please stop blowing up the forest, and telling every monster out here exactly where we are?"

"Sorry!" I waved, showing everything was okay. "My fault!"

He turned back around, and they went back to walking.

I got Jess back to her feet and slapped her awake. "Hey, snap out of it. That was impressive for a first spell, but you can't go passing out every time mana leaves your body. You need to control how much you push out at one time. Don't allow yourself to lose too much all at once. Otherwise, the shock to your system will knock you for a loop."

"Got it." Jess straightened up, forcing herself to stand on her own. "I'm okay now. I just got really weak all of a sudden."

"Because you pushed out all of your own mana along with mine. It will be a bit before we can try again. Probably close to sundown." I passed over the bracers that had belonged to Cross. "And next time, I want you to wear these. I'm pretty sure they enhance whatever spells you use. I'm hoping they also help control how much mana passes through them. We'll have to see if they help you or not."

"Thank you, James." Jess put them on. They were loose, but not so loose that they would fall off. "I'll take good care of them, I promise. Although I will have to hide them under my sleeves when we get to any villages. Anyone who looks at them will be able to tell they came from a high-ranking Warden."

I pointed at her upper arm and biceps. "With how big Cross's forearms are, you could wear them on your upper arms and under your sleeves without too much trouble. Just be smart about it, and you should be fine. I'll need to look them over later, but you should get used to wearing them for now." I would make a rubbing of the runes later, so I could study them. If there was anything new, I could probably make something custom for myself with them. Maybe a ring would work, and then I wouldn't have to take off my hand cannon or shield bracelet. "Let's hurry. We need to catch up to the others. They're too far ahead."

We stepped it out, and by the time the next village was in sight over the next hill, we had caught up to them. The trail ran straight through the middle, with a high earthen wall surrounding the cluster of buildings that hugged the thin ribbon of packed dirt that ran through the forest. I was looking forward to buying some new clothes if they had any, getting some hot food, and maybe trading some of the raptor hides for some local currency before we got to Greendown.

As we approached the gates, Jess tugged at my sleeve.

"I just realized something. You said there were two things bothering you, but only told me about one. What's the other problem you are worried about?"

I didn't answer right away, instead looking at the pile of dinosaur skins on the horse's back. "You have velociraptors here, right?"

Jess nodded yes.

"Well, the thing that's really bothering me is what else might be out there."

"What?" Jess followed my eyes to see what I was looking at. "What else are you worried about?"

I swallowed hard. "Have you ever heard of something called a tyrannosaurus rex?"

CHAPTER 18

"A what?" Jess seemed confused at my question, and I sighed in relief.

"That answers it, thank you."

Our conversation was cut off by the gate guards standing outside the walls. There were four of them, and none looked like professional soldiers. More like farm boys wearing antiques, doing their best to come off as tough. The fact that one of them was using a pitchfork instead of a spear ruined their chances of being taken seriously.

"Halt!" The only one old enough to need to shave more than once a week took a step forward, dropping his rusty spear to block the entrance. "Who goes there?"

"We're the cliché police, and you are under arrest." Everyone turned to look at me like *I* was the crazy person. "What? You have to admit, it was a pretty cliché thing to say."

Leedy just shook his head at me before turning to look at the gate guards. "We're on Warden business, just passing through on our way to Greendown. Let us pass."

The lead guard stepped back but squinted hard at Cross. He had the same build and general appearance of the other two Wardens, but wasn't armored like them. It was enough to pique his interest. When his eyes met the slitted catlike eyes of Jess, it was too much for him to handle. "This doesn't look like any Warden business I've ever seen before. Let me see your guild signs!"

"Oh, for the love of all that is good and holy, would you shut up?" I might have been feeling a little testy. I wanted some clean clothes and a hot meal, and this kid was holding me up. "Even if we were up to no good, do you genuinely think you could stop us?"

He gulped, taking a step back to put himself in line with his friends. Until they took another step back, isolating him once again.

"See? Your friends get it. Just move out of the way and point us to the nearest general store and inn."

His face turned red, and his knuckles turned white on the haft of his weapon. I had hurt the fragile pride of a young man. Which, to be fair, was a very frail thing on the best of days. He didn't give us directions, but he did move out of the way and let us pass. Considering the layout of the small village, it didn't take long to find what we were looking for anyway.

Private Murphy went with Jess to a tanner farther back from the main path to trade some skins, while Leedy took Cross to the local inn to get them started on some meals for us. I went into the only general store, and quickly traded four raptor claws for two more sets of clothes and a sewing kit so I could make some alterations. I got a small purse of silver bits in change, and felt better about having some local spending money beyond the larger denominations I had taken from Cross.

The shopkeeper and I talked for a bit about the local rumors, and I learned that they had been seeing more signs of bandits, undead, and goblins moving through the area. It explained the guards at the entrance. He was very upset that the Wardens and Hunters' Guild hadn't been answering their requests for help, and hinted at them demanding bribes before the people would get any help. It was hard to know how much of what he was saying was hearsay and how much was truth, so I took it all with a grain of salt. Either way, the fact the shopkeeper was okay with voicing the rumors to a complete stranger meant he was comfortable with the idea of the corruption being commonplace. It wasn't a surprise, but I still hated hearing it.

After securing everything in my ruck, I went out to track down the others so we could eat and move on while there was still daylight. Which was when things went to shit.

"Look what we have here! Where did all your friends go, tough guy?" The kid from the front gate was waiting for me, this time with more than three friends. There were seven, to be exact. Definitely enough that holding back could end with me getting seriously injured if they decided to pull out weapons. Thankfully, none of them had pulled any yet. "I'm surprised to see you all by yourself. It's a shame there aren't any Wardens nearby to protect you. In case you have an accident, I mean."

"Ah, crap. Listen, kid. I'm sure you are the big cheese around here and everything, and I hurt your feelings earlier. You aren't used to people talking to you like that, and now you want to prove how tough you are. Maybe to yourself, or maybe to your buddies who were on gate guard with you. None of that is a good enough reason for you to push your luck and end up getting your face wrecked." I could immediately tell that I was just wasting my breath. Mr. Dumbass-With-a-Fragile-Ego wasn't listening, and his friends were all following his lead.

He smirked at me, and flicked his hands to motion everyone to move in.

"Well, I tried."

I fought back the urge to twist my staff and pop out the spearpoint, and instead spun the base into the shin of the tough guy coming in on my right. The increase of five stat points in my Strength apparently had as significant an effect on my physical combat as the increase in Mind had on my magic, because even when I pulled the hit, I still managed to accidentally snap the bones like they were dry twigs. My own inner sense of justice wasn't happy about such a debilitating blow against someone who wasn't a serious threat without a weapon in his hand.

"Look what he did to Yang! Get him!" The kid leading the group held back, encouraging his lackeys to rush in instead.

Super courageous, this guy was not.

The accidental escalation had a very detrimental effect. Three of the six remaining pulled knives, and what was supposed to be a dust-up turned into something deadly serious. I snatched my mace off my belt with my left hand and used the haft to block a swipe from one, while I swept my staff across horizontally to keep them back with my right.

"Stop. I don't want to hurt you, but I will defend myself." My words fell on deaf ears, and they rushed in once more. I jumped backward, setting my back against the wall of the building to keep them from surrounding me. They formed an arc, and I shifted my grip on my staff so I could hold it easier with one hand. "Fine. I'm done talking."

The next person who swiped at me with a knife had their arm broken when I slapped it away with my mace. This time, my inner voice didn't have a problem with it. The other two with knives tried attacking at the same time, so I clocked one across the face with my staff and broke his jaw and sent teeth flying in a spray of blood. The other one surprised me, and dove low enough that I missed the block with my mace. He slashed me across the upper thigh, making a shallow cut that stung my feelings more than my leg. Before he could back away, I snap-kicked him in the nuts hard enough that his future grandkids would still be feeling it.

"What's going on out here?" A bear of a man came bursting out of the building across the street onto his porch, meaty fists resting on his hips. He was huge, with heavy muscles on a frame hearty enough to handle it with no problem. A heavy gold pendant, combined with the fine clothes he wore, marked him as someone of importance. The group surrounding me all turned to look at him with guilty looks on their faces, distracting them for a brief moment. "I smell blood, and everyone knows there is no fighting inside the walls!"

Since this wasn't my first goat rodeo, I used the diversion to finish the fight. I dropped my mace and used my staff to crack each of the young men still on their feet on either their arms or legs. I didn't hold back, purposefully breaking forearms and shins without remorse. The kid who started the whole thing tried to run, so I threw my staff like a spear, hitting him in the lower back hard enough to send him sprawling onto his face in the street.

"What are you doing?!" The big guy stepped off his porch and moved to stand between me and the guy I knocked down. "You can't be doing this!"

"He started it. I'm finishing it." I went back, picked up my mace, and clipped it back on my belt. "They ambushed me as I came out of the store. They thought I was a pushover. I tried to warn them I wasn't, but they didn't listen."

"That doesn't give you the right to do all of *this*." He gestured to the six young men groaning on the ground between us. "You could have killed them!"

I shook my head and tried to get around him to the kid who was slowly getting back to his feet. There were some things he and I still needed to discuss. "They could have killed me. Especially when they pulled knives." I pointed to a blade near the man's foot. "I was within my rights to kill them, but I didn't. Besides, this isn't just about me. If they get away with this kind of behavior now, they'll do it again. And next time, that person might not be able to defend themselves. Now, get out of my way. The one who started all of this is trying to get away."

The big guy moved to block me, and the kid finally got to his feet and started to run. "I think you've done enough. It's going to be months before the rest of them recover."

I ignored him, instead taking a step to the side. I made the hand symbol for a wind blade and flicked my wrist, sending a minor spell at the retreating figure. It clipped him across the back of his leg, hamstringing him. The kid dropped to the ground with a scream, holding his injured leg. A severed Achilles was a devastating injury that would take a long time to heal, if it ever did. It would probably take several months of saving up for a healing potion to properly fix. Plenty of time for him to think about the consequences of his actions. The niggling feeling of my Judge mantle trying to surface faded, having meted out punishment to everyone involved.

"Now I've done enough. Consider this a learning lesson for them." I picked up my staff off the ground and turned to walk away. "Next time, maybe they'll think twice before they try to hurt someone. It will stop them from being murderers, and save the life of their next victim."

I didn't hear the big guy move, so I was surprised when his hand grabbed my shoulder and jerked me to a halt.

"There was no need for that. I would have spoken to his father about what he did, and made him pay for the others to be healed. Now that won't work, so you need to pay for their healing."

"Pay to heal the people who tried to hurt me?" I turned and pulled free of his grip. The leg that had been cut was still bleeding freely—although my Vigor stat was doing its best to close the wound already—and I pointed at my pants that were slowly getting stained red. "I don't think so. They attacked me, and paid for it. I think we're even."

"It doesn't work like that." The big guy shook his head, motioning to all the people on the ground. "Our village can't afford to have so many able-bodied young men down all at once. You need to provide the money to heal them, or I will have to take it from you."

"I just took down seven of your warriors, and you think you are just going to take my money? I don't think that would be a good idea." I shook my head. "This might be the craziest little village I've ever visited." That was most definitely an exaggeration, especially considering how nuts the people were in most of world eleven. And world fourteen, with the nonstop dancing and singing. Ugh. The *singing*. "I'll be going now. You have a wonderful day, big guy."

"You leave me no choice." The man took off his heavy pendant, and I took a step back.

The moment it left his neck, I could feel the weight of it on my senses. It was enchanted enough that I could sense it from several paces away.

His voice dropped into a gravelly growl. "I'll do my best not to kill you. Like you did the boys."

His whole body sprouted hair, and his clothes ripped off him as he dropped onto all fours and magically put on another two hundred pounds of flesh. He roared in anger and pain, his face extending into a snout as ropes of bloody spittle sprayed out of his muzzle. The bear-like man was a werebear.

I dropped into a crouch, twisting my staff to snap the blade in place. "Fine then, Mister Werebear. Let's dance."

CHAPTER 19

The werebear leapt for me, easily clearing the very frightened young men still on the ground. I didn't know how tough his hide was, so I avoided the obvious move of planting my spear-staff in the ground and allowing him to fall on it. If his skin was too thick, it would snap the thin blade. Repairing it would be impossible without finding a high-quality blacksmith shop, so I really wanted to avoid the hassle. Instead, I dove out of the way, rolling to my feet just off the main road between two buildings. I backed between them, knowing it would force him to come straight at me.

I squared my shoulders and got ready to play danger-tag with the lycanthrope. The fact he was willing to openly shift in full view of everyone, combined with the obviously expensive enchanted pendant, told me this guy was a sanctioned shifter. For him to earn that honor, he must have been important, and had *very* good control of himself. Until I had a better grasp of the politics in the region, I had to be careful with people like him. That meant no silver, fire, or removal of limbs. Even out here in the middle of nowhere, he could be a major player who I couldn't afford to kill. That, and my sense of justice told me it would be wrong to kill a guy who ultimately was just trying to take care of his people.

The werebear barely paused before rushing in to attack me. I stabbed forward, poking him hard in the front shoulder. He reared up on his hind legs and swiped my spearpoint to the side, his movements fast and precise enough to catch it just behind the blade. I shoved, and the shifter's claws dug furrows in the dirt as I pushed him back. The werebear's eyes widened in surprise, my Strength stat more than enough to equal the bear-man's thick muscles.

"Told you, big guy. This wasn't a good idea." I twisted and pulled my spear-staff out of his grip, slicing the thin blade across his palm.

He growled in pain and lunged forward. I dodged out of the way, but my rucksack on my back bumped into the wall of the building beside me, stopping me from getting fully out of range. His claws raked across my left shoulder and arm, causing a flash of pain like lightning in the corners of my vision. I was mad. Mostly at myself, for making such a rookie mistake and not dropping my ruck, but still plenty angry at the werebear. I thought about activating my shield bracelet, and immediately discarded the idea. It wouldn't stand up to the heavy attacks anyway.

I stuck my spear-staff into the bear's side as it moved past, angling the blade to slide between his ribs. His hide was tough, so I put some umph behind it. I had to let go of the weapon, because only my right arm was listening to my commands. The wounds to my left were deep enough to sever something important, and I was losing blood fast. As the werebear turned to set himself, I ran my index finger through my own blood and drew a circle on my forehead, sending a burst of energy into it to heal at least some of the damage.

Since I wasn't concentrating on anything besides 'make me better,' the quick and dirty spell didn't close up any wounds except my leg. But the bleeding actually stopped completely, and even some of the wounds across my chest and arm showed a noticeable change for the better. I really was going to have to test the extent of my new magical strength, and soon. For now, it was good enough to finish this fight.

As the bear-man got set to charge—my spear-staff still sticking out of his side—I surprised him by running right at him. Before he could do more than take a step back, I punched him in the face with everything I had. The sharp crack of bone was accompanied by a moan, and he dropped flat on his stomach with a broken jaw. Then I jumped straight up and gave him an atomic elbow, dropping with all my weight onto his forehead. The crack of bone told me I cracked his skull, and the werebear's eyes rolled back in his head as he was knocked unconscious.

"Well, that was exciting."

New Title Earned: Werebears Aren't Care Bears

-Defeating an Alpha Werebear without killing it has granted you a new title!

Skill Imparted: Your attacks have a 5% chance to stun any ursine opponents. Staring down an ursine opponent has a 2% chance of intimidating it into submission.

"I swear, the titles I earn are only getting weirder." The new bonuses would be nice if I ever had to fight more werebears, and fighting mundane bears always made me feel bad about killing them. Now, I had an option to avoid fighting them in the first place.

After dealing with the notification, I finished healing myself while the lycanthrope shifted back into his human form. I made sure to pull my spear-staff free before he became a man again, which meant his naked body was completely free of any wounds by the time all the extra hair fell away in a disgusting carpet around him. "It really isn't fair how quickly they can heal. There isn't even a scar."

"You are only saying that because you don't know how bad the change hurts."

I spun quickly to see Jess standing there with Murphy. She had her hands full of packages wrapped in soft furs, and Murphy warily eyed the sleeping man, holding his halberd.

"If you did, you wouldn't envy them so much."

"But I thought you couldn't shift?" I watched carefully as her eyes darted to her feet before quickly looking back up at me.

"I can't. Anyway, what happened here? We were coming back from the tanner's place when we heard the commotion."

Jess was telling the truth, but not the whole truth. I didn't push her, figuring she would tell me when she trusted me enough.

Instead, I accepted her change of subject. "He asked me about my car's extended warranty, and I finally took the chance to get even for all those annoying phone calls." They both looked at me like I was crazy, which was a fair assumption. "I'm just kidding. I got jumped by one of the guys who stood at the gate, and then this guy tried to make me pay for their healing after I won the fight with him and his friends." I motioned for them to follow me out onto the main street, where the young men I had beaten were still laid out. "I disagreed, and you can see the results of our little argument."

"Good decision, not killing the mayor." Murphy walked over and poked at the unconscious lycan. "He's the father-in-law of the Vice-Admiral of the Sailors' Guild. They control most of the shipping along the Mighty Reka. One word from him, and every bounty hunter from both sides of the river would be after you."

"Well then, why don't we get out of here before he wakes up?" I hurried between the two, moving along the backs of the buildings fronting the main road. "Are you coming?"

They shrugged and followed me to the back of the inn, where Leedy and Cross were waiting inside. I didn't bother knocking, instead barging inside as if I owned the place. We walked through an empty and cold kitchen area before emerging behind a long bar that had seen better days. The only people inside the common area were ours, and they sat empty-handed at a table near the front door. They both stood as we entered, and I frowned as I saw a distinct lack of meals present.

"Leedy, please tell me you found some hot food." He shook his head at me, and I growled in frustration. "Damn. Well, what did you get?"

He approached the bar like a soldier walking to an execution. I was confused at first, until I realized what I must look like after the fight with the werebear. Tattered and bloody didn't look good on anybody. I mean, I pulled it off better than most, but that was due to my unique charm and decades of practice.

"We have a problem. This region has been dealing with a sharp increase in threats since I last moved through here. Bandits have become so brazen that they openly scout the town from the road, daring someone to come after them." Leedy's ramrod-straight posture told me he was uncomfortable, but he pushed on. "The innkeeper left for Greendown with a contingent of their best militia members over a week ago to ask for help. They should have been back yesterday, but there has been no word."

"That explains the guards we met at the gate. The regulars are all gone, so they had to use their youngest members to fill in." Murphy looked at Leedy for a brief moment, and the two had a silent conversation that ended with him giving his corporal a grim nod of agreement. "We have to find them. They might be lost in the forest, or they could have been captured."

Both of them looked at me, and Leedy held out a hand. "I swear, on my honor, that we will join you at Greendown as soon as we can. Our oaths won't allow us to ignore these people's plight."

Cross snorted, and everyone turned to look at him. He ducked his head in shame, knowing by the looks on our faces that his cynicism wasn't very appreciated.

Instead of reacting to his outburst, I thumped my fist on the worn bar top. "It isn't just bandits. There have been sightings of undead and goblins as well, according to the shop owner I talked with. All these things happening at once can't be a coincidence."

"But what would cause something like that?" Jess had set her packages on the bar and was fiddling with her bracers. Cross was eyeing them with obvious hunger, until I flicked him in the forehead and shook a finger in his face. Nobody noticed our interaction as she started putting things in piles from her stack of items. "It isn't like the three groups would be working together."

Leedy nodded in agreement. "It's almost like when a new apex predator moves to an area. The entire region gets shuffled around, with the original predators figuring out new territories and hunting grounds." He turned to look back at the front door, pausing to think for a second.

I silently agreed with his idea. It would explain the wendigos we had fought, as well as the raptor pack clashing with the big cats before the vampires interrupted them. Predators forced to relocate and find a new place to live.

"I know the mayor. He should have some idea of what might have changed recently. At the very least, it should give us a starting point."

"Um, about that…" Leedy spun to look at me.

I shrugged. "He's taking a nap right now, and we shouldn't disturb him."

"How do you know he's taking a nap?" Leedy crossed his arms and narrowed his eyes in suspicion. "What did you do?"

"They fought, and he knocked the mayor unconscious." Murphy dodged the kick I aimed at his shin. "We should probably get out of here soon, before he wakes up."

"Great! Now we have to go out there blind." Cross finally spoke up, and he shook his fist at me in anger. "How are we supposed to help people when you keep attacking the leadership of every town and village you visit?!"

"What can I say? Today I woke up and chose violence." My joke was met by flat stares. Some people just don't have a sense of humor. "Look, they started it—I just finished it. And besides, you stopped caring about the people out here a long time ago, so stop pretending before I take the other hand. Faker." I held up a hand and curled my fingers, trying to form a small ball of fire to emphasize my point, but my lack of control was still a problem. A column of fire shot straight up from my hand, scorching a burned spot in the ceiling. I played it off like I meant to do it, considering I had an image to worry about.

"Okay, okay, just calm down!" Cross held up his hands in surrender. Well, one hand and a stump, really. "I'll shut up now."

"Well, we should probably get out of here then." Leedy decided to ignore my interaction with Cross, instead going over to where they had been sitting and collecting his gear. "We'll meet you in Greendown as soon as we can. Just be mindful of how you handle Captain Cross when you approach the gates. They'll recognize him even without his Warden armor on."

"About that." The group turned to look at me, and I leaned on the bar top, moving clear of the piles of packages Jess was still organizing. "I'm not going to let you go by yourselves to help these people. I'm not blind to their problems. You are trying to hold true to the tenets of your organization, and I respect that. We'll all go together."

Both Leedy and Murphy gave me sharp nods of appreciation. Murphy's seemed like more of a confirmation of something he already knew, while Leedy seemed a bit more thoughtful.

"Besides, I have a feeling I know exactly who is causing all of these problems."

"Before we go, everyone needs to come and get their presents." Jess patted each neatly stacked pile, practically jumping with excitement. "You're going to love them!"

CHAPTER 20

"Presents?" Leedy approached the bar cautiously, acting as though he were afraid they would bite. "What kind of presents? How did you afford them?"

"Oh, don't be like that." Jess pushed one of the smaller piles at him. "Murphy and I did a great job bargaining for half of the raptor skins at the tanner. For some reason, the man at the counter just went along with whatever I suggested!"

The smirk on Murphy's face as he looked the woman up and down told me it wasn't the raptor skins the tanner had been interested in.

She pushed the largest pile toward me, oblivious to Murphy's actions. "We saved the other half of the skins for when we get to Greendown. The skins are heavy, sure, and I'd rather just sell them here for the coin and lighten our load, but there's only so much demand for the stuff in such a small town. For now, these will definitely help. Just open them and find out."

I carefully untied the wrapped packages one at a time, revealing a set of wood and leather armor, along with a thin cloak that had an oversized hood and matching leather gloves. Everything was dyed a dark green, which would blend well with the forest and surrounding hills. By reflex, I cast my Identify spell, and I was surprised at the results.

Item: Woodsman Scouting Uniform (Cloth and Leather with Wood reinforcement)

Type: Light Armor

Grade: 6/10

Description: Leather vest and pants with wooden sections that protect the chest, back, shoulders, thighs, and shins. Waterproof cloak and gloves improve stealth in rural and forest environments. Only effective for camouflage in urban areas during night operations. Above average protection without sacrificing flexibility or mana absorption.

"Wow. Thank you, Jess. I don't know what to say." I looked at what the others had received while she blushed at the praise. Leedy and Murphy only got the cloak and gloves—they had Warden armor, after all—while Cross and I had the full set. Well, Cross didn't get any gloves. Probably a tactful choice by Jess. I was sure he couldn't pull off the Michael Jackson look. She had gotten herself one a few shades lighter in color, with smaller sections of wooden disks that overlapped one another instead of being a solid piece. I approved of her getting herself the best set, considering she had the least amount of time as a warrior.

Jess pulled her own armor on over her clothes, settling it in place while she talked. "I know we can get much better armor in Greendown, but I thought it would be good to have something now, especially considering what we have been through so far. And this way, the group can hide better in the forest."

"Wh-why did you get these for *me*?" Cross looked like he didn't know how to feel. The young woman he tried to kill had just given him an obviously expensive gift, intended to protect him from harm. "I'm a prisoner. I don't need armor."

"No, you're not a prisoner, Cross." Jess gave the disgraced captain a smile somewhere between genuine and feral. Which was definitely something interesting to see. "You're one of us now, whether you like it or not."

"There's no way I'm one of you. Once we get back to a proper city, I won't be a prisoner for very long. In fact, I think you'll be surprised at how quickly our positions are going to reverse." Cross glanced at me quickly after he spoke, trying to make sure I wasn't about to give him a thumping for opening his mouth.

Before I could, Jess dropped a truth bomb on him that hurt far more than anything I could do to him.

"Oh, poor man. You haven't figured it out yet?" Jess pointed to her own neck, tapping her jugular. "Those vampires marked *you*, not any of us. Your best chance of survival is sticking with James." Cross paled, but she wasn't done with him. "As far as the Wardens' leadership goes, do you think they'll be happy with how you handled all of this? If I were in your shoes, it wouldn't just be the vampires I was worried about."

"It's not like that…" Cross's brows furrowed in deep thought. "The Commandant won't punish me for something out of my control. No one could have known how strong the wanderer really is."

"Because your organization has proven itself to be so upstanding and lacking in any corruption whatsoever, right? Maybe they won't punish you for losing to him, but you certainly can't be a captain anymore. You can't perform magic, so you aren't qualified. The *best* thing you can hope for is a quiet retirement, where you get a small stipend to train other Wardens. There's always the chance you can take a demotion to private and serve as a foot soldier, I'm sure. Unless you are the kind of person who enjoys doing paperwork. You could certainly be a secretary for the next captain." Jess pushed the armor and clothes toward him. "Or, you could redeem yourself. Join us, and try to make things better. Help people, like you swore to do all those years ago. Wash the stains off your soul."

Cross sat down heavily on the nearest stool, holding his wrist where his hand used to be. "You want me to join the person who maimed me?" He looked up at Jess, his eyes rimmed in red as he tried to hold back tears. "Why would I ever do that?"

"Because deep down, you know what happened was justice. You might have been a good man a long time ago, Cross, but you aren't any more. Look at me, Cross."

He unsteadily met her gaze.

"You still can be. You know James is telling the truth. He's here to help people, and punish the ones who deserve it." She motioned to Murphy, and the young man somehow knew exactly what she wanted.

Which made one of us. Both Leedy and I were shocked at the entire exchange. Nothing she was saying was wrong, but trying to recruit him to our side? That was crazy, even for me.

She accepted the sheathed sword that Murphy had gone to collect from his pack. The sword with the markings of a captain of the Wardens running up and down the sheath and hilt. Jess gripped it tightly, and slowly pointed the hilt at Cross. "Will you join us, and change your fate?"

Cross looked up, and slowly reached out to take the hilt of the sword. He took a deep breath and instead of taking it from her, he pushed it away. "No. I won't join you. I know how this story ends, and I want nothing to do with it."

"Fine." Jess took the sword back and set it on the counter. "It's your choice. Even if it is a bad one. Hatred will only poison your soul."

"I think that's enough attempts at recruiting for the day, Jess. Let's get this gear on and try to find those lost villagers." While I admired her flash of wisdom and ambition, I had no hopes of Cross joining me in any positive fashion. If anything, I expected him to say he'd join long enough to get a weapon in his hand so he could stick it in my back at the first opportunity. I put my own armor on, tucking the gloves behind my belt. I wouldn't need them unless it was cold outside, and wearing them might mess with my wrist gun. The armor set was a little uncomfortable when I put my ruck back on, but I would get used to the way it rested on the back armor. Otherwise, it was a vast improvement over the whole bunch of nothing I had as armor before.

Cross was the last person ready to go. Getting armor on without two hands was quite the chore, but he was unwilling to accept help from anyone. Once we were all ready to leave, I had to admit we looked a little intimidating as a group. Cross was still unarmed—Murphy had his sword slung across his back—but the cloak hid that fact from any onlookers.

"Are we going to have any problems leaving?" Leedy had his hand on the door handle, trying to look outside through a crack in the door. "Should we go out the back?"

"We'll find out together." I motioned for him to get a move on. "Just let me do the talking if the werebear tries to stop us."

"Of course. I'm sure nothing will go wrong with you in charge of negotiating."

Leedy's sarcasm was noted, but I chose to ignore it.

Our motley group of five exited the inn, and walked down a deserted main street that shouldn't have been empty at this time of day. It was barely past noon, yet not a single person was out and about. Images of Western movies with a showdown in the streets flashed through my head again, like in Jess's village. I moved to the front of our group, my staff in one hand and a wind blade ready in the other. The feeling of impending violence was palpable, and when a stout woman with gray peppering her dark hair stepped out into the street to confront us, our group spread out across the road. Well, most of us did. Cross just stood behind Leedy with his hood pulled low.

"Ah, there it is. Time for the showdown, I take it?" I tapped my staff on the ground, and looked behind us to see a young woman with features similar to the lady in front of us leaning against the side of a building. "Or is this supposed to be some kind of ambush?"

The stout woman shook her head and stepped within range of my staff. "That depends on you." She put a hand on her hips and pointed a finger in my face. "What were you thinking, beating up on my husband like that? Don't you know the kind of trouble you've caused?"

"Your husband?" I looked her in the eye and saw her dark-brown eyes flash yellow. "Ah, the bear shifter. I take it you're one too?"

"That's right." She raised her chin toward the young woman behind us. "And that's my oldest daughter, April."

Everyone around me tensed up when they realized they were surrounded by two bear shifters. Jess even let loose with a low growl in her throat, her own shifter instincts coming to the fore.

"Well, before things get any more interesting, why don't you tell us why you're keeping us from leaving town?" I tried to motion for Jess to calm down, but she was completely ignoring me.

"I want to know why you beat up my husband, and hurt all those young men. What did our village do to you, that you think it's okay to act like this?" She crossed her arms in a huff and gave Jess some side-eye. "And if I don't like your answers, we'll just see how well you handle *two* angry bears."

I sighed, doing my best not to grind my teeth in frustration. I couldn't wait to leave this crappy little town. "Look lady, like I told your husband, *they* jumped *me*. All I did was defend myself. I hurt them bad enough to make them think twice about trying to do it again to someone else later. Your husband demanded I pay for them to get healed, and I refused. He didn't like that answer, so he went all 'bear-man-angry' on me, and I knocked him out."

"So, you're telling me that a man capable of handling an alpha werebear was threatened by a bunch of young men barely old enough to grow chin hairs?" She shook her head, and her fingernails started to grow. "I don't think so. I think you need to be taught a lesson about respect." Hair sprouted along her arms and she took a few steps back as she started to shift.

I twisted my staff, the spearpoint snapping into place. I was going to put her down hard. Two werebears at once was no joke, so taking her out quickly was my best option.

"Stop!" An almost-naked man stumbling out into the street, shouting at the top of his lungs, would make most people pause— and we were most people, so we all froze. "Michelle, calm down. There's no point in continuing this." He limped over to his wife and put a hand on her shoulder.

In my personal experience, telling an angry woman to 'calm down' had never ended well, but just this once it worked. The hair and fingernails went back to normal, and everyone let out a collective sigh of relief.

"I'm glad to see you up and moving, Mayor." I twisted my staff, the blade disappearing back inside the shaft with a snick. "Now that this is settled, we'll be leaving."

"This isn't settled yet. You aren't going anywhere." The mayor's frown would have probably had more impact if he had been wearing more clothes. Although, the threat of having to fight three werebears did carry a certain amount of gravitas. "The fight with me shows you aren't a killer, but my wife has the right of one thing. If you can beat me, you could have handled those boys without hurting them so badly."

I took a deep breath and let it out slowly, pulling the mantle of Judge about myself with an effort of will. My bearing shifted as that ephemeral weight settled onto me once more. "Let me try to explain this in a different way. In just a few days, I have witnessed the abuse of power of a small-minded counselor in a small-minded town." I gestured to Jess to prove my point, considering she had been exiled from her home for the terrible crime of standing up for what was right. "I have seen the Wardens who, instead of policing the region with fairness and equality, persecute the innocent while defending the guilty."

I looked behind me at both Murphy and Leedy, who had the good grace to look ashamed. Cross managed to hold my gaze for a moment, before he, too, looked away uncomfortably. Baby steps. I turned back to the mayor and his wife. "I come to your fine town, and what do I see here? The same rot, only entrenched in a group of impressionable young men. Barely men, but if given the appropriate reality check, they might still turn themselves around into proper examples of citizens. Then, the mayor of this town not only actively fights against my just cause, but attempts to rob these young men of a vital lesson. A lesson that, if given the opportunity to sink in, might one day save their conscience, if not their lives. Because make no mistake. I, or someone like me, will return one day, and if the lessons of justice, character, and righteous execution of responsibility don't stick… I think you can imagine just how that scenario will play out."

They all visibly winced, knowing how that story would end.

I shook my head. "When confronted, they chose violence because they thought they understood the relative balance of power. Because they thought they could get away with it without facing consequences. They were wrong. When they faced a stronger opponent than expected, they pulled blades. The way it ended was on their heads, not mine. What if they did the same thing to someone less capable? Would they be morally justified in light of your argument that the weaker party couldn't 'have handled those boys'? This is about them learning to not be in that position in the first place."

"But—I'm not trying to..." The mayor stuttered at my accusations. He raised a flat palm to his face, before running a conflicted hand through his thick hair. "Look. They're not bad kids. They're not as rotten as you seem to think. They made a mistake and they've learned their lesson. Which is why you need to pay for their healing." His frown only deepened when I shook my head. "Okay, how about you only pay for the boy who started it? I can still pressure his father to cover the healing for the others, but only if his own son is uninjured."

"In what world do you live in, that learning a lesson means being absolved of the consequences of your actions? That road leads to entitlement and the very abuse of power that I am fighting against. Their need for recovery was my *goal*, not an unfortunate side effect of my actions. It was, in fact, the very *purpose* of them. Convincing the boy's family of his responsibility isn't my job. Offering each of those young men the opportunity to choose their path going forward? That *is* my job. Their wounds are both the execution of justice and the execution of grace, Mayor, and I am finished arguing with you about it."

I turned to leave, and he grabbed me by the arm. I allowed it. The boys weren't the only ones I was giving a choice to.

He tried to squeeze, and seemed surprised when I easily pulled my arm free.

"We've already seen how this ends."

"Sir, this man is on Warden business. We're trying to leave so we can track down your missing people." Leedy stepped between us, throwing back his cloak to show off his armor marking him as a Warden. "Please, allow us to do our jobs."

"I've seen you before, haven't I?" The mayor looked Leedy up and down. "Aren't you the corporal who covers the region a little farther to the west?"

"Yes, sir. I'm on a mission that requires us to go to Greendown." Leedy looked back at the inn we had left before turning to face the mayor. "When we heard about your people who went missing, all of us agreed to search the region between here and the city to help find them. Please. Let us help you."

His sincerity seemed to get through to the stubborn man, and he finally backed down. "Fine. If this man can beat me on his own, I'd much rather have him out looking for my missing townsfolk than going for a second round." The mayor turned and growled at me. "Even if he does deserve a good thrashing."

"Oh, shut up, would you?" I dropped the Judge mantle and went back to being just James. I was done dealing with this place and its crazy inhabitants. "I'm leaving, and if you try to stop me again, I won't go easy on you this time."

The mayor snorted in disbelief, but I wasn't willing to warn him again. He would either fuck around and find out, or leave me the hell alone. Either way was a win for me.

Leedy pulled the mayor and his wife off to the side to talk, probably to try to get more information about the routes their people might have decided to take.

Jess and I left, heading for the gate on the far side of the village. As we walked out, I was surprised to see only a single guard. I guess the werebear hadn't been stretching the truth about how short-handed they were. They would just have to make do with the bare necessities.

CHAPTER 21

Leedy and the others were taking their sweet time, so Jess and I waited just out of sight of the village. I extended my senses toward the shifter girl, and I was pleasantly surprised by how much she had recovered from our earlier spell practice.

"So, are you ready to try again?" I nodded at the spell enhancement bracers she wore. "I think you have enough mana, if you want some practice."

"Do you even need to ask?" Jess stepped off the trail and took a moment to pick an innocent tree to mangle. Once she had a target picked out, she looked back at me. "What spell should I cast?"

"Well, wind blades come to mind because of their simplicity, but I think you should start with something a little more versatile." I held up a closed fist and rolled my wrist, then stuck out my thumb as the power started to take form. Usually my weakest element was earth, but I didn't even have to utter the spell name to get the ground in front of me to respond to my will. I said the name of what I was doing anyway, so Jess could hear it. *"Earthen Wall."*

I had intended to raise a foot-thick section of hard-packed dirt about the size of a normal door, something perfect for hiding behind when an area attack spell was sweeping through where I was standing during a battle. Instead, a sheet of solid crystal quartz three times the size of what I wanted erupted from the dirt, throwing dust, pebbles, and uprooted tree roots into the air past the height of the forest. The power drain was a shock, and I sagged against the wall for a moment while I caught my breath.

"Holy Trinity! What was that?" Jess poked her head around the wall after things settled down a bit, her eyes wide enough that I could see the whites all the way around her catlike irises. "You expect me to do this?"

"No, I think something smaller and less dense would be a good place for you to start." I played it cool, not letting on that I was more surprised than she was at the sudden appearance of a sheet of crystal that had to be worth more than the combined value of everything inside the village we had just left. Maybe several of those villages. "Go ahead and try the spell while I get this one to go away."

Jess gave me a look that said she saw through my façade and walked off to give it a try. My keen hearing picked out her saying something about not being the only one who needed practice, but I ignored it as the magnanimous and upstanding individual I was. I immediately inspected the magical structure holding the wall together, looking for a place to unravel the energy that thrummed in my senses. Something like a regular earthen wall would fall apart in a few days, but this looked as though it might still be holding strong when it was time for me to go to a different world a year from now. To make things worse, I couldn't find anywhere to pull on a frayed bit of spell structure to tear it apart.

"That's it. No more spells until I get a handle on what's going on." I put my hand on the wall and tried to drain the energy from it, but after I felt full enough to burst, it still had plenty of juice left. That definitely wasn't right. It shouldn't hold more power than I put into it. Looking closer, I realized the wall was pulling in mana on its own to sustain itself. That part of the spell looked unstable, so I picked it apart to see what I had done. Subconscious magic was what made a mage, a *mage*, but this process was one I didn't think I could repeat on demand. Another thing to add to the list of stuff to experiment with when I was in a more controlled environment.

I immediately broke my no-magic rule and opened up the earth under the wall until it dropped low enough to be flush with the ground. I didn't use any control words this time, which thankfully made it easier to manage the mana that left my hands. Once it was impossible to see unless you were practically standing on it, I sat down to try and recover the energy I had used. It was a good excuse to use the time to think.

It was becoming clear to me that using both hand motions and activation or control words put too much force behind the spells I was casting. I would have to do either one or the other, unless I wanted something completely overpowered to happen, or until I gained more practice and control. Thinking over my meeting with the wendigos, I wasn't ruling out the need for ridiculously powerful magic in my near future.

"Stupid spell! Work!"

I looked over to see Jess raising up knee-high mounds of dirt that fell flat after a few seconds.

"James, I don't know what's wrong, but I can't get a wall to form at *all*."

To my eyes, Jess was simultaneously holding back too much mana, and she was trying too hard. "Instead of forcing the spell to move exactly the way you want, try giving it some slack. Give the magic a chance to form naturally, without your intent disrupting the natural flows of the earth around you. And stop limiting how much mana goes into the spell. Let the power come from within, like you are a spool of thread and the spell is pulling out as much as it needs."

Before she could try again, the sound of a twig snapping caused both of us to turn and look back up the trail. At first, I suspected it was Leedy and the others, but I got to my feet when the smell of something rotting reached my nose. It was clear Jess had noticed it too, because she moved to stand next to me.

"Undead." She took in a deep breath before coughing. "Smells like zombies. More than one."

"Just to make sure I know what I'm dealing with, what kind of zombies are we dealing with out here?" I reflexively enhanced my senses, listening for anything sneaking up behind us. I was also surprised at how much I had recovered since burying the wall. My mana wasn't as full as it had been when I tried draining the wall, but it was close. Probably something to do with the ball of energy behind my belly button that sucked in mana like a sponge. "Are these the kind that shamble, or run? And if they bite me, do I turn into one too?"

"You ask the strangest questions. Of course you turn into one if you get bit, if you don't get treated in time. They aren't vampires, where they have to swap blood or something." Jess looked away from me and dropped into a crouch. "As for how fast they are? That depends on how long they've been dead. The older ones usually aren't hard to handle. New ones are the dangerous zombies. They are even stronger than they used to be when they were still alive."

"Great. So, the worst kind of zombies. Got it." I let loose a long sigh. "Why did I even ask? Of course this world would have bad ones. At least a bite isn't instantly fatal." A low moan came from behind us, forcing Jess and me to stand back-to-back. "We need to finish these off fast. Otherwise, Leedy and Murphy might stumble into them."

It was moments like this that made me *really* wish I had figured out some kind of rifle from my original world. Racking up some headshots—from a healthy distance—would be some serious stress relief. Instead, all I could do was once again snap out the spearpoint on my staff, raise my shield—more to cover any blood spray coming into contact with my mucus membranes than for protection—and prepare some wind blades in my left hand. I could use the spear to keep them at a distance, and the wind blades to slice them up.

"Uuhhhnnn."

A chorus of moans greeted my preparations. Of course, that plan only works if there's a handful of zombies to deal with. When more than a dozen rotting corpses come stumbling out of the trees all around you, keeping them at distance suddenly becomes more of a chore.

"There's too many! Run!" Jess darted away, somehow weaving through the first few undead so she could scramble up a nearby tree that was big enough to hold her weight. The zombies immediately closed ranks, making it impossible for me to repeat her trick. Jess saw the predicament she had suddenly put me in, and pulled free her dagger to try to stab the ones in range in the top of the head. "Sorry! I'll try to thin out their numbers for you!"

Not wanting to get bit, I immediately cast the prepared wind blades at the undead closest to me. The zombies were all rotting and bony, meaning they were of the older variety, so the impacts were enough to blast them off their feet. When two of the five started getting back on their feet, I mentally kicked myself for not taking the extra bit of time needed for headshots.

A bony hand grabbed my shoulder, so I spun out of reach while sweeping my spear-staff across at ankle height. Two more zombies went down, and I had enough room to run. I sprinted down the path before turning around to face them once again. Since nothing ever seems to work right on this stupid planet, they completely ignored me and surrounded the tree Jess was hiding in. She was trying to climb higher to get away from them, but the tree wasn't big enough to support it. A branch she grabbed snapped, dropping her back down to the lowest set of tree limbs.

"Help!" Jess stabbed the arms grabbing at her ankles, chopping off fingers while trying to hold on with only one hand. "Don't let them eat me!"

My mind flashed back, to a different girl, on a different world.

"James, help! Don't let them—"

I was powerless to stop the swarm of giant centipedes as they covered her legs, biting and chewing their way up her body. Her shouting stopped abruptly as the venom reached her heart, making her spasm violently before the light left her eyes. The healing magic I was trying to push into her arms could do nothing for the dead. My vision went blurry as I let go, allowing her body to fall down the cliff, landing on the broken bridge that had given out as our group traversed the gap.

"It's too late for her, James. Bianca's gone. We need to get out of here before we're next!"

I ignored the knight standing behind me, his blackened armor hiding his face in the shadows of the stinking rainforest. This quest was his idea. His plan, to hunt down the warlock hiding in the ruins of an ancient city dedicated to the dark gods, was what had brought us to this point. In that moment, I hated him for it.

I got to my feet, crushing the first centipede that poked its ugly head over the edge of the cliff with my heavy boot. The rage building inside me needed an outlet. The rage of seeing another friend die a senseless death, of being a part of an unfair mission caused by another in an endless stream of evil overlords, of yet another world I was forced to journey to without any real help or guidance, and most of all, rage at the pointless endeavor to bring 'justice' to a people that didn't even want it.

The growl building in my chest exploded into a roar of frustration and anger, and I instinctively raised my hands as pure power erupted from them, washing away all the arthropods, plant life, and everything else in its way. I scrubbed the ravine clean, leaving only the bedrock below. Before I passed out from the sudden loss of energy, I heard the knight behind me gasp.

"By the gods, he's not a Paladin! He's a Mage!"

World nine, the moment I gained my Mage class. The emotions running through me as I saw another comrade in trouble were more intense than I expected. My vision blurred as I raised my hands, and with a wordless shout, lightning erupted from my upraised hands.

The zombies were ripped apart by the violence of the attack. Their flesh burned to ash, and their bones were blasted back up the trail. Jess was accidentally caught in the electrical discharge, her body seizing up as she somehow managed to cling to the tree. Seeing her getting shocked, I calmed down enough to bring my magic under control. The lightning trickled off into sparks that jumped around my body, stinging my exposed skin.

My head started to pound, and the ball of mana behind my belly button ached in sympathy as it tried to suck in as much energy as possible to refill itself. Oddly enough, it wasn't the same kind of tiredness I had felt when accidentally raising the wall of quartz. Instead of it feeling like I was going to pass out from lack of energy, this was more like I had just done wind sprints and I only needed to catch my breath before doing it again.

Lightning had always been my weakest element, and this seemed like it was more of a jump than even my stronger abilities would account for. Could it be from the lightning Jess had seen in my mana? I kicked myself for not taking the time to examine my mana as I'd told myself I would. There just hadn't been time yet.

I shook off the stray thoughts and hurried toward Jess, who had dropped bonelessly to the ground. I slowed down as she sat up, groaning as she brushed herself off. She looked up at me, her hair sticking out all over the place. Her eyes widened in fear, and for a heartbeat I felt crushed as I thought she was afraid of me. Then I noticed her eyes were looking over my shoulder.

I was already moving as something snarled behind me, causing the hair on the back of my neck to stand up, and I dropped to one knee as I spun around, bringing my spear in line to intercept whatever was coming. The undead creature that backhanded the spearpoint out of the way was—to my eyes—what would happen if the Hulk had an illegitimate child with a giant skeleton, and then that child won a fight against an oversized blender. Basically, it was big, green, angry, and had bone spurs sticking out all over the place.

Instead of holding on to the spear-staff, I let go as the undead monster smacked it to the side to avoid the swing. I had to roll off the path into the bushes to dodge the follow-up kick it aimed at my head. The speed and strength it displayed were at least on par with the wendigos I had fought, but this one was really pointy.

The roll into the bushes caused my mace to come loose from its clip, leaving me with only my ninjatō and wrist gun. I unsheathed the magic-eating sword as I got to my feet, holding it with both hands in a low guard. I chose low guard not because it was the best position for fighting a larger opponent, but because it allowed me to point the barrels of the gun at the monster without it realizing what I was doing. Considering the undead's speed and strength, I didn't want to make any assumptions about its intelligence.

It stomped a bush flat as the creature moved toward me, thankfully ignoring Jess for the moment. I dodged a sweeping roundhouse punch aimed at my head, waiting for the perfect moment to blow its head off.

"*Me eat man-meat. Hold still.*" The creature spoke in a gravelly rasp, and I was shocked enough that I missed a great opportunity to shoot it while it was talking.

"This thing can talk?!" I knocked aside another punch, leaving a line of blackened flesh along its forearm from the edge of my blade. It looked surprised that I had managed to hurt it.

"Ghoul! Kill it with fire!" Jess shouted at the top of her lungs, before dodging out of sight when the creature turned to look at her.

Not wanting to give up the opening she provided, I aimed and let loose with all three shots in my wrist gun at the back of its head.

I nodded gravely. "Nuke it from orbit. It's the only way to be sure."

Because my hand was vertical, the silver bullets hit in a line from the base of its neck to the top of its skull. The heavy rounds did massive damage, tearing off huge chunks of rotting meat and spraying brain matter farther up the trail as half of its head disintegrated. The monstrous undead stumbled forward, leaning against a tree before turning around to look at me with its one remaining eye. Most of its throat was torn out from the exit wound as well, making its roar of anger more of a disturbing gurgle.

"Damn. I didn't think it was possible, but you just got uglier."

The ghoul didn't appreciate my comment, and charged at me once more. The damage I had inflicted only seemed to have accomplished limiting its vision on one side. Even though its brains were leaking out of its shattered skull, the undead somehow kept going. Considering silver bullets had no effect, but my sword did, it most likely meant that ghouls on this planet were animated by some kind of magic instead of a virus or disease like in the movies, where ghouls were usually a type of super zombie or dead flesh-eater.

The undead monster leapt at me, barreling through the lower tree branches of the forest as if they weren't even there. I curled my fingers and hurled a fireball to knock it out of the air, halting its trajectory and setting it on fire. From the way it reacted, the ghoul's blood seemed to have some kind of flammable properties. The creature went up like it was soaked in gasoline, and rolled on the ground to try to extinguish itself. I waited for an opening, and meticulously started hacking its legs off. It was honest work, and I was happy to do it.

It was able to mostly put itself out by the time I managed to remove all the ghoul's limbs. I took a step back to get a fresh breath of air and looked over to see Jess stomping out the few places where the forest was trying to catch fire. "Thanks for doing that. A forest fire is the last thing we need right now." I thought about what I said for a bit. "Actually, that might be exactly what this place needs."

"Ha-ha, real funny."

Jess thought I was being sarcastic. I wasn't, but I didn't push the issue.

"Why haven't you finished killing it yet? Trust me, ghouls are too stupid to answer any questions, and you made it so it can't talk any more with that booming attack."

"Because this thing smells like a high school trash can that got left out in the sun over a long weekend before getting molested by a rabid skunk." I saw the confused look on her face and waved my hand. "Don't ask. Just know that it's something that would stink almost as bad as this thing does."

"I'll take your word for it." She grimaced as the wind shifted and she got a taste of the full experience. "Ugh, that is *nasty*."

Before I could agree with her, the sound of a twig snapping nearby interrupted me. Without a word, we both dropped into a crouch and ducked behind nearby trees.

Something else was coming.

CHAPTER 22

"What in the Trinity happened here?"

Leedy's voice coming from farther up the trail let both of us relax. Jess went over to intercept them and explain what happened, while I walked back over to get a closer look at the ghoul.

This wasn't my first experience with one, but every world was different. Past run-ins were only guidelines, and I was looking at the proof of that right now. I had never run across an undead that could still keep moving and fighting after their brain had been pulped. Even ancient vampires had to heal the damage before doing anything else, and liches abandoned the body they were inhabiting and returned to their phylacteries. For a much lower-tiered undead like a ghoul to keep on swinging, there were either some very different rules this world followed, or I was missing something.

I poked at the burnt torso with my sword while holding my breath. The others eventually joined me, after piling up the more mundane zombies in a nearby clearing. While I was doing my inspection, the ghoul still rasped at me, its single eye following my every move.

Cross stood nearby, so I walked over to talk to him. "Has anyone ever figured out why destroying the brain doesn't kill these things?" I wiped off my sword before sheathing it, not wanting to dirty the scabbard. "Or do other kinds of creatures keep fighting with most of their brains missing?"

"Oh, there's plenty that can keep fighting without a brain. Golems, trolls, certain kinds of giant insects, bone fiends, you. All kinds."

I looked at him with a cocked eyebrow while I collected my spear-staff and mace. I had to give it to the man—he managed to keep a straight face before glancing back at the ghoul.

"But, to answer your question, no. There hasn't been a lot of study on how ghouls work, considering how hard it is to catch one without destroying it. Not to mention, there aren't very many of them. Ghouls are one of the rarest forms of undead out there. I've only seen them farther north, and even then, this is only my third." He gestured toward the limbless and still-struggling torso. "There are plenty of stories about them, but most are just retellings of battles during the last great undead incursion, which was long before I was born."

"Fair enough. I suppose it's worth checking to see how this thing ticks." I crouched over the chest of the monster, making sure not to let it touch my clothes. That was a smell that would never come out. I pulled out my folding knife and checked to make sure it was sharp. The blade on my spear-staff would work, but it was too unwieldy for fine work.

"What are you doing?" Murphy stood next to me, his hands gripping the haft of his weapon hard enough to turn his knuckles white. "Do you need help killing it? That tiny knife won't do much."

"I'm doing something called an autopsy. Most of the time, it's what you do when you want to know how someone died." I started the incision, cutting around the bony plates of its armor. "In this case, I'm doing it to find out how this Monty Python wannabe *didn't* die."

"You are an odd man." Murphy turned and left, joining the others in their attempt to finish cleaning up after the battle. Leedy poured oil over the corpses to burn the remains, while everyone else made sure there were no body parts or stragglers left behind.

While I was not a trained medical examiner, I had enough experience through my own admittedly crisis-driven medical practice to know what should be inside a human-like creature, and what shouldn't be there. After poking around for a bit, I finally came across something. Besides all its organs being oversized to the point of ridiculousness, there was a small black orb about the size of a marble settled behind its heart.

The moment I touched it, the limbless creature tried to thrash and bite me. I tugged the glass-like object free, and it was like unplugging an overly excited blender. It just stopped, going completely still. While holding the orb, a screen flashed in my vision.

Quest Update!

Rare Quest: Track down Silver Star – Ongoing

-You have discovered a clue to the location of the lost airship. Continue to gather information and items that will help you solve the mystery behind what caused this world's greatest invention—and future ruler—to disappear.

After getting an update like that, I immediately inspected the orb I held with my magic.

Item: Lesser Monster Core

Type: Undead/Darkness Aspect

Grade: 2/10

Description: A core of condensed mana used to empower or control rare subspecies of undead. Can be used to empower enchantments, or absorbed to boost mana capacity. Undead aspect makes this unsuitable for consumption by the living.

****Warning****

This is an Object of Power not native to this plane of reality. Handle with care.

Now *that* was unexpected. Monster cores were something I had read about in the great libraries of the elves in world eight, but in their archives, any monsters that created them had been hunted to extinction by greedy hunters looking for easy power. No other worlds had mentioned them, and I guessed they had either never had them, or the beasts had met similar fates long before I had shown up.

And the warning? That was something new. As far as I knew, the only 'Object of Power' jumping between worlds was *me*. For me to find this meant either the ghoul was a traveler like me, or something that allowed it to gain a core came from a different planet. Just what kind of things were on this lost airship?

"What's that?" Jess snapped me out of my thoughts, and I stood up from my crouch over the corpse.

"It's what allowed the ghoul to keep going after I blew most of its head off. And I bet it's also why my sword was able to hurt it so badly." I held up the core. "This is condensed magic. It's very dangerous and unsafe for anyone but me to handle."

"Doesn't look like much." Jess leaned forward to get a closer look. "What are you going to do with it?"

I put it in the same shielded pouch I kept my other enchanted items in. "I'm thinking about using it to power some runes. Maybe use it to make a trap, or bomb. Something that otherwise I would have to actively power with my own mana."

"Can I help?" She kicked over one of the severed limbs of the ghoul toward the pile, making sure not to stab herself on the pointy parts. "I would like to learn how to make something like that."

"Sure, but only as an assistant. You have to learn how to control your own mana before trying to empower runes into actual enchantments." I found a thick stick to use to roll the torso. Getting my own staff dirty wasn't something I wanted to do. "After all, you just went through an entire battle without trying to use a single spell."

Jess grimaced and gave the limb an extra hard kick. "I forgot. It's still not real to me." She waved her hands, as if casting a spell. "Magic isn't instinctual yet. Running away and ambushing anyone who chases me is what I'm used to doing."

"That's not a bad thing. Standing and fighting overwhelming odds is a good way to end up dead. Now you can ambush them with magic." I levered the torso onto the pile, causing it to shift and almost collapse. "Oops, sorry guys. This thing is heavy."

Leedy was pinching his nose closed to avoid the smell, and already had a burning brand ready to throw on the pile. "Don't worry about it. Let's get this over with and try to find those missing villagers." He put action to words and lit the oil-soaked remains.

We cleaned up as best as we could while the fire burned down. Murphy and Cross had to take the horse farther down the trail, since the smell was too much for the poor animal. It was almost too much for the humans as well, but we couldn't leave an untended fire in the middle of a forest. I was still on the fence about burning the whole thing down, even if rash decisions made in anger were seldom seen as good ones the next day.

As the flames started to die down, Murphy came back to talk to us. "I think you should see this." I went to follow him, but he held up a hand to stop me. "Not you. Corporal Leedy. You haven't been through here before, so you can't know if the trail has been moved."

"Moved?"

Murphy ignored my question, and Leedy hurried off with him while I stayed with Jess. Thankfully, she answered before I could ask.

"He doesn't mean the trail was *literally* moved from one place to another." Even though she didn't roll her eyes, I still felt it. "Sometimes, bandits or other people will clear out a new path—even mimic the markings on the trees—and cover up the old one with bushes and stuff. It's a lot of work, but it lets them set up an ambush site of their choosing."

"Ah, I see. At first, I was thinking there was some kind of earth mage running around playing pranks on people." I thought about it for a second. "This is much worse, though. If that's what happened, the bandits are very organized, and there's a whole bunch of them running around out here."

The two of us fell into silence, both contemplating what it meant. Although I had no idea what Jess might be thinking, I was trying to put it all together. Missing villagers, wandering bands of undead being led by a rare ghoul, roving well-organized bandits, wendigos, dinosaurs, and a bunch of vampires being led by an unknown pretentious person who called themselves the Destitute. How very punk. Add in the quest update for the missing Silver Star, and I was starting to get the feeling that everything connected somehow.

"Do you think it's burned down enough that we can leave?" Jess kicked at what looked like a charred femur, knocking it back into the hottest part of the dying fire. "Those villagers aren't going to save themselves."

"Why don't you try and put the fire out with magic?" I pointed at the center of the fire. "You can try to cast a water spell to put it out, but that's the easy way. The one you should try is visualizing taking the heat from the fire and dispersing it into the ground. Being able to bend reality—or brute-force it—into whatever you want is a great way to strengthen your willpower. Think of it as proving you have what it takes to handle more complex magic."

Jess gave me a sharp nod of agreement before focusing all her attention on the fire, squinting hard in concentration. It was hard not to smile. She practically vibrated with excitement. If she managed to pull it off, I would start her on mana exercises that would make it easier for her to expel more energy from her body at once. If she couldn't do it, I would have her practice elemental control. No sense in being able to cast more powerful spells if you couldn't exert the willpower to manage them.

While she was busy, I reloaded my wrist gun and refilled the makeshift powder horn. After that, I looked over the rubbings of the runes on the bracers she wore. I was a qualified Runesmith, so it was easy to see how mana would flow through the symbols. What wasn't easy to see was how the separate runes came together as a whole, creating the enhancing effect I knew had to be the ultimate result.

Being from another world and all, runesmithing should have been hard for me. Instead, I had looked at them like electrical circuits in a machine. Each rune had a different job. Some runes were conduits, some were resistors, converters, storage, and of course the runes that executed the purpose of the circuit. Most series of runes created a type of closed circuit, with the power source funneled through 'positive' conduits until it hit the rune that gave the desired result of the formation, and a 'negative' conduit that ensured the mana going through the execution rune was at the proper power limit, so the whole thing didn't explode.

A basic light enchantment had a rune that held mana, another rune that funneled mana into the actual 'light' rune, and another rune that took any unused mana and sent it back to the storage rune. Almost exactly like a battery with a positive wire leading to a lightbulb, and a negative wire leading back to the opposite side of the battery. If I wanted to make a flashbang, I would just leave off the 'negative' rune that led back to the storage rune and allow the light rune to overload and explode. More complicated enchantments were usually run like a series circuit, or a string of lightbulbs. It made it dangerous if a rune failed, because it would cause a cascade failure that usually destroyed the object the runes were carved on. That was why most people stuck to simple enchantments.

In fact, one of the crudest versions of bombs that I had briefly thought about creating was using high-quality materials and feeding the positive conduits with energy using, say, a recently acquired beast orb. Then, not adding in any negative conduits to limit the flow. Once the materials reach their maximum capacity, I would get a boom with varying degrees of awesomeness. The upside being I could put one together fast and dirty on the fly with a wide range of materials. The downside being it was very difficult to calculate just *when* the whole collection of baling wire and chewing gum would explode, and how powerful that explosion might be.

All in all, it was a pretty simple way to look at runesmithing, but it had worked across every world I had come to so far. Even though I didn't know exactly what each rune on the bracers did, I could see how the mana would flow through them. The confusing thing about what I was looking at with the rubbings from the bracers was it should be a singular closed circuit. Instead, it was a parallel circuit, where every execution rune had its own direct link to the much larger power supply rune, with a shared negative link. It made them safer individually, but if the power supply or negative rune failed, it would mean more than the bracers would be ruined. They would go off like a stick of dynamite.

"Hey Jess, I think it might be a good idea for you to give me those bracers back." I glanced up to see her drenched in sweat, her face still scrunched up in concentration. She was either too focused to have heard me, or decided to ignore me completely. "Jess!" I snapped my fingers, and she finally looked at me. "Why don't you take a break? Straining yourself too much will only slow down your training. And hand me those bracers so I can make some adjustments to make them safer to use."

Jess handed me the bracers before flopping to the ground and staring sullenly at the dying embers. "What am I doing wrong? I can't seem to do anything right." She pulled out a waterskin and took a few sips. "Maybe I'm not meant to be a mage."

"You've been practicing for one day and are already prepared to quit?" I shook my head as I packed away the bracers. "If that's how you are going to act, I guess you really aren't meant to be a mage."

"That's not what I meant!" Jess jumped to her feet. "I'm not going to quit that easily. You just wait and see. I'll get this done, even without those bracers to help." She stormed off, moving to the other side of the fire. As she left, she shouted back at me, "You know, it's okay for people to vent from time to time!"

I fought the smile that tried to turn up the corners of my mouth. Angry determination was still determination. With her distracted, I got back to experimenting with the core. I tore off a strip of torn clothing from my pack and tied a knot in the center around the black monster core. There were two equal tails coming off each side, and I stretched them out on a nearby rock.

Pricking my thumb, I used the tip of my pocket knife to write runes in my blood. It would have been better to use crystal dust mixed with some kind of oil and somebody else's blood, but I wasn't exactly drowning in useful materials at the moment. I would just have to risk the possible backlash if I messed up.

The first rune I drew was meant to connect to the orb as a power source, instead of drawing in ambient mana, or mana imbued by the user. I made sure to use the strongest rune I knew, even though it was far stronger than the material could handle. It was better that the fabric overloaded from rune failure than the orb.

Next, I used a connection rune that led to a series of runes that created a light spell meant to cast a cleansing aura. It was what almost every entrance to an elven nature temple used as a way to ensure no corruption or undead could pass, with the theatrical side effect of making people feel a sense of awe when going inside. They were the very first runes I had ever learned and were a strong baseline I could use for future experiments.

Since I was secretly a rebel without a cause who just wanted to blow stuff up, I also wanted to see what would happen when the runes used were the exact opposite of the elements contained in the core. 'Cause, ya know, science and stuff.

I repeated the sequence on the opposite side of the knot, pricking my finger again so I could have enough blood to get the job done. Having two rune sequences would either let me run the same test twice, or one time with double the power. Either option would have to wait, because Leedy ran into the clearing, his sword already drawn.

"We've found them, but it isn't good." Leedy motioned for the two of us to follow him. "Come on, before it's too late."

CHAPTER 23

The three of us quickly caught up to Murphy and Cross, who waited near a felled tree that looked as if it had been torn up by its roots. I was surprised to see Cross wearing the breastplate of his armor over the clothes Jess had given him, and he held his sword in his only remaining hand.

"What's he doing?" Even though Jess had offered Cross his sword back not long ago, she was still tense seeing him standing there with it. "Did you decide to join us after all?"

"No, I'm not joining you." Cross rested his blade on his shoulder. "But that doesn't mean I'm willing to let those bandits run free if I can help stop them."

"The more people we have fighting, the better our chances of saving more villagers." I gave him a nod of approval. "I would expect nothing less of you. And, it's why I left you with one hand instead of none, like that noble. You can still be useful." The glare he gave me definitely wasn't from someone who was appreciative, but I was man enough to let it go.

Some people just don't know how to say thank you.

"*Anyway…*" Leedy redirected the conversation over to the fallen tree. "Here is where the path was moved. The old one was blocked by this tree, and then covered up by people planting ferns and shrubs to hide it." He picked up a large fern that popped free with only a light tug. "It wasn't long ago. Probably happened right after the group from the village left for Greendown."

"How is it not obvious that the trail was moved?" I motioned to the 'new' trail, where several stumps from freshly cut trees were clearly visible from where we stood. "I mean, who falls for this?"

"It's obvious that the trail was moved, but there are all kinds of reasons why it could have been done on purpose. A washout farther down the trail, a new nest of monsters, or even a mushroom farmer tired of people getting too close to his grow spots. And with no warnings posted, a traveler wouldn't know it was done by bandits, unless someone in town told them." Leedy pulled two crossbows from the saddlebags and handed one to Murphy. "Let us lead, and the rest of you flank around to the back. We'll give them a chance to surrender once we see where they are keeping the rest of the prisoners."

"We should secure the prisoners before they get the opportunity to use them as hostages." I pointed a thumb at Jess, considering she had recently been one herself. "No sense risking them if we don't have to."

"I'm not going to kill them without giving them a chance to surrender first." Leedy didn't want to acknowledge the dig about Jess. "We're professionals. We know what we're doing."

"How do you know they even have prisoners?" Jess rubbed her eyes, obviously tired from an already very long day. "Did you see them being held somewhere?"

Murphy shook his head, frowning. "No, all we could see were a few people wearing chains while they worked on the roof of the waypoint. They expanded the building, and had a few smaller sheds nearby. There were only a few bandits watching over them. The rest of the bandits are probably waiting along the new trail to ambush someone." He tucked a few spare crossbow bolts into his belt before vaulting over the fallen tree. "If there aren't any more prisoners somewhere, it means this group has killed a *lot* of people."

With that, a feeling of tense anticipation fell over the group. I decided to let Leedy take the front and made sure to bring up the rear as we started on the older trail. It was almost dark by the time we made it to the clearing where the waypoint was, and we split up to cover as much of the ground as we could. Letting them get away to warn their friends wouldn't be ideal.

Jess and Cross waited in the tree line while I got close enough to get a better look at what we were dealing with. I saw an enormous pile of dirt behind the building, and my stomach sank. It looked suspiciously like a mass grave. I had seen too many of them to mistake it as something else. When I got back to the trees, I took off my pack and propped my staff against it before unhooking my mace from my belt. My Judge aspect didn't have any mercy to spare today. It told me these bandits would die, and I was more than happy to listen.

After giving a thumbs-up to Leedy and Murphy to show we were ready, we crouched low while they approached in the open. A shout from somewhere inside the building caused everyone to stop what they were doing and spin to face the two Wardens. The two armored men held their crossbows in the open, but they weren't specifically pointed at any of the people in the clearing.

"This is your one chance!" Leedy stepped forward, making sure his breastplate and uniform was clearly visible. "Surrender, and we'll take you to Greendown for trial."

I quietly cursed him in my head for giving away the element of surprise. He was only making things harder.

Another shout from inside the building had everyone running for cover. A bandit tried to drag one of the prisoners into the cabin, but Murphy's crossbow bolt made sure that didn't happen. The bandit fell to his knees with a shaft in his stomach, while the chained man sprinted around the side to get clear.

Cross moved into the clearing when no one ran his way, intercepting a pair of bandits who were trying to sneak up on Leedy, who was trading shots with someone inside. His sword was a blur, pushing back the two men without giving them a chance to break away.

By then, Murphy had already shot his few bolts, and was running to cross blades with someone who had to be the leader of the bandits. It was a woman, wearing a full suit of red-stained plate armor and carrying two scimitars. She looked like she knew how to use them, and had Murphy on his back foot after the first exchange.

I would have helped him, but I had my own problems. Four bandits had tried to run, with two more going for something in the sheds behind the main building. Jess moved to stop the pair, while I took on the four trying to run for help.

"I've got him! You go and get Rich—"

The bandit most definitely didn't have me. I hit him so hard I crushed the side of his head in with a single move. My mace came free with a squelch, and I twisted to avoid a long-handled axe swung by a man big enough I had to look up to meet his bloodshot eyes.

Keeping my momentum from the dodge, I let go of my mace like it was a shot-put and I was king of the power throw. It took the quickest of the three remaining in the back, thunking into his spine hard enough to shatter organs and knock him on his face. He was super dead, making it two against one. The big guy swung his axe again, so I took a half-step back and let it swing past. Before he could set himself, I rushed forward and grabbed the haft of his weapon.

I was surprised at how strong he was, but I still managed to take his axe away by twisting it in his grip. He swung a haymaker at my face, and I moved the blade in the way. It didn't end well for him.

Hissing in pain, he tried to back away to make room for his friend wielding a pair of daggers. I was still holding the axe near the head, so I threw my own haymaker and punched the big man in the face with the pointed hook of sharpened steel.

He dropped like a stone, and then it was just me and the dagger guy. The smaller man froze at the sight of his three downed members and turned to run away, giving me time to line up a throw that split his skull in two. The axe had a nice balance for something unenchanted. I reminded myself to look at their equipment closer. Between the quality of that axe and the leader's full plate, these bandits were much better equipped than they should be.

A shout from Jess made me look over to see her dancing between her two bandits. I grabbed my mace to go and help, but then I realized she would be fine. Both the men she was fighting weren't able to move because their feet had sunk into the ground. Jess had finally remembered to cast a spell, and it was a well-executed one.

She finished them off while Murphy and Cross were working together to bring down the woman in armor, and Leedy cleared out the waypoint cabin. I copied Jess and used a spell to swallow the bandit leader's rear foot with a fold of earth, giving Cross the opportunity to chop his blade into the weak metal gorget protecting her neck. She dropped her swords to try to stem the fountain of blood that erupted when he stepped back, but it was too late. She died gurgling on her own blood.

"Is that all of them?" Cross fell back on his instincts, taking charge of the aftermath. "Anyone need healing?"

Leedy was the first to answer. "In here! Hurry!"

The rest of us ran over to see what was wrong. When we stepped inside, I was immediately hit with another flashback.

Stepping inside the temple, our entire team froze. The rough stone walls were studded with large, heavy spikes of metal. The missing caravan we had been searching for was mostly refugees running from the invasion pushing northward. It had given the worshippers of the dark gods plenty of sacrifices, and they had impaled their captives onto the spikes in patterns that recreated the blood runes meant to summon their unclean masters from the Infernal Realms.

"By the Lady, what have they done?" The cleric next to me dropped to his knees before retching.

The smell of fresh blood and offal combined with the stink of his vomit, making me fight to hold down my own supper.

"We...we need to get them down, and bless the bodies before something manages to possess them." Our leader of the expedition, Mitchell, was the first person to step deeper into the room. He was the highest-ranked adventurer in the region, and had been the first choice of the Society to track down the missing people. "Even if we killed all the cultists, their black magic only needs time to attract enough fiends to push through the veil."

I helped the cleric back to his feet, and he gave me a nod of thanks. Everyone was exhausted by the series of minor battles that had brought us here, but the cleric and I were the weakest of the group. The two of us were the last to follow, letting the other, more experienced warriors go first.

It was the only reason why we survived.

Mitchell was the first to die, as the body of the woman he tried to pull free pounced on him, ripping his throat out with an ear-splitting screech that was the signal all the others had been waiting for. Bodies tumbled from the walls, the possessed corpses bending joints in all the wrong ways, moving in sharp, jerking motions that were impossible to predict. The warriors didn't stand a chance in such an enclosed building, and were torn to shreds before the cleric and I could do anything to help.

I snapped out of it when I heard one of the men nailed to the wall groan in pain. My reflexes almost made me blast him to smithereens with a fireball, but I was able to redirect the spell into the ceiling. The roof exploded, throwing wood shrapnel all over the place. Everyone turned to look at me with wide eyes, and Cross was holding his sword like he was ready to run me through.

Jess was the first person to speak up. "What in the—"

"Sorry, my bad." Once again, I reminded myself to hold back on the spells until I had a better gauge on what my new power levels were at. "I guess I'm a little jumpy."

"How about you *not* kill the people we're trying to rescue, huh?" Leedy let the matter drop and immediately moved to help the man who was showing signs of life. "Help us get these people down. Murphy, keep watch outside. We don't want the rest of them sneaking up on us while we're all inside."

Everyone jumped to work, and I started casting healing spells on the villagers in the worst condition. They hadn't been nailed to the wall like the poor souls from my second world, where I had changed my focus from Healer to Warrior. Being a straight Healer had been an abject failure, but being a simple Warrior hadn't been much better. I had failed my second world the same as my first. Bringing permanent change in only one year to a world that wasn't even asking for it was hard, but for the weak, it's impossible. That didn't mean that being a Healer was useless.

"Are they going to make it?" Jess hovered over my shoulder, watching as I focused energy into the circle of blood on the forehead of the man in front of me. "They don't look so good."

"That's because they nearly suffocated. Being crucified, even without getting nailed to the wall, is still fatal. The weight of their body dragging down on their arms and chest makes it impossible to breathe. Slow suffocation is a terrible way to die, and it takes a long time to heal properly." I slowed down the push of mana so she could get a better look. "You shouldn't try doing this until we have gone over some information on how the body works, but the trick is to use a symbol to focus the power. I use a circle, which means rejuvenation to me. Life and rebirth. It's imagery I took from a distant and ancient group of religious believers called the Buddhists. It ensures the mana goes to where it's most needed first. If I want more power to push through, I add things to the symbol."

"With you blowing the roof off buildings, it's a good thing you have that symbol to control things." Jess smirked when I looked back at her. "Well, you can't deny it."

"Yeah, I get it." I stopped the flow of mana, using the rasping breath of the prone villager to let me know to give them some time for the healing to settle before continuing. "After another round or two of healing, we should be able to move them safely."

Leedy crouched over the first villager, a deep frown on his face. He sat up and looked at me. "We may not have time for that."

"Why? What's wrong?" Jess made sure that Murphy still stood in the doorway, with Cross on lookout. "They haven't said the rest of the bandits are coming."

"No, it's what he managed to say before passing out again." Leedy checked the necks of everyone lying on the floor. He let out a sigh of relief, but still drew his sword.

"Are you going to keep us in suspense?" I got to my feet, picking up my staff off the ground. "What did he say?"

Leedy started for the door, stepping over the villagers. "Just one word. Vampires."

CHAPTER 24

"Vampires?" Jess backed toward the door, stepping away from the unconscious villagers. "I thought we were dealing with bandits?"

Leedy thought for a moment before moving for the door. "I'll go ask the people who were on the roof before this all started. I'm pretty sure they're hiding in the sheds behind the building after 'Mr. Judge' over here blew the roof off earlier." He left, leaving Jess and me by ourselves in the former waypoint building.

"What do we do now?" Jess was still keeping her distance from the injured. "Should we go outside too?"

"You can if you want. I'm going to finish healing these people." I pricked my finger with my pocket knife, causing a spot of blood to well up so I could draw a healing circle on the villager Leedy had been speaking with. My new healing speed was fast enough that the tiny wound was already closed before I even touched his forehead. "No matter what's going on, we'll need to get them back to their homes before we can finish our trip to Greendown."

She let out a long sigh before coming back to help me. "Sorry. I'm letting my fear override my better judgment." Jess started sorting through the room to try to find clothing and shoes for the villagers to wear. What they were in now was soiled enough to make burning them the only real option. "It's just…" She looked down at her feet. "It's just, ever since we fought those vampires in the clearing, I've been worried about running into them again."

"I understand. Vampires are scary. They are walking nightmares that you've witnessed firsthand." I finished my healing spell and stood up as the breathing of my patient turned back to normal. "Think of it like this. You know a stove is hot, so you don't touch it with your bare hand. But, you still use it to cook. That's because you understand the danger it represents."

She gave me a slow nod of understanding. "You're saying I need to ready myself, and have the necessary tools prepared."

"Basically. Remember, victory doesn't care about right and wrong, or good and evil. It favors the prepared." She didn't need to know I was basically ripping off a quote from my home world. After all, I might be the first person on this planet to say it. That basically gave me dibs.

"Wise words. But I'm afraid words won't help us much now." Leedy came back in and dropped a large sack that jingled as it hit the ground. "According to the survivors, this group was getting paid to provide fresh food to a vampire nest somewhere nearby."

"Odds are, we've already run into that nest. That means we don't have any extra enemies to deal with." I moved over to the last patient, pricking my finger again so I could heal them. "We just have to wait for them to come to us."

"They said there's always at least one vampire with the group out there now, and there could be more. I'm not willing to risk their lives on the possibility of there being several bloodsuckers coming here." Leedy started haphazardly scooping up the loose items inside the room into a few sacks laying around. "We need to get them back to safety behind the walls of the village as soon as possible. Help me grab anything of value."

"You're robbing the robbers?" Jess raised an eyebrow. "I didn't expect you to do something like that."

"Not for me. It's for them." Leedy motioned to the survivors. "They deserve some kind of compensation for what they've been through."

The three of us got to work, collecting up what we could. After the first of the survivors started to stir, we grouped back up with Cross and Murphy to make a plan.

"We all know this group is going to move slowly." Leedy looked over Murphy's shoulder at the small cluster of people huddled near the sheds. "Even the uninjured are malnourished and weak."

Cross nudged his way in front of Leedy. "Don't forget about the rest of the bandits. They'll eventually come back here, and I don't think any of them will be happy." He motioned to the tree line in the distance. "We could set up some traps to slow them down. It won't take care of all of them, but it should keep them from catching up to us."

"No." I pushed my way through the group and sat my pack down against the wall of the cabin. "I'm not willing to let them escape judgment. The rest of you take the survivors to the village. I'll wait here for the remainder to come to me."

Jess shook her head sharply. "I'm not leaving you here to fight them on your own. You don't even know how many there are, or how strong they are. And what if a bunch of hungry vampires show up, wanting their payment of blood?" She set her own pack next to mine. "You need at least one person to stay with you, to watch your back."

I looked at the three Wardens, who seemed equally determined to stick around. "Fine. One person can stay, but it shouldn't be Jess. Even her small amount of magic could save lives." I motioned to Cross, who gave me a sour face. "He should stay. Fighting in the open will be easier for him with only one hand, and if anything happens on the way back to the village, the three of you should be able to handle it."

Leedy and Murphy instantly agreed, which forced Jess to grudgingly accept the plan. Cross didn't say anything, which we all took as him being okay with it. As Cross moved to the tree line to set up traps, and Leedy and Murphy got the survivors ready to move, Jess pulled me aside.

"Are you sure you can trust Cross to watch your back?" She turned to put her back to the tree line, in case the disgraced captain tried to spy on them. "It's pretty obvious he isn't going to try very hard to help you."

"Do you remember what the vampire said in the clearing?" I waited while Jess thought for a moment, but she shook her head no. "It's what you talked about back at the empty inn. They marked him somehow. In case it's the same group, I don't want them to be able to track the group back to the village." I snapped my fingers, causing a jolt of lightning to dance across my knuckles. "And it isn't like I really need him to watch my back. Unless there's an ancient vampire running loose, I should be just fine."

Jess let out a long sigh. "I still don't like it."

"You don't have to like it, Jess. You just have to listen to what I say." I smiled to take the sting out of my words. "Besides, I have plenty of tricks up my sleeve you haven't seen yet. I'll be fine."

One of the newly revived villagers stumbled out of the waypoint door, and Jess rushed to help them. I decided it was as good a time as any to catch up with Cross. I had no doubt Jess and the two Wardens could figure out how to wrangle everyone by themselves.

The disgraced captain was easy to find, considering how loud he was cursing at the contraption he was trying to place on the ground. I made sure to make plenty of noise to let him know I was approaching.

"What do you want?" Cross didn't look up from his task. "Come to gloat over the man you crippled?"

"Oh, shut up." The urge to smack the man was hard to ignore, but I pushed it down. "Would you rather I had cut your head off instead? You do realize that was the alternative, right? Look, we aren't friends, and I don't owe you a damn thing, but as far as I'm concerned, you don't owe me anything either." I motioned to his stump. "You paid for your crimes, and how you choose to live going forward is a clean slate in my book." I waited while he used his foot to step on the base of the trap and levered it open with his remaining hand. "We've been over this. I could have killed you, but instead I judged that you could redeem yourself. Was I wrong?"

Cross stood up, his hand gripping his sheathed sword hard enough that his knuckles were white. "And what gave you the right? You are an outsider, who doesn't know our ways. You don't understand how things *work*." He shook with rage, tears forming at the corners of his eyes. "So you come here, on your high tower, and decide that *you* determine right and wrong?"

"First off, don't you *dare* try to convince me that what you had become is good and righteous in any way. Just because you *could* get away with acting like a huge twat-waffle doesn't mean you *should*, and you know it. The shame in your eyes tells me so." Taking a deep breath, I let out a long sigh. "And second, to answer your question, when did it become my job to decide who to punish? To determine who lives, and who dies? Do you think I want this job? Do you think I had a choice?" I shook my head, pushing down memories of the worlds I had already visited. "I could say it was the gods who saddled me with this responsibility, but that wouldn't be the full truth. Those truly responsible are people like you, and the ones who pulled your strings."

"What? I never—"

"Yes, you did. The moment you thought your actions would go unpunished, you became the kind of person who lords their power over those who can't defend themselves. You were a captain, which meant you were a leader of men, and I witnessed you give the same wrongful orders to your men that you received from your own leaders. You carried the same seed of twisted ideology that they still hold. Well, I'm here to balance the scales. I'm the judgment the universe sent. I'm the person who ensures you reap what you sow. And a rotten harvest it was, Cross."

Suddenly, the sound of a branch snapping in the distance reached our ears. "I thought for a moment that the corruption didn't run to your core. Now is your opportunity to either prove me right, or decide I was wrong. Will you take your punishment and choose to become a better man—and protect those people who are running for their lives—or become a bitter soul I should have put out of their misery?"

Cross didn't answer me, instead walking past me back into the clearing. I followed, happy to see the back of Murphy disappearing down the trail. They had managed to get the prisoners out just in time. Behind me, I could hear the sounds of several people moving through the dark forest. Cross had disappeared between the small huts near the rear of the waypoint, and I twisted my spear-staff to eject the tip of the blade free with a quiet snick.

The occasional shout told me the returning bandits and potential vampires weren't aware of our presence yet, so I ducked behind a pile of debris left over from the roof I had blown off the building. A screech of metal followed by a scream of pain silenced the bandits. One of them had found a trap.

"Oy! What idiot decided to put traps out here?" Silence was the only answer to the voice coming from within the forest. "Hey 'Tilda, you smarmy bitch! You think this is funny? Somebody better answer me, or they'll pay for it with their heads!"

"Silence." A second voice cut through the forest like a knife. "It smells like smoke. And death. Fresh death."

It was obvious the vampire had spoken, and I could feel the malevolence and wrongness it put into the region like a pressure on my chest. This one was old, and old meant powerful. Leave it up to me to find a true opponent with only a single one-handed warrior as backup. Oh well. Looks like it was time for some good old-fashioned fisticuffs. Or, explosions and stuff. That might work better.

CHAPTER 25

The twang of a few more traps going off without associated screams of pain meant Cross didn't hide them well enough after the first one was found. The tree line seemed to waver as a veritable wall of people walked into the clearing. It was a struggle not to sigh when I saw how many of them there were. I was getting tired of feeling like I was rushing from one proverbial fire to the next. This whole planet was a train wreck, and I was ready to get off this ride already.

As they moved out of the shadows, the two leaders were immediately obvious. The bandit leader looked like he could have won any amateur weightlifting competition on my home world, as long as they didn't care about personal hygiene standards. His long, stringy hair was matted together in clumps that looked like an octopus was living on his head. I could tell from where I was crouched that being around him too long would require me to burn my clothing to get the smell off me. If at all possible, I would get Cross to fight him.

The real standout was the vampire. I wasn't sure how culture bleed-through worked across the universe, but I had no doubt I was looking at a Mayan. The misshapen skull looked like every one of the shaped skeletons from that ancient culture I had seen in museums on my world, and the obsidian-edged plank of wood he carried looked just as deadly as those ancient sword-like clubs had been. His aura pushed on me like a weighted blanket, confirming my concerns about him being an elder. It wasn't the strongest I had felt, but this guy was no pushover. If I were a betting man, I would say he probably ranked as a lieutenant for the big guy running the show, the Destitute.

"Spread out. Find them. Take them alive. Otherwise, *you* will be the next blood sacrifice." The vampire held completely still after giving his orders, the creepy kind of stillness only the undead could manage. His burning gaze was a physical force that cut through the night like a cone of contained hatred. It made the hair on the back of my neck stand up as it passed over where I hid, but it moved on without pausing.

As the group of bandits spread out, I counted almost twenty enemies. As long as there weren't any surprises, it wasn't an impossible situation, but I was going to have to take the gloves off this time around. They moved slowly, taking their time to poke at the grass to make sure there weren't any more traps. More than a few of them kept glancing back nervously at the predator waiting to pounce behind them. I didn't blame them. The leader motioned for them to keep searching, hefting a heavy single-bladed axe to help prove his point.

"I can smell you…hear your heartbeat." The undead moved fast enough to be a blur in my vision, stopping with a swirl of wind several yards closer to where Cross was hiding. "You were marked by one of my kind. Are you their servant, or their prey?" It let out a gravelly chuckle. "It doesn't matter. You are *my* prey now."

There was no way the disgraced Warden could fight the vampire, so I started to gather power in the palm of my hand.

Instantly, the creature's head snapped around to where I was hiding. "Another? Excellent. And this one has *magic*. A soft little wizard, ready to be plucked. It makes me…hungry."

Clenching my hand into a fist, I punched the ground in front of me. I wasn't a wizard, damn it.

The wave of power that erupted from my punch disappeared into the terra firma, vanishing with a ripple. A tremor went through the ground before a grasping hand of stone erupted from the earth, snatching the vampire out of the sky as it tried to leap away from the surprise attack. It squeezed him hard enough the sounds of snapping bones were audible all the way to where I was hiding. I knew it wouldn't hold him forever, but it would give me enough time to deal with the others. Another wave of dizziness hit me as ambient energy rushed into my body to replace what I had used, keeping me on one knee for a moment.

Even though Cross was a terrible Warden, he was no fool. The distraction caused by my spell was the perfect opportunity for him to leap from the top of a shed, his sword cleaving through the skull of the bandit closest to him. He showed his experience by maximizing the surprise of the moment, not pausing to admire his minor victory. Ripping his sword free, Cross swirled into the nearest cluster of bandits. Their screams spoke of his effectiveness against them, and threw the rest of the group into more confusion.

I went to capitalize on the vampire's current situation, but the bandit leader came to its rescue. He leapt from the edge of the clearing, forcing me to jump back in a hasty dodge. The man was an obvious bruiser, his swollen knuckles showing scars from hundreds of fights.

I was also *absolutely* correct about how bad he smelled.

"I guess I need to show this wizard who's boss!" He smashed his knuckles together, creating a small shockwave. "Better be careful, little spellcaster. I don't want to kill you before the bloodsucker is done with you. Take your beating like a man, and—"

The paper-thin blade of my yari-like spear tip cut through his throat with a splash of blood. It was a great way to shut him up. He grabbed at his wound, but there was a distinct lack of panic in his face. I let loose a quick sigh. Definitely a strong healing ability for him to not be freaking out right now. "I knew I should have let Cross fight you."

"You're gonna have to do better than that, little man." He coughed before spitting out a glob of blood. "That little pigsticker ain't big enough to do me in." Then he rushed me, using his powerful legs to leap right at me.

I wasn't intimidated.

A boot to the chest stopped him cold with a crunch of ribs. I followed up with a short punch to his face, breaking his nose in a spray of blood and mucus. The big guy took two rapid steps backward, but I didn't give him time to regroup. A quick thrust of my spear caught him in the groin, and he doubled over in pain. "Look, now you're the little man!"

He looked down in a panic, and I stabbed him through the top of the skull. He spasmed before dropping onto his face.

That should do it.

"Not just a soft little wizard after all?"

I turned to see the Mayan vampire walk out of the shadow of the upthrust stone fist he had been trapped in, looking no worse off than when he had first walked into the clearing.

"I might need to turn this one. It's so hard finding capable people." A thick fog bank suddenly appeared around him, obscuring everything but his suddenly glowing red eyes that tinted the ground around us as though it had been soaked in blood. "But first, I want to see what else you can do."

"I *hate* elder vampires." I tried to cast a wind spell with a wave of my hand to blow away the obscuring fog, only managing to set it swirling as his magic battled mine. "Fine. I guess I'll show you a few tricks."

The red glow disappeared as I threw my spear at the glowing eyes, with a burst of wind magic to help it along. I heard a grunt of surprise, and the fog seemed to thicken in response. For him to have advanced control of the weather like this, it meant I had underestimated him. He was more than a lieutenant. This guy might be second in command. I drew both my ninjatō and mace in either hand, and dropped into a low crouch as I shuffled to my right.

A flicker of movement was all the warning I had before the obsidian-edged club flashed out of the fog, clipping me on the upper arm. Obsidian holds a sharper edge than surgical steel, which meant it cut through my armor like a hot knife through butter. It deflected off the bone, severing muscles and making it impossible to use the hand holding my ninjatō. The maxed Vigor stat of a human just couldn't hold up to the strength of an elder vampire.

I heard a low chuckle come from the opposite side, forcing me to spin and block another attack with the handle of my mace. He disappeared back into the fog with a snarl. "Hmmm…your blood smells different. Exotic. Where are you from? Of the thousands I have tasted, you stand unique." More flashes of magic came from within the fog, but they were distorted and hard to pinpoint.

Concentrating on healing my arm, I decided to keep him talking to buy me some time. "Oh, you know, here and there. I like to travel, take long walks on the beach, and my Zodiac sign is asparagus. Any other questions, you overgrown leech?"

"What? Did you sacrifice your sanity in a deal with a demon? Or perhaps you are a World Traveler? No, you are too weak for that. And too human. You would be ripped apart by the forces between. It must be a bargain." His voice came from directly behind me, forcing another spin. "No matter. Your conversion will make any agreements with the denizens of other planes void. I'll be sure to keep you on a tight leash until I know how deep your instability has grown."

Holy shit. A World Traveler? What did this guy know about that? If he was just a little weaker, I could risk trying to capture him instead of killing him. Too bad that probably wasn't an option. "Thanks, you're a real peach. I could almost overlook the biting problems you have, but using teeth like you do is a real deal-breaker for me." I had use of my arm again, but I didn't give it away, instead letting it dangle with my sword in a loose grip. "I just don't see this working between us."

A quiet growl was his only response.

"Hey, before I kill you, I gotta know. Are you this 'Destitute' character everyone keeps talking about?"

"You think I'm the Destitute?" His voice seemed to come from both in front and behind me, the swirling fog making it even harder to figure out where he was. "Oh, you are but a candle in the presence of a bonfire, unaware of the burning sun over the horizon. The Destitute is the most powerful vampire this continent has ever seen. I'll be sure to introduce you once your transformation takes hold."

"A bonfire, huh?" I started funneling energy into my mace, causing sparks to jump between the blades that made up its head. "Let's see if I can't make you eat those words."

The quiet scuffle on my sword hand side was what I had been waiting for. At their core, vampires are predators. They can't help but act upon those instincts. A wounded opponent makes for easy prey, and attacking their weak spots was the best way to bring them down. But, instead of a wounded arm that couldn't even lift a weapon, the elder vampire's rush was met by the sharp point of my magic-eating sword.

It took him high in his chest, on the opposite side of where his undead heart sat as an unbeating vestibule of his power. "You missed the important part. The heart." He swiped at me with a smile, using his deadly weapon in an attempt to hack into my shoulder.

I caught the attack using my mace, stopping his hit cold.

"No, you're right where I want you." The look of shock on his face was priceless. He had been expecting to overpower me, but I was just a little bit stronger. My mace pushed his weapon aside, knocking it wide and leaving him open for another hit. Three blades of the mace impacted his shoulder, dumping the load of mana I had been charging it with like a thunderbolt. The sword was always hungry, and immediately pulled in the uncontrolled energy. It created a tunnel of destruction that ripped straight through the vampire, vaporizing most of his upper body, including his heart.

Bug, meet bug zapper.

The blanket of fog started to fall apart, giving me a good view of the undead fire in his eyes slowly fading away.

"Look out!" Cross barreled into me, knocking me aside as my own spear tip erupted from his chest.

I looked over to see the bandit leader stumbling forward as a newly raised undead. The ghoulish zombie gripped my fallen spear in corded muscles fueled by unholy strength as it shoved the spear further into Cross's body. I was entirely focused on the vampire, meaning he had been the one to raise him at some point while the fog obscured him. The vampire collapsed to the ground as Cross stumbled to the side, dropping to his knees as the spear ripped free in a spray of blood.

I cast a fireball at the new zombie, the impact blowing it back into the middle of the clearing, where it flailed as it burned. Climbing back to my feet after the dizziness from using so much of my magic passed, I walked over to see the vampire trying to reach the fresh blood that Cross had leaked all over the ground. "I don't think so." I grabbed the dying elder vampire by the ankle and dragged him over to the still-struggling form of his newly risen underling. "Burn." Tossing him onto the flames turned out to be anticlimactic as the monster simply curled up on itself as it quickly turned into charcoal.

It turned to look at me as it died, baring its fangs in one last hiss. *"My death will bring the green flames. You will die, a prisoner in your own body."*

He was full of shit, because there were no green flames when he fell into a pile of dust.

Looking back over to where Cross was, I let out a sigh. Depending on where the spear would have hit me, he might have just saved my life. I guess I needed to return the favor before he bled out.

CHAPTER 26

Leaning over Cross, I saw it was bad. The spear had punctured a lung, and he was quickly bleeding out. He looked up at me as I applied pressure, trying to slow the bleeding.

"You…didn't expect that, did you?" Cross winced as I pulled out some debris that had managed to get in the wound. "That I would save you?"

I looked at him, wiping my thumb through the blood foaming from his lips. "Well, I wouldn't have put money on it, but I'm not exactly upset about it." I used his blood to draw a circle on his forehead, slowly letting in a trickle of mana to start healing him. Sucking chest wounds meant a collapsed lung, so I needed to take my time and do it right. "Try not to talk. I don't want you choking to death on your own blood before I can heal the damage."

"Do…do you really think I can be better?" Cross coughed, sending out a spray of blood. "Be worthy?"

"I think in the heat of the moment, you chose to make a sacrifice. You knew I could heal you, but you also knew it was a risk, and there would be pain. But, it takes more than one action in the heat of the moment to make up for a lifetime of deliberate decisions." I boosted the amount of mana a bit more when I felt the entry wound on his back finally close up. "Keep making those kinds of decisions, and you will find yourself on the right path. Now, shut up, and let me finish."

The rest of the healing process for Cross didn't take long, and then the two of us picked through the bodies of the dead bandits. The entire time, I was kicking myself for missing out on the opportunity to use the monster core experiment on an elder vampire. It had been the perfect chance to see what it was capable of, but I had completely forgotten about the stupid thing.

"I think that's it." Cross dropped a heavy sack down between the two of us, kicking it open so I could see what was inside. "There wasn't much besides a few coins and some weapons. Most of their armor wasn't worth the time it takes to get it off them. All told, it's probably worth five or six gold."

"You can keep all of it. Call it thanks for taking that hit for me." I didn't miss the grimace that crossed his face. "What? Were you expecting more or something? Okay, here goes. Good job killing all those scrubs, Mister Professional Ranger-Killer-Man with a jawline sharp enough to cut glass, and thanks for watching my back while I killed the most dangerous monster I've ever seen on this gods-forsaken planet."

"What's a scrub?"

Cross cocked an eyebrow, and I really wanted to punch him in the face for some strange reason. Either his face was more punchable after I healed him, or I was getting tired. I studied Cross closely enough that he began to shift uncomfortably. *Definitely* more punchable, I decided.

"A scrub is…you know what? It doesn't matter. Pick up your sack of goodies and let's go. I need to wash myself after dealing with that vampire. Just being close to it made me feel dirty." I tracked down my own pack and made sure all the straps were still in place.

"If your life is only worth five or six gold coins, I suppose I shouldn't be surprised that you call this good enough." Cross grabbed the bag and slung it over his shoulder. "We should hurry if we want to catch up with the others."

The sky beginning to lighten meant sunrise was coming up soon.

I pulled my straw hat out of my pack and plopped it back on my head. It was a little squished from being stored for so long, and it didn't match my current woodland-themed clothing, but I was tired enough that my eyes felt scratchy and I didn't want the sun in my eyes. Should I try and make sunglasses again? My last attempt had been on world ten, when I gained my Blacksmith profession. I was much better now, and maybe I had a chance at getting the lenses right.

Anyway, back to the adventure filled with suck. "Fine with me. I'll let you set the pace."

Cross took off, weighed down with his normal stuff and the bag of loot. I expected him to tire quickly, but the stony warrior kept it up the whole way back to the split in the path. He paused to rearrange the bag before hefting it again. "Their tracks are fresh. We should be catching up to them soon."

I looked at the ground, easily picking out the tracks of our group. The edges of their footprints were sharp, meaning Cross was right. "They should have made much better time. Something must've happened." I set the pace this time, and Cross could barely keep up. As we ran, I kept a close eye on the trail. The occasional splatter of blood made me even more worried. It was probably from a wound that opened on one of the former prisoners, but I couldn't keep dark thoughts out of my head. Even though I hadn't known Jess or the Wardens long, I was already growing attached. And I hated myself for it.

Every time, I made the same mistakes. A year was plenty of time to make friends. Enough time for someone to sneak their way deep into your heart and rip it to pieces when they were stripped from your life in an instant, one way or another.

Well, that was enough of that. I wasn't some angsty teenager. I acted like a real adult and put all my feelings in a box before shoving them deep inside and ignoring them. There now, much better.

"I think that's them." Cross was half a pace behind me, trying extra hard not to show how winded he was getting.

I looked up and saw what he was talking about, and it most definitely wasn't our group.

"No, it's another cluster of those roaming zombies. Where are all of them coming from?" I looked over to Cross, who only shrugged at me. This time, I didn't forget about the monster core and pulled it out and double-checked to make sure the runes were still correct. "Wait here, I want to test something."

I was forced to stay on the path to approach them, considering how dense the undergrowth was on either side in this area. It made sense why they kept showing up on the trail. They must walk through the forest until they hit an easier way to move around and just follow it.

At least, that's what I figured. Every world had minor differences in the levels of intelligence of their undead. World eleven flashed through my memories. Those undead had been almost as smart as they were while alive. The fact their intelligence meant they didn't form hordes was the only reason there were still living people on that entire planet.

Shaking my head clear of the fog of the past, I readied the cloth-wrapped orb. The group was walking away from me, so I was able to sneak close enough to lob it into the middle of their cluster before they noticed me.

The bit of mana I pushed into the rune circuit as the makeshift device left my hand activated the sequence less than a second after it hit the dirt. The area immediately surrounding the core erupted into a hazy fog thick enough that I couldn't see what was happening to the zombies inside. Only the few stragglers closest to me weren't engulfed, but their reaction was enough to tell me I was glad not to be inside the heavy mist. They dropped to the ground, groveling as if the most powerful undead in existence was pressuring them to their knees with its aura. Standing outside the mist, the only thing I could feel was a curtain of dense mana. I probably had to be undead to feel its full effect.

A popping sound was the only warning I had before the mist vanished in a blink, like it was never there. The runes most likely overloaded the fabric, and it failed. The undead that had been inside the mist were outright flattened, meaning the pressure exuded had been *real*. Or, at least real to the undead. I definitely didn't want to test it to find out, given the burst bodies of the affected undead.

Unfortunately for me, squished zombies weren't dead zombies. Their rotting corpses started to clamber back to their feet, so I snapped the blade on my yari spear in place and waded into their midst before they could recover.

Going through them was much easier when they were mostly still on their hands and knees. The spear-staff gave me the range to keep out of easy reach, and all of them were permanently dead in less than two minutes. None of the undead had the capabilities of the ghoul to continue to function with a mangled brain. I bent over and picked up my homemade rune device. The fabric crumbled off of the core and scattered into dust. I inspected it to see whether there were any changes.

Item: Lesser Monster Core

Type: Undead/Darkness Aspect

Grade: 1/10

Description: A core of condensed mana used to empower or control rare subspecies of undead. Can be used to empower enchantments, or absorbed to boost mana capacity. Undead aspect makes this unsuitable for consumption by the living.

****Warning****

This is an Object of Power not native to this plane of reality.
Handle with care.

The grade had dropped from a two to a one, meaning I had degraded it somehow with my experiment. It felt cold, as if I held a piece of ice. I shrugged and put it in the same pocket that held my gemstones. Maybe I could find some more with a better charge, and sell this one. Were they rechargeable? Maybe I could get an early jump on the magical battery industry before it really took off. The core swirled in glittering colors of purple so dark it looked black, and I had no doubt it would make me a lot of money at any jeweler's shop.

"I've never seen a spell like that one before." Cross walked up behind me, looking fully recovered from our run earlier. "What's it called?"

"Not sure yet." I shrugged and started to walk. "I thought about naming it 'mind your own business,' but that doesn't have the same punchiness as 'ask me about it again and I'll use it on you.' Both of those are pretty long-winded for such a simple spell, though. I'll think of something else."

Cross huffed at me before quickly falling in step. "You don't have to be such a jerk all the time. I was just asking a question."

"*You* telling *me* not to be a jerk? That's hilarious." I gave him a smile to take the sting out of my words. "I'm tired, and the day's just starting. All these ambushes and running from one fight to another is starting to wear me down. Once we get to Greendown, I want to spend a couple of days at a nice inn doing nothing."

"Did you forget that you're a criminal? You won't be resting at an inn. You're going to be in prison." Cross pointed a thumb back at the heap of dead zombies. "Even if the Wardens don't find you, the guilds most certainly will. You've cost them a fortune by now."

I snorted in disbelief. "Do you really think I'm worried about the guilds? Besides, they are the ones who've allowed this situation to fester, so any blame rests on their own heads. They should be paying me a fortune for cleaning up their mistakes, not chasing me down for doing the jobs they can't be bothered to do."

Cross just shook his head at me. "You'll see. You think you know how things work around here, but you have no idea. I give it three days from the moment you walk into Greendown before you're in jail."

"So, what you're saying is, conclude my business and get out of Greendown within two days? I think I can do that." I laughed while Cross spluttered.

"I thought for sure you were going to stay there for a while, clean up the city and judge people by cutting off random body parts." Cross waved his stump at me. "You know, your 'mission from the gods' and all that other crazy stuff you go on about."

"Don't you worry. I'll tackle the guilds at some point, but first I need to take care of the exterior threats. There's a process to this whole thing. No sense tearing down walls when you might need them for protection." I squinted against the harsh morning sun that somehow made its way through my straw hat. "Whoever the Destitute is, I see them as a much bigger threat to the common people. There isn't any sense in making a better government for the people if all the people have been eaten."

Cross frowned in thought. "I guess that makes sense, even if you are an idiot for thinking you have any chance of winning against a bunch of world-spanning organizations."

"We'll just have to see, won't we?" I sped up once more, increasing the gap between us. I wasn't interested in convincing Cross. I already had a plan coming together in the back of my head on how to handle several of the guilds at once, but I would have to get a look at their 'communing with the gods' book before I could finalize things.

About the time I felt like calling another break, we finally caught sight of the others. They were strung out in a line barely visible through the trees, hurrying as quickly as they could manage as another cluster of zombies shambled after them. I let loose a long-suffering sigh and looked over at Cross.

"Come on. Let's go save them. We wouldn't want all our hard work to count for nothing." I shook my head as a flood of memories flashed through my mind, all examples of my past failures. This wasn't those worlds, and I had learned from my mistakes. A jaw-cracking yawn snuck up on me before I could fight it off. "And then, we take a nap."

CHAPTER 27

The black marble halls of the Hunters' Guild were nearly empty, an oddity for any day, but most especially for this time of year. It should have been overflowing with members turning in kills, picking up missions, and ringing from the clash of steel echoing from the practice fields as new members were trained and tested.

As Gleason hurried to the west wing, where the Western Wardens' regional headquarters was located, he only saw the occasional member hurrying from one room or hallway to the next. The sense of tension that permeated the area seemed to push down on them, causing hunched shoulders and furrowed brows. Sharp increases in undead and beast activity had drained the Guild of every available hunter who had completed even the most basic levels of training.

Checking his reflection in a polished sheet of brass, he made sure his black hair was properly slicked back and his posture was straight, smoothing out any wrinkles in his white uniform. Whip-cord thin and hard as iron, he knew his ice-chip blue eyes were properly intimidating, no matter the hint of gray creeping up his temples. Succumbing to the pressures brought about by the current situation was a sign of weakness he refused to show.

The empty and boarded-up east wing—where the Eastern Marshals used to keep a nominal presence—had been reopened, and plans were already underway to turn them into a small hospital for those few Wardens and Hunters' Guild members who managed to make it back to civilization after suffering a wound in combat. Gleason knew it was mostly a waste of time. If someone was injured severely enough to be sent back to Greendown, there wasn't much chance of them recovering. The weak didn't deserve the resources it would take anyway. If they couldn't handle putting down some beasts or undead, they didn't belong in the Guild in the first place.

After announcing himself to the lone secretary wearing a black tabard, Gleason took a seat. Commandant Beck always made visitors wait, no matter how important they thought they were. Gleason understood why it was important that the Commandant reminded people of their place, but it didn't make the practice any less boring.

The secretary, obviously an old and weak member of the Black, was a badly burned veteran of the Fire Brigade. Gleason didn't know why such a man would be allowed to still serve after being such an obvious failure.

One day, when he took the Commandant's place, such oversight wouldn't be ignored. His flawless record and family connections already caused more than a few rumors about his impending promotion, but *The Oracle* hadn't announced it yet. As far as Gleason was concerned, it was only a matter of time until the Trinity rewarded his dedication and devotion. Patience was another weapon he had no problem using, and now that Captain Cross had gone missing, he knew that more opportunities were on the horizon.

He distracted himself from his thoughts of conquest by casting Long Eye throughout the city with the help of the heavy amulet he had created that hung around his neck. Only the strongest of wizards could manage such a spell, and most of those could only manage to look over short distances. It was something he did often, finding it to be a useful way to root out rule-breakers and curb the growing number of dissidents, as well as a subtle display of his strength. He was powerful enough that his spell could reach most of the city from the Guild Hall, which sat in the center of Greendown, as was proper. The most powerful deserved the best position, and the Hunters' Guild was only challenged in strength when both the Healers' Guild and Alchemists' Guild banded together.

Jotting down the location of a young woman who was skinning a brace of rabbits behind her small cottage—a flagrant violation of both the Tanners' Guild and the Butchers' Guild that he would pass on to an underling—was interrupted when the heavily engraved door opened with a quiet creak. The secretary motioned for him to enter with a hairless hand. "The Commandant will see you now."

Swiftly sweeping into the room, Gleason was mildly surprised the old man he had come to see wasn't alone. He was still speaking with a member of the Blue, who was red-faced and spitting mad.

"Sir, we can't just *leave*. The northern camps will be wiped out in a matter of days! All the able-bodied hunters are already working on trimming beast numbers, which only leaves my men to fill in the gaps." The Warden stabbed at the map spread out on the wide oak desk with the thick fingers of a practiced swordsman. "If you would allow a small, well-armed group to travel southwest and find the Captain, we could—"

"That's enough, Sergeant. There will be no searches for the lost Captain Cross by your Wardens, and any who wish to stay when we pull back closer to the city will have to fend for themselves."

Gleason hid the smile that wanted to creep across his face. Cross failed his secret mission, and now the house of cards was falling down.

Commandant Beck tapped another point on the map with a dull thud. "Gather a third of your men behind the walls to begin preparations for a siege, while the others maintain the slow withdrawal. These orders come straight from *The Oracle*. It's clear that either the witches or the vampires are preparing for something big, and the Hunters' Guild are the only ones allowed to fight what's coming."

"Yes, sir. Will do." The sergeant saluted before he turned to leave, ignoring Gleason as he stomped past.

Gleason only snorted in amusement. Members of the Blue were always so dramatic. They didn't understand that the *true* threat to the guilds came from people, not monsters. Having to regroup behind the walls only proved how weak the Wardens had become in recent times.

"Commander Gleason, I'm glad you could make it here on such short notice." The Commandant stood to shake his hand.

It was clear the current troubles were making him lose sleep. The white hair on his head was thinner than the last time Gleason had seen him, and the dark circles under his eyes were more pronounced than normal. Although he looked like a man barely in his sixties, Gleason knew the Commandant was close to a century in age. Magic and a youth spent in battle had given Beck the figure of an old warrior still capable of lifting a spear, but time behind a desk had softened his midsection. His grip was still firm enough that Gleason had to keep the wince off his face.

"I know you're a busy man."

"I'm never too busy to visit my uncle." Gleason's mother had died when he was young, so he didn't know her side of the family well. Of course, that certainly didn't deter him from using the connections her blood provided. "You should never hesitate to call if you need me, no matter the reason."

"No matter the reason, you say?" The old man let out a heavy sigh. "Nephew, I've received more complaints about the Investigations Division in your six months of leadership than the last ten years combined." He sat back in his chair and opened a drawer, pulling out a hefty stack of papers and slapping them on the desk. "This isn't the first time we've talked about these things. Excessive use of force, unnecessary investigations, torture, heavy-handed sentences for the accused, and even claims of planted evidence." He looked up at Gleason, his gaze carrying the weight of a wizard holding his rage in by only the barest of willpower. "Explain to me why I shouldn't relieve you of command right now."

Gleason shook his head, reaching for the pile of papers. "Uncle, let me handle these 'complaints' for you. They are most certainly from dissenters and troublemakers, looking to sow distrust among the Wardens. I'm sure a quick investigation will prove—"

"I know exactly what it will prove, Commander Gleason." The Commandant pulled back the papers and dropped them back in his drawer.

Gleason couldn't hold back the wince at the switch from 'nephew' to his rank and name. It wasn't a good sign.

"We have enough problems plaguing this region without members of my own leadership eroding the faith of the people in the Guild! I'll bet my coin pouch that you've already found some trivial misdemeanor this very day, and have passed it on to your subordinates to 'fix' the issue. Well? What is it, washing clothes in the river without a permit? Begging outside of the Temple on a workday? This needs to stop, Commander. Our resources are not unlimited, as you seem to believe. There are much more important matters to be handled than this nonsense. That is putting aside the ill will your actions aim at our organization. Instead of giving citizens the slap on the wrist these incidents warrant, you instead cut off the hand!" He took a deep breath to calm down from his shout. "No matter. I have a task that someone with your…proclivities would excel at. In fact, you were named specifically."

"Uncle, while I understand you are frustrated at the moment, simply reading *my* reports would show you that everything I have accomplished in the last few months has been *necessary* to uphold the laws set forth—"

Gleason cut off what he was saying when a snap of lightning flashed between the clenched fists of his uncle.

"Or, I'm sure whatever you have in mind would be better."

"You will address me as Commandant. While you might be the child of my sister, I'm disheartened to learn you are far more like your father than any of my blood. How someone so powerful could be so unaware of reality, I will never know." Beck stood, leaning across the desk to loom over Gleason. "Slapping you in irons and demoting you to a private under the Blues is what you deserve. It might even fix your *perspective* on things enough that you could be redeemed."

Gleason felt a wave of indignation. Hadn't he followed every law to the letter? Hadn't he ensured the people of Greendown were keeping to their roles as outlined by each Guild Charter in the city? Bending the occasional rule was fine for *him* to do, obviously, since he was entrusted to enforce them, but the common citizens all knew the consequences of not following the rules they were sworn to follow. He opened his mouth to argue, but thought better of it when he saw the Commandant reach down and pull out a slip of silvered paper from under the map on his desk. There was only one place where silver paper came from, and it meant his plans were still working exactly as he thought.

"I received a dispatch straight from *The Oracle*." Beck held it out for Gleason to take. "Not long ago, I handed Captain Cross an order just like this one. He should have returned to the city by now, but he has gone missing." Beck rubbed his eyes with his thumbs, as if trying to push away a headache. "Apparently, the Trinity thinks you will succeed where he failed. In addition to what *The Oracle* has ordered, I want you to determine the fate of Captain Cross, and, if possible, return with him once your mission is complete."

Gleason saluted the Commandant, his uncle's earlier words of reproach already gone from his mind. What did his uncle's opinion matter in the face of *The Oracle*'s decree? His hard work had finally paid off. The Trinity had deemed him worthy. "I'll gather my most trusted men and make preparations immediately, Commandant." He turned and left, not even waiting for his dismissal.

His mind burned with the orders of *The Oracle* as if they had been implanted there by the Trinity themselves. In a way, they had been. With a twist of his fingers, the slip of silvered paper burned to ash. The words still floated in front of his eyes as he stormed out of the Guild Hall.

> **To**: Commander Gleason of the White
>
> **Priority Level**: Urgent-Immediate
>
> **Mission**: Kill the Wandering Warrior and his accomplices
>
> ***Kill James Holden.***

CHAPTER 28

I woke up with a splitting headache and a queasy feeling in my gut, which was stupid. I knew from past experience there wasn't anything physically wrong with me, beyond the exhaustion that came from using too many spells in rapid succession. Especially when I couldn't properly control how much energy I was putting into them. This felt like something more. An instinct built from long years of experience. I needed to get out of town. Something out there needed my attention, and it needed it now.

Cleaning up the few undead that had been going after the other group had only taken a few minutes with all of us working together, and returning with the survivors had produced a much different greeting from the people of the village the second time around.

The innkeeper had unfortunately not made it through their ordeal, but the mayor had been more than happy to let us use the empty rooms in the ownerless building as a place to get some rest. The light coming in from the small window told me it was well past lunch, meaning I had gotten at least three hours of sleep. Just like most things in life, it wasn't as much as I wanted, but more than I probably deserved.

I sat up and quickly got dressed. The feeling in my gut told me I didn't want to spend the night in the village if I didn't have to, so it was time to get moving. While I packed everything up, I thought about how quickly Jess had taken to learning magic. She was genetically predisposed to magic flowing through her body from being a shifter, and I knew from past experiences I was a good teacher, but I wasn't *that* good. For her to be casting spells so soon spoke to a natural talent, one that I wanted to explore as we traveled.

After loading all my gear and double-checking my weapons—including making sure my shield bracelet was charged—I left my room and immediately made a bunch of noise. Slamming my door, banging pots and pans in the small kitchen, shattering an empty clay pot in the common room, the basics of a homemade alarm clock meant to wake everyone up.

"What's going on out here?" Leedy came stumbling out of his room first, his eyes bleary and hair a mess. "Are we under attack?"

"Nope." I slowly pushed another empty pot off the edge of the counter, making sure to keep my face neutral as it shattered on the floor. "Just redecorating."

Leedy winced at the loud crash and looked at me with narrowed eyes. "Sometimes, I really don't like you."

"Just sometimes? I need to try harder." I gave him a wink before I glanced back into the kitchen, looking over what was still available to cook. Murphy, Cross, and Jess finally came out of their rooms. "Nice of you to join us! One of you get started on cooking something while I go let the mayor know we'll be leaving."

"You want to go now? Why not spend the night and get a fresh start tomorrow?" Jess looked the most tired of everyone. Heavily using magic for the first time could do that to you. "It would make more sense than leaving with half the day gone."

"Because we've been held up enough as it is, and I'm not waiting anymore. There's too much to do in too short a time remaining." My mental to-do list already included fixing the Wardens, the structure of the law regarding the guilds, and figuring out their stupid 'Oracle' book. That was on top of tracking down this Destitute character, including his vampire cohorts, and all the quests that the system had given me. Plus, the gut instinct telling me to get a move on. I looked over my stat sheet and quest list again to make sure I wasn't forgetting anything.

Name: James Holden (Earth v7.1)

Title: Chief Justice/Arbiter/Justicar/Executioner/etc.

Level: 100/MAX

Rank: 1/10

Age: 27 (Physical) 47 (Actual)

Class: Warrior/Soldier/Knight/Paladin/Mage (5/5)

Profession: Healer/Alchemist/Blacksmith/Runesmith/Judge (5/5)

<u>Status</u>:
Strength – 55
Flexibility – 55
Vigor – 55
Mind – 55

<u>Mission</u>:
Mythical Quest: Deliver Justice – World Count 20/???
Legendary Quest: Return Home – Requirements not met
Epic Quest: Find out why – Requirements not met
Rare Quest: Track down Silver Star – Ongoing
Unique Upgrade Quest: Find ten places of power – 1/10

I had been on this world for less than a month, and I already felt overwhelmed by how much I had to do. A year could pass by before I knew it, and wasting time made my skin itch.

"Fine by me." Murphy walked past me into the kitchen. "I'll get something going." He looked back at Jess. "Mind helping me?"

Her cheeks blushed a light pink before she gave him a quick nod. "Let me get cleaned and packed up, and I'll be right there."

"That's it? You're just going to go along with this madness?" Cross leaned against the doorframe, awkwardly crossing his arms. "I vote we should stay, instead of spending the night stuck in the forest. With the waypoint destroyed, we'll have to sleep in the middle of nowhere, where anything could find us."

I shouldered my pack and moved to the exit. "I don't care how you vote. This isn't a democracy—it's a totalitarian dictatorship that I rule with an iron fist. Specifically, two fists to your one, so I automatically win even if there were votes. Now pack your stuff and get ready to go."

Leedy rushed over to stop the man from doing anything foolish while I walked out the door. My head hurt, and I knew I was picking an unnecessary fight, but I didn't care. I stopped by the well out front and drank my fill before starting my search for the mayor. While I knew it wasn't a regular hangover I was suffering from, it still made sense to me to keep hydrated.

The small village was a ghost town as I walked around. It wasn't exactly hopping the last time I was here—besides the fighting, of course—but literally *no one* was out and about during what should have been the busiest time of the day. The atmosphere didn't feel very welcoming, and I could feel someone watching me. If it was night, I would expect an ambush at any moment.

Eventually, I found what had to be the mayor's house. It was bigger than most other houses, and it had a big snarling bear carving on the front door that screamed 'fuck off' louder than an actual person saying it. I kinda liked it.

I knocked on the door with the butt of my staff and took two steps back, just in case the big guy was feeling feisty after our last interaction. After a long wait and two more knocks, the door finally opened, and the mayor's wife poked her head out.

"Why aren't you at the meeting with… Oh, it's you." She stepped out onto her porch, closing the door behind her. "What do you want?"

"I came to let the mayor know we were leaving." I thumped my staff on the top of my foot, feeling out of place for some reason. Her eyes were piercing enough they reminded me of my grandmother, who could almost boil water with a heavy glare. "I'm sure you can pass on the message to your husband. Have a nice life." I turned to go, but she stopped me.

"Wait. I think you should go to the church." She motioned to the only building with a multicolored slate roof near the wall. The green, black, and brown colors made it look like a bad camouflage job. "My husband…he might have something for you."

"He and I didn't exactly get along the last time we met. I think it would be better if we went our separate ways." I motioned back to the street, where we had clashed. "I don't feel like going for round two at the moment."

She growled before shaking her head. "It isn't like that." Now it was her turn to feel out of sorts. "Please. Go there. They weren't expecting you to leave so soon, and I know they wanted to ask a favor of you."

"Lady, I don't owe you people anything. I've already done more than any of you could reasonably ask. Why should I do this crappy little village another favor?" Once again, I knew I was being a bit of a jerk, but this time I didn't feel bad. I mean, they had *attacked* me. Twice. "You seem capable enough to take care of yourselves."

"It isn't like that." She moved into the yard to stop me from leaving. "Look, we're sorry. *I'm* sorry. We didn't treat you right, and my husband's temper got away from him."

I ignored her and started to step around her.

"They might even pay you!"

"Do I look like a mercenary to you?"

She looked me up and down with a raised eyebrow.

"Okay, don't answer that." I rubbed my aching eyeballs. She had apologized, and seemed genuine about it. My stupid Arbiter title—which was a finicky thing most of the time—poked at me. I had gained it when I picked up my Judge profession, and it hadn't come with a description like most of my titles. The only reason I knew it was the thing pricking my brain was a general sense of right and wrong that came from the place where it sat in my head. "Fine. I'll go *talk* to your husband, but I'm not promising anything."

"Thank you." She gave me a hint of a curtsey. "And thank you once again for saving our people." She looked toward where the inn was located. "Those who you could, anyway."

"Sure." I stepped around her and walked toward the second-rate camo building they called a church. "Good luck."

She was already most of the way back inside her house, the door slamming my only answer as I made my way up the hard-packed road edged in drying mud. "Such fine people, and a great atmosphere to boot! Why isn't this the vacation destination for everyone?" I looked up at the sky, seeing another low cloudbank was moving in. More dreary rain for a dreary place. It matched my mood, somehow making me feel better. It didn't diminish the feeling that I was needed elsewhere.

When I got to the church building, it became obvious where most of the people had gone. The shouting from inside was audible from the street, and as I walked up the cobbled path to the oversized front doors, I could hear what they were yelling about.

"—ing isn't our job! Do you know what would happen if the guilds found out?!"

"The guilds don't give a damn about us! They never have. With how many there are roaming the forest right now, it's pretty clear they aren't jumping over themselves to come help!"

"Does it matter? We're Loggers and Farmers, not Hunters! We should go to the Timber Guild, or even the Carpenters' Guild for help! They'll be able to negotiate better than we can by ourselves!"

Huh. There seemed to be a guild for everything in this place.

I pushed the doors open hard enough that they hit the walls with a bang. Well, one did, while the other smacked some guy, sending him stumbling back. I looked at him and shrugged. "My bad. You're a victim of my flair for the dramatic."

"What do you want?" The mayor, who stood behind this place's version of a pulpit mixed with an altar—I didn't want to call it a dais, because I hated the word dais—was red-faced and angry. As per the usual. "Can't you see this is a private meeting?"

Looking around the crowded building, I saw mostly unwelcoming faces. Whether that was because they didn't like me, or they always looked like that, I had no idea. It was packed deep enough that most of the aisles between narrow pews were standing room only, making it impossible for me to approach the mayor privately. Oh well, I didn't want to be here in the first place. "I just came to tell you we're leaving. I tried your house, but your wife asked me to come. Since I'm clearly not welcome here, I'll go."

Silence was my only reply, so I turned and left, heading back down the path to the inn. I half expected someone to come chasing after me, but it didn't happen. By the time I made it back to where the rest of my group was, the wind had picked up. Rain would be hitting soon, and I knew the trails would be wet, muddy, and miserable. Lightning flashed in the distance, and thunder rumbled across the skies.

Seriously, this world sucked *huge* goat-balls.

CHAPTER 29

After eating a simple meal and double-checking everyone's equipment, we left the inn as a group. I was starting to feel better after getting some food in my system, and now it seemed everyone was bound and determined to ruin any positive gains by complaining about anything and everything they could come up with.

"Rust is going to set in, just you wait and see." Leedy kept trying to hold his waterproofed cloak over his scabbarded sword, failing miserably. "It's going to take hours to clean and oil all of our equipment."

I activated my shield bracelet and adjusted the beads holding the rune structures, causing it to function like an umbrella. It was a terrible waste of its charge, and I would have to shut it off eventually, but I couldn't resist. In fact, it was an excellent opportunity to test out the mana generator that now sat inside me after completing the first step of the places of power quest. Just how long could I keep this umbrella going? I glanced over at Leedy with a smile. The longer the better, as far as I was concerned. "I don't see what the big deal is. You are wearing a nice, waterproof cloak thanks to Jess, remember? And I'm perfectly dry."

Murphy let out a snort of amusement, but when Leedy snapped his head back to glare at his subordinate, he had his normal stoic look plastered on his face. Murphy was my favorite Warden for a reason. I gave him a thumbs-up while Leedy wasn't looking.

"James, why is it so important that we leave right now? It doesn't make sense." Jess had her hood back, allowing the rain to soak her hair. "Waiting until tomorrow morning would only change our arrival at Greendown by a few hours. At most, we're only gaining about half a day!"

I didn't answer, knowing that it would be impossible to explain the instincts that were telling me it was important that we keep moving. Instead, I held my first two fingers up like the letter 'V' and twisted them sharply while imbuing a tiny fraction of energy into the motion. It caused a small tornado to form around me, quickly drying the small amount of dampness that had managed to set in before I had activated my shield. It only made Leedy's glare even darker.

"Don't bother. I've seen leaders like him a thousand times." Cross rubbed at his stump while he talked, the weather obviously causing it to ache. His horse plodded along behind him, looking equally miserable. "As long as *he* isn't inconvenienced, he doesn't care. It's just the kind of man he is."

I turned my head to look at him and cocked an eyebrow. "Oh, and you're the *master* of proper leadership? I distinctly recall you using magic to slap around your subordinates, and trying to torture and kill innocents." That shut him up quickly and dropped the group into silence. I sighed, deciding I couldn't leave it there. "Look, I know you don't understand my decision, but you should have a little faith. Something, some instinct, is telling me I need to get somewhere, fast. Half a day can be the difference between victory and defeat on the battlefield, and that's exactly what this is. A battle—no, a war—that we're going to have to fight on multiple fronts. And my intuition is telling me that we need to get to Greendown—or somewhere along the way—as fast as possible." I motioned to the four of them. "If you weren't here, I would have left before even eating a hot meal and had trail rations as I walked. It may not seem like it, but I am making concessions for you."

We rounded the corner before anyone could reply, and saw a group of villagers blocking the gate. In front of them was the mayor, who was pacing back and forth. The moment he saw us, he marched toward our group like he wanted to fight.

All of us tensed up before Jess held out her hands in a patting gesture. "Calm down, everyone. We saved some of their people, remember? I'm sure they don't want to fight."

The others relaxed at the reminder. I just changed my hand from a fireball to a sand trap formation.

"Wardens, may I speak with you?" The mayor walked up to us, completely ignoring me and focusing on Leedy. "I need to discuss some things. Privately." He gave me some pretty serious side-eye, so I shrugged and kept walking.

"Sure, Mayor, we can take a few minutes to talk." Leedy looked my way with a frown. "Would you mind waiting for Murphy and me by the gate?"

Cross stayed hunched up in his hood, unwilling to face the mayor.

"I'll walk slow until you catch up." The crowd parted in front of me as I kept walking. I saw the group of punk kids who had tried to assault me at the fringes of the group, trying to keep as many people between us as possible. I guess some people *can* learn.

Jess and I had to remove the crossbar and open the gate ourselves, but we managed to get out without further incident. I had half expected the mayor to try to stop us from leaving. I was mildly disappointed that he hadn't. Getting to fight him a second time might have been fun. It wasn't out of petty spite or misplaced angst. Or that I just wanted to punch his stupid bear face. Okay, it wasn't *only* because of those things, at least.

The changes to my stats had me truly concerned in a way that I hadn't been in a long time, and the opportunity to flex those metaphysical muscles in a method that was low stakes was a valuable opportunity. If it came with the side benefit of being emotionally cathartic…well, that was just icing on the proverbial cake.

The three of us walked for well over an hour before Leedy and Murphy finally caught up to us. Cross and Jess had been quietly arguing the entire time about the best spices to use in this world's version of pancakes, so I was actually happy when they finally rejoined the group. One more comment about 'sprinkle bark' and I might have punched something.

I stopped for a moment to let them catch their breath, and to deactivate my bracelet. It had been running fine with the mana generator in my body supporting it, but I didn't want to push things. Now that we were in the trees, the constant downpour caused heavier drips to fall from the leaves and branches, which were managing to make it through the settings on my makeshift umbrella anyway.

"So, what did they want?" Jess unconsciously moved to stand closer to Murphy. "Were they trying to convince you to stay?"

Leedy shook his head. "No, they just had a bunch of letters they wanted us to deliver. I tried telling them that the Western Wardens weren't a messenger service, but he made some good arguments about the risks involved in them doing it themselves." He shrugged and held up a small messenger bag. "I agreed to pass them on in exchange for some additional supplies."

"We should change your name to the Pony Express." I chuckled at the confused looks on everyone's faces, before examining the messenger bag. Frowning, I held out my hand. "Let me see those." Leedy pulled the bag away, and I dropped my hand. "I'm not going to do anything to them. I just want to know who they are trying to contact."

"Why do you care? They're just asking for help." Cross looked between the bag and me. "Are you trying to learn how much political pull a small village might hold? Because I can tell you right now, it isn't much."

"Just give me the bag, please. I'm not going to keep them from asking for help." What I didn't say was that I *would* keep them from stabbing me in the back, if that's what they had in mind. Leedy finally passed the bag over, and I thumbed through them quickly as we started to walk again. The wax seals all had the symbol of a bear, meaning they came directly from the mayor.

I had a certain special touch with wax seals. Controlling temperature in a small and localized area was simple compared to making bullets. I focused on the space between the wax and the paper and pulled gently with my will, careful of my new strength as I leached away the heat. The wax quickly gathered a rime of frost around its connection with the paper. After that, it was a simple matter to separate the seal fully intact from the letter. When I wanted to reseal the letter, it was an easy process to warm the wax enough to melt the bottom layer and reattach it.

Most of the missives were intended for various guilds that would care about their plight. From the symbols, it looked like they were for Carpenters', Hunters', Farmers' Guilds, and even one for the Church of the Trinity. But it was the smallest letter that caught my attention. The small image of a boat that served as this world's crude address system meant it was intended for the Sailors' Guild. The mayor was trying to use his son-in-law for assistance, and I wanted to make sure it didn't mention a certain disagreement the mayor might have had with me.

I cracked the seal and motioned Jess over. "Do you mind reading this for me? I still haven't learned your written language."

"Sure! Although, I'm pretty sure you weren't supposed to open it."

I shrugged.

She rolled her eyes and took it from me, reading it silently while I watched her facial expressions. Her eyes widened momentarily before squinting. "Uh, James? I think you should hear this part."

"Just tell me what it says. You don't have to read the whole thing out loud." I started cracking the seals on all the letters. "And based on that expression, I'm going to need you to read the rest of them."

"Well, it's mostly about how they need help, and how he's asking for them to speak with the Hunters' Guild on their behalf." She paused, and I motioned for her to get on with it. "The last paragraph is about you, and how you broke the law by assaulting people in the village, killed some bandits, and stole bounties for all those undead."

"I knew it. Petty assholes. You have to be *paid* to 'steal' bounties, you assholes!" I yelled back in the direction of the town. It was pretty par for the course for me. I bet that prick of a mayor was grinning ear to ear at the thought that I was going to deliver these condemning letters with my own hand. Mayor Yogi back there must have had hibernation-induced brain damage if he thought he could pull one over on me. He'd have to wake up pretty early… No, that was one too many puns, even for me. I sighed mournfully. So young. So naive. It always seemed to go this way. People like these made it even harder to find the motivation to make their lives better.

"No, it's not like that." Jess pointed to a line near the bottom. "He's saying it in a way that makes it seem as if you are the kind of person they might want to recruit."

My brain did a little hiccup. Reboot failed. Okay, *big* hiccup. We were totally off script here. "You mean, he's *not* trying to turn me in to the authorities? Demanding some kind of bounty or something?"

Jess shook her head. "It's more like they want you to join them for some secret group." She handed the letter back to me. "Maybe the Sailors' Guild is looking for fighters?"

"It's possible." My thoughts raced, trying to put things together. What was the connection between sailors and—I considered the context of the letter again—vigilantes? If *sailors* are the Batmans of this world, I officially quit, right now. I tilted my head back to the sky, opening my hands as if to beseech the heavens for answers. I gave up after two seconds. Divine intervention was a snowball's chance in hell, in my experience. It's not like I was spoiled for choices.

I considered the possible angles this provided. "Or, more likely, I might have just had a stroke of luck." I didn't say it out loud, but I might have just stumbled across a secret cabal of disgruntled people who weren't happy with the way things were going. Had I already found a resistance group? How organized were they? Were they merely political, or did they have a more active resistance? If the group already had members like the second-in-command of a powerful organization like the Sailors' Guild, where else had they spread? I passed over the rest of the letters. "Read the rest of these, please."

She found a similar paragraph in a letter intended for the Farmers' Guild, which made sense to me. Farmers would be some of the worst affected people when monsters and undead went on a rampage, meaning they had a lot to lose under the current regime. The recipient was someone called a 'Plow Shaper' who seemed to be highly placed as well. It spoke to a more political leaning, which suited my purposes just fine. If I could find a way to tap into them as a resource, I might already have more of a start than I thought.

"What is it? Why are you smiling like you're a fox that managed to get in the hen house?" Leedy looked over at what I was holding and came over to try and snatch the letters out of my hand. "Give those back! You weren't supposed to open all of them!"

"Calm down." I concentrated for a moment, warming the bottom of the wax and pressing my thumb down on the seal for the Farmers' Guild letter. The wax softened and soon it looked as if it had never been opened. "There now, no harm done." I repeated the process for the rest of the letters and put all of them except the Farmers' Guild and Sailors' Guild back in the messenger bag. "Here. You can make sure those get delivered to where they need to go."

"And what about those two?" Leedy watched as I pulled off my rucksack and carefully tucked them away. "Are you going to keep the villagers from getting help from those guilds?"

"Nope." I got my ruck settled properly and started to walk, the others hurrying to catch back up. I gestured over my shoulder with a thumb toward my pack. "These, I'm going to deliver myself."

CHAPTER 30

As we made more progress, it wasn't much longer until we reached the fork in the road where the bandits had created the artificial split in the trail. Jess had been at the front with Murphy, and the pair stopped and looked back.

After a few moments of them conferring with one another, Jess shrugged and raised her voice. "So, which way should we go? The fake path made by bandits, or the original one that will bring us past the waypoint?"

I shrugged in return. "I don't really care. Although, it might be better if we went the way we haven't gone before, the one the bandits made. I imagine there's going to be some predators lurking around all those dead bodies by now."

Nodding, the pair took the path. Cross, Leedy, and I walked in silence, the three of us keeping alert for anything nasty that might be about. Cross had the lead to his horse in his remaining hand, and the bedraggled creature kept nudging him for a treat. The surly man ignored it. After another fair bit of time, another pop-up filled my vision.

Title Upgraded: Lucky Instinct II

-Your instincts save you again! Keep making good decisions, because staying alive for a guy in your position is a miracle in itself!

Skill Imparted: You become 1% → 2% more likely to follow your intuition in a way that benefits you. Decisions made under duress will have a 0.5% chance to improve the probability of your victory.

The title had been one I had first earned back when I had picked up my Paladin class. I hadn't thought about it in a long time, mostly because I had written it off as just another useless title that didn't have any purpose beyond the snarky commentary pissing me off. Now, though, I was replaying the need to leave despite the rain. And more importantly, what had I avoided that was so dangerous? The urge to turn around and face whatever it might be was almost overwhelming. I wasn't exactly the shirking-from-danger type of guy. But, as annoying as the title system might be, it was never wrong. Maybe it just wasn't the right place to face whatever was—

"Is there a reason why we stopped?"

Cross snapped me out of it, and I looked around to check our surroundings.

"Well? Did the damp melt your brain?"

"Ah, thanks for asking, Cross, but I'm fine, buddy. How are you doing? Everything okay? Any two-handed tasks you need help with?" I didn't wait for him to answer, instead shooting him finger guns and walking again. "That's great. Better keep up, though. You're only missing a hand, not a foot after all."

His sputtering complaints fell on deaf ears, until Leedy came up beside me while Cross lagged at the rear. "You know, you don't have to needle him like that." He leaned in closer so he could keep his voice down. "It may not seem like it, but I really do think he's trying."

"Trying to do what, Leedy?" I motioned to the wet woods around us. "Trying to save his own skin by hanging around? It isn't like I've forgotten that he was marked by a vampire somehow, and I'm the best chance he has at surviving that eventual confrontation." Leedy tried to argue, but I held up a hand to stop him. "Look, I get it. He even stepped in front of a spear meant for me when it was just him and me fighting together. There's signs of improvement in the man." I thought for a moment about how I wanted to say what I was thinking. "Right now, he's at a crossroads. On one hand—pun intended—he could choose to be a new man. The kind of man he was supposed to be, given his role in society. On the other hand— still funny, sorry—he could become an even worse person. Bitter, angry, and with just enough power and skill to ruin countless lives."

"So why are you trying to make him angry?" Leedy turned away from me. "It's almost like you *want* him to go bad."

"First off, I'm not ribbing him *that* hard. And second, I want to push him." I pointed a thumb at myself. "I went through the same thing, once upon a time. I was given a shitty bingo card in life in the first place, and interdimensional travel wasn't even on it." I ignored his confused look when he turned back to me. I guess they didn't have bingo here. Too bad. "That option was so over-the-top unexpected it didn't even register as possible. Then, I immediately followed up that terrible life event with a series of nearly fatal mistakes because I was dumb, and didn't understand how the world—well, worlds—really works. I was stubborn. Still am. A trait I share with a certain captain. If I'm being honest, he's more like me than either he or I would be willing to admit. At least, not to each other, in any case. I turned real bitter because of it. I almost gave up. I had to make a choice, to change. But to get to that point, I had to get pushed."

"Bean-go?"

Leedy was clearly still stuck on the bingo thing.

"Listen, the important thing is, most people, especially tough guys, don't like to take a long look at what's in the mirror. Actually *see* the kind of person they are, and *think* about what kind of person they want to be. That kind of introspection doesn't come easy, or naturally. You have to be pushed down that path." I glanced back at the wet and miserable Cross. "Luckily, I have no problem being the person pushing him."

"So, you think the way to make Cross a better person is to make him want to kill you in your sleep?" Leedy took an unconscious step away from me. "Remind me not to share a tent with you."

I couldn't help but laugh a little. "Basically, yes. My goal has been, and hopefully always will be, to give people a chance, and a choice, when possible. The former leads to the latter. I admit it might not be fair that I get to determine the definition of what's possible, but that's the paradox of power for you. One of them, at least. As for Cross? The stakes here are that I'm the direct challenge to the way Cross used to see himself—to the way he was before. If he can kill me, he can go right back to the mostly evil, egotistical man he was before, hiding behind a set of loose morals that poorly mask the kind of person he was on the inside. The kind of person okay with killing an innocent shifter barmaid for doing nothing wrong. But, if he can figure out how to move past this part of his life in a positive way, he can grow into a good person. Maybe. For someone with his past, good might be asking too much. Relatively decent might be a better goal."

"That means, when he saved you, he made the choice to be a better version of himself." Leedy nodded in agreement. "I knew he had it in him."

"Don't get ahead of yourself there, skippy. That was a snap decision. It bodes well, but it wasn't deliberate. And deep down, he knew, same as the rest of you, that as long as he wasn't outright killed, I could heal him. And after taking a spear for me, how could I not heal him? I *owe* it to him after that, right?" I shook my head, adjusting my cloak. "His true test will be how he acts when we get to Greendown."

"Because that's when he can betray you?" Leedy looked down at his feet, obviously thinking about how things might go when we reached the city. "I—I don't know what he'll do. It was hard to read him *before* you came along. Now, it's almost impossible." He looked at me with a frown. "And don't call me 'skippy' ever again. I don't skip. Ever."

"Because that's when he'll have the *power* to betray me. Power and choice are as intertwined as light and shadow. One results in the other. The more power you possess, the more choices you have at your fingertips." I waved away his glare. He really didn't like nicknames. "Don't get so wrapped around the handlebars about things. What will be, will be. Every person has to choose their path for themselves. Cross is no different."

I looked back at Cross, and he was obviously doing his best to listen in on us while trying not to look like that was exactly what he was up to. Leedy seemed to realize that he was listening to us and decided to change the subject.

"What are handlebars? And bean-go?" Leedy tapped his sword hilt. "Are they some kind of weapons from where you're from?"

"Definitely. Very dangerous weapons. You don't want to face down an elderly person with a bingo card if you don't have to, especially if it's a winner. They're lethal."

He gave me a slow nod, obviously picturing some kind of super-weapon.

Sometimes, keeping a straight face was hard. "Anyway, how far until the next village? Do you think we can make it, or should we start looking for someplace to stop?"

Leedy looked around, paying close attention to the trees around us. The path wasn't as well-formed since it was bandits who had made it, and there weren't any markings on the trees like there should have been to tell us how far things were. "I can't be sure, but

I *think* we can make it if we hurry. Cross could ride double with Jess, while you, Murphy, and I all run to keep up."

I gauged the appearance of the group. Even though we had just left a town, the others looked like they could use a warm fire and a dry bed. The weather on this planet was the worst. "Okay, let's do it. I don't want to sleep in mud any more than the rest of you do."

Everyone seemed happy enough at the plan, and the three of us running had no problems keeping up with the overloaded horse. We were all mud-splattered and nearing exhaustion by the time the walls of the next village came into sight. Well, I wasn't *physically* tired, but mentally I was ready to do something else. Running can get pretty boring after a while.

The trail the bandits had roughly cut had barely been better than a deer trail at some points, and everyone had been slapped in the face by a dripping tree branch at least a few times. It had put everyone in a bad mood, including me. After all, who likes getting bitch-slapped by nature?

I looked up at the gate as we approached the village, the setting sun providing enough light for us to see. It was like a thousand other villages the worlds over, a wooden palisade built atop mounded dirt created by a shallow dry moat, but this one had a stubby tower next to the thick wooden doors. A ragged-looking young woman poked her head up over the lip of the tower and waved a yellow flag with a black dot in the center. It made us stop in our tracks, and I let out a sigh.

"Please tell me that doesn't mean what I think it means?" I looked at everyone's faces, and saw them all grimacing. "It's a plague flag, isn't it?" Some universal constants seemed to always remain the same, and for some weird reason the symbols for warning people of sicknesses were one of them. It may not tell me the exact disease, of course, but sick was sick.

"That's the symbol for the twisting sickness. We need to get out of here, right now." Cross turned the horse, trying to lead it around the village. "They should have placed markers farther out, so people know to avoid this place instead of risking getting so close."

With his words, my vision went fuzzy, and suddenly I was all the way back on my first world.

The moaning of so many people kept me from getting any sleep. I was no doctor back on my world, so I had no real idea of what I was dealing with. Vague memories of smallpox and scarlet fever images from pamphlets during an emergency room visit made me think that might be what I was trying to heal, but this could be something completely different. Each world would certainly have their own terrible forms of disease.

Given that I could do magic now, maybe it was even a magical sickness. They all had a high fever at the start, and a red rash that spread across their body by the end of the second day. After the fourth day, they couldn't drink anymore, their throat and tongue too swollen for liquids. It was only a matter of time until they died after that point.

My spells could heal people, but I didn't have enough energy to do more than a few every hour. More if they didn't have the rash yet, fewer if their throats had started to swell. Waiting for my body to recharge so I could do it all over again was a lesson in agony, one that I learned over and over again as they brought more people to the tent where the guards had set me up, next to the river so it wasn't so hot all the time.

A shout by the entrance forced me out of my cot. I had been in a state of permanent exhaustion for weeks, stick-thin and nearly as pale as my patients. The line of people waiting outside weren't happy about someone cutting the line, but no one was willing to attack the King's Royal Guard while they traveled in such well-armed groups.

"Healer!" The man wearing a steel breastplate edged in gold pushed aside a young man sitting on the floor next to his sick mother's cot. "Where are you? I need to speak with you immediately."

"What's the rush?" I tied the belt of my white robes closed, covering up the stained and worn blue jeans that I had been wearing when I had been sucked into this world. "I know the line is a problem, but like I told the last set of guards, I'm healing people as fast as I can."

The guard grabbed me by the shoulder with his gauntleted hand, squeezing hard enough that my collarbone creaked in distress. "You are coming with me. Your King has need of you."

"Get off me." I jerked free of his grip and took a quick step back. "I'm no subject of the King. I'm not from here. I'm just a wanderer, trying to help where I can. And as you can see, I'm very busy. Now please leave, I have work to do."

"One of those types, eh?" He motioned to his men, and they all unsheathed their weapons. "Don't like to do things the easy way. That's fine."

"If you hurt me, your King will get no healing." I stood strong, not backing down an inch from the imposing man. "I'm not saying I won't go and see him. He'll just have to wait like everyone else."

He smiled, his eyes dead as a shark about to strike. "Oh, I know I can't hurt you, little healer. You're too valuable." His dagger cleared its sheath faster than I could move, and he buried it in the eye of the woman on the cot next to him.

Her son shouted in disbelief and tried to tackle the guard, not paying attention to his men waiting behind him. He never saw the sword that hacked into the side of his head, and he dropped to the ground bonelessly, dead before he hit the ground.

"But, I can kill all of these people, and there's nothing you can do to stop me."

I stared at him in shock, still too new to understand that I wasn't on my world anymore. Rules and laws didn't mean anything if no one was willing to enforce them, if there were even rules and laws to begin with. He laughed at me and motioned once again to his men. They spread out as they raised their weapons, every one of them prepared to kill as many innocent people as it took to get what they wanted.

"Wait!" I held up my hand, motioning for them to stop. "I'll go. Just…just don't hurt them."

"See? Now that wasn't so hard, was it?" The guard motioned for his men to sheathe their weapons. "Let's go. The faster you do what we want, the faster you can get back here and heal this rabble."

As we left the tent, I looked back and saw the puddle of blood growing beneath the butchered mother and son. Both were victims of the tyrant I was about to see, and I swore to myself that I wouldn't heal his sorry ass, the hollow promise meaning nothing to the dead.

"Stop." I grabbed the reins of the horse before Cross could get away. The feeling in my gut that had been telling me to hurry, that I needed to be somewhere, had finally settled. This was where I needed to be. That feeling of being controlled, of something out there telling me where to go, combined with memories from my first brush with a scarlet fever outbreak—and the asshole in charge of world one—put me in a foul mood. "We aren't going anywhere until I know more."

CHAPTER 31

"Describe to me, in exacting detail, what this 'twisting disease' does to people." It had nearly come to blows, but I finally had everyone calm enough to answer questions. Honestly, it was like they had no faith in my abilities as a healer. Once I explained that I could heal more than injuries, they had stopped arguing with me. "I need to know everything I can before we go in there."

Murphy cleared his throat before stepping forward a bit to speak. "It usually starts with a fever. Their head hurts, and they get really weak. It's just like a bunch of other things, which is why it can sneak up on people before they know how bad it is." He grimaced, obviously dealing with some kind of memory from his past.

I knew exactly how he felt. I motioned for him to continue.

"They start throwing up, and then their neck gets stiff. That's the first real sign people know to look out for." He tapped at his legs. "Eventually, if they keep breathing, their legs get all twisted up and they can't walk anymore."

One of the benefits of increasing my stats was how it changed my brain—an advantage I didn't have when I was on my first world. Most of the time my past was pretty hazy, but when I concentrated, I could pull up information about some things, like when I remembered garlic was a natural antifungal. Running through the most likely suspects, it sounded like a form of polio. That meant it was viral, which was bad. Bacterial infections were easy for my healing to fix. Viruses were a little more finicky. I could heal the symptoms easily enough, but stopping it before then wasn't. 'Vaccine' wasn't a function of what I could do. I looked back up at Murphy.

"Tell me, does it hit children the hardest?" I waited for his nod to confirm what I was thinking. "Okay, do any of you know what the Healers' Guild normally does to treat it?"

Cross and Leedy shared a glance before looking down at their feet. Jess laid a hand on Murphy's back before she finally answered me. "The Healers' Guild usually hires the Hunters' Guild to enforce a quarantine anywhere it pops up. The Hunters' Guild sends Wardens to keep people from entering, even if there are citizens willing to take the risk."

Murphy squared his shoulders and brushed off Jess. "That's the real reason why I joined the Wardens. One Warden was asleep on the job and let my mother into the village. She wanted to get back to my brother and me." His fists shook as he glanced at the closed gates, his voice going dead with a forced neutrality. "She was safe, visiting her sister on the coast. She didn't care, though, and came rushing right back the moment she heard." He took a deep breath and let it out with a shudder. "I lost my brother first, then her. Both of them just…stopped breathing in their sleep. I…I never got sick. After that, I swore to myself I would join the Wardens, and make sure something like that never happened again. If the Warden keeping people out had done his job, I wouldn't have lost both of them."

"Murphy… I'm sorry you went through that. And you are absolutely right, no one should go in there if it's what I know as polio. Honestly, it's a miracle you made it through all that." I took off my pack and handed it over to him, along with my weapons. Stripping out of my armor took a little longer, and I put everything except my shield bracelet and one healing potion in a pile at his feet. I only had a loose shirt and pants on. Even my boots went in the pile. I wanted to keep my losses to a minimum. "I'm going in there to see if I can help, and when I come out, I'll burn these clothes. You four set up camp somewhere upwind. I can't remember if polio is airborne or not, but chances are it is. I do know for sure it usually comes from drinking dirty water, so I will check their well first. To be safe, only drink water we brought with us. It could be in the streams nearby."

All of them looked at one another in surprise.

"You know what causes the twisting disease?" Jess grabbed my hands. "Do you understand how big this is? How many people can be saved?"

"I'll be sure to write down what I know about diseases, where they come from, and how to treat them when things get more settled down." That had been something I had done on every world I had visited once my Mind stat had hit the low twenties, in world nine.

Not everyone had believed me about washing hands and avoiding poop, but at least I tried. It had taken several millennia on my original world for it to sink in there, too. "For now, I need to see what I can do for this village." I turned and headed to the gate, where the young woman was still standing. "Oh, and one more thing. Fill every pot we have with water and start boiling it. I'm going to need it when I come out."

They looked confused, but I had faith they would listen to me. As I got closer, the girl started visibly freaking out. She tried motioning me away, so I waved like a happy idiot right back at her. Giving up, she hopped down out of sight. A few moments later, just as I was close enough to push open the gate, a different person poked their head up over the wall.

"Ho there, stranger! What do you think you're doing?" The speaker was an older woman, looking well into her sixties with white hair and a stooped back. "Didn't you see the sign?"

"I did, but as it happens, I'm a healer. I'd like to help." I held out my hands to show I wasn't holding a weapon. "If you let me inside, I could do some good."

"We don't need any help. It's the twisting disease. Once it runs its course, we'll be fine." The old woman waved me away. "Now git, before you mess around and find out how sick the twisting disease makes you."

I crouched before leaping upward and catching the top of the wall. The spiked wood was roughly cut, and if my skin wasn't toughened, I would have had a nasty collection of splinters. Another push-off, and I stood on top of the tower, looking down at the hunched old woman next to me. Below us, the young woman stared up at me in shock. It wasn't every day that you saw someone perform a twenty-foot vertical leap, after all.

"Boy, you are a special kind of stupid, ain'tcha?" She shook her head at me before turning to head down the ladder. "Thinkin' jumpin' around like a jackalope is gonna keep ya from gettin' sick. I swear, every generation is jus' gettin' dumber. Pretty soon, they'll be nothin' but a buncha stumps-for-brains walkin' 'round these parts."

From how she was acting, this woman was obviously important in the village. I wasn't going to get anywhere without her help, so I grabbed her and spun her around. She had a wavy dagger in her other hand faster than I expected, understandably ready to stab the stump-for-brains who put his hands on her without permission, but I ignored it as I spit on her forehead and drew a circle through it with my other hand so fast my movements were a blur.

Before she could stab me in the face, I shoved enough energy through the connection to freeze her in place. The shock of my dense power made her drop the blade, and I heard the girl below shout something. Instead of worrying about whatever trouble she was brewing up, I focused on what to do with my magic. I still wasn't in full control of how much energy I had used, but it was thankfully far from the point of making her pop like a meaty water balloon.

The first thing I did was focus on her spine, encouraging it to straighten and strengthen back into something more normal than her current hunch. A good bit of power went to her joints, especially her swollen knuckles on both hands. Minor injuries accumulated from a hard life lived on a dangerous frontier added up to a lot of issues, and her body took every bit of the magic I had pushed into her. Decades of wear and tear slowly diminished, until she had nothing left for me to fix. I pulled the small excess energy that still remained back into myself, where it settled without a problem.

She collapsed into me, and I gently laid her down on the rough planks of the tower's floor. I looked over the side and saw a cluster of villagers already forming, the girl gesturing wildly as she pointed up at where I was standing. When she realized I was looking at her, she let out a yelp and ducked behind a broad-shouldered man wearing a leather apron that screamed 'blacksmith' louder than he could have with a megaphone. I had worn one just like it when I was on world ten and got my own Blacksmith profession.

"What did you do to Granny Crow?" The blacksmith held a metal bar still hot from the forge. "You better not have hurt her, fella!"

I looked back at where she was still recovering. She already looked about ten years younger, and I could tell it would only be a few minutes until she was back on her feet. "She's fine, just recovering from my spell. I'm a healer. All I want to do is help."

"You've got to be the worst healer in the Healers' Guild if you came here, then. Everybody knows you can't do anything but wait out the twisting disease." The blacksmith shaded his eyes from the setting sunlight as he looked up at me. "Now, step away slowly from Granny Crow, before there's any more 'misunderstandings' between us." His eyes flickered to the side, and I saw a man holding a crossbow trying to hide behind some stacked crates.

"Granny Crow is just recovering from the healing. Give her a minute to recover before you try shooting holes in people." I backed away from the edge, ruining any chance of catching a bolt. Granny Crow was finally coming around, so I helped her back to her feet. She was still unsteady, but rose to her full height, stretching her back and working her hands open and closed. "How are you feeling?"

"Well, I'm feelin' a mite foolish, one might say." She shook her head and finally focused on my face. "You even fixed my eyes?" Granny Crow rubbed at them before looking back at me. "I apologize, young man. I shoulda known someone strong enough to jump the wall woulda had more th'n a few tricks an' such up their sleeve."

"Granny Crow! Are you okay?" The blacksmith's shout drew us back over to the edge of the tower, where the villagers could see that she was unharmed. Hell, now she was *better* than unharmed.

"I'm fine. Don' get yer pants in a twist!" Granny Crow pulled me up next to her. "This here's the real deal! A healer who knows his business." She turned around with a spring in her step and scooped up her dagger. "Come on, fella. There's a lotta folk that ya need ta see."

While she climbed down the ladder, I hopped down to the ground with a flick of the wrist, creating a gust of wind strong enough to let me drop to the ground gently. The not-so-subtle display of power was calculated, and from the murmurs coming from the villagers, it had worked as intended. I was wasting energy, but I figured it was worth the cost.

"Granny Crow, what's going on?" The blacksmith, still serving as a human shield to the nervous girl, came stumping up to her as she hopped off the ladder. When she rose to her full height, the blacksmith took a quick step back, accidentally knocking the girl into the dirt. He glared at me for a moment before looking back at her. "Wha-what happened to you? He's not wearing a healer's uniform, or carrying their symbol. Is he some kind of rogue wizard who cast a glamour on you?"

"What happened?" Granny Crow danced a little jig, doing a medieval version of jazz hands blended with Riverdance. "I'm young again! Do ya think I care one whit if he's wearin' the right clothes or not?"

I walked over and motioned for her to calm down. "No, you aren't young again. You're just healed. Rejuvenated." I gauged my recovery rate from the excessive healing I had done on her. I could either do two or three more big healings like I did on Granny Crow, or several minor healings on people without such a large number of chronic issues. "Why don't we hurry this along? You guys can keep talking after you take me to the sick people." I chose to ignore his comments about me not displaying any affiliation with the Healers' Guild.

"Oh, right." The blacksmith turned and saw the girl still sitting in the dirt. "What are you doing down there, Lilly?" He reached down and hauled her back to her feet. "You take this young man over to the tents, and we'll be along shortly, after we've had a chance to talk about…things." His eyes flickered over to me before looking back at Lilly. "Make sure you get him *whatever* he needs."

"*Me?*" Lilly's voice came out more like a squeak than words. "You could send—"

Granny Crow waved away her concerns. "Quit bein' such a plucked duck. He ain't gonna eat ya."

Apparently, being a plucked duck was quite the insult here, because Lilly snapped her mouth shut and her cheeks went flaming red. "Fine." She motioned for me to follow her. "This way."

CHAPTER 32

The smell of a field tent overflowing with sick people was always the same, no matter what world I was on. It brought back a flood of memories, all of them awful. Instead of letting them wash over me, I focused on what was in the here and now. Over thirty rickety cots were crowded into the large canvas shelter they had erected on the field in front of their church, and the tent had been here long enough that the grassy ground was turning yellow from lack of sunlight.

"Who is the worst off?" At first glance, it was pretty obvious to me that the row of smaller cots near the entrance were the priority, but I wanted to see what Lilly had to say before I jumped straight in. I watched as two caretakers in the robes of the local clergy walked between the tight rows, chanting prayers and wiping faces with damp cloths.

"Old Man Cromegas. He's having trouble breathing." She pointed me toward the back corner of the large tent, where a gnarled old figure was curled up in a fetal position. "He probably doesn't have much time left."

I squeezed my way over to him, and drew a small circle on his forehead with my index finger. There were too many people here for me to repeat what I had done to Granny Crow, so I used a small flush of energy to feel how bad his system was doing. I was shocked to discover he was another shifter, this time some form of tortoise. I didn't even know there were tortoise shifters, and visions of Raphael and Donatello—my favorite brothers—ran through my memories. Man, I missed television. I shook my head wistfully, giving up on thoughts of hope and fun.

"You can't help him?" Lilly was halfway leaning on me, peeking over my shoulder. Apparently, seeing me do magic made her forget that I was supposed to be threatening. "He's our village's only carpenter. Saving him would mean a lot to the people here."

"He isn't a kick-ass ninja who defeats crime?" She just looked at me like I was speaking a different language. That was fair. "Disappointing, but yes. I can save him."

I invested another chunk of mana into his body after licking my finger and drawing a larger circle. Focusing the power on his spine allowed his brain to reconnect to his nervous system, and his breathing immediately got easier. I cleaned up his lungs—years of wood dust had left them in rough shape—which made his color improve almost immediately. A moderate amount of power remained, and I felt some leach into an unseen outlet in a familiar way that I knew meant I was dealing with a virus. I still hadn't worked out how to fine-tune my senses on a nanoscopic level to deal with viral diseases, but I could brute-force the healing at a greater energy cost. I did it now to confirm a virus as the cause, but couldn't afford this level of mana output as a standard procedure. It worked to confirm my diagnoses, however.

I cut off the directionless flow of healing, preventing my mana from being wasted on inefficient methods. The greater the healer's ability to mentally 'see' and focus the effects of their healing, the less mana intensive the act was. Without being able to see the virus, I shifted my attention and focused back on the specifics that I could manage. One last pass to get rid of his fever and reduce the swelling around his spine and joints, and I called it good enough.

As I sat up from leaning over Old Man Cromegas, Lilly gasped in surprise. "You really did it! You healed him!" Her shouts brought the attention of the clerics, but they thankfully kept to their work instead of coming over to talk to me. "Are you an important person in the Healers' Guild? You have to be, with magic like that."

"Nope." I looked around, seeing a teenage boy who was almost as bad off as Cromegas had been and scooted over to his cot. "I'm not in any guild, actually. I'm just passing through on my way to Greendown."

Her mouth dropped open in surprise.

"Greendown?" Old Man Cromegas shifted uncomfortably as he spoke in a rasp, the strength in his own voice surprising him most of all.

"Shhh, rest now." One of the clergy swooped in to calm him down, tossing me a grateful look laced with incredulity.

I gave them a nod of recognition before turning back to Lilly, continuing to talk while I started to heal the kid in front of me. "Almost every village I come to along the way has some kind of serious problem. I swear, it's like there's something out there trying to keep me from getting to my destination. Although, all these problems have really driven home the fact that the current guild system isn't working for the people. Take the Healers' Guild, for example. Do you see them here right now?"

I pointedly looked around as feeling came back to the boy's limbs. "No. I see some clergy members offering comfort, but no actual *healing*. Even a halfway decent herbalist would be able to treat the fevers here with willow bark if they were available, but they aren't. Maybe the guilds were a good thing a long time ago, but now? It just provides roadblocks for people to fend for themselves, and political clout for a select few who want money and power. Wouldn't you agree?"

Lilly was doing the gasping-fish-mouth thing, so I shrugged and moved on to the next patient. By this point, I was pretty sure I was dealing with some kind of polio. Most of the damage I was seeing centered around the spinal cord, so I quickly focused on getting through everyone still waiting for healing. All of them would eventually recover. Keeping new infections from happening was the next step.

When I got done, I was beyond drained. The low mana of this world was still a problem, no matter what upgrades I had gained. I was also incredibly hungry. "Lilly, do you guys have some place I can get some food around here? I need to eat and rest a little before I track down where the twisting sickness came from."

"Um, we can see if Granny Crow is cooking something. She always makes extra, in case people don't feel like cooking for their evening meal that day." Lilly led the way out of the tent, the two of us leaving behind thirty people who were rapidly looking like they could go home.

We walked in silence for a bit before she finally worked up the courage to talk to me again. "I don't know if I agree with you, mister. Not about everything you said."

"What do you mean?" I was only halfway paying attention to her. A section of the village had fallen into disrepair a long time ago, most notably a bunkhouse and horse stables near the wall. It looked as though the village had hosted a contingent of soldiers at some point. Rain had caused mold to run rampant, the stink of stables left to rot was overpowering, and the combination was playing hell with my stomach. "What don't you agree with?"

"About the guilds. They do help us." Lilly motioned to the opposite gate from where I entered. "We're close enough to Greendown that they come here only a few days after we ask."

"Really? Every time you ask, they come running?" I cocked an eyebrow, the disbelief obvious on my face. "Kid, if you believe that, I've got some beautiful oceanfront property to sell you in the great state of Arizona."

"Huh?" Lilly must have been a quick study, because she moved right past the part she didn't understand. "No, they don't come every time. But they do when it's really important, and they have the members to spare." She shrugged. "We're not the biggest village, so we don't have top priority all the time."

We stopped in front of a house that had seen better days, but it had a nice garden out front with bright flowers that didn't seem to mind how gloomy this place seemed to be most of the time. Lilly knocked on the door, and the two of us waited.

"Okay. For as far back as you can remember, how many times has a healer from the Healers' Guild come to your village when they were requested, and how 'important' did the situation have to be?" I bent over to look at the flowers, noticing that it was a blend of chamomile and jasmine, along with a bunch of stuff I didn't recognize. Familiar herbs were a good sign. Jasmine could be used to help stomach aches, and chamomile was great for nausea and fevers, especially for children. "Looking at this situation, my guess would be not much. If this isn't 'important' enough to warrant their help, then nothing is."

The door was yanked open, and a very spry Granny Crow stood in the entryway. "Ha! A real healer, like I said. Notice my little helper garden, did ya?" She reached out and snatched Lilly's arm, dragging her inside. "Get yer hind ends in here. I jus' put a pot on the stove."

We were herded to a table in the middle of a small kitchen, where pleasant smells drifted out of an honest-to-the-gods witch's cauldron. It bubbled happily in the stone fireplace, making my stomach grumble in anticipation. The house was lit by an obscene number of candles, which gave off a pleasant floral scent that blended nicely with what was cooking in the cauldron. As we waited for Granny Crow to deem the food ready to serve, she sat across from me with a serious look on her face.

"I heard ya askin' the girl 'bout the guilds, an' I got an answer." Granny Crow glanced at Lilly, measuring her with her eyes. "Ya were a young'un when the red fever took a third o' the village. 'Twas when yer ma passed, and yer older sister. We asked the guild fer aid. Three times, we asked. Each time, their answer was ta wait it out, same as it been the las' dozen times there was a real sickness 'round these parts."

"But, they came when Miss Crawford had problems with her baby, and when Mister Douglas broke his leg." Lilly seemed smaller at the mention of her mother and sister passing, her voice losing the strength it had before. "I've seen all kinds of guild members come when we call."

"No, girl. Ya seen 'em come when there was enough coin ta make it worth their while." Granny Crow reached out to grab Lilly's hands. "If the risk is too big, their fee goes out o' our reach. They don't like ta risk their own scrawny necks."

A heavy silence settled on the room, and I cleared my throat before breaking it. "How fast do you think they'll come when they hear a nonmember was healing people without permission?"

Granny Crow snorted in amusement. "How fast can a horse gallop?" She waved a hand like she was brushing away a fly. "It don' matter. They won't hear nothin' from us."

"So, I don't need to worry about the blacksmith reporting me?"

Both Lilly and Granny Crow gave me a guilty look.

"Ya noticed that, did ya?" She shook her head. "He knows better'n ta say somethin' without talkin' ta the council first."

Lilly nodded in agreement, sitting up straighter. "And since you just saved the life of a council member, I don't think you have anything to worry about."

"Let me guess, Old Man Cromegas?"

Both of them nodded yes. Any further conversation was interrupted by the pot bubbling over, and Granny Crow deftly had bowls of thick stew placed in front of us in no time. Like most old ladies, she knew how to cook, and I was quickly getting seconds.

"If it settles anyone's conscience, I will be applying to the Healers' Guild as soon as I reach Greendown."

Granny Crow studied me a moment before nodding. "Aye, knowin' that'll go a long way'n your favor, I reckon."

"Well, I'm glad that helps." While I waited for my second bowl to cool down, I remembered something important, pointing toward the bubbling pot. "By chance, where do you get the water you cook with?"

Granny Crow pointed to the rear of her house. "I got rain barrels, like most folk. Walkin' back an' forth to the well is for the young."

"For the young…" I murmured thoughtfully, considering the mostly younger patients in the healing tent, and polio's more adverse effects on younger people. "And where is this well, by chance?" I happily started eating again, thankful that I wasn't eating tainted water. Even though I could heal myself, that didn't mean I wanted to ingest poop water.

"Why do you want to know?" Lilly seemed genuinely curious, so I took a few minutes to explain all the bad things that could happen when drinking water that was contaminated. Both of them were immediately concerned, and Granny Crow pulled her cauldron off the fire before rushing off into the deepening twilight.

Lilly tried hurrying me out after her, but I was determined to finish my meal. I needed to fuel my body if I was going to be casting any more spells.

"Hurry up! We need to keep people from drinking from the well before it's too late."

"Calm down." In my experience, telling a frantic girl to calm down had given me some very mixed results. This time, as expected, it didn't seem to work. "I have no doubt Granny Crow already has things well in hand."

By the time the two of us made it to where the well sat, half the town was there in an uproar, torches waving about like they were ready to burn down somebody's castle. Granny Crow was browbeating people into listening to her, so I let her keep at it. They might believe a healer who had just healed a bunch of people, but I wouldn't hold a candle to the forceful and familiar persona of Granny Crow.

Instead of getting involved with the question-and-answer session, I walked over and inspected the well. Placing my hand vertically with my palm facing me, I crossed my ring finger over my pinky and middle finger over my index finger, forming an upside-down '*V*' that I pointed at the well. It was too dark to see the bottom, but I had magic to help me.

Sitting and eating had recharged me enough that it was easy to cast what I considered a delving spell. It was a pulse of mana that was similar to my inspection spell, but less focused. My control over the new power level was steadily improving, and running low on mana made it even easier to make sure my spells stayed in the acceptable range of what I considered to be normal. The sonar-like bounce told me the well was a deep one. It relied on the water table to refill it instead of going to an aquifer or underground stream. That meant I already knew the problem.

"Granny Crow." I didn't raise my voice, but the crowd finally fell silent the moment I spoke. "I think I know what's causing people to get sick. Who owns that run-down set of stables polluting your groundwater?"

CHAPTER 33

Leaving the village wasn't nearly as dramatic as my entrance. Despite the hour, most of the village was busy cleaning up the stables, so only Lilly and Granny Crow were there to see me off. They had agreed to keep under quarantine for at least another fifteen days before opening up their gates to the city, which would keep anything from spreading if I had missed someone. It rained enough that those who normally used the well would be able to get by for a short time, while they drained and cleaned it to make their water safe again.

"Be careful, young man. If'n you plan on challengin' the guilds, you need ta watch yer back." Granny Crow gave me a wave, and I felt a minuscule pulse of magic come from her that washed over me. "Blessin's o' the traveler will keep ya safe."

Lilly only gave me a tiny nod, still unsure of herself given recent events.

"Thank you, Granny Crow." I turned and left, looking for Jess and the others. A quick glance showed me the gates were already closing behind their retreating backs. At least one village I had left in my wake didn't hate my guts. Not that they had asked me to stay the night. They didn't like me *that* much.

As I was beginning to realize was the norm, the stars were quickly being covered by clouds that threatened rain. The increased darkness made it easier to find the flickering campfire through the trees, so I got closer before stopping on the edge of the trail. Before I met with everyone else, I had to burn my clothes.

First, I drank the healing potion I had saved from Jess's village. I might have been a little paranoid, but I wanted to be sure I wasn't a carrier. I may not have had the capability to magnify my perception to a level that I could 'see' viruses, but the healing potion didn't have the same requirements—or limitations, for that matter. It worked to boost the existing immune system, which at fifty-five Vigor, was already potent stuff, and snuffed out any budding viral spread before it could get started. While it was tingling through my system, I stripped down to my birthday suit and flash-fried my clothes. The cool air made my skin break out in goosebumps, forcing me to push away a shiver. As I approached the fire, I was surprised to see the camp was empty. The only things showing it belonged to my people were the several pots of water boiling away over the fire pit.

A twig cracked in the forest, snapping my attention off toward the darkness. I expected to see Jess and the others, but instead I found a familiar and very unwanted sight. I let out a groan. "You again. Didn't get enough of me last time, huh?"

The last time I had seen the female vampire, she had been dressed as a noble. This time, she wore clothes that made her blend into the wilderness, with a heavy bow in her white-fingered grip, a thick rune-covered arrow already nocked on the string. "I told you I'd find you again, sorcerer. Although, I didn't expect to find you so…vulnerable."

I looked down at myself. Being caught out completely naked with nothing but my shield bracelet and low on mana wasn't exactly the best situation I could have asked for. I mean, it was better than the time I had been tied up by the woman 'training' me to get my Soldier class on world three. I had been expecting a more *fun* training session, but after she had tied me spread-eagle to a bed frame, the crazy woman had let four men I had pissed off earlier that week into the room. It was hard not to wince at the memory. "You might be surprised to hear this, but I've been in more vulnerable situations before."

She laughed, the sound grating on my ears. "Oh, I do believe you. Now, I've been ordered to bring you and your friends to see my boss. They want answers, and you're going to give them." She waved a hand, and Jess, Leedy, Murphy, and Cross were all yanked into the light. All four of them had been stripped down to their underwear, and looked like they had lost a fight with a really angry weed-whacker. They each had a vampire holding one arm, bringing the enemy count up to nine. I suspected there was at least one more hiding out of sight, probably more. "We've already captured your followers. Come along quietly, and we won't hurt them. Much."

I smiled and held up my hands as if waiting for them to be shackled. "I can't believe I get to say this, especially since I'm technically an alien to *your* world, but…take me to your leader."

The female vampire didn't know what to say, so she simply motioned for someone behind me to come forward. Two more vampires came out of the woods, one of them holding a set of silver shackles that had more carvings than an elven princess's chastity belt. I definitely didn't want them to get those things on me.

I looked up at the others to gauge how capable they might be in a fight at the moment. Both Leedy and Murphy looked as though they had fought hard, and were in rough shape. Surprisingly, Cross was in even worse condition. I guess the constant worry of the vampires coming back for him had been weighing on his mind for a long time. Jess only had a goose-egg lump on her forehead, meaning she had probably gone down fast and early. The glazed look in her eyes worried me. Head injuries were nothing to play around with, and she needed healing immediately. Basically, I wasn't going to get much help from the four of them.

"Be careful. We still don't know who his patron is. There could be a curse on his flesh that destroys anyone who touches him without permission." The female vampire pulled up her bow and drew back the arrow, aiming it at my midsection. "Tell me, sorcerer, will we die if we touch you?"

"Die if you touch me?" The fire hissed as some of the water boiling bubbled over. I looked at it, thinking about its intended purpose. The reason I had told Jess and the others to boil so much water was because I was going to have them dump it on me while I was healing myself, ensuring I was completely disinfected. It was an extremely painful way of doing things, but it worked, and I was no stranger to pain. Now, it was going to serve a different purpose. "I couldn't have said it better myself. In fact, you're already dead. You just don't know it yet."

My shield bracelet activated with a snap, and a flick of my wrist caused the boiling water to be thrown at the line of people and vampires across from me. They all went down in a screaming tangle—vampires, humans, and shifter alike. I felt a little bad hurting Jess, Leedy, and Murphy—not so much Cross—but I could heal them when this was over. The female vampire let loose her heavy arrow, and I caught a lucky break. It deflected off my shield and hit the undead dude holding the silver shackles in the throat. He dropped like a sack of potatoes, and I spun and grabbed the other vampire next to me, who was too shocked at the sudden violence to have reacted yet. I threw him at the female vampire hard enough that when they collided, the sound of snapping bone was audible over her scream of outrage. They tumbled into the fire, and the screams of outrage turned into screams of pain.

I grabbed the first weapon I could find, which was the arrow sticking out of the vampire's throat. I yanked it free and stabbed him again quickly in the heart. He wouldn't be getting up again. Then I jumped over the pair still rolling around in the fire to take on the eight vampires the others were tangled with. Two were already getting back to their feet, so I stabbed them each through the heart with two jabs before they even realized I was in front of them. A third vampire grabbed me by the ankle, yanking me off my feet before I could pull myself free of its grip.

My shield blocked a stomping boot from crushing my head as another vampire made himself known. The stupid horse ran past, with all our gear and equipment on its back, meaning this guy had probably been holding it when the fight started. He cocked his leg back to try again, which gave me a very odd angle to deal with. So, I threw the arrow I was holding like it was a dart as hard as I could, straight up his poop-chute. That definitely distracted him.

While that guy was screaming and hopping around, I kicked my leg free of the vampire holding onto me. In the scrum, Leedy had found a big rock and was busy crushing the skull of a vampire who was face-first into the dirt. Murphy had pulled Jess free, and was keeping two vampires at bay with a pointy stick. Cross was either dead or unconscious, burned badly by the boiling water. That left the one who had grabbed me, and two more that were unaccounted for. They had already disappeared into the forest, the sound of their retreat crashing through the trees.

The vampire who had grabbed me was easily killed when I stomped his head into paste, and the one with an arrow up his honey-hole was even easier. I grabbed him around the throat with one arm, the shoulders with the other, and ripped his head off. Sometimes, extreme violence was cathartic.

Murphy used the distraction of my violent execution to stab one of the two he was facing in the chest, and the last one ran off when I took a step in his direction. I checked on the two that had fallen in the fire, and I was pretty sure they were done. The older a vampire became, the more flammable they were. The female had been old enough that she might as well have been soaked in oil. I deactivated my shield bracelet with a pop once I felt we were in the clear.

"Are you okay?" I checked on Leedy first, considering he was on his back, gasping for breath. "Did you break anything?"

"I was sure we were dead." He groaned as he sat up, the burns on his face and hands making me wince. "They got us with their mind tricks. We barely fought at all."

"I don't think we'll have to worry about them for a bit. Now tell me, did you break anything?" I had the mana to heal his soft tissue injuries, but bone and organ damage would cut it close. "It's important."

"No. I don't think so, anyway." Leedy winced as he looked at his boiled skin. "Nice trick with the water, by the way. I don't think anyone could have expected it."

"I learned it from a great hero where I'm from, named Keanu Reeves. 'If a bad guy has a hostage, just shoot the hostage.' Or something like that, anyway." I drew a circle on his forehead, avoiding the worst of his burned skin, and healed the worst of the damage. He had some torn ligaments in his left elbow that were going to have to wait until I had some time to recharge. "Take it easy for now. Let me check on the others."

Murphy was the least burned, but made up for it with bruises. He stayed silent while I healed him, only looking at Jess while I worked. He finally found his voice when I knelt to check on her. "Do you think you can save her? The sound she made when they hit her…it wasn't good."

"I think so. I can heal most injuries, as long as I get to them in time." I thumbed back her eyelids, checking for any response. One pupil looked normal, but the other was blown wide open. Shit. Looking the rest of her over, most of her burns were on her torso, and they were bad enough she already had large blisters swelling across her abdomen the size of potatoes. "Has she said anything since they hit her?"

"No." He swallowed hard, pushing down his emotions once again. "They were going to kill us as soon as you surrendered. All of them were laughing about it while we waited for you to show up."

"We're going to track down the ones who got away as soon as everyone can move, and show them the error of their ways. Now, let me see how bad she is." I bit my cheek to get some blood in my saliva before spitting on her forehead. Using both my index and middle fingers, I drew a large circle with '*James H*' on the inside. I wanted to use as much of a connection as I dared to check her brain. It was dangerous to connect too deeply. I didn't want to lose myself, and spend the next day or two trying to find my way back into my own body. Also, leaving myself undefended was a dangerous thing.

I looked back up at Murphy. "Guard me while I do this." He gave me a serious nod, and I dove in.

Using only a trickle of mana to conserve energy, I ignored her burns and focused on her head. Her shifter constitution was already working to heal the burns, so I gave it a small boost. Removing the scars later would be easy. Now came the hard part. I had to delve deep to find the problem, and such finicky work always carried risks in seriously delicate areas of the body. The thread of mana that ran through her brain bumped into an area where pressure from blood leaking into her cranium was causing problems. I found where the blood was leaking and healed it first, then I brought down the swelling. Being so deeply intertwined with her body disconnected me from my own, and I could faintly feel my heartbeat starting to slow. I had been here too long. Falling into a coma was a bad idea. Pushing in another burst of energy, I let it diffuse through her body unguided. It would catch anything I missed. By then, I was almost bone-dry on mana, and my body was running on fumes. It would have to be enough.

Pulling my consciousness out of Jess, I came back to find both Leedy and Murphy watching over me. "How long was I gone?" The vampires were still crackling in the fire, so it couldn't have been too long.

"Less than an hour." Leedy motioned to Cross. "Do you have enough power left to save him?"

"Forget Cross—is Jess okay?" Murphy missed the look Leedy gave him.

I don't think he would have cared even if he had seen it.

"Will she remember who she is?"

Looking between the two of them, I decided to answer Murphy first. "I've done what I can for now. The brain is the trickiest thing to heal." I considered my statement for a moment, having slipped into full-blown Healer mode. "Well, specifically, it's the *mind* that's the trickiest to heal. Although the two are intrinsically linked, they aren't the same thing. The brain is a bitch to fix, but it's the ailments of the mind that even specialized archmagus have a hard time with." I pulled back her eyelids, and thankfully they looked more normal. Still not perfect, but much better. "Her shifter nature should cover any gaps I might have missed."

Murphy let out a long sigh. "I hope so. I can't lose her, not now." He looked up sharply at Leedy and me. "I mean, the group can't lose her. She's an important member of the team."

"Whatever you say, Murphy." Leedy just shook his head. "Now can we go check on Cross?"

I stood up, immediately feeling the lack of mana. "I won't be able to do much, but I can at least check on him." As I got closer to him, I could see the steady rise and fall of his chest. "Well, he's at least still alive." The skies chose that moment to open up, and a heavy downpour immediately soaked me before I could activate my shield bracelet again. "Would you track down that horse and find me my clothes, please? I would really like to not be naked anymore."

"Sure. It's trained to not run far." Leedy walked off, keeping his sore arm tucked against his body. As he walked past the fire, he tossed a few more logs on it to keep it going despite the rain. It was near enough to the sheltering boughs of a tree that it would keep burning as long as it stayed hot enough.

"All right, Cross. Let's see what we're dealing with." The moment I touched him, a spark jumped into my body, and I couldn't move. A voice spoke in my head, powerful enough to make my eyes rattle inside their sockets.

Hmmm…and what do we have here?

CHAPTER 34

The mental assault by whatever this was had caught me flat-footed. I was tired, hungry, cold, naked, uncomfortable, sore, and empty on mana. Basically, the worst position to be in for putting up a mental defense. If it weren't for my time fighting mind flayers on world fourteen—the one with all the goddamned singing—I would have been about as well-off as an armless man in a bitch-slapping competition.

What are you? Human, for the most part. More than human in other parts. Your soul has been branded though, scarred and warded enough that even I can't touch it. Still, this body would make an excellent *vessel. I must have it.*

"Kinda…occupied." I forced the words out, pushing against whatever was trying to take me over. "Piss…off…dickcheese."

Dickcheese? My, I wasn't expecting such an eloquent host. Dominica, be a dear and show him that it is important to show me proper respect. Not too rough, now. I still want this one for myself, no matter his patron.

When nothing happened, I could feel a sense of anger and shock from them. It gave me a toehold to push against the mental pressure, and I shoved them back, gaining control of my body again. "You mean that lady vampire you keep sending? She's busy doing a really good impression of a burnt piece of toast, which is exactly what you're about to become." I gathered my mental willpower like it was a fist, and smashed the invader with it as hard as I could. The entity recoiled in pain and surprise, and flinched away from my second attempt at hitting it.

You are proving to be quite the thorn in my side, sorcerer. One I'm going to enjoy plucking very soon. Before I go, know that I marked the rest of your friends, to make it easier to find all of you when I'm ready. If you had come peacefully, they would have been left alone. Now, they will pay the price for your hubris. Until next time…

I knew whatever this thing was had probably lied about leaving my friends alone, and it was only messing with my head, but it still pissed me the fuck off. Putting a target on my friends meant he had shifted to the top of my to-do list.

The spark jumped out of my forehead, shooting into the ground near the fire. The burnt skeletal remains of the female vampire—Dominica, apparently—jumped up with a clatter and hiss. Both Murphy and I leapt to our feet, ready to fight it, but the crispy critter ran off into the woods in the same direction the other vampires had gone. Toward Greendown.

"What was *that*?" Murphy was wide-eyed, looking around with his fists raised. "Have you ever seen a vampire come back from the dead like that?"

"The vampire was dead as a doornail." I wiped at my nose, where a trickle of blood was running down. "*That*…was something else. Something we are going to have to track down and kill, if we ever want to be free of it. Either a lich, psionic demon, or a mind flayer who has managed to live without its original body for a long time. Considering how it animated that dead body, my money is on lich." I rubbed my temples, feeling the headache set in. I had just fought a lich in the last world I had left, and now I had to face another one?

"Liches are a terrible enemy to fight. Time means nothing to them. They're immortal magic users who have centuries, sometimes millennia, to perfect their spells. Rituals and traps that are built up over generations, plans within plans that make it almost impossible to work through in an assault of their strongholds. Some are so powerful that people worship them as gods." The one on world nineteen had been like that. A god-emperor who ruled over a continent. It had taken almost the entire year I was there to bring it down. At least this thing didn't feel as overwhelmingly powerful. If it was a lich, it couldn't be over a thousand years old. Still bad, but not world-destroying bad.

"How do you know that? Have you fought them before?" Murphy took a few steps over to the fire and tossed some more logs on it, making sure to break up the skeleton of the remaining vampire while he did so. With the rain, the lich leaping around had almost put it out. "I've only heard of those in stories."

"Yeah, I've fought all of them at one time or another. Mind flayers are weak physically, and can usually be killed easily from a distance." I shuddered, remembering a dark cave filled with brain-dead mind slaves we had found after putting one down. They had started screaming the moment it had died, and didn't stop until they were silenced. Permanently. "The other two, liches and psionic demons, aren't as easy to deal with."

"I thought demons were just a myth, a story told to scare children?" Murphy walked back over to Jess and angled his body to protect her from the rain. "There hasn't ever been a real one, according to the Wardens."

"Oh, they're real." I carefully touched Cross again, this time ready for an attack. Of course, there was nothing. "They aren't native to this dimension, and have to be called here by someone. Demons, devils, fiends, and daemons can all be summoned if you know how."

Murphy looked at me like he thought I was making stuff up. "You just said different words for the same thing."

"Nope. Common mistake." I started to heal Cross, using a small circle and as little energy as possible. He was tough as old boot leather, and would survive if I took it easy on myself. "They are all similar, but they come from different dimensions, and all follow different rules. Devils are evil, but they follow a certain set of codes and laws. Where I'm from, we call it 'Lawfully Evil.' Demons are evil too, but they are agents of pure chaos, so they are called 'Chaotic Evil.' Daemons are more of a cosmic force of evil, focused on the annihilation of everything, so they are 'Neutral Evil.' Fiends come from a less physical realm, and usually embody evil concepts instead of an actual manifestation. They're what most sorcerers make deals with in return for power."

"That all sounds great, but I don't actually care." Murphy shrugged and turned back to Jess, shifting so he covered her better. "Probably won't be a Warden anymore when we get to Greendown. I'd be surprised if I was even still a member of the Hunters' Guild." He looked down at his hands, still crusted in the black blood of vampires despite the rain. "I'll be lucky if I can join the Farmers' Guild after everything comes to light."

I laughed, breaking the connection with Cross. He was healed enough that he could fight, as long as the lich hadn't melted his brain. "Murphy, sometimes I forget how young you are." He cocked an eyebrow at me, probably because we *looked* like we were close to the same age. "I've seen this play out a bunch of times. It's gonna go one of four ways." I held up one finger. "Either they'll try to cover everything up, so they'll kill you." I held up a second finger. "They'll try to cover everything up, and throw you in the deepest, darkest prison they own." I held up three fingers. "They'll act like everything was a big misunderstanding, and promote you." I held up four fingers. "Or, they'll really piss me off, and I'll end up passing judgment on everyone, and you'll get promoted by the survivors." I leaned in and whispered conspiratorially. "My vote's on number four."

"Huh. I guess I never thought of it like that." Murphy straightened up a bit. "Those aren't the best options, I suppose, but at least I don't have to stop being a Warden."

"*I'm glad I could make you feel better.*" *I* certainly wasn't feeling better. I was sitting in cold mud, naked, with a headache that was only getting worse. I decided to focus inward, to the mana generator sitting behind my belly button. All my recent activity had drained it to almost nothing, and it throbbed in time with my headache.

Deciding to experiment, I mentally prodded at the dregs of mana that sat at the bottom, causing them to swirl sluggishly. An unexpected side effect was that my body seemed to pull in the faint amount of ambient mana in the area around me, recharging me just a tiny bit faster. After seeing that, I kept doing it, poking at the mana until it sang.

Yes, it actually made a sound, like a low humming off in the distance. I checked to see whether Murphy could hear it, but he didn't react. The swirl became a tornado, going faster and faster as the energy around me was drawn into my body. It hurt, like the way it hurts to stretch a stiff muscle. Lightning formed inside once again, sending tingles through my body. It danced through my muscles, causing me to twitch and jump.

That was enough to break my concentration, and the tornado went back to a whirlpool, the lightning dying down until it was only inside my mana generator. It wasn't back to full, but I was far from empty now. Almost as if I had rested for a full six or seven hours. My headache from the mental assault had also stopped getting worse. Although I didn't have time to deeply assess what had just happened, I had the gut feeling that whatever it was had just changed the game forever. No more reliance on passive mana gain when my personal stores of mana had been exhausted? How often could I use this? What were the limits? Concentration and time, for one. As things stood, there was no way I could concentrate and control that hurricane of power mid-battle. But if there was one thing I'd learned through the years, it was that I was capable of acclimating to nearly anything.

I turned my attention back inward, my curiosity at such a new and powerful tool in my arsenal simply too much to ignore. Maybe I could get the thing spinning just a little bit faster…

"Uuunh, what happened?" Cross sat up, rubbing his head. "Lieutenant Lucente, where did you put my clothes after—" His eyes widened when he saw me—still naked—sitting across from him.

"Morning, sunshine! Hope last night was good for you, because it sure was for me." I grinned at his look of horror, and then I saw when it all came back to him. His shoulders slumped, and he looked sullenly at the stump where his hand used to be. He must have really gotten a good whammy if he had forgotten *me* for a few minutes. "Back with us now?"

"Unfortunately." Cross looked around, his expression becoming more somber at seeing the mess that the campsite had become. Bodies were still lying around, and one was even bent over with an arrow sticking out of its keister. "What did I miss?"

"Remember those vampires who were going to track you down?"

He gave me a sharp nod.

"Well, they did. We managed to fight them off, but a few got away. As soon as Leedy gets back with the horse and our gear, we're going to track them down and finish them off."

"My horse will come if I call it." Cross tried to stand, and immediately flopped onto his face.

I watched him struggle for a minute before I took pity on him and helped.

"Leedy can handle it. I've got some questions for you before we leave, and they're important ones." I waited for him to agree before I continued. "Do you remember how they marked you? Was it a physical thing, or a mental one?"

Cross shook his head. "No, but I'd assumed it was based on my scent. That is how most vampires hunt, and once they know you, there is little you can do to escape."

"Have you been hearing strange voices the past few days? Perhaps someone whispering to you, or thoughts that might have seemed out of place?" I watched his eyes carefully to check for a reaction, but he was completely deadpan.

"I've had nothing of the sort. Why do you ask? Even for you, these are odd questions." Cross scooted back a little, getting some extra space between us. "Did you do something else to me that I don't know about?"

"Not me, the vampires." I motioned to the fire, where the skeleton of one still burned. "There were two bloodsuckers in there, but one got up and ran away when the lich hiding in your head failed in its attack against me."

Cross didn't say anything, stunned at the thought of a lich being inside him.

"I was afraid that the 'mark' they gave you was the lich hiding inside you all this time, but now I think the vampires brought him when they attacked. There's no way it could lay dormant that long without revealing itself."

"Have I fallen so low, that an abomination can take control of me?" Cross tried to stand again, this time flopping onto his side. "What have I become?"

I stood and walked over, licking a muddy finger before drawing another circle on Cross so I could heal him again. "That lich gave *me* a run for my money, and I'm far more powerful than you are. It's strong enough that I bet your guild leader would fail against it, so don't beat yourself up so bad. Now, hold still so I can figure out why you have no balance."

A quick inspection showed me a lesion at the base of his brain, in the cerebellum. I had missed it earlier because I hadn't been looking. I pushed a quick burst of healing at him, and it went back to healthy tissue. Now that I knew where the lich liked to hang out in people's minds, I could surgically target him next time we met.

"Try to stand now, you should be okay." I backed up, and Cross got to his feet with only a single wobble. "Better?"

"I think so." For a moment, Cross looked as if he were going to thank me. Then, the sound of something coming through the trees interrupted, and the moment was gone. "I think I hear Leedy returning with our things."

"Yeah." I walked over to check on Jess. Now that I had more power, I could do a better job on her too. And I could fix Leedy's elbow. Then we could track down those vampires and finish them off. I stopped and thought about it for a second.

First, I should probably put some pants on.

CHAPTER 35

Jess was still fuming, upset at herself about how things had gone down. "I should have *smelled* them, at the very least. They stink like you wouldn't believe." She punched her palm, grinding her fist into it. "I'm going to show them how it feels to get blindsided like that."

"Instead of talking about what you're going to do, why don't you practice the spell I showed you some more, so we can gauge your progress?" I was very interested to see how quickly she was going to learn something completely different from the earth spell I had shown her before. If she got it as quickly as the last one, it meant she was some kind of savant. "Start at the beginning, and take it slow."

She was trying to learn a lesser version of the fireball spell, something similar to a fire dart. It took less time and energy to form, but without the splash damage, it meant you had to be more accurate. For someone with shifter reflexes, I was hoping it wouldn't be a problem.

"Why am I learning this one again?" Jess held up a curled index and middle finger, like she was throwing an invisible knuckleball. "Wouldn't an actual fireball be better?"

"Sure, if your body could control the mana to power one big enough to matter." I held up my hand in a mimic of hers and swung, casting a swarm of five fire darts, sending each of them perfectly into a thick tree sapling. One dart wouldn't have been enough to do much, but the five combined worked together to chop it down like an elemental chainsaw. It fell to the ground with a crash. "Trust me, this spell has its uses."

Jess swallowed hard and looked at her hand. "Okay, I see your point."

I watched as the mana in her body swirled down her arm as she swung forward, and a single spark shot out, burning her hand.

"Ah! What was that?" She blew on the burn, trying to soothe away the sting.

"That was a more normal response." I reached out and drew a circle on her hand, quickly healing it. "Now, try the earthen wall spell again."

She did as ordered, and a hard ridge of earth appeared a few feet off the trail from where we were walking. It was even better than the last time she had used it. "That was easy. Are fire spells harder than earth spells?"

"For you, apparently." I showed her how to do a wind blade. "Try that one. I want to see something."

"Okay." Jess put too much energy into it, and ended up causing a large gust of wind that blew the leaves off the nearby trees. She also managed to exhaust over half of her energy supply, and sagged to one knee. "Um, that one didn't go as well."

I helped her back to her feet and gave her a strip of dried jerky to help her recover. "Give it a minute before you try anything else. I think I know what's going on, anyway."

"What is it? Am I broken?" Jess looked around, making sure the others were out of earshot. "Will I not be able to become a mage?"

Shaking my head, I could only laugh. "No, you are just lucky. How you are with other spells is how you should be with earth spells. A total noob." I ignored her raised eyebrow. Noob should be a universal term, and damn any language morphology. "I think you have an affinity."

"What does that mean?" Jess took a swig of water to help swallow the jerky. "Can I only cast one kind of spell?"

I concentrated for a moment and formed four tiny balls of energy above the palm of my hand. "There are all kinds of spell elements, but most of them can be broken down into the four major ones. Water, earth, fire, and air." I gave them a mental push, and they started to spin. "Most mages have a favorite element or two that they focus on, usually because they find it easier to control. That's called an affinity. It's not usually anything drastic, just a slight preference." I allowed the earth element to grow until it was twice the size of the other three. "For you, it's *very* pronounced. Any earth spells, or mostly earth spells, are going to be much easier for you to cast. You're just average with all the others."

"So, what do I do? Only cast earth spells now? What if I want to become a death mage, or metal?" Jess mimed stabbing out with a sword. "I might have an affinity for something else."

"Life and death are something called esoteric magics, but even they have some aspects of the main four. And a metal mage is basically just an earth mage with excellent control. But to answer your real question, what you should do is keep practicing everything." I showed her how to cast Earth Spike, and then a smaller rock version that could be thrown similar to the Fire Dart. "Since we're about to go into a fight, you might want to concentrate on spells that are immediately useful to you. Earthen Wall, Earth Spike, and Rock Dart should give you an edge."

Jess immediately cast the Rock Dart spell, her pinky thrust forward like she was stabbing someone with it. The one I had shown her looked similar to a crossbow bolt, fully formed and with rudimentary fletchings to help control its flight. Her version was more like a sharpened pencil, and stabbed into a nearby tree with a twang. "What do you think?"

"I think it's a good start. Keep practicing." She gave me a thumbs-up, and I left her to it, jogging forward to check in with Leedy. "Any word?"

"Murphy said he lost the trail, so he went to try and find Cross. Since he hasn't come back yet, that means he's picked it up and is still tracking them. Or, they got him again, but that's unhelpful and I'm doing my best to stay positive." Leedy patted the horse's nose, wiping away the dripping rain. "The fact that they can find anything in this weather is a miracle."

A flash of lightning lit up the skies, and the mana inside me thrummed in response. It was loving this storm. "Well, you did say Cross used to be in charge of a scouting team. I'm sure he had to pick up some tricks here and there if he wanted to stay in command."

"Either way, they seemed to still be running parallel to the road. All we have to do is see where they veer off, and we'll be able to follow them straight to their base." Leedy closed his hand into a fist, his knuckles whitening. "There's not many places to hide between here and Greendown, so I know we have to be getting close."

"I think the sun came up awhile ago, but with this storm, they might still be able to stay above ground." Another flash of lightning crackled across the sky, and I only counted to one before the thunder followed. It was getting closer. "If this gets any worse, we might have to seek shelter."

Leedy shook his head. "There's no place to go. We're going to start running into the farms and inns that surround Greendown before you know it."

We walked in silence for a few minutes before he spoke again. "You know where they are already, don't you?"

"I can't be sure of anything, but I can make an educated guess. After all, the best place to hide is always in plain sight." I motioned to the forest around us. "Not to mention, do you see a lot of food for vampires around here? If I was in charge of a bunch of undead, I would want to be close to their food source to keep them from getting grumpy. Put all that together, and the only population center large enough to cover up the occasional missing person around here is Greendown."

"What about the hints that their headquarters is farther north, in the mountains? Didn't you say that's where the Destitute's Mausoleum is?" Leedy pointed straight east, along the trail. "That's not where Greendown is located. In fact, I'd say it's a little south of here."

"The Destitute is a vampire, not a lich. We're tracking down the equivalent of an undead guild house, and that lich is in charge of the closest one. I've probably got at least another two or three boss fights to get through before I fight the *big* bad guy." I wiped the rain off my face, shifting my hat down to keep me from getting wet. "There's the witches we need to worry about too, plus I need to figure out where that super ghoul and its core came from."

"Have you given up on your quest to find the Silver Star, then?" Leedy smirked at me when I let out a long-suffering sigh in response. "I'll take that as a no. People can't resist the thought of all that treasure."

I rummaged around for a second and pulled out the black marble-like core, holding it up for him to see. "I told you, it isn't about money. *This* is connected to the Silver Star. I don't know how, or why, but it is. And I found it inside a ghoul that could keep fighting after I exploded its head in half." I tucked it back in my pack. "There's no way all of this is separate. I'm going to figure out how they connect, and then I'm going to tear it down."

A spike of dirt erupted out of the forest next to us, toppling a tree and scaring the horse. Leedy was busy fighting with it while I slowly turned around and glared at a guilty-looking Jess. She gave a tiny wave and mouthed 'Sorry' before ducking her head under her hood.

"You trying to kill us or something?" Leedy finally got the horse to stop bucking, before shaking a finger in my face. "That was entirely uncalled for!"

"That wasn't me, it was Jess." I cast the same spell, and a much more compact version erupted next to the one she had cast. "See? That's what my version of the spell looks like."

"Stop doing that!" Leedy gripped his sword hilt, looking around nervously. "You'll anger the Pauls."

I just stared at him, not understanding what he was talking about.

"Of course you wouldn't know about the Pauls. They own the forest around Greendown. Everyone leaves them alone, because they don't bother humans unless they try chopping down the trees in their territory."

"What are these 'Pauls'? Are they another kind of undead?" I was surprised to see Leedy acting so nervously. He hadn't seemed so worried when he was facing velociraptors. "And how dangerous are they?"

"They aren't undead. Nobody really knows for sure what they are. Maybe some kind of fae, or just an odd kind of monster." Leedy slapped at a leg, doing a little hop at the same time. "They've only got one leg, but don't think that makes them slow. Pauls dart about all over the place, kicking people in their rears the moment their back is turned." He positioned himself so he was closer to the horse for cover. "A single Paul can ruin your whole day. Trust me."

"I'll...take your word for it." I could only shake my head in disbelief. Don't get me wrong—I believed Leedy. It was just crazy to me that a race of one-legged ass-kicking monsters named Paul were running loose in the forest. This entire planet was off its rocker. "Anyway, does Greendown have any kind of sewer system, or underground tunnels of some kind?"

"What?" Leedy was paying attention to our surroundings more than he was listening to me. He was genuinely worried. "I'm sorry, I missed what you said."

"I asked if—"

The horse jerked itself out of Leedy's grip and trotted farther down the trail, disappearing around a curve before I could finish my sentence. The two of us started to run after it when both Cross and Murphy came into sight, with the horse already in tow. At least we knew where its loyalties remained.

"Finally!" Leedy seemed excited to see them, and I didn't blame him. I was ready to be anywhere except in this storm. "Did you find them?"

Murphy stayed silent while Cross passed the horse's reins over to him and crouched to draw a map in the mud of the trail with a finger. "Here's Greendown, and this is the northern gate." He drew a cluster of spots farther north, and a line connecting the two. "This is the old patrol base the Hunters' Guild gave over to the farmers years ago. Now, it looks like they've taken it back. There's signs of heavy fighting, and the tracks lead in that direction."

Leedy knelt to fill in a few more details, including the east–west trail we were on and some more dots that were probably the farms and inns he had told me about. "Where do their tracks branch off?"

Cross made a mark shortly before the first set of dots on the map, causing Leedy to frown.

"I don't trust it. Why would they charge straight into a place where there are more Wardens and Hunters? There's plenty of room left for them to double back and go somewhere else."

"That's what I was thinking." Cross nodded, looking up at us. "It means they know we're on to them, so we need to look out for an ambush."

"Do me a favor." I took a step to the side as Jess finally caught up to us. "Draw in the details of the rest of the surrounding area, especially any abandoned buildings and underground locations."

Cross quickly added dozens of spots, and both Leedy and Murphy helped where his memory might have left any gaps. Jess stole my hat so she could use it to shield the makeshift map from the rain, and we all carefully looked it over for clues.

"If they headed north, what are the odds that their actual base is south?" Murphy pointed to a series of farms that stretched along a road that led toward the coast. "They could have taken over any of these places, and no one would know for a long time."

"No." I shook my head, pointing to a spot closer to the city. "Their neighbors would notice, and they wouldn't want to draw attention. Not only that, they wouldn't want to travel far for food. What's in this location again?"

Leedy leaned closer, checking distances before answering. "That's the old dairy farm and cheese factory. It's supposed to be a storage site for root vegetables during the winter, but I imagine it's empty now."

We looked at one another, all of us coming to the same conclusion.

I stood up, putting my hat back on my head. "Let's go."

CHAPTER 36

We decided to cut down on the chances of being reported by anyone, and swung south through the forest instead of following the trail. Surprisingly, even Cross agreed that going straight to the city and turning south was too big of a risk. Either he wanted to put off the confrontation we all knew was bound to happen, or crushing the undead threat was a priority to him as well. The few farmhouses and cabins we could occasionally spot through the thinner sections of trees were far enough away that we didn't see a single person, despite being so relatively close to the city. Our only time spotting another living thing was when we crossed the main north–south road, and that was just a pack of feral dogs that ran the moment they saw us.

"Something's wrong." Jess was sniffing as we threaded our way through the forest. She had taken a break from spell practice to recharge and was walking up front with Murphy again. "I don't smell woodsmoke."

"It's not exactly a cold day outside." Murphy shrugged, causing his cloak to shift and a bunch of water that had collected at the base of his hood splashed to the ground. "Good thing, too. Otherwise, we'd be even more miserable."

I held up my hand, causing everyone to stop. I took a moment to expand my senses and confirmed the same thing. Not only was there no woodsmoke, but I couldn't hear the sounds of any animals in the area. We were close enough I should have at least heard a chicken or something. Also, we all needed a bath, and Leedy might have athlete's foot. "No, she's right. The farms and forest are empty around here. They probably have been this whole time."

"With the fighting to the north, the city might have evacuated the countryside. Everyone could be inside the city walls. If not, it's too late for them already." Cross took a moment to look around at where we were. "I'm pretty sure we've only got another mile or two until we run across the trail that will take us to the dairy farm. It was paved a long time ago to allow the heavy wagons easy access when it rains, so we can't miss it."

Leedy nodded in agreement. "If I remember right, there should be an old trapper cabin somewhere nearby. We could rest for a little and prepare ourselves, and leave the horse there while we fought."

"I was planning on riding my horse into battle, as is proper." Cross patted his horse's neck with his stump. "We've seen many battles against the undead together."

"That's great, Lancelot, but we're going to be fighting indoors, remember? I don't see the need for a cavalry charge in the near future. Besides, the Code of Chivalry has firm guidelines—any jousting inside should be done without pants on." I motioned for Leedy to take us to the cabin. "We'll go with your plan. It's well past lunch time, so we should hurry. Even with the clouds, I'd rather fight them during the day than after dark."

We got to the cabin at what I would say was close to two in the afternoon. The log shack was barely standing, but it was good enough for our purposes. Instead of risking the chimney, I started a fire in front of the collapsing porch and quickly got some trail stew started. I only used three of the prepared packets that had been given me instead of a full five. In my experience, it was bad to fight on an empty stomach, and even worse to fight with a full one. This would give us enough to get by without getting sluggish. Leedy poked around inside while the rest of us ate around the fire.

"Are you ready for this?" Murphy leaned close to Jess, pitching his voice low so nobody else could hear. I hadn't turned down my senses yet, meaning I still could. "It's going to be a hard fight. If it was a group of Wardens going after a nest like this, we would have at least twenty people to help."

"Well, we don't need twenty people. We're more than enough to handle this." Jess shifted to be a little closer to the heavily muscled Warden. "I don't believe in the Trinity very much, but have you thought about what it really means that James is here? There's a god somewhere who wants our people to be safe. They want things to be better than they are. And I want to help make it that way."

Murphy made sure not to look directly at me, but he slowly shifted so I was in his peripheral vision. "Do you really believe that? That they would send one person to change everything?"

Jess shrugged, taking another bite of food. "I don't really know for sure. What I do know is that things are already changing. How much safer are the western roads now that so many monsters are dead? I bet trade goes up because of it, and that will make the villages expand. Who knows what else is going to happen?"

I decided to tune them out, and double-checked all my gear. Wrist gun was good to go. Ninjatō and mace were secure on my belt. Yari spear-staff opened and closed smoothly. Armor was clean and strapped in place. Shield bracelet was fully charged, and glowing yellow.

Wait.

Glowing yellow?

"Enemies in the camp!"

As much as I didn't like Cross, the man was solid in an ambush. He was on his feet as fast as I was, sword in hand. Murphy and Jess weren't far behind, and the four of us were ready to face the line of zombies that came stumbling out of the trees. A trio of robed figures—probably the magic users who had set off my bracelet—were behind them, along with two more of those super ghouls I had fought before.

"I guess they know we're here." Murphy had his spear and stepped in front of Jess. "Let's do this."

"No." I held up a clawed hand, forming a dense orange fireball. "They know enough about us now that it's obvious there aren't enough of them to be a serious threat. This is meant to wear us down, so we aren't a threat by the time we make it inside their base. We aren't going to fall for it."

"Ha! Not a serious threat, sorcerer? I think you underestimate us." One of the robed figures held up his own hand, and started forming a throbbing ball of black necrotic energy that hurt my eyes to look at. "Allow me to show you the error of your ways!"

"Oh, shut up, bitch." I dumped extra energy into the spell from my center, causing it to turn into blue flames laced with lightning. I tossed it underhand like a softball pitcher, spreading my fingers so it would expand as it flew. The drain on me was more than I wanted, but after everything this world had put me through, I was getting used to it.

The fireball washed over the center of their line, lighting up the zombies like candlesticks. One of the super ghouls tried to dive out of the way as it rolled farther backward, but was stopped by the lightning that shot out in front of the flames. The robed man screamed as a bolt struck him, and his own spell devoured his arm whole. His screams were cut short when he inhaled the blue flames, ending his life, along with his two compatriots. The only survivors were a few zombies on either end, and both super ghouls who were doing a good impression of crispy critters.

"What did I miss?" Leedy came running out of the cabin, still strapping on his armor. He looked around at the mess and unsheathed his sword. "I guess we lost the element of surprise."

Now that they had lost their controllers, the remaining zombies focused on Leedy's voice and started to stumble in his direction. That snapped everyone else into action, and they quickly finished off what I hadn't killed. I took a minute to manipulate the ball of energy inside me to increase my mana levels before going over to inspect the dead super ghouls, and the mystery men who had led them.

"Anything interesting?" Jess had only cast a single spell—a well-aimed rock dart that had nailed a zombie in the temple and dropped it like a bad habit—so she was the first to join me. "I didn't recognize what those people were wearing."

There wasn't much left to look at. I used my pocket knife to peel back a section of burnt and crumbling fabric, exposing charred skin underneath. It was hard to tell with all of the damage from the fire and lightning, but I was pretty sure some of the discolorations he had were from intricate tribal tattoos. "Any idea what kind of magic user or cult uses tattoos like these?"

Jess shook her head as she looked over my shoulder. "No, not really. At least, no group around here. Guilds use uniforms and badges, not tattoos." She motioned over to the others. "Maybe they'll know something."

Of course, they didn't. Leedy and Murphy only shook their heads after looking the three over. Cross did a more thorough inspection, taking his time to go over what little evidence was left. At the end, all he could do was shrug his shoulders in defeat. "They could be from anywhere across the seas to the south, or maybe the far east. Those regions use tattoos more often than ours. An Eastern Marshal might know more, but I haven't seen their match in my travels."

Deciding to give up on them, I tried to find more of those black orbs in the super ghouls. Surprisingly, the larger of the two didn't have anything, but the smaller one had a pea-sized core that was rough and bumpy instead of smooth and pretty like the other one I had found. To figure out why, I dug around a little and found the smaller super ghoul had a larger brain, with denser bones and muscles. The ghoul must have been the stronger of the two, despite its smaller size. It was a good reminder that size wasn't everything. For some people, anyway. I cast my Identify spell on the bumpy orb, and the results were a surprise.

> **Item**: Artificial Crude Monster Core
>
> **Type**: Undead/Darkness Aspect
>
> **Grade**: 1/5
>
> **Description**: An artificially created core of condensed mana used to control rare subspecies of undead. Can be used to empower enchantments. Imperfect and crude aspects make it inefficient and unstable.

To me, the fact it was missing the warning about being from another reality was the biggest clue. It had been made *here*, by someone trying to recreate the monster cores from elsewhere. I hadn't seen anything else like it before, and a feeling of dread settled into my stomach. "This isn't good. We need to get to that cheese factory as fast as we can."

Except that one time I had a quesadilla-related emergency, I never thought I'd have to say that out loud.

I calmed myself, assured in the knowledge that whatever we would face here couldn't possibly be worse than the enemy I'd battled that day.

CHAPTER 37

Gleason slapped the bear shifter again, dropping the burly mayor to his knees. "I'm tired of your excuses, lycan. I'm tired of these little, worthless villages, and their worthless little people. I'm tired of chasing this worthless man around this stupid forest, and I'm quickly running out of the capability to care about collateral damage. Now, tell me everything you know, or you will find out what happens when I reach the end of my patience."

The morning sunlight was like daggers in his eyes, and it made him more irritable than normal. Even seeing a full platoon of thirty White Wardens in their immaculate uniforms did little to make him feel better. He motioned for his man holding the mayor's daughter to provide a demonstration, and he punched the girl in the kidneys hard enough to make her gasp in pain.

"Enough!" The mayor's wife struggled against the shackles she was held in, trying to break free from another of Gleason's men. "He's told you everything he knows!"

"*Silence*!" The man holding the mayor's wife's chains jerked them hard enough that she fell awkwardly onto her back, the shackles causing her to cry out in pain as they dug into her flesh. "You will only speak when spoken to."

Murmurs from the crowd surrounding the spectacle were quickly turning hostile, but Gleason had no concerns. His pristine white uniform told them everything they needed to know. You might be able to argue with a Blue Warden, or even fight with a member of the Black. But no one *ever* stepped out of line around the branch that specialized in investigations and executions.

"Why don't we start from the beginning." Gleason's tone made it clear it wasn't a question. He snapped his fingers, and one of his men ran over with a camp chair so he could have a seat. "Tell me what happened, from the moment this stranger walked into town, to the moment he left."

As the lycan spewed forth more lies, Gleason thought back to how close he must have been to meeting his target on the trail the first day he had set forth from Greendown. If it hadn't been for those foolish bandits creating a second path through the forest, he could have ended his mission before going through all this trouble. Considering how easily the bandits had been defeated by Holden and his few followers, all the testimonies of their former 'captives' were hardly believable. A bare handful of people—even if he believed that one of them was Captain Cross—wouldn't have been able to take down an organized group of any proper size.

It was far more likely this village had been working in concert with a small band of miscreants, and the undead were a fabrication used to scare those not in on their plans. Gleason didn't think the *entire* village was bad, after all. But when they let a dirty *shifter* lead them, they were barely better than the dregs of society. That was why he was back here, in this flyspeck on the map, trying to learn more about his target. If they'd had even a modicum of capability or competence, he'd never have been sent here to correct their many mistakes. Although he was vastly overqualified for the task, he was nothing if not a servant of the people, and would see his mission completed with the humility and grace he was renowned for.

His men had already tracked his target back along the trail to a village stricken by some kind of plague, and lost them shortly after. Let the Healers' Guild do their job for once, and enter that Trinity-forsaken place. He knew no one else would, after all. It was clear that they'd done the only sensible thing and left the village to its fate and moved on. Even Gleason's Long Eye spell couldn't follow them through the dense forest. It was too much ground to cover, and he had no place from which to start his search, even if he had the mana to spare. There was no way they would have risked the sickness in the last place they were spotted, so that left this village as his best chance of finding out where James Holden was going next.

"...and then, they left. None of them spoke of going anywhere else, besides heading to Greendown, like I said before." The mayor wiped at the trickle of blood running down the corner of his mouth. "That's all I can tell you."

"And you expect me to believe that. Do you think I'm a fool, mayor? If what you said was true, they would have reached the city days ago. I've certainly received no word of them, and I would be the first to know." Gleason stood, pulling out his boot knife. "I think, perhaps, you've misunderstood the situation you're in. Maybe you just aren't *hearing* me." He reached out, viper-quick, pulling the mayor's ear out from his head before slashing it off in one stroke. "Perhaps this will help you listen." Gleason moved to cover up the motion with his body so the crowd couldn't see it at first, waiting to see how effective it would be before revealing his actions.

The bear shifter only gave a short grunt of pain, barely reacting to losing a portion of his flesh. It disappointed Gleason to see the lycan was so resilient, but he couldn't help but feel the flash of excitement at what it meant. To find the man's limits, he would have to try something else. He stepped back and tossed the ear aside as he unlimbered the whip coiled on his belt.

"No!" The daughter, upon seeing what Gleason had done, managed to pull free of the White Warden holding her. While the mayor and his wife were in shackles meant to control shifters, they didn't have enough sets to use on the girl. They were expensive, after all, and Gleason wasn't in the habit of taking shifters prisoner. The girl immediately started to change, heavy claws growing from her fingertips as her face elongated into a snout and thick fur sprouted from her body. Surprisingly, she still managed to speak during her transformation. *"Leave him alone, you monster!"*

The shifter girl, now a three-hundred-pound grizzly bear, slapped another of Gleason's men away as he tried to rush toward her. Blood flew as the shifter's claws slashed his man's chest, staining his white clothing red.

Smiling, Gleason flicked his wrist in an almost lazy fashion, cracking his whip across the mayor's chest and upper arms, flaying his skin to the bone. This time, the stoic man couldn't hold back the scream that erupted from his throat. The magic embedded in the leather, silver, and steel braids made any wounds burn like they had been doused in salt and acid, compounding the agony the man felt.

"Come, little bear." Gleason's ice-chip eyes seemed to burn with excitement, and sparks danced from his free hand. "Let me show you what happens when you defy a White Warden."

She charged him, rumbling forward on all fours. The onlookers gaped at the spectacle, taken aback by the sudden turn of events. They knew—they all knew—that the moment the girl had struck a Warden, her life was forfeit.

Gleason's favorite part of his job was being an executioner. Even though he hated being outside the city, it did have its perks.

Like getting to decide *how* to execute criminals. Inside the city, he had to bow to his uncle's orders. Here, *he* was the highest authority. Gleason could make much better examples of criminals, so things like this in the future didn't need to happen. He was more than happy to sacrifice the shifter girl so that others would make better choices in their lives. It would give some meaning to her worthless life, and that made it an even better reason for him to enforce the law.

He let her get close enough to think she had a chance, then leapt over her, scoring her back with his whip. Gleason was impressed that the girl didn't immediately collapse, and instead spun around, ready to charge him once again. To encourage her, he cracked his whip at her father, neatly splitting the knuckles of the hand clenching his chest.

The bear reared up on two legs, letting loose a chest-shaking roar before charging at Gleason once again. This time, he used his free hand to cast a spell that caused a fist of air to punch the shifter hard enough to stop her dead in her tracks. He slashed his arm back and forth, leaving two thick lines of bleeding flesh across the bear's chest and stomach. This time, it was too much for the young lycan to take, and she dropped to the ground, trying to back away. Gleason whipped her again, this time catching her across the snout.

The bear whimpered in pain, and tried to turn and run. His whip caught her around the trailing foot, nearly severing it as he jerked backward hard enough to pull the heavy shifter off her feet. She whimpered once, before falling unconscious, the pain too much for her to take. Her naked form slowly started to change back into that of a human, and Gleason rolled his wrist, ready to whip her again.

"Stop! *Please!*" The shifter woman, still on her back, tried to get to her feet. The White Warden standing over her put his boot on her abdomen, holding her in place. "Have *mercy*. She's just a *child!*"

"I'll-I'll tell you anything! Just leave my daughter alone!" The mayor had sprouted hair along his cheeks and arms, but the magic in the shackles kept him from doing more. That he could even push through enough of the magic to do what he had was impressive, and showed how powerful of a shifter the mayor was. "I know things! Important things!"

Gleason let loose a sigh. He had been hoping the mayor would have been able to provide at least a little more of a break from his boredom. His whip, as if it had a mind of its own, uncurled from the girl's ankle and rolled back up. He made sure not to dismiss the spell that inflicted pain on the wounds, though. There would be no escape from the agony for these unclean things. If left unattended, it would fade naturally after a few weeks' time. Some were driven insane by it. But those who made it through came out changed for the better. Just another perk of Gleason's position, helping to improve the little people beyond what they could ever achieve on their own. His eyes swept over the mob of witnesses, who all flinched back after his display of power. It was good they knew their place, now that he had reminded them of it.

"You are not in a position to bargain with me, Mayor." Gleason flicked off a bit of fur-encrusted flesh from the end of his whip as he approached. "You are going to tell me everything you know. And I do mean *everything*. At the end of our conversation, I'm going to finish punishing your daughter for assaulting a White Warden."

His wife wailed in distress, but was cut off by a thump from his man.

"The severity of her punishment will be measured against the quality and quantity of the information you have provided me. Now, I would encourage you to hold nothing back, as her survival surely depends upon it."

This time, as the mayor started to talk, Gleason paid close attention. Their discussion went on well past lunch, and finally, as early afternoon started to pass, the mayor ran out of things to talk about. His rasping and dry voice trailed off, and he looked up at the leader of the White Wardens with nothing but fear in his eyes.

"Good. You have done well, Mayor. I think you might have even told me enough to save your daughter's life." Gleason motioned to his men, who had fashioned a pair of posts while he had been interrogating the mayor. "She still needs to be held up as an example to anyone who learns of this, but she can do so by telling the story herself."

As his men strung her up, he ignored the pleading of the mayor and his wife. Gleason had already explained to them what was going to happen, and felt no remorse for their unlawful ways. Knowingly consorting with people who were actively planning to weaken the guilds was always going to end up with them paying the price in blood, and he was here to collect.

The girl's shifter nature had allowed her to heal some of the damage over the last few hours, which only allowed him to push the limit even farther. Gleason's control of his whip was precise enough that he never cut too deep, only flaying open the girl's skin in careful layers over her back and abdomen. He made sure to take one eye, and scar her face evenly on both sides. At some point, one of his men cut out the mother's tongue. She had probably said something to deserve it. The mayor had dropped to his knees, tears running clean streaks through his dirty cheeks. He was a defeated man, without a spark of defiance left. No one else in the village would meet Gleason's eye, all of them only looking at their feet.

"There. Now, the spirit of the law has been followed and enforced. Beyond punishing the mayor himself, of course. Since his wife and daughter are crippled, I choose to leave him whole, so they won't starve to death out here on the frontier. I can *certainly* show mercy." Gleason looked around at his men for approval, and they all murmured their agreement. He then pointed at the heavy emblem hanging from the mayor's neck. "Oh, and he isn't the mayor anymore. No lawbreaking lycan should be in charge of a frontier village in need of strong, *proper* leadership. Choose someone from yourselves to take his place, or I will do it for you."

A haughty older teen, just shy of his twenties, broke from the group and took the pendant from the man, shoving the old mayor in the dirt before putting it on his own neck. "I'll take it, Mister Warden."

"Fine. I'm sure you will be an upstanding example."

The new mayor turned to leave, but Gleason cleared his throat to stop him.

"Give them a day to gather their things, and then run them out of town. If anyone stands against you…burn their house to ashes."

The young mayor seemed happy to get Gleason's orders, as any small-town leader should. The crowd quickly dispersed, leaving the platoon of Wardens to their own devices. A few villagers collected up the bleeding wife and daughter, while the former mayor followed them numbly.

"Let's go. Perhaps taking a look at the farmhouses around Greendown will reveal the location of our wayward targets."

As Gleason and his men prepared their horses, he thought over the past few days. He had learned much from this excursion. There was a growing rot all throughout the city, and it was his job to dig it out, one he was looking forward to doing.

After, of course, he killed James Holden.

CHAPTER 38

We made it to the cheese factory well before dark, but the heavy clouds made it seem otherwise. It couldn't have been much past four in the afternoon, yet everyone except Jess and I were nearly stumbling around in the dark. She had stayed back with Murphy and Cross while Leedy and I had moved up to check the front of the long stone building. While I was still checking it out, my vision filled with text.

> **Title Upgraded**: Werebears Aren't Care Bears II
>
> -Your involvement has caused an entire Werebear family extreme pain and agony!
>
> **Skill Imparted**: Your attacks have a 7% chance to stun any ursine opponents. Staring down an ursine opponent has a 4% chance of intimidating it into submission.

> **Title Upgraded**: Law of Unintended Consequences IX
>
> -Your past actions have led to innocents being unnecessarily injured, maimed, or killed!
>
> **Skill Imparted**: Physical and magical damage is reduced by 9% while attempting to right the wrongs of your past—but only while in combat against those responsible. No one is perfect, but you should do better.

"Damn." I clenched my fists, quietly grinding my teeth. Apparently, something had happened to the mayor of the village we had been to, and it was my fault. It wasn't the first time I had earned the 'Unintended Consequences' title, but it still felt like a punch to the gut. While I wasn't the biggest fan of the mayor, I had no bad feelings toward his family. They had done nothing wrong. The family's connection to the Sailors' Guild was even a very important key to my future plans. I looked over at Leedy. "Remember how Cross was supposed to kill me? What would your Commandant do after he didn't report back?"

"You want to talk about that right now?" Leedy and I were still crawling forward in the grass, moving slowly so we didn't draw attention. "It isn't exactly the best time."

"Just, humor me." I peeked above the grass, still not seeing any movement. "Let's say your *Oracle* got impatient and sent someone else. Who would it be?"

Leedy grunted as he pulled himself over a sharp rock before answering. "Oh, I'd say it would be his nephew, Commander Gleason. He's the person in charge of the White Wardens. They're who should have been sent in the first place, but everybody knows Gleason is barely better than a rabid dog." Leedy grimaced at some past memory. "He's broken inside, like a puzzle that's missing the most important pieces." Leedy described to me some of the rumors he had heard, along with a few facts about how the man went about enforcing the law. "His family is important, though, so he always seems to end up in charge, even if someone else might be a better choice."

"Wow. This guy sounds like a real piece of work. So, you wouldn't be surprised if he were to hurt someone to get information about us?" I angled my approach so I could get close to a building next to the road. "Say, that bear shifter mayor and his family?"

He grabbed my leg to stop me. "That is *very* specific. Did you cast some kind of secret magic or something that told you this?" Leedy's grip tightened on my calf. "I'm serious. This isn't the time to joke."

I let out a long breath. "You could say it was a kind of magic, I guess. All I know is someone attacked them, and it has something to do with me. I don't know if they're dead or alive, but I do know it happened recently."

"How recently?" Leedy let go of my leg and looked back in the direction we had come. "If it was the White Wardens, they're probably riding chargers. They could make it down the trail in a fraction of the time we did if they ran them the whole way."

"There's nobody in that town who knows where we are." I pointed a thumb at the cheese factory. "We're in the middle of nowhere, remember? They might have some kind of spell to track us down, but if it was that easy, they would have already used it. Either way, there's nothing we can do about it at the moment. Now, we should finish this. Before we run out of time."

Leedy nodded in agreement, and the two of us refocused on the vampires. I wouldn't be able to help the werebear family if I was drained of blood, or inhabited by a lich. I finally made my way to the hut that had once served as the guard house to the facility.

"I don't like this." Leedy was crouched next to me in the tall grass. "I know the sun is hiding behind those clouds, but it won't matter much to the vampires."

"Don't bet on it." I looked to the west, where I knew the sun had to be. "Maybe a younger vampire can run around, but an elder vampire is sensitive to even the slightest ultraviolet radiation. They aren't going to get zapped by a full moon or anything, but direct rays, even through heavy clouds, will cook them up like a bucket straight out of a Kentucky Fried drive-through."

Leedy looked at the side of my head, probably trying to see if my brains were leaking out of my ears or not. "I swear, half of what you say is pure nonsense."

"You're not wrong." I shucked my pack and leaned it up against the building, making sure it was out of sight. We had both already seen that the only entrance on the front side of the building was blocked off by an overturned wagon, meaning we needed to find an alternate way inside. "Tell everyone else to drop their stuff off here, and I'll swing around the south side while you all swing north. We meet on the back side and plan our entry from there."

He gave me a thumbs-up, and the two of us split apart.

I stayed low, keeping below the top of the grass. I had almost completely maximized my perception, making it easy to see where I was going. It was also easy to smell the scent of old blood and rotten meat, mingled with rotten milk. Time to dial back the ol' sense of smell a bit, before I went nose blind to the funk. Not that it would have been a bad thing, but I didn't want to rob myself of an early warning system if I didn't have to.

What I wasn't getting a lot of was noise. Either the stone walls were incredibly thick, there wasn't anything inside, or they knew we were here and were keeping quiet. Given the smell and my luck, it was definitely the last option.

I had to wait a good five minutes for the others to catch up with me on the opposite side. It had given me enough time to spot three likely places we could enter, which made all of them bad choices. A large, empty window frame, a set of double doors warped open by age and neglect, and a smaller door on the western side that looked to still be in working condition were all we had. The five of us grouped up behind a pile of rusted-out milk containers less than fifty feet from the largest entrance at the rear. I laid out what I had seen, and we quickly agreed on one thing.

"It's definitely a trap." Murphy peeked through the containers at the double doors before ducking back down. "There's no way that's not a trap. They want us to go in there."

Cross pointed the way they had come. "We saw another window on the side that's been boarded up. We could go in there." He looked at the open window near the double doors. "Not that it's a better option."

"Why don't we just throw spells at them until they have to come outside and face us? We could use bigger spells, coordinate attacks, and keep from getting overwhelmed or cornered. Wouldn't that be easier?" Jess looked around at us, obviously confused as to why we hadn't already just said so. "Am I missing something?"

"It's as good a plan as any, Jess. There's only one problem." I held out my hand in an upside-down '*V*' and prepared the delving spell that I had used on the well back in the quarantine village. One cast, and I could already tell that there was an extensive underground area. "There's a big basement, and I think they've expanded it. They can just retreat down there and wait for us to run out of spells."

"You're assuming they're smart enough to do that." Leedy tapped his nose at me. "Not every enemy makes good decisions."

"But to hope for their stupidity is to plan for failure." Cross pointed at me. "We all know the best plan is for you to send in a big spell and set off whatever ambush is prepared for us. The rest of us can fight what comes out. After that, we go in and clean up what's left."

I shook my head. "I don't think a full-frontal attack on a lich is the best option. Well, it is, but we need to be more surgical. It would be better to create our own entrance by punching a hole through the ceiling all the way to the basement, and take on the strongest enemy while we're at our best. The vampires won't be able to run while the sun is out, so after the lich is gone, we focus on them. Zombies, ghouls, and whatever else can get mopped up after we're done with the greater undead."

"And how, exactly, do we survive being inside the basement long enough to kill the lich without getting ripped apart by the rest of them?" Surprisingly, Cross didn't sound combative. He sounded genuinely curious. "Because that would be quite the trick."

"Remember when it was just you and me, and I tried out that strip of fabric that messed up all those undead?" He nodded, and I held up the artificial monster core. "I think I can do it again, but better this time."

Once Cross was in on the plan, the others quickly agreed. Instead of fabric, I used a strip of wood this time. It only took me a few minutes to carve out the runes with my pocket knife, and I had to prick the finger of everyone present to include their blood in the creation of the device. The majority of the blood was mine to ensure it would be strong, but using theirs would ensure they would be excluded from the aura when it activated. Seating the lumpy piece of hardened mana in the hole I cut for it was a chore, since it wasn't a perfect circle. I had to wedge a few slivers of wood in the gaps so it wouldn't fall out, and I knew it wouldn't hold up if someone bumped it too hard. It would have to do.

"Is it ready to go?" Jess had been looking over my shoulder while I worked, literally breathing down my neck. "It doesn't look like much."

"Yep, it's ready." I passed it off to her. She took it with wide eyes, almost dropping it. "When things kick off, I'm going to be too busy to watch over that thing. It's up to you to guard it." I pointed to the section of the rune sequence that activated the pull on the core. "Just push a bit of mana in here, and set it on the ground. Once it goes off, we'll have a good five to ten minutes before it burns out."

"There's a big difference between five and ten minutes, James." Leedy didn't seem amused at such an unspecific time frame. "In a fight, that's a *huge* difference."

Looking back at him, I shrugged. "Well, considering I've used one of these once, with a piece of fabric, it's the best guess I can make. What I *can* say for sure is, anything strong enough to withstand the aura it creates is going to do their best to destroy that thing. So, protecting it needs to be a priority."

"I'll help Jess." Murphy had his halberd ready to go, with a short sword on his hip. His breastplate and helm were polished, and the runes on both thrummed with unused power. He was certainly ready. "They won't get through the both of us."

"We're wasting daylight. Come on." Cross led us to the side of the building with the boarded-up window, where we took turns helping each other onto the roof. It was made of slate, giving it a stone look like the rest of the building, and flat enough that we didn't have a problem finding footing.

For once, I didn't have a memory to remind me of something. Assaulting an undead stronghold through the roof with only four people to back me up? Definitely a first. I cast my delving spell again, picking the place that seemed to be most central to the underground area. It was actually near the front door of the building, which would have been the last place we would have been able to easily access had we gone through the rear entrance.

"Is everyone ready?" I looked around, getting confirmation from each of them. We had checked and rechecked our gear so many times it was pointless to do it again. "Okay. The first spell is going to clear the way, the second is going to make room for us, and the third is going to let us drop down without getting hurt. The moment we confirm the lich is nearby, or we start to get overrun, Jess activates the core. She and Murphy guard it, while the rest of us kill as many of them as we can." I held out my hand, forming a fist. Lightning danced around it as I forced mana into the spell that built across my knuckles. "Here we go!"

My punch slammed into the roof, shattering tile downward in a funnel of destruction. The spell I had used was a variation of Earthen Spike, but I hadn't properly formed it into something solid. By leaving it more 'free,' it allowed the energy to explode downward in a cylinder shape that took what materials were available instead of creating any from mana. Basically, it was a homemade tunneling spell that dropped a tube of stone pulled from the building into the basement.

Screams from undead throats echoed out from below, and I answered them with a swarm of fireballs. Instead of one big spell like in the clearing, I cast a series of smaller ones to reduce the strain on my mana reserves. A wave of heat rushed out of the hole, so I twisted my wrist, causing a small vortex to form. Flames leapt upward, carrying with them the smell of dust and roasted meat. Rotten roasted meat. The column of flames shot so high that it seemed to touch the bottom of the clouds.

"How are we supposed to go down there?!" Leedy was missing part of his eyebrows after trying to look down the hole, and I wasn't sure whether the redness on his face was from the heat or if he was mad at the surprise makeover. "We'll be cooked alive!"

"I'll admit, maybe fire wasn't the best choice." I moved over to the other corner of the roof. The underground section here wasn't as deep, but it was still wide open enough to give us room to fight unobstructed. "What can I say? I'm not perfect." I punched downward again, casting another makeshift cylinder digging spell. Air rushed in, feeding the flames before black smoke came pouring out. I cast a series of wind blades to clear it enough to see, and I deemed it clear enough to risk it. "Come on, before they realize what we're doing!"

As everyone jumped, I used the vortex spell to slow our fall enough that we could reach the bottom without breaking our legs. It was still a hard fall, and the uneven ground caused by the chunks of stone covering the ground from my spell meant it was easy to twist an ankle. Murphy let out a curse as he came down, and I rushed over to help him to his feet before he could ask.

"That wasn't fun." Murphy grunted in pain as my healing spell straightened out his leg. It had been a complete dislocation, meaning it was going to be extra sore for a long time. It was one of those injuries that stuck with you no matter how much healing energy you dumped into the body.

My eyes asked him the obvious question in the flickering light of the fires caused by my spells.

"I'm good. I can walk. Just don't ask me to run anytime soon."

The room we had landed in had probably once been meant to store wheels of cheese, but the wooden racks had long since gone to rot. The dividing walls had been smashed to rubble, turning the entire basement into one large open area with the occasional section left standing to hold up the building above. I could see the dug-out section of the basement where my first breeching attempt had gone off, flames still leaping high enough that the floors above were burning. Suddenly, I was glad we hadn't landed there. It had been their refuse pit, and the source for the raw materials the lich necromancer needed to make his undead abominations. As we watched, several amalgamations of bone and flesh tried to climb free of the pit as the magical fire ate away at their substance.

A high-pitched scream meant to freeze a man's brain into slush hit us with a physical force, causing the runes on everyone's helms to light up. My shield bracelet glowed red, telling me it was repelling an active magical assault. A charred skeleton came clacking into view, its blackened fangs somehow more prominent than any vampire I had ever seen before. Its eyes glowed with green eldritch flames, scorching the skull's sockets as they rolled wildly in the dark. When it finally spoke, it did so straight into our minds, despite our protections.

How nice of you to present yourself to me, my new vessel. You have no idea how much trouble it would have caused if I had been forced to chase you halfway across the known world. As a reward, I'll have to do something nice for you. Perhaps a pleasant dreamscape for your soul to reside in, while I take control of your body? Hmm? Would that be nice?

Jess glanced over at me before looking back at the vampire skeleton. "I guess we found the lich."

CHAPTER 39

We only had a moment's warning that more undead were coming, when a rain of pebbles dropped from the hole we had just fallen through. The first thing that came through was a zombie that was little more than a skeleton, and the fall caused it to shatter into pieces. Jess backed away from the new avenue of attack, cornering herself in the back of the room. Murphy followed, killing the next creature that fell through the hole by lopping its head off before it could even fully stand. It had either been a young vampire or a fresh zombie, but in this case it didn't matter much.

"Should I do it?" Jess had the plank of wood held behind her, out of sight of the lich. "There aren't as many as we thought there were going to be."

"Wait until the right moment. You'll know it when you see it." I gave her a thumbs-up for encouragement, and twisted my yari spear, snapping free the blade. "It's time to make this bastard pay." A vampire came flying out of the darkness at me, so I used a flick of my wrist to help boost its jump straight into the burning pit of flames. A certain Johnny Cash song popped in my head, and I chuckled as I focused back on my primary target.

Somehow, Cross had managed to get in front of the lich before I could, his sword at the high ready. His stump was held out to his side, helping to balance him like a professional fencer. "You were in my head, creature. I demand payment for this injustice."

I had to give the one-armed bandit some credit. He certainly still had both huevos.

Yes, I suppose I should have left you better off than when I arrived. It's poor form for a visitor to leave a mess, even if it was for a short while. The lich waved a bony hand, and a bolt of pure darkness shot out of his fingers.

Cross managed to mostly dodge it, catching a glancing blow on his breastplate. His sword slashed downward, clanging off the lich's forearm bones as if they were made of steel. The possessed skeleton grabbed Cross by the groin, picking him straight up off the ground and throwing him over his shoulder, where he bounced across the ground twice before going still.

Never mind about the both huevos thing, I guess.

A follow-up bolt of darkness from the lich caught him in the back, and Cross jerked in pain.

While they were fighting, the rest of us hadn't been idle. Leedy had been killing everything that tried dropping through the hole, while Jess and Murphy were fighting off the lone burning flesh amalgamation that had made it out of the pit. I was closing in on the lich while beating off the occasional vampire who showed itself—and by beating off, I meant violently dismembering.

"Hey, Sparky, why don't you pick on someone your own size?" I cast a bolt of lightning empowered by my mana generator, and it seemed to have an effect. A pair of ribs got blown off, and it looked like the fires in the lich's eyes weren't burning quite as bright. "Glad I could get your attention. You know, I've got a nine-volt battery I think you would really get along with. Maybe you just need to meet someone to bring out the best in you."

I think I've changed my mind about the pleasant dreamscape. Instead, I will be removing your fingernails for eternity.

The lich grabbed for my throat, trying to subdue me.

I had to admit, he was fast. But I was faster. I dodged the grasping hand, and stomp-kicked his knee the wrong direction. If it had been a living person, that would have ended the fight rather quickly. Instead, it only made the lich stumble back into a pile of rubble.

"You know, Sparky, things would go a lot easier if I knew where your phylactery was hiding." I cast an earth spell, holding out my pinky in a sweeping motion and forcing the stone to enclose around him like a cage. It struggled for a moment, but it was quickly obvious there was no escape with me standing in front of it. "I would make things go way quicker for you. Even with your threats, I promise, it won't even hurt very much."

I didn't want to do this, vessel. Your unwillingness to understand your position has forced my hand. Just know, the results of this day rest on your head. The green fires of its eyes flashed, and what we had thought were solid walls fell away, revealing undead packed together so tightly that they had shown up on my delving spell as solid material. An enemy force that numbered in the hundreds now counted in the thousands.

I was looking at generations of people the lich had dug up and enslaved for his army, and it pissed me off.

"Jess, now!" My warning shout was unnecessary, because Jess and Murphy had been backed up against two of the walls that had just come down. They were already neck-deep in angry undead, and only Murphy's furious fighting and Jess managing to cast Earthen Wall spells had kept them alive long enough for her to place the piece of wood on a flat section of the floor.

When the spell activated, the difference between wood and fabric was immediately noticeable. Instead of a dense fog focused on the immediate area, a gray haze covered the entire underground space, blanketing it in a light coating of heavy oppression. Even the lich seemed cowed, trying to double over in his stone cage.

"Now's our chance!" Leedy was the first to capitalize on the opportunity, rapidly maximizing his time available by removing the heads of everything within reach of his sword. "Kill them all while you can!"

Everyone exploded into action, taking out as many undead as they could. It was obvious to me almost immediately that it was no use. Even with thirty minutes, we wouldn't be able to kill the lich's army of undead with conventional means. We were going to have to retreat and do it some other way. The distraction did give me a chance to check on Cross, who had miraculously been left alone after getting manhandled by the lich.

A quick inspection showed me his body had been infected by the necrotic energy the lich had used. Considering we were still in the middle of a battle, I couldn't completely empty my mana in an attempt to heal him. Instead, I focused on just getting him back in the fight. A quick pulse of healing energy with a circle on his forehead was enough to make his eyes flutter open.

"You back in it?" I saw his eyes focus on my face, and Cross grimaced in pain before giving me a sharp nod. "Good, because we need you."

"Help me up."

I pulled him back to his feet, and Cross wobbled a bit before standing firm.

"I'm good."

He definitely wasn't, as I could see the veins of necrotic energy pulsing under his skin.

"Okay man, you go for it!" I put his sword in his hand and slapped him on his back, sending him stumbling toward a horde of zombies.

He turned the stumble into a charge, and was quickly chopping off heads and limbs like a pro. I'm sure he'd be fine.

Your struggles are pointless. It's only a matter of time until you and your friends are overwhelmed. If you give yourself to me now, I will allow your friends the opportunity to join my army as something more than just the fodder that you see before you now.

"I have an idea. How about you shut your bitch-ass up?" I channeled my mana and worked a slab of kinetic energy into a certain slapping spell I'd seen Cross perform once before, and that I had practiced once or twice in my free time. The nearly translucent form of a hand manifested as the spell bitch-slapped the lich across the face hard enough to knock his bottom jaw loose. It was every bit as satisfying as I hoped it would be. The lich's jaw dangled free by a strip of flesh, swinging back and forth like a macabre metronome. "Too bad that won't actually keep you quiet."

There is nothing you can do against me. None of your magic can do me permanent harm, and because I am not a fool, my phylactery isn't anywhere nearby. Even if you defeat me here, for an immortal it is but a temporary setback. It is only a matter of time until you—

An explosion rang out from up above, stunning us both. We looked at each other carefully, gauging whether the other was responsible.

"That wasn't either of us, was it?"

The lich shook its head, and I jumped to my feet, casting a spell to reinforce the stone prison trapping the skeleton. Its struggles intensified now that there were party crashers, but my mana was still too densely layered in the stone for it to break free. While it fought to get loose, the lich must have ordered a sizable portion of its forces to go up and battle whatever had come to visit, because the back ranks of the horde disappeared into the darkness.

There was another explosion, and a scream from up above told me it was at least a human in persuasion who was invading. And from the sounds of it, there were a lot more than just one. Leedy and Cross were already closing in on the wooden plank where Jess and Murphy were fighting, so I moved to join them.

It was as good a place as any to make our stand. Either the new person or persons would get killed and we would end up facing the rest of the undead, the undead would get wiped out and we would make some new friends, or the undead would be unalived for good and we would fight some new and exciting enemies. Either way, we were in for a long evening. The basement walls getting ripped out made the entire structure unstable, and any overly destructive spells would certainly bring the building down on our heads. We would need to wear them down slowly, as long as our stamina could hold out. No matter what happened, I had to make sure my mana stayed above a quarter of my total reserves. I still had a date with Sparky, and there was no way I was taking a rain check.

"Focus on the bloodsuckers!" Jess cast her version of Stone Dart, taking a vampire through the eye. "They're still weak from the aura!"

Now that I could focus on the fodder, I realized how many vampires there actually were. Under the influence of the aura, they weren't moving around much better than the zombies. There were a couple of elder vampires herding groups of their brethren forward onto our blades, so I targeted them first. A couple of surprise flame darts didn't finish them off, but it certainly distracted them from helping.

The four men stood back-to-back, with Jess standing in the middle. She cast her Stone Darts over our shoulders as fast as she could, keeping anything from flanking us. Our weapons worked with practiced efficiency, and I cut down undead by the dozens. The blade of my spear was a blur as it cut through anything that dared walk in front of me.

I was just starting to feel like we were making progress, and everyone else seemed to notice that the density of enemies was easing off, when the aura helping to slow down the undead flickered. The only thing the lich could move was its head, and it swiveled its broken skull to look at me.

It's almost time. You won't believe the things we can accomplish together. If you would only acquiesce to the inevitable, you would see that this isn't such a bad thing for you.

"Right back at you, bub." I cast another fireball at the center of the basement for emphasis, providing us with more light and taking out another wave of reinforcements before they could close in.

As if to answer, another fireball—this one more red than my blue—flew down the stairs on the opposite side of the basement. It splashed over the stone steps like water, washing away the undead like they were sandcastles built too close to the waterline. It was the closest thing to napalm I had seen since world five, where I had gained my Alchemist profession and had actually seen some used to clear out Creeping Reaper Vines.

"Commander, down here!" The first person down the stairs was a Warden dressed in a similar style to what I had first seen Cross, Leedy, and Murphy wearing, but he was in all white instead of blue. He had the unfortunate luck to run into the aura our artificial core was producing, and immediately dropped to his knees before tumbling down the stairs into the fire.

Oops.

Cross immediately turned to shut off the device, but I held out the butt of my spear to block him. "Not yet. We've still got a few minutes left. Kill as many as you can while it still lasts."

He was furious with me, but gave me a quick nod before getting back into the fight. There hadn't been time to tell him about the werebear family, or perhaps seeing another member of his Guild die reminded him that he was supposed to kill me. Either way, he wasn't opposed to killing more undead.

The rest of us redoubled our efforts, doing our best to thin out the undead as much as possible while we still held the advantage.

Considering the situation, I started to let loose a little more with my spells. I tried to keep them small, using things like wind blades to extend the attacks with my spear, and earthen spikes to shape the battlefield to our advantage for when the aura finally dropped.

When it started flickering, the fight quickly got more dangerous. It was hard to predict the jerking attacks of the faster zombies, and the vampires were smart enough to start using the brief moments of unrestricted movement to actually *throw* zombies at us.

"Get closer!" I quickly erected two walls to either side of us, only leaving two directions to defend. With both Murphy and I using polearms, the thrown enemies weren't as much of a problem. The spikes I had placed earlier made it harder for them to flat out rush us, so Cross stood with me to cover the front while Leedy and Jess joined Murphy in the back. "If it gets too rough, let me know and I'll close up this side too. We'll be trapped, but we can focus all our strength on one side."

"Don't worry about us—you just handle yourselves!" Murphy's halberd chopped into a particularly juicy zombie, slamming it off to the side where Leedy could finish it off. "We've got this."

I looked over at Cross, who was somehow moving even faster than when we had started. "How are you feeling?" The black veins that covered his body throbbed with his heartbeat, strong and steady despite the situation. "You don't look so good."

"I…I feel better than good." Cross took two quick steps forward and cut a vampire's head off with a flawless rising draw cut. He was so fast, the undead creature couldn't attempt a dodge, even with the flickering death aura. A single jump backward, and he was in position next to me again. "See?"

"Yeah, I definitely see." I reached out a hand to try to diagnose him, but a shout from the stairs stopped me cold.

"*James Holden*!" A man wearing plate armor covered by an immaculate white robe was standing there, looking straight at me. At least, I thought he was looking at me. It was dark, and he was wearing a helm, but I was pretty sure. He cracked a whip that exploded the head of another vampire who tried to charge him up the stairs, and somehow still managed to remain spotless. "I've been ordered by the gods to come and kill you."

"You're going to have to go back up top and check in with reception to get a number." I gestured at the undead. "There's a line, and these guys were here first."

The lich poked his head up again, looking between the two of us. *Oh my. Things just got interesting…*

CHAPTER 40

The aura device didn't seem to bother the Warden as he came down the stairs. He was forced to deal with the undead trying to swarm him just as much as we were, but his whip sliced through them like they weren't even there. It had to be powerfully enchanted, on top of him pushing a hefty amount of mana into it.

"James, I think that's the guy I told you about!" Leedy shouted back over his shoulder at me while he fought against a vampire who was using a femur like a club. "He's probably the one who hurt the mayor and his family!"

"What's he talking about?" Cross moved so quickly that his sword was a blur to everyone but me, clearing some space so we could talk for a few uninterrupted moments. His job was made harder because his weapon was starting to warp from all the action we were seeing, probably made worse from clanging off the hardened bones of the lich earlier. "Who hurt what mayor?"

I cast another row of Earthen Spikes a little farther out on our rear to reduce the pressure on the others while I answered. "A type of magic informed me that the werebear family we met was injured because of me, so Leedy and I made an educated guess that it was some guy named Greasy."

"You mean Gleason. Commander Gleason, the man in charge of the Greendown Division of the White Wardens." Cross squinted at the armored man slowly making his way over to us in a storm of violence. "That certainly could be him. It…sounds like something he would do, and he does prefer using a whip."

"Well, you know what I'm going to do to him if he really was the one. Are you going to be okay with that? Or are you going to try and stop me?"

We were interrupted when I had to deal with another zombie thrown by a vampire who had been hiding behind a pile of rubble. Using a bit of mana around the blunt end of my spear, I whacked it away like a gruesome version of baseball. The vampire wasn't expecting the line drive to come right back at him, and the pair of undead went down in a tangle of limbs. "That's at least a double."

Cross brushed off the baseball commentary and looked at me seriously. "James, I…" He looked down at his stump of a hand for a moment, ignoring the battle around him. When his eyes met mine again, they were harder than stone. "I don't know if I will ever forgive you for taking my hand, but I understand now why you did it. You brought me low, and showed me the rotten foundations I stood upon. For that, I thank you." He glanced back over to the whip-wielding Warden, who was now more than halfway across the basement to us. "And to answer your question, no. I won't help you to fight the Wardens, but I won't stand in your way. Especially Commander Gleason. In fact, I'll make an exception for that one. He's everything that's wrong with them, all rolled into one person."

A section of the floor suddenly dropped, cutting off the direct path Gleason had to where we were standing. The ground shook as a meaty arm flopped onto the ground, and the mother of all super ghouls poked its head out of the hole in the ground.

"Well, shit. I better go handle that. Think you can stop Mister Fifty Shades of Grey reject over there while I handle the goliath?"

The man never even batted an eye at the movie reference. That alone told me that he was well on his way toward developing a sense of humor. Hallelujah. Either that, or he was just getting used to me. Cross simply gave me a sharp nod and started fighting his way over to where he would intercept Gleason as he circled the new pit in the ground.

I sprinted forward toward the giant ghoul, dodging a heavy punch that turned the zombies that were too slow to get out of the way into hamburger meat. The monster was too big to get out of the pit, but that didn't make it any less of a danger. If anything, it made killing the stupid thing even harder. I would normally hamstring something this big, then take it apart piece by piece. Since that wasn't an option, I had to play whack-a-mole, with me filling in for the mole. Every time I dodged a swing, I took a chunk out of the monster's arm. It had those annoyingly sharp bone spurs covering up most of its exposed flesh, making the task even more difficult.

Eventually, the ghoul made a mistake. It raised a hand to crush me, and one of its bone spurs got caught in the ceiling. The delay cost it an arm.

"Ass whoopin's for sale! Only costs an arm and a leg!" I cackled in glee as I cast an overpowered wind blade and followed up right behind it, using my spear blade to slide into the elbow joint and remove the limb with a pop. It made with the angry roars of pain, and I danced out of reach while it flailed around.

I glanced over to check on how Cross was doing, eagerly looking forward to the epic showdown. The culmination of my redemptive efforts. The proverbial straw that would break the camel's back of corruption. The crescendo of my labor to reach one lone Warden for the betterment of humanity. The snowflake that would unleash the avalanche of change in this world. I could even hear the orchestral soundtrack in my head as Vader confronted the Emperor. Grinning in anticipation, my eyes landed on the two embattled foes. The grin slid from my face and into the same confused head tilt of a dog watching its owners doing the horizontal mambo.

They were just…yelling at each other? What is this shit? A domestic dispute? Did Daddy slap Mommy at the dinner table? Get your shit together guys, and make with the stabbing! I rolled my eyes in exasperation as I dodged another reckless swing from the ghoul, its brain not computing that it was missing a good four feet of the distorted appendage.

"You were always a disgrace to the Wardens, Cross. But I can't believe you would deny *The Oracle*!" Gleason halfheartedly snapped his whip at Cross, who dodged it easily. "I'm going to enjoy showing you what it means to betray your oaths!"

"*I'm* the disgrace? You're barely human!" Cross tried to dart forward, slashing at Gleason's leading leg with his sword. His boosted speed surprised Gleason, but the White Warden's armor easily deflected the hit. Cross danced back as the whip cracked through the space where he had stood. "I've heard all about the things you've done to people. The lengths you'll go just so you can hurt someone."

"That's because they deserve it!" Gleason's whip cracked out, and this time Cross couldn't dodge in time. It cracked across his left forearm, scoring a line of searing pain just short of where he was missing his hand. "I'm the only one willing to go far enough to dig out the corruption you allow to rot!"

Whatever happened next was between the two of them, because I had to deal with a one-armed giant ghoul that figured out it could pick up its own severed limb and use it like a club. The good news was the wild swings were easier to dodge, and cleared out any interference from the other undead crowding the basement. The bad news was it got a lot harder to do any damage to the stupid thing.

I had to use another wind blade to cut the back of the ghoul's wrist as its arm swung past, cutting deep enough that the momentum caused the joint to give way. It tore its own hand off, sending the heavy arm it had been using as a club into a cluster of zombies near the stairs. The ghoul watched the lost limb disappear with a forlorn look on its face, so I used the opportunity to throw my spear through its eye into its brain. I must have hit something important, because it went limp. That might sound stupid at first—the spear went through its friggin' brain, after all—but the last super ghoul I'd fought had still stepped up to the plate with half its head missing. Apparently this one wasn't in the same caliber. It must have used all of its 'super-ness' on getting big instead of tough. I was also not prepared for it to die that fast, so I didn't manage to dodge out of the way when it collapsed forward onto me.

"Umph!" My breath exploded out of me as the heavy corpse squished me to the floor. I was stuck under its chest and shoulder, with only my right leg and arm sticking out like a squashed bug. I immediately tried wiggling myself free, but my armor was caught somewhere on one of the ghoul's bone spurs.

Of course, that's when a zombie noticed me and tried to take a chunk out of me, the opportunistic bastard. The undead creature tried to drop down and bite my face off, so I punched it in the chest. Even without good leverage, the dry and desiccated animated corpse was dusted. I looked past the crumbling body and saw Cross wasn't doing so well against Gleason. It was looking like it wasn't going to be a clean breakup. Damn, I hated the clingy types. I hoped Cross learned his lesson well. You never put your metaphorical religious dick into crazy.

The much better armored White Warden was like a bull, charging at Cross and waiting to see where he dodged before cracking his whip at him. Cross was bleeding from multiple wounds, mostly across his arms and legs. The black veins throbbing under his skin leaked a dark sludge that was streaked with his blood. Cross occasionally got a few hits in, but he was overmatched. His poor captain's sword was getting wrecked against the enchanted armor protecting Gleason, making it even harder for him to inflict any damage.

Knowing that there were going to be more frisky undead trying to get a piece of me, I doubled down on trying to wiggle myself free. The awkward position I was in made it way harder than it should have been, so I started to carefully raise earthen spikes under the ghoul, being careful not to stab myself or shift more of its weight onto me. Just as I was about to get free, I heard Cross shouting.

"No! James, look out!"

That bitch Gleason had realized that I was the home-wrecker, and I was now trapped ass-up in the dryer. I wasn't about to go out like that. I pushed harder at the dead weight with both my strength and magic, a thrill of fear and premonition shooting down my spine.

He yanked a medallion of some kind off his neck—forcing a simply gratuitous amount of mana into the thing, if the sudden influx of energy I felt was any indicator—and lobbed it underhand at me. Commander Assbutt just stole a page out of my playbook. The White Warden had just overloaded a high-quality rune device, and it was going to explode. It seemed to tumble through the air in slow motion, gathering in power as it flew over the hole in the floor.

The moment drew itself out into a sharp, silver-edged thread, as though pulled by fate itself. Even the trajectory was perfect, the mana straining the failsafes of the rune sequences, more than sufficient for its grim purpose. My bulging arms were bars of forged titanium as they strained against the weight pinning me. But it was the weight of the moment that truly held me in thrall. I shoved mana into the Earthen Spike spell, pushing the ghoul off of me and slicing a deep cut across my left hip as the bone spur that had caught on my belt was yanked free. I'd already known the bitter truth from the time the medallion left Gleason's fingertips, however. It wouldn't be enough.

My mind spun with calculations and angles, the vast weight of personal experience working each possibility in the potential of that one moment—and in the end, came up wanting. A grim determination settled on me even as my focus never diverted from the four and a half rotations the medallion had made in its flight. I was going to have to—

The broken, bent, and chipped blade of a Captain entered my narrowed vision like a mandate from the heavens, striking the artifact as if to deny the very gods themselves. Cross's bloodied and battered body had made a decisive lunge, his movement so fast that he was blurred, even to my superhuman senses. Unbowed, he struck at Gleason's surprise attack while a steely resolve furrowed his creased brow, even as he overextended himself, dropping any pretense of defense.

Stunned, I couldn't do anything but watch as Cross slapped the medallion away in midair with his sword, scoring the already strained runes and causing the artifact to explode. The blast sent him tumbling head over heels, bouncing off the torso of the ghoul I had finally forced to the side. I heard the crunch of bone and tearing muscle as he ricocheted away, and came to a sliding stop a few feet away. Like a morbid bank shot on the world's worst pool table, the collision forced the body of the ghoul closer to the sunken pit it had crawled from, pitching grotesquely as it slowly dropped back into the hole in the ground, and disappeared from sight. I limped over to Cross and grabbed him before we could be swarmed by more undead, dragging him back to where Jess and the others were waiting.

Gleason was immediately forced to fight off a fresh wave of zombies, led by a regular-sized super ghoul that forced him back for the moment.

"Are you two okay? That was crazy!" Jess ran over to help me pull him into cover. "What was that explosion?"

I checked over the unconscious man, seeing that he was in rough shape. The impact with the ghoul had definitely broken some ribs, and the whip injuries looked pretty bad. Somehow, he was still holding on to his sword. I was genuinely impressed. "That was Cross, making a choice. Even with my shield bracelet, there's no guarantee I'd have come out the other side of that explosion in one piece. Last time, he dove in front of a spear for me, knowing that the big bad guy had been defeated. He understood me, even then. Knowing he would be healed. This time, he didn't know how this fight would end."

My voice began to shift in tone, the patterns of speech becoming something more, something old and resonant with power. "He chose a Path. Even though he knew not the way, he found it nonetheless." I looked carefully at Cross and made my decision. I might regret giving up so much mana all at once in the midst of battle, but I could make it up with a few minutes of uninterrupted focus with my mana generator.

The mantle of my Judge profession settled heavily on my shoulders, and I grabbed Cross by his empty wrist.

His eyes snapped open, the sudden pain shocking him awake.

"You were judged for violating your conscience. You chose an easy evil, a wrong action, instead of making a hard, good, and right decision. Hiding behind an organization you were a part of to give yourself the ability to justify murder." Cross tried to pull away from me, but I didn't let go. "The purpose of your punishment was so you could see the error of your ways. And while there are many methods to fake true repentance, I believe you truly have seen the error of your actions."

Cross stopped struggling, and didn't try to pull away as I bit my inner cheek and spit the blood on his stump. He coughed, trying to clear his abused lungs. "How do you know I'm not faking it? That I'm not pretending to have changed?"

"Because, Cross. You've seen both sides of the coin now. You have judged people in the past, been judged yourself in turn, and didn't let it break you." I drew a circle across the top of his stump with my palm, smearing my blood and spit. Water and life. "Then, you did something that showed what is hiding inside yourself. When you described Gleason, you said 'he's everything that's wrong with *them*.' Meaning, you don't count yourself among 'them' anymore. You went and fought him, giving it your all. Then, when you were given a choice, you picked the wellbeing of another over yourself. I don't know about you, but it doesn't sound like you belong with the Wardens anymore. And it just so happens I know an organization that's *very* low on members that you can join." I waited a moment while he processed what I told him as I readied the ritual.

My eyes were lodestones that gripped and held his, even as the magic took me—the words ancient and not wholly my own. "Alexander Cross, former Captain of the Western Wardens, the Judged and Redeemed, the Crippled, Lich-Touched, and now, the Worthy." I had never even known his first name, the knowledge was suddenly there, provided by the magic of the ceremony. The mantle of Judge throbbed with power, the swirling ambient mana of the region ebbing as it coalesced around the two of us. Magic gathered into a primal Working, outside my control. It was a function of the Old Ways—a magic so fundamental and primordial that its roots ran into the very core of each world I had been sent to. It was a power so old and deep that the scraps of information I had gained on ancient tablets and sources tucked in dusty corners of elven libraries had hinted that it came from the same place as the gods themselves. That power—no, that *Power*—now gathered around Cross in a shroud, and called to him as it had called to me all those years ago. There weren't words, but it was a contract and a commandment all the same. It was a Covenant wrought in the very foundations of existence itself.

I held up my right hand. "Do you so swear to uphold the tenets of righteousness and justice? Do you swear to defend the weak and the oppressed, to show grace and mercy toward the innocent? Do you swear to Judge their oppressors and the unrighteous, and to take up the heavy burdens of responsibility? Alexander Cross, do you accept the Office of Judge, and all the inherent authorities, requirements, and privileges therein?"

His eyes widened when he realized what I was offering. A chance to become a Judge. The words came to him, the same way they did me. From elsewhere, and everywhere. "I make this blood oath of my own free will. I swear to be a defender of the weak, a guardian to those unable to defend themselves. I swear to be a warrior for good, a bulwark against those who wish darkness upon the innocent. I swear to punish the unjust, fairly and without bias. I swear to balance the scales. I swear to be a Judge." He gave me an almost imperceptible nod right before the mana I had called—but didn't fully control—rushed into him, flooding his body with healing energy. Time seemed to slow as I undid what I had before, changing it so his hand could regrow.

Most of the gathered mana funneled into Cross and broke into uncountable threads that wove their way through his body in a way I couldn't hope to understand. The Old Ways were making a Judge. I focused my attention on what I *could* control. His healing.

At first, everything was fine. His broken bones and various wounds acted normally. I tried to heal the rest of him while I was working, but the black veins didn't want to cooperate. There was immediate resistance from the necromancer's energy, and I found it impossible to push it out of his body. As his hand regrew, the dark magic left the rest of his body and funneled into the regrowing flesh. No matter what I did, I couldn't force the foreign power from him. Instead of spending more time duking it out with the black energy, I formed a shell of energy to block it from reentering the rest of Cross's body, and ensured his own mana would keep it powered.

Figuring out a more permanent cure would have to wait. As I released him, the still moment that had been created burst like a soap bubble, and I pulled him to his feet as we both had to immediately defend ourselves. The brief lull was over, and the two of us fought furiously for several seconds before we could speak again.

"What did you do?" Cross held out his new hand. It was a solid dull black, as if it drank in any light that touched it. A perfectly straight line divided normal healthy tissue from the black flesh right below the bend of his wrist. "It feels cold."

"I don't know what happened. The lich's power wouldn't leave, but I managed to lock it all away into your new hand. Can you use it?" I watched as he tossed his mangled sword back and forth from one hand to the other, without fumbling it. "I'll take that as a yes."

"There's no sensation. It's numb, but I can still move it." Cross rushed forward to kill three more enemies who got into his range. I noticed his speed wasn't what it was a few moments ago, but it was still more than normal. When he came back, he was shaking his new hand. "It's going to take some getting used to."

"Can you cast magic again?" I saw the realization hit him that his magic might be available to him once more.

He just shrugged.

"Well, try it out."

"I don't have my gauntlets." Cross saw the look on my face and his mouth closed with a click of teeth, immediately giving up on getting his old gear back. He flicked his wrist, casting what I recognized as his slapping spell. The nearest zombie who was trying to make its way between earthen spikes got folded like a paper airplane, dropping to the ground with a crunch. We both looked at each other with Pikachu-surprised face. "Yes, I can do magic again."

"I'd say so. Looks like someone got an upgrade." I looked carefully at Cross's hand, and noticed that the pristine line separating the dark and light skin wasn't quite as defined. Him using magic must have disrupted the power keeping it separated from the rest of his body. "Although, you might want to hold off on too many spells until we understand for sure what's going on with you."

Cross immediately saw what I was talking about and quickly agreed. We then had to fight off another group of zombies and one more vampire. I looked back and saw that Leedy and the others were looking tired, but they were still in the fight. After healing Cross, my energy levels were barely below a quarter, right at the threshold of where I wanted to be to handle the lich.

The undead I could see still numbered in the high hundreds, but the piles of corpses were making it more difficult to tell. In that regard, the lich was actually helping us. His eldritch power would occasionally flash out, devouring the defeated to empower those still able to fight. If he hadn't been doing that, we might not have been able to move just from the sheer weight of bodies.

The White Warden was dealing with that exact issue at the moment. He was bogged down less than fifty yards away, but couldn't get any closer due to how crowded it was around him. His whip was certainly effective at taking down the undead. That didn't make it a bulldozer capable of pushing stuff out of the way.

If I was going to fight Gleason myself, I would have to go to him.

"Cross, take this." I handed him my spear. His sword was barely better than a strip of dull metal by this point. "Try not to break it." He gave me a nod, and I turned to the others. "Hey, I'm going to block off your side. You three come help Cross hold this side while I fight the other guy."

A quick spell later, and we were all bunched up on the only open side of a cube. Everyone was amazed at Cross's new hand, but there wasn't time to explain much.

Jess grabbed me by the arm before I could leave the relative safety of our little fort. "James, be careful. The White Wardens have a reputation of being tough for a reason. You saw what he did to Cross."

"I'll be fine. You just hold the line." I pulled free of her grip. "This won't take long." I planted my foot against an earthen spike and drew both my ninjatō and mace. The familiar weight of the weapons felt comforting, and mana unconsciously danced along the mace before sparking over to the ninjatō, where it was absorbed.

I used the earthen spike as a springboard to launch myself toward Gleason, bowling over the undead in my way. My shield bracelet almost immediately overloaded, shattering at the multitude of impacts. The gap I had made closed up behind me, but I was already within striking distance of Gleason. It took him a moment to comprehend what had just happened, which gave me enough time to hit him with an uppercut from my mace. It caught him in the breastplate, flipping the Warden onto his back with a heavy thud.

His breath exploded out of him, and he struggled to get back to his feet.

"Commander Gleason, I presume? You and I have a few things to discuss."

That was the exact moment the flickering aura finally gave out completely. The undead rushed me with a vengeance, and I was forced to defend myself with my full concentration. Just because I was super strong and fast didn't mean I couldn't be overwhelmed by huge numbers. The strongest human ever was still only an even match for an average vampire. While I had broken the shackles of the strongest human, I still had limits. The prolonged fighting was beginning to wear on even my enhanced strength and endurance.

I lost sight of Gleason for a moment, until the Warden erupted from the crowd with a flurry of sweeping whip swings. He managed to catch me across the back of my left arm with the tip of his whip on a backswing I underestimated, and I almost dropped my sword from the sudden shock of pain. His weapon packed a real punch.

"Mired in the filth of the plague of undead? It's no wonder why *The Oracle* wants you dead." Gleason cast a spell that was enhanced by his armor, and his speed doubled. He blurred forward, but his long whip was hindered by the surging undead.

My shorter weapons didn't have that problem, so I stabbed at his leading leg with my ninjatō as my mace blocked his swinging arm. Surprisingly, the magic-eating sword didn't penetrate right away.

"Just as the disgraced Captain Cross learned, you are no match for the ancestral armor of the Gleason Family. It has been improved for generations, and—"

The tip of the sword finally ate through whatever was blocking it, and the strength of my arm allowed it to puncture straight into his leg.

"I'm going to make you pay for what you did to those werebears, asshole." I twisted the sword before ripping it free, tearing an even bigger hole in his armor.

He staggered back, where a super ghoul was waiting to grab him. It tried to bite through his neck armor, but Gleason's family actually *had* done a good job at reinforcing it.

I killed a vampire and some zombies that tried to grab me as well, just in time for Gleason to break free of the ghoul and kill it with his whip. I set myself, flinging gore off my weapons. With a growl, the two of us rushed at one another, and light flashed in the darkness as his whip cracked.

Trying to trap Gleason, I held my sword out from my body to make it an easy target. He took the bait, his whip snapping out and wrapping around it as he tried to yank it from my grip. Lightning danced along the edge of the blade where it met the whip, and he quickly pulled it free before his weapon was destroyed. He was an idiot, anyway. Anytime you're in plate armor, you should be more concerned about blunt weapons. Like, say, a mace.

I could tell Gleason had been trained to use a shield, because he reflexively lifted his arm to block my mace. He wasn't using a shield, so my hit crunched into his elbow hard enough to move his whole body sideways about six inches. The sudden pain and whiplash stunned him, so I hit him again, this time aiming for his thigh. I really put some mustard on it, and I heard his femur snap as his armor buckled against my full strength. The runes seemed to be more for magical and piercing attacks than blunt damage, so I took full advantage.

He dropped to the ground with a scream of agony. To give the guy some credit, he managed to whip me across the face in his fall. It caught me right under the chin and followed my jawline all the way to my ear. The cut burned like it was on fire, but my Vigor stat was already fighting against it. A twisted and malignant magic infected the cut, making the pain spike excruciatingly. It was a disgusting use of magic that could only belong to a sadist. I swiped a finger across the wound, concentrating as I cast a quick spell that cut off sensation around the wound, undercutting the magic at its foundation and not giving the spell any handhold to execute its dark work. His whip being imbued with this spell in particular reaffirmed Gleason's position as a bug that needed stepping on. It also made me want to rip his head off with my bare hands as I imagined its use on the mayor and his family. A healing spell later would make sure I didn't have a scar.

I had to kill some more undead that had closed in before I could do anything else, but when there was another brief lull, I stood over Gleason and met his eyes through the gap in his helm. "I would normally go through a long spiel about how I'm a Judge, and it's my job to punish those who do wrong." My mace rose and fell, crushing the femur of his other leg. His scream of pain was cut off when I slapped him with the flat of my sword blade.

"Considering the situation, I don't think all of that is necessary. I'll just skip to the end, where I sentence you to death for being an absolute piece of shit." Two more quick blows and both of his forearms were shattered. "I should leave you like this and let the undead finish you off, but I don't have the time to make sure they do it right." I stood up and readied my mace to crush his skull, which was more merciful than the little rat deserved.

"No!" Gleason flailed around, trying to stop me. "It can't end like this! I was meant for *more*!"

"You were meant to be a protector, fuckstick. Instead, you became a nightmare to the people you were supposed to protect. Try to do better in your next life." I raised my mace over my head, but before I could swing it down, the floor under him gave way. Meaty tentacles from some undead abomination reached up from the sub-basement, forcing me to scramble back so I didn't join him.

His screams disappeared as he was dragged away into the darkness below.

"Okay, I guess that works too." I gave a shrug, and my mantle faded into the background.

More cracks were forming, showing the places where the sub-basement had been dug out by the undead. Over by the stairs, I saw a group of White Wardens fighting. They weren't making much progress, and seemed to have a denser mix of vampires than my group did at the rear of the basement. It was definitely time for us to get out of there. This was no place for the living.

CHAPTER 41

We had been fighting for well over twenty minutes, maybe more. That kind of exertion would make anyone feel like they were about to fall over dead.

"Did you finish it?" Cross was the only one still steady on his feet, but the line of darkness on his wrist had grown jagged in the short time I was gone. "Is he dead?"

I looked back to where Gleason had disappeared into a hole in the ground. There was no way I was going down there right now to confirm the kill. "I didn't see him die, but I would bet my spear you're using that he isn't coming back after the undead are done with him." Not that it mattered much anyway. He had been pretty easy to beat. "If by some miracle he lives through this shit and wants a round two, I'll just kick his ass all over again."

Jess gave me an exhausted thumbs-up. "Great. Why don't you get over here and give us a hand?" The blood of the undead made it look like someone had splashed her with black paint in a poor attempt to recreate a Pollock painting. "I could use a break."

I had to jump over a pile of bodies to get to them. Our group had been putting in some work. "I know you guys really want to finish off what's in here, but what do you think about getting out of here?"

"What about the lich?" Leedy had to brace himself against the wall to stand upright, but he didn't have an ounce of quit in him. "There's no way we can let something like that run wild. It's too big of a threat."

"Oh, I've got a surprise for that thing." I sheathed my sword and hefted my mace. "It doesn't know how screwed it is."

Cross stepped forward. "Do you need us to do anything? Maybe I can hurt it now that I hold some of its power."

"No. What I need you to do is hold a perimeter around me while I handle him. Then, we'll need to move fast. My spell will allow us to follow his soul back to his phylactery, but the trail only stays visible for a short time." I pointed to the stairs, where the other White Wardens were still getting their asses kicked. "There's no telling how far away it is, so I might have to leave you behind for a while. If we do get split up after we plow through those guys, find a place nearby to recover and I'll find you."

Everyone agreed, so we readied ourselves for a fight to get back over to the lich. I only had enough mana for the first part of what I needed to do, meaning I would have to take the time to recharge when I got to the lich's phylactery. If it had extensive wards or guards, I might be in trouble. I was betting on the thing going for stealth over a good defense. Its brief time in my head gave me a few hints at its personality, and it felt more like the kind of thing that prided itself on outsmarting its enemies by being sneaky, and gloating about hiding things in plain sight. Considering how things had gone in the basement, I couldn't be sure of anything. One could always hope, anyway.

You still don't seem to understand your position, future vessel. Nothing you can do to me can cause permanent damage. It was still struggling against its bonds, and I could feel the stone prison weakening as we got closer. *Destroy this body, and I will find a hundred more. Eventually, you will give in. Surrender yourself to me now, and save us both the time and trouble.*

When we got to the lich, the fire burning in its eyes had died down to mere embers compared to the scorching flames I had seen before. The others formed up around me, keeping close so they could help one another as needed. I waved my hand over the center of the stone prison, allowing the mana there to pull away and expose the lich's bony chest. I held up my mace and took a deep breath, gathering my power. I looked down at the lich and smiled.

"There's something you should know about me, Sparky. Something you definitely didn't account for." The blessed star metal mace lit up a vibrant blue that clashed with the eldritch green light from its eyes. "I'm also a Paladin."

The embers of its eyes flashed, but it was too late to do anything. It had been too sure of its power over me, and its safety with its phylactery somewhere else, and it knew it.

"Smite."

I swung the mace down hard enough to shatter the skeleton as if it were made of glass. Pieces of bone flew everywhere, and I watched as the skull bounced out of sight, the embers flickering out as it rolled away. I made sure to keep mana from the Paladin spell flowing into my mace as the lich was forced out of the vampire's remains so I could still see the form of the lich as it coalesced in front of me.

The Smite spell was one of four I had received when I gained the Paladin class, and it could banish or destroy all sorts of evil spirits, demons, devils, and so on. It had varying effects based on how strong they were. For something like a lich, it didn't matter how powerful or ancient it was. The undead creature would be forced back into its phylactery for at least a short period of time to recover, which gave me a chance to kill it for good.

As I watched, the sickly green mist that was the lich swirled around the basement before shooting up the hole I had cut through the roof. Its essence left a trail that I could see like a streamer of neon in the dark of the basement. "This way!"

I ran for the opening, clearing out space for us with brute force provided by a second wind. The adrenaline rush of tracking down and killing the lich had banished the exhaustion that had been creeping up on me, making it possible for the others to keep up without getting bogged down. It also helped that the majority of the undead seemed to lose interest in us as we ran deeper into the basement. They were more focused on the noisier and flashier White Wardens, who were still getting mangled over by the stairs.

Cross and I helped Leedy and Murphy up to the next floor, where they immediately started fighting more undead. Cross jumped up to help them while I planted a knee so Jess could use it as a springboard and leap up herself.

After I jumped up, I saw the mess that Gleason and his men had made. They had walked straight into the ambush we'd avoided earlier, consisting mostly of super ghouls and a few elder vampires. Torn bodies were strewn everywhere, and I was shocked to see how many undead they had killed up here. Jess stood next to me, looking as sick as I felt. "If we had come through one of those doors, it…we might not have made it."

"No kidding." I pulled her away from the hole, toward the wide-open doors on the opposite side of the building. We only had to fight a single ghoul as we left the building. It had been trying to catch the horses staked outside by the White Wardens. Their lone guard left behind to protect them had been killed by the ghoul, and the undead had been wearing ruts in the grass as it ran in circles after the chargers that hadn't managed to pull their staked-down ropes out of the ground. "You gather up our gear and pick the best horses. I'll follow the trail and send up a signal if I need you."

I didn't wait for them to agree. Instead, I took off running. The trail led out into the forest behind the cheese factory, weaving between treetops like a single strand of the northern lights. It was fading fast, mostly because my own mana was running dangerously low. Concentrating on my breathing, I tried to bring in as much ambient mana as I could as I sprinted through the trees.

Somehow, the lich realized I was onto it. There was nothing it could do about refusing to return to its phylactery, but it could make sure that it threw in as many zigs and zags as possible before getting sucked back into its home like a third-rate genie getting pulled into a dusty-ass lamp. I was forced to juke my way through five or six briar and thorn patches before I changed up the dynamics of the situation.

Instead of running around and wearing myself out, I found the tallest tree in the area and quickly climbed it. I quickly realized the damned lich had been running me in circles around a small clearing in the forest. While the lich had the capability to delay its return, creating extra work for me as it did, the limitation was that the direction of travel had to always be a little bit closer toward its phylactery. It was too dark to see details, but I thought I could see a few boulders or possibly a stone hut in the center of the clearing. That *had* to be the place. I decided to take a chance and beat the lich there.

Jumping from one tree to the next, I made quick time over to the location. As I got closer, it was obvious my hopes of the lich leaving his phylactery undefended were misplaced. What I had seen from the tree was a ring of stones similar to a miniaturized Stonehenge that had been carved with wards meant to keep everything—and I do mean everything—out. Not even grass was growing inside the ring. In the middle was a tiny stone hut no bigger than an outhouse.

Over my head, I saw the energy signature of the lich finally catch up. It shot straight into the outhouse, causing the single visible window to glow an angry green. The irony of the lich's phylactery hiding inside a shitter wasn't lost on me, but now wasn't the time for laughter. I tried to push my way into the clearing, but it was like going up against an invisible brick wall.

Nothing happened as I tried to shove my way through the barrier with raw strength, marshaling all of my considerable physical stats. I strained—veins stuck out in stark relief against my arms and chest as I pushed against the barrier. I let out an explosive breath as I stopped trying to brute-force my way in and changed tactics.

"Magic barrier, huh? Well, I got something special meant for things just like this. Annoying shield-thing, I'd like to introduce you to ancient elven engineering."

I drew my sword and slashed horizontally in one smooth motion. The ninjatō smashed against the barrier in a ripple of explosive light and sound. The energy of the blow created a backlash on my body, knocking me backward and nearly taking me off my feet. The barrier pulsed once in response but didn't diminish in any noticeable way. This wasn't working fast enough. By the time the mana-leaching properties of my sword brought down the shield, I'd be too late, and the lich would've escaped. I couldn't let this bastard get away, but I was quickly running out of options.

A cold knot tightened in my stomach as I faced the possibility of failure, the knowledge that all the sacrifices of our party and the many victims—the generations of undead we had seen in that basement—could be wiped away in front of this last obstacle. I was just so damned tired. Physically, yes, but in a much deeper sense that had been growing year by year, as I faced world after world without any reason, direction, or answers.

Oh, I had answers, all right. I'd learned more than I'd ever thought possible in these twenty years, but I had none of the answers that really mattered. Who did this to me? Why? What was the purpose of it all? Would I ever get my fucking *life* back? Would I ever get to taste root beer again? Was it my destiny to be a tool of the uncaring forces of the universe that had upended my entire existence? It would be so easy to toss in the towel. Say fuck it, and just go fishing or something.

Just then, a subtle sensation broke through the fog of despair and self-pity. One I had been experiencing ever since I drew closer to the house, only I had never stopped to truly examine it. It was a feeling I had only experienced once before, when the vampires had sent their velociraptor attack dogs against us. I finally made the connection. Whatever was powering this thing had some serious mojo, much more than a single lich should be able to gather on its own. In fact, it hadn't done it on its own. I slid my sword smoothly back into its scabbard and stepped closer to the barrier, one hand reaching for its polished surface. Only this time, I reached *into* the barrier. A message popped into my vision.

> **Quest Update!**
>
> **Unique Upgrade Quest:** Find ten places of power –
> 2/10
>
> -Absorb the power built up at the location to increase
> your level.

It was clear to me that the lich had somehow converted or parasitized the collected magic of this place of power's energy well. I sucked in a deep breath as I considered the danger of what I was about to do. Books had been written about the folly of drawing in magic that had been tainted by the sentient will of another. Even after twenty years, there was so much out there about magic that I didn't know it could fill libraries—literally—and this was certainly a subject I wish I had studied more. I also knew it didn't matter.

I was going to do it anyway.

Putting both hands against the barrier and closing my eyes, I envisioned the wall as a white mist. I immediately thought of the energy blocking me like a battery that I could drain, making it easier to start drawing it into my body.

At first, it didn't want to budge. Pulling free the first few wisps of power was like dragging heavy chains with my hands taped shut. When I finally got the first one to flow inside my body, it got a lot easier. In fact, it got too easy. Energy started to flood my body, and I was suddenly drinking from a fire hose.

You think you can steal my *power? The hubris of those who think themselves strong is truly staggering. Your dirty tricks won't save you now. I wanted you as a vessel, but after injuring me, I think I will have to use a different option. Let me show you what happens when* true *strength shows itself.*

The lich somehow had control of the wards even from within its phylactery, and I was locked in place by the mana pouring into me. My only defense was to keep it from pooling inside my body and burning me up like a wooden pitcher trying to hold lava. Instead of trying to escape, I pushed my mind against the river of energy to try to force any kind of movement. It felt impossible. The rush of power felt like a solid bar of metal burning its way deeper inside my body. For the briefest of moments, I felt a flash of doubt, before I crushed it mercilessly. This piss-face lich and his stupid booby trap weren't going to kill me. I doubled down on my focus and shoved with all I had.

Blood sprayed from my nose as something inside my head gave way, but the energy finally swirled into motion. It lazily curled around my body, burning me on the inside, until it hit the mana generator in my center. The mana was pulled violently toward it, creating a whirlpool that felt like my organs were getting dragged into a black hole.

Zero stars, do not recommend.

As more power poured into me, it scoured my body from the inside out. I was being scrubbed with dense flames, every part cleansed in a fire of agony. All the energy that formed the dome of protection was moving toward me now, and I was forced to focus all of my attention inward. The mana compressed as it was pulled deeper, making me feel like an overstretched water balloon about to burst. Keeping myself from popping was both a physical and metaphysical struggle, centered around the whirlpool of my mana generator.

Finally, the generator couldn't hold anymore. It had condensed down from liquid fire into a solid ball of marble laced with lightning that suddenly burst outward in a flash of thunder. I heaved uncontrollably, and foul black sludge poured from my mouth out of nowhere.

While I was trying to puke up the barrel of rancid crude oil I didn't remember eating, the generator reformed. It looked almost exactly the same as it had before being turned into a solid rock, except now its interior walls were crystalline in nature. Almost like a blue geode, but filled with dense gaseous mana that was lit with the occasional streak of silent lightning. A less dense version of that same mana now filled the rest of my body, making me feel like an overtightened spring about to shoot loose and bounce around all over the place.

A series of dings accompanied a screen that popped in my vision, telling me I had accomplished another step of the quest.

Name: James Holden (Earth v7.2)

Title: Chief Justice/Arbiter/Justicar/Executioner/etc.

Level: 100/MAX

Rank: 2/10

Age: 27 (Physical) 47 (Actual)

Class: Warrior/Soldier/Knight/Paladin/Mage (5/5)

Profession:
Healer/Alchemist/Blacksmith/Runesmith/Judge (5/5)

Status:

Strength – 65

Flexibility – 65

Vigor – 65

Mind – 65

Mission:

Mythical Quest: Deliver Justice – World Count 20/???

Legendary Quest: Return Home – Requirements not met

Epic Quest: Find out why – Requirements not met

Rare Quest: Track down Silver Star – Ongoing

Unique Upgrade Quest: Find ten places of power – 2/10

My stats had all grown by ten points this time, along with my version and rank increasing by one. It should have been a moment to celebrate, except for the projectile vomiting, of course. Jumping for joy and crushing the soul-home of the undead magic user would have been the logical next step, if I had been able to move. Once I was done involuntarily heaving, I realized I was frozen in place, still stuck as if I were reaching out to touch the invisible dome that I had already absorbed. I tried to drop my arms, take a step, cast a spell, do anything other than stand there and breathe, but I couldn't. It seemed only my involuntary bodily functions were working. Something had paralyzed me.

I'm surprised you survived such an influx of power.

The lich's smug voice was more annoying than fear-inducing, but I could feel as I broke out in a cold sweat when my arms dropped to my side and I took a single step toward the hut on top of the hill without telling my body to do so.

As surprising as you are, you still don't understand many things. Such as what happens when you take power that is not your own, and fail to claim proper ownership of it.

I took another step, almost falling forward onto my face.

This isn't the usual way I take control of a body, but I suppose it's better than nothing.

Thinking furiously, I did everything I could to stop myself from haltingly making my way up the hill. I tried to throw myself backward, but there was no response. All I accomplished was giving myself a terrible headache. Again. The power humming inside my body was controlling me like I was a puppet, and no matter what I did, the lich didn't even seem to notice. It had said that I hadn't claimed ownership of the power, but that wasn't a real answer. Not that I could do anything about it now anyway. Even the mana generator inside me refused to react when I tried to manipulate it.

I had known what I was getting myself into when I absorbed the mana from the shield. However, knowing the danger and experiencing the reality of it were two completely different things. I tried to calm my racing thoughts and work through the problem. Tried, and failed. Panic was a flame in my chest as one attempt after another met with zero success. I was totally fucked. I knew it, and based on how the lich somehow managed to move my limbs with a smug sense of superiority, the lich knew it too.

Well, what should I do with you now?

My body came to a stop in front of the hut, and my hand reached out to drag open the heavy stone door.

First, since you have wounded me, you shall help find a new home for my phylactery and guard it until I have healed. I will think upon your future while repairing the damage to my soul. That Paladin magic makes you unsuitable as a permanent vessel for me, but perhaps I can force you to take the step into immortality. You don't have to be willing to participate in the Ceremony of Endless Night.

He was talking about turning me into a lich. That would be bad.

When the door opened, I saw a small, ornate wooden table covered with runes. Around the edges were various pouches filled with uncut gems, thick gold and platinum coins, and what had to be different kinds of colorful swirling monster cores in more than just the undead variety. All in all, it was an absolute fortune that rivaled the treasuries of some city-states I had visited.

In the center of all that wealth and power was what I could only describe as a glass spray bottle. The old-fashioned kind with a squeeze ball my great-grandma kept around that used to hold perfume. The type that smelled like baby powder, before it had dried up sometime around the end of Prohibition. Inside the perfume bottle, swirling green energy from the lich marked the out-of-place item as the phylactery. Somehow, despite the hold on me from the undead creature, I managed to snort in amusement.

What? You find something funny, mortal? Has your own impending doom caused your composure to shatter like your frail mind?

The lich relaxed control of my voice, and I took a moment to spit out the foul taste in my mouth before answering, noting with relief that the lich needed me to communicate verbally. Although it had control over my body, it couldn't read my mind. It was a small edge, but this bastard had me dead to rights. "No, it isn't that. I was just wondering what cheap-ass antique dime store dumpster you found that thing in. The last lich I killed had a really badass dagger crafted from the fang of an ancient viper and the skulls of his enemies or something respectable like that. But you? Nope. *You* go with a perfume bottle. I mean, seriously. Did you say to yourself, 'Self, baby powder and wrinkly old ladies are what really get me going, so let's tie our soul to something that represents both of those things at the same time!' Or was there some other process that made you decide on such a shitty home for all of eternity?"

As it turned out, the lich didn't appreciate my sense of humor. They probably had no idea what I was talking about. I'm sure that the bottle was used on this world for something other than perfume, but they were very sensitive about it, regardless.

The lich ripped free my sword from its scabbard and stabbed me through the leg. Impressively, it avoided hitting anything important, like a major artery or bone. It still hurt like hell.

The next time I let you speak, it would be good for you to remember that I can cut out your tongue anytime I feel the need. Now, time grows short. I'm sure your friends will be along soon, and I want to be in a secure location before they do.

Without my agreement, the lich used my body to start stuffing his pouches of wealth into a black leather pack covered with protection and camouflaging runes that had been left under the table. The runes on the table sparked and sent jolts of electricity through my body as items were removed, but the lich was happy to let me suffer through the pain instead of taking the time to deactivate them.

My new Vigor stat of sixty-five meant my body could take the abuse. The real problem was the sword sticking out of my left thigh. The regenerative effects of Vigor tried to close the wound immediately, but the lich decided to leave the sword where it was, continually cutting and healing as I moved. Preoccupied as it was by the wealth of items on the table, the lich didn't notice the blade on my ninjatō glowing subtly as my blood dripped onto the floor. My *magic-eating* sword.

Without letting on that the stolen mana inside me was diminishing, I tried to wiggle my toes. My big toe moved up and down twice, but only on the side where the sword was. Since the mana inside me was stagnant instead of flowing freely, the ninjatō was affecting my left side faster than my right. My left hand was holding the bag, so I tried to move my fingers. They twitched, causing the lich to pause.

It thankfully brushed off the involuntary movement and went back to what it was doing.

After a few minutes of carefully packing the leather pack and sealing it up tight, the lich went to reach for the phylactery.

It was time for me to make my move. Somehow, I knew that if I touched it, the lich's chances of winning the battle for control of my body would swing in its favor. Holding its center of power was a bad idea, especially when I was still filled with mana it somehow had control over. The runes protecting the perfume bottle were more stout, so it took the time to disarm them as it slowly held out my hand.

Almost done. I have a secondary location nearby, and once we use the blood of a sacrifice to contact the Des—

It was reaching with the right hand, so I used the bag in my left to swing at the spray bottle. The lich was so caught off guard that it didn't even try to stop me. I smacked the phylactery off the table, where it clattered off the floor and bounced out of sight. I knew that the crystal or glass it was made out of was supernaturally reinforced by the lich's soul, so the fall wouldn't hurt it. The runes reacting to the phylactery getting disturbed sure as hell did, though. Hurt, I mean. Well, it hurt *me* at least.

My body was blown out of the tiny building by the explosion. All things considered, the explosion was pretty small compared to what it could have been if the lich hadn't already been deactivating them. I landed a few yards away, rolling on the ground and shouting in pain as my sword was ripped from my leg, tearing open a huge wound that sprayed blood high into the air. Today was not a good day. Really, it was going in my top twenty of days that sucked the worst. Maybe top ten.

You think to defy me*! Entire kingdoms have bowed to my greatness. For centuries, I was worshipped as a* god*! I've had enough of you, and your ridiculousness.*

My right hand clumsily flopped around before finding where the hilt of my mace was clipped to my belt. The lich repeatedly punched me in the huevos while trying to pull the weapon free.

Definitely moving into the top-ten category.

You'll die by your own hand!

The carabiner-style clip was confusing for the lich, which only bought me a brief moment to think of a way to keep me from splattering my own brains across the barren hilltop. The blessed star metal mace was the most lethal of all my weapons, and I didn't want to get into a pointless tug-of-war that only risked my own life. All it would take was one slip and I was dead, and at no point in that confrontation was the lich in any danger.

When the bad guy takes a hostage, you shoot the hostage.

Aiming my left hand at my right forearm, I fired the leftmost barrel of my wrist gun. Amazingly, I didn't lose the hand. My new stats had toughened my body enough that I managed to only suffer a shattered radius and ulna, and lose a hefty chunk of meat in the process. Still, at such close range, it was a miracle it wasn't blown off completely. By doing it to myself, I thought the shock of getting shot would be lessened. I was wrong.

What an interesting spell. I'll have to explore that later.

I groaned as I tried to pull myself back up the hill while still lying on my back. It was awkward, and lacked any good leverage. I also couldn't heal myself, otherwise I would have to just shoot myself again. Slipping in my own blood, I didn't stop. I kept inching my way back up the hill.

You're determined, I'll give you that. You know, I was rather intrigued by that slapping spell you cast on my avatar in the basement. What do you think of my version?

The lich raised my injured arm and started slapping it across my face. It couldn't kill me with force, so it seemed like the lich would do it with indignity, instead. Indignity or not, it certainly didn't feel like getting hugged by a basket of kittens.

Quit hitting yourself. Quit hitting yourself.

"There is no James, only Zuul…" The lich didn't get my joke, because it was an uncultured savage living in a world severely lacking in a proper entertainment industry. "I'm going to kill you like the bitch you are, lich." The hut finally came into sight, and I found a fresh burst of energy. Getting to my feet was impossible, so I started crawling for the open doorway. I still couldn't move my right side properly, but with my body using up the remaining mana inside me to heal all the damage, the lich was losing control. "You're gonna be super dead. D-E-D dead, motherfucker." It was possible the blood loss was affecting me.

I finally got within arm's reach of where the phylactery was lying on the ground, and managed to unclip my mace from my belt with my left hand. Instead of Smite, I prepared myself to cast the Paladin spell Cleanse. Because the lich was already suffering the effects of the former, the latter should finish it off. As the spell started to take shape, it fizzled out, and there was a stabbing pain in my head, renewing my bloody nose.

You don't have the control necessary to cast another one of those Paladin spells with my claimed mana still flowing through you. I'll tear you apart from the inside the moment you try to cast another 'holy' spell like that.

"Damn." I lifted the heavy mace and slammed it down on the spray bottle with a dull thud. Neither the mace nor the phylactery seemed to have suffered any damage from my weakened blow.

Ha! You're nothing. You're too weak to break something that has been reinforced by my soul, even after you injured me. It's a good thing I found a better vessel. I would have found you disappointing.

"So, you're saying a physical blow *could* still break it. It doesn't need to be magical." I carefully clipped my mace back on my belt and scooted back a few feet, using the hut to shield most of my body from the phylactery. "I'm just not hitting your lame-ass perfume bottle hard enough." Taking a moment to select a title I barely used, I activated it.

> **Title**: Executioner
>
> -End the lives of the guilty, so their presence can no longer sway the world.
>
> **Skill Imparted**: Your next attack is 25% stronger. An additional 25% will be applied if the target is restrained. Can only be used on those who are deemed guilty. Useable once per day.

The power of the Executioner hummed through me. "You aren't exactly the Necronomicon, but let me show you my Boomstick, asshole."

Wait, no, I—

I lifted my wrist gun and fired first the middle barrel, then the top one, lining up both shots so they would hit at nearly the exact same spot, one barely above the other. I did it so fast that the two shots sounded more like one. The first round hit lower, causing microfractures to spread across the glowing green crystal and popping the bottle up in the air for a split second before the next round shattered it into oblivion. The resulting explosion was far larger than the little hut could contain, and it sent me on another trip down the hill, where I was stopped violently by my lower back cracking across one of the boundary stones.

I barely hung onto consciousness as pieces of burning hut and dirt rained down around me. I looked up just in time to see a familiar leather bag—a very *heavy* bag—descending straight for my face. "Son of a—"

The fucker *did* make it into the top ten after all. I closed my eyes, resigned to taking the hit.

A good nap was probably what I needed anyway.

EPILOGUE 1

Everything had been going perfectly. Gleason had left the village behind, and his scouts had brought him to where they had lost the trail for James Holden just in time for a beacon to light up the evening skies in the far distance. It was as if the Trinity was lighting the way for him. He could feel their gaze settle upon him, urging him upon his divine quest. Gleason and his men had nearly killed their chargers in their rush to catch their prey.

Gleason had used his Long Eye spell to spot his quarry sneaking around the roof of an old building, and had immediately ordered his men to don full armor and go in after them. That was when things had started to turn for the worse. When the gaze of the Trinity had fallen from his shoulders.

Although he knew that the undead weren't normally a threat to the Wardens—and most especially the men under his command, who he had personally trained—they had been confronted by a new type he had never seen before.

At first, he had waited outside the old building while his men dutifully followed orders and attempted to clear the building themselves. After all, if their commander had to do all the work himself, what good were they? A runner had come to tell him of the fierce fighting inside, and of the mounting casualties they were being dealt.

Gleason ordered all his men but one to join in the fight, leaving his newest Warden to guard the horses. He did what any good commander would do, and followed behind, bringing up the rear so he could better organize his men as they fought.

Instead, he watched as his men were ripped to pieces by foes that should have been killed by the wounds his men inflicted. An undead who could still fight with a spear through its head was unlike any undead he had ever heard of, with the exception of those very few ancient vampires that lived in the far north, or across the seas in the southern deserts.

He was forced to join in the battle, dirtying himself with the ichor of the undead monsters within minutes of entering the building. Gleason was so incensed by the *audacity* of the unclean filth that dared touch him, he cut a path almost by himself straight to the strongest source of magic he could feel in the entire building.

That was when he had seen him. *Him.* James Holden, the man who called himself a Judge. A monster, condemned to die by the gods themselves, claiming to be something more than a pig wallowing in filth. He was covered in it, stinking of the undead, as if he had been down in the basement with them for days.

Gleason had always known himself as one of the best fighters in the Hunters' Guild. Out of the hundreds of Wardens he had sparred with in recent times, only the Green Wardens could defeat him soundly. He knew his worth, and it was far more than most men could ever aspire to reach. Then, he fought James Holden.

It was like fighting a Green Warden, but without any of the pride or honor they exuded. He knew then that Holden was a monster in truth. Gleason had given his all, and was found wanting. In fact, he knew that Holden had beaten him without much effort. The lazy confidence the man showed was evidence enough of that, not even breathing hard during their fight.

Then, to make matters worse, instead of being given a clean death upon his failure, Gleason had been pulled underground, where a slavering monster had dragged him through what had felt like miles of tight tunnels until he was brought before this creature, a wizened old vampire who felt heavy with mana. Gleason knew it was a powerful undead, at least at the level of an elder vampire.

"What have we here?" The raspy voice sounded like the monster hadn't spoken out loud in a long time. It reached out, flipped open the visor of Gleason's helm, and sliced a ragged, dirty fingernail across Gleason's cheek. The vampire licked the blood that dribbled free, taking a few moments to taste it as if it were a fine brandy, picking through the subtleties and secrets it carried. "I think the master would like you. I think he would like you *very* much."

Behind Gleason, the tentacled creature that had brought him here made a burbling sound, and produced a charred skull that had very pronounced canines. The elder vampire snapped his fingers, and the tentacled creature gently handed it over. As Gleason watched, the vampire focused on the skull, and a faint green glow radiated from the empty eye sockets. A disembodied voice seemed to come from nowhere and everywhere at once, fading in and out to Gleason's ears.

…keep it…different vessel, without holy magic…injured badly. Tell the Destitute that I…not what we thought…need to hurry, before it's too late…demons can't hold him forever…

"Yes, milord. I'll do as you say." The vampire turned to face Gleason, and smiled wide enough to show yellowed fangs in all their unholy glory. "Today is your lucky day, young Warden. You get to become a part of something important. Something bigger than yourself. All you need to do is…survive."

Gleason's mouth was so dry, he had to try twice before he could speak. "S-survive? What do I need to survive?" There was a faint flicker of hope in his chest. Perhaps the Trinity didn't leave him completely forsaken. "You aren't going to kill me?"

The vampire moved faster than Gleason could hope to avoid, grabbing his helm and twisting his head to the side. He pulled it up enough to expose a gap between his breastplate and gorget, baring a strip of flesh around his neck. Gleason tried to struggle, but the vampire's grip was like a vise.

It held up the skull like a dagger before plunging the twin canines into his neck, and Gleason felt like two icicles had been stuck into his flesh. Coldness flooded his body, numbing his broken limbs as his chest slowed its breathing. He managed to look down enough to see that thick black veins were writhing beneath his skin. Gleason could feel them stretching to cover his body, living snakes twisting through his organs, invading his brain. Then, the skull exploded.

"*No!*" The elder vampire jerked back from the flash of green fire, pieces of its own hand blown off in the sudden violence.

The cold invading Gleason was interrupted by the green flames getting sucked into the twin holes in his neck, before it flashed orange and was gone.

"What did he do? What does this *mean*?"

Gleason, now forgotten on the floor, was dealing with problems of his own. The black veins and green fire that had invaded his badly injured body caused a catastrophic grand mal seizure. His body contorted so hard that he fractured more bones, knocking free his helm and exposing his sweaty head and face as he foamed at the mouth. The black veins had sunken out of sight, leaving him looking as normal as a man in his position could be expected to appear.

Staring down at the broken man, the elder vampire scoffed. "So many grand plans, gone to waste. The outworlder must have managed to destroy the lich after all." He looked at his damaged hand, and the barely breathing Warden. "No sense letting good blood go to waste. Especially since I need to heal myself before I can report to the Destitute all the failures of the lich."

Grabbing Gleason by the back of the neck like he was a stray kitten, the vampire lifted him up to his mouth and bit him, drinking deeply from the Warden. He intended to drain him completely, not wanting to chance a newly risen vampire in a few days' time that he would need to babysit. They were little more than beasts, thinking only of their thirst, and with the knowledge of magic already in his mind, the former Warden would have been a nightmare for the elder vampire to deal with.

As it took a second drink, Gleason's eyes snapped open. His body moved by instinct, trying to grapple the elder vampire to break free of its grasp. The many broken bones he suffered from made him weak, and the elder vampire fought him off easily. Not wanting to draw things out, it took a third drink from Gleason, enough that the man should have passed out from blood loss by now. Instead, black veins erupted to the surface of his skin, giving him enough strength to pull free of the vampire's grasp.

"Curious. The lich's gift should have died when it did." The vampire stood, intending to finish the job the old-fashioned way as he pulled a dagger from his belt. "No matter. I'll make this quick."

Even with the boost provided by the black veins, Gleason could do nothing to save himself. He watched silently as the vampire approached, holding up its weapon as it prepared to kill him. For Gleason, it wasn't even the first time he had faced a similar scene that day. In his last moments, he cursed James Holden for beating him, he cursed the Wardens for sending him on a fool's errand, and most of all, he cursed the Trinity for forsaking him in his hour of need.

Before the knife could strike home, the elder vampire stopped, grabbing at its abdomen. "What?" He looked at Gleason, obvious confusion on his face. "What did you do to me?"

A realization struck Gleason as his lips cracked and bled in a crimson smile. It made sense now. All this—he wasn't forsaken by the Trinity. He was being *tested*. Tested for greatness. Laughing maniacally, he croaked out a familiar sentence. "All you need to do, vampire…is survive."

As Gleason watched, a familiar black vein crawled up the vampire's neck. The already wrinkled appearance of the vampire seemed to worsen, and more black veins spread across his visible skin. The powerful undead monster was brought low, doubling over in pain as it whined like an animal caught in a trap. That only lasted a few more seconds, before the vampire dropped to the floor, completely still. Its body rapidly shrank, turning into little more than a withered skeleton.

From its back erupted a mass of black ropey tentacles that flung itself at Gleason. He could do nothing except close his eyes and await a similar fate as the tar-like mess slammed against his breastplate. Gleason held his breath, waiting to die.

When nothing happened, he looked down to see nothing was there. The black veins were gone, leaving nothing beyond a clean spot on his armor. A few heartbeats later, Gleason knew it had somehow gotten inside him anyway. He was suddenly flushed with a cold so intense it burned, turning his breath into a mist as he exhaled.

Gleason expected the end to finally come, but once again, it didn't. The burning cold seemed to rejuvenate him. Heal him. *Restore* him. Gleason finally sat up, fully whole and hale, more energized than he had felt in *years*.

"I… I'm *alive*." Gleason patted himself down, confirming he was truly okay. Staring down at his body, he could only come to one logical conclusion. "I truly *am* destined for more. The Trinity have not forsaken me. They have *blessed* me." He felt his neck where he had been bitten by the vampire. Gleason knew from all the literature and from past hunts he should be feeling feverish already, and that the change into an undead monster was inevitable. Somehow, that didn't bother him right now. He didn't feel feverish, and even if he did change—which he might not—he knew deep down that he wouldn't be like a regular bloodsucker. Gleason had been chosen for *more*.

He reviewed his memories over what the vampire had said. Apparently, the skull it had used to poison him was supposed to impart some kind of gift from a lich. When it had exploded, the vampire had assumed that the lich had been killed, but Gleason knew different. The Trinity had changed the unclean gift from an undead monster into a blessing from his deity. That meant his mission from *The Oracle* was so important, it warranted direct interference from the gods themselves. Gleason dropped to his knees in supplication, raising his hands above his head.

"You have chosen me to be your agent on this mortal plane. I will not fail you. Corruption will be cleansed, torn out by the root. I will raise your praises with my voice, and fulfill your orders with my hands." Gleason stood, not noticing the black veins tinted with green and orange flames as they flickered across his body. "This I swear."

In his heart, Gleason was most happy that the only real order he had ever received was to kill James Holden. After what he had learned from that dirty shifter mayor, it made what he was going to do to Greendown all the sweeter.

EPILOGUE 2

The windows that overlooked the snow capped mountains had long since been repaired, but the signs of the explosion that had rocked the room were still apparent. Scorched stone, blackened walls, and missing tapestries made the cold chamber feel even more unwelcoming than it had before.

"Milord, there's still no word." The messenger knelt near the entrance, afraid to enter without permission. The three figures standing around the table in the center of the room were all unnaturally still, contemplating whatever was displayed on the piles of maps and wooden figures spread across its surface. "Would you like me to convey another set of orders?"

The attention of the vampire dressed as a noble fell on the messenger like a physical weight, pushing the much younger vampire into the stone floor and causing a trickle of blood to leak from its eyes.

"Nothing, you say? Not even from the elders stationed nearby?" The Destitute stepped away from the table and walked over to the mantel over the fireplace. He picked up a small bottle, tapping it with a finger before holding it up to his eyes. "Hmm…"

"Don't tell me, the lich is dead?" The woman stood up straight, grabbing a steel staff capped with a clear diamond the size of a fist off the table. "I can't believe the snake finally bit off more than it could swallow."

The shortest of the three leaned away from the woman, afraid of being included in any backlash the Destitute might visit upon her. "Milord, what would you have us do? If this new enemy has the power to kill one of the lich's strength, we can't face it alone. Perhaps we should—"

"Oh, quit sniveling. I thought the Duergar were supposed to be a tough race, but you're nothing but a coward." The woman sniffed in disdain, turning her back. "I don't know if I should even trust you to fix my ship."

"Coward?" The gray dwarf clenched his heavy fists, anger causing them to tremble. "Say it again, and I'll pull my support so fast your pointy fangs won't know what happened! Let's see how far you get without me, or my engineers."

The diamond on top of the woman's staff started to glow with a faint silvery light, and she bared her fangs at the duergar. "If you think you can just walk away after everything I've done—"

"I think that's quite enough." The Destitute didn't raise his voice, but it wasn't necessary. The weight his words carried were enough to silence the bickering between the two, and caused the messenger to cough up blood. The noble vampire went to place the bottle back on the mantel before thinking better of it, and tossed it into the flames. It immediately started to melt, spitting sparks over the ever-burning logs in the fireplace. "The lich failed. That doesn't mean our new opponent is strong, just that the lich failed. We need more information before we jump to conclusions." He turned to the gray dwarf. "Production will need to increase by a quarter. I'll send the extras south, to bolster the witches. The rest will continue to fight the demons, as normal."

"And you want me to have the coven kill the interloper, right?" The woman reached into a pouch, pulling out a locket and walking toward the door.

"No, Princess."

She stopped and looked back at the Destitute.

He smiled, showing an elongated fang. "Tell them to learn everything they can, and then report back to you. We'll plan our next steps from there."

The woman gave him a sharp nod and swept out of the room.

He turned back to the fire, thinking over what orders to give to his remaining forces in the south. In the flames, he saw something interesting.

Bending over, he plucked free the melted glass remains of the bottle he had used to mimic the phylactery of the lich. Instead of boiling away into nothing, there remained a tiny glass figurine. An upraised fist, in the same shape the Wardens used. The Destitute turned to look at the messenger who still waited near the stairs.

"Get parchment and ink. I don't want you to forget anything. I've many commands, and there's no room for mistakes." He turned back to watch the flames as they danced across the logs that never burned. "After all, we're trying to save the world."

AUTHOR'S NOTE

Well, how about that? I hope you liked the story. Wanna know something crazy? This literally started as a fever dream. No joke— I was super sick, and it popped in my head. During the fever haze, I started writing. The first five chapters were done before I knew it. By the time I realized what I was doing, the story and characters were too permanent in my head to leave alone. So, now you get to reap the benefits. At the very least, I'm in for a trilogy, and maybe more if the people demand it.

There's a few folks I need to say thank you to, like my publishers, editors (James Kelly and Faith Williams are magical), beta readers, Patrons, friends, and family. You know who you are, and yes, that means you, Brian. But, most *especially*, my wife. I've been married to her for over twenty years now, and I can't believe she still puts up with me.

I'm writing several stories at the same time, since my brain is all kinds of wonky and that's just how it works for me. Come check them out on my Patreon page if you want to see them all. I've got *Threads of Fate*, *Year of The Sword*, and *Wandering Warrior* mixed in with short stories, maps, artwork, and random updates as I get them. You can also message me on Patreon, Discord, or Facebook, and I tend to be pretty responsive. Also, I have a website where you can get merchandise! That's right, I have merchandise, and it's pretty cool.

Last, but not least, I want to say thank you to you, dear reader. I wouldn't be able to keep doing this without your support. If you feel like leaving a review, I'd appreciate it, but just reading this and spreading the word to people you know means the world.

Until next time,
Michael

www.michaelheadauthor.com

PATRONS AND PATREON

The people who support me directly every month deserve some extra credit, and a whole lot of extra love. Those who support at the higher tiers, get even more. Thank you all so much for helping me do what I do.

Jeff Williams

Cromegas Flare

Justin Novack

If you would like to join their ranks, or check out my exclusive content you can go to:

www.patreon.com/michael_head

Thanks again, you legendary champions!

ARC AND BETA READERS

ARC and Beta Readers are an integral part of turning a rough draft into a finished book, and the ones I had on this project were fantastic. If you see them out and about in the online community, be sure to poke them and say hello.

To each of you, all I can say is you are amazing.

Brian Nordon

Shawn Weeks

TJ Lombardi

Clark Tyler Phelps

Scott Reid

Ben Oliver

Richard Griffiths

Nathan McGraw

I'll talk to you all soon for book two, if not sooner. (Look out your window, Brian. I might be there…)

QUEST ACADEMY

By Brian J. Nordon

A world infested by demons. An Academy designed to train Heroes to save humanity from annihilation. A new student's power could make all the difference.

Humans have been pushed to the brink of extinction by an ever-evolving demonic threat. Portals are opening faster than ever, Towers bursting into the skies and Dungeons being mined below the last safe havens of society. The demons are winning.

Quest Academy stands defiantly against them, as a place to train the next generation of Heroes. The Guild Association is holding the line, but are in dire need of new blood and the powerful abilities they could bring to the battlefront. To be the saviors that humanity needs, they need to surpass the limits of those that came before them.

In a war with everything on the line, every power matters. With an adaptive enemy, comes the need for a constant shift in tactics. A new age of strategy is emerging, with even the unlikeliest of Heroes making an impact.

Salvatore Argento has never seen a demon. He has never aspired to become a Hero. Yet his power might be the one to tip the odds in humanity's favor.

Buy on Amazon

ARISE ALPHA

By Jez Cajiao

When you steal a hundred grand from some very bad people, the best way to survive is to stay small and quiet...

Possibly its not to save a pair of drowning girls, not go 'viral' on social media and certainly not to let the local police take your passport, trapping you on a small 'party' island in the middle of the Mediterranean Sea.

But Steve isn't the average guy, he's ex-military, ex-enforcer and ex-human. He's a one man nanite fueled nightmare for those that cross the line, and he's decided that its time to clean up his act. He's going to make up for the things he's done, and save 'the little guys'.

It's a nice fantasy, but even he has to admit, it's really just a justification, because he's a very bad man, with horrifying abilities, and he's only just learning what he's capable of. He needs a reason to not go to the dark, and if that's hunting down the creatures of the night and beating them to death with their own femurs?

Well, he's just the man for the job.

Stolen money. Greek Islands. Werewolves and Enforcers... What could possibly go wrong?

Buy on Amazon

KNIGHTS OF ETERNITY

By Rachel Ní Chuirc

When Zara awoke in chains she thought she'd gone mad.

She was Zara the Fury - mistress of flame and fear. Her name was whispered across the land, from ramshackle taverns to the royal court. Even the heroic Gilded Knights thought twice before crossing her path.

She was feared—*respected*

Now she was curled up on a dirt floor on her fiance's orders. Valerius, leader of the Gilded, mocks her cries for help. And the kingdom is on the brink of war over the missing Lady Eternity…

But that wasn't why Zara thought she had gone mad.

The reason why is that the last thing she remembered was blood, an arcade screen, and the gun that changed everything.

But no chains can hold the Fury, and when she gets out?

The world is going to *burn*.

Coming soon!

FACEBOOK

There's also a few really active Facebook groups I'd recommend you join, as you'll get to hear about great new books, new releases and interact with all your (new) favorite authors! (I may also be there, skulking at the back and enjoying the memes…)

www.facebook.com/groups/LitRPGsociety/

www.facebook.com/groups/LitRPG.books/

www.facebook.com/groups/LitRPGforum/

www.facebook.com/groups/gamelitsociety/

www.facebook.com/groups/litrpglegion